THE VOYAGE OF THE
GOLDEN HANDSHAKE

THE VOYAGE OF THE GOLDEN HANDSHAKE

Terry Waite CBE

SILVERTAIL BOOKS • *London*

First published in Great Britain in 2015 by Silvertail Books

www.silvertailbooks.com

Copyright © Terry Waite 2015

1

The right of Terry Waite to be identified as the author
of this work has been asserted by him in accordance
with the Copyright, Design and Patents Act 1988

A catalogue record of this book is available from the British Library

Typeset in Ehrhardt Monotype by Joanna Macgregor

Printed in the UK by CPI Group (UK) Ltd, Croydon, CR0 4YY

ISBN 978-1-909269-19-4

This book is dedicated to all my fellow passengers and crew with whom I have sailed on various ships across the years. All characters in this book are fictitious and any similarities with any living persons are entirely coincidental.

The lovely thing about cruising is that planning usually turns out to be of little use.

Dom Degnon

If the highest aim of a Captain were to preserve his ship, he would keep it in port forever.

Thomas Aquinas

Being in a ship is like being in a jail, with the chance of being drowned.

Samuel Johnson

1

It was a raw winter's morning in Grimsby. Albert Hardcastle braced himself to step out of bed into the chill of a bedroom that was a stranger to warmth. Central heating had yet to be installed and, given Albert's meagre salary as a lowly shop assistant at the local Co-op, it was unlikely ever to be, despite government promises of special help for the elderly. His wife of forty years, Alice, slept soundly on as she always had done. It had been Albert's practice for as long as he could remember to stumble down the stairway of their modest terraced house and make an early morning cup of tea, and he was just about to leave the warmth of his bed for the sub-arctic temperature of the kitchen when he stopped.

'Good God!' he cried, to the consternation of Alice who sat up in bed with a start. 'Eh, Alice luv, no more work. I've just remembered – I'm retired this very day!'

'Does that stop you making tea?' queried Alice, somewhat crossly.

'Well no, not exactly,' replied Albert, 'but it does mean I don't have to get up right at this very moment.'

'Don't get idle, Albert Hardcastle. You may have finished with the Co-op, but you've still to do a few simple tasks in the home. It's a cold morning, and a cup of tea would be very welcome, thank you.'

Accustomed as he was to obeying the instructions of his wife, Albert gingerly levered himself out of bed. Fine start to retirement, he thought as he padded across the bedroom looking for his trousers and his carpet slippers. In a few moments he was dressed and in the kitchen making tea.

Yesterday, the fifteenth of December 2013, had been his final day at the Co-op. Albert had spent all his working life in the grocery business, starting life as a van boy delivering orders, progressing to being in charge of the provision counter, and when the conversion to a semi-supermarket establishment took place, he spent the day packing shelves and collecting the trolleys and baskets that customers left littered around the shop floor. He wasn't a bit sorry to leave a job that had now become drudgery.

Meanwhile, many miles away at 'The Bridge', in Frinton-on-Sea, a late-Victorian residence with views across the bleak English Channel, retired Rear Admiral Sir Benbow Harrington also prepared to face a new day. Although the Admiral had been retired from the Royal Navy for many years, his life was by no means devoid of activity.

Sir Benbow Harrington had had a very full life in the Senior

Service and (contrary to the opinions of his superiors) considered that he had had a successful career. Admittedly, he had
been rapidly promoted to remove him from the scene of several
disasters and thus render him harmless. As a junior officer, the
part-sinking of a destroyer under his command was, he claimed,
an unfortunate accident. From there on, he spent the major part
of his career in various shore establishments where, alas, trouble
followed him as the proverbial lamb followed Mary. There was
an unexplained fire on HMS *Otanga* in deepest Devon; a mutiny
when he was in command of HMS *Pitcairn*, and reams of missing files when for a year or so he was lodged with the Admiralty
in London. The latter incident stimulated the Navy to move
him still further higher up the chain of command and then prematurely retire him - much to the relief of the noble Sea Lords.

Admiral Benbow was not a man to give up the sea lightly,
however, and in no time at all had established himself as the
proud owner of a small passenger vessel which he renamed the
Golden Sovereign. During the holiday season the Admiral could
be seen at the helm of this ancient packet, ferrying bemused holidaymakers from Frinton along the coast to Harwich and back.
Lady Felicity Harrington supervised the culinary requirements,
which in the main consisted of a variety of fish-paste sandwiches
and home-made sponge cakes.

For the first time in his less than glamorous career the Admiral was at long last experiencing the sweet savour of success.

The *Golden Sovereign* made a modest profit and thoughts of expansion crowded into its owner's ever-fertile mind. As a first step, building on the name of his flagship, he established a new company which he grandly named Golden Oceans. Now, well on the road to becoming a shipping magnate, he acquired a second vessel, the *Golden Crown*, which enabled holiday-makers to view the delights of Poole Harbour. In no time at all, the *Crown* was joined by the *Golden Guinea*, which sailed on a daily basis along the Thames between Greenwich and Westminster Pier.

Since leaving the service of Her Britannic Majesty, nothing but success seemed to have followed the old Sea Dog. On the very morning that Albert Hardcastle in Grimsby dipped a spoon into the tea caddy to make a warming brew, Sir Benbow Harrington down in Frinton-on-Sea was planning a major development which would bring these two unlikely characters together in adventures that neither could ever have dreamed of, nor possibly foreseen.

2

Sunday morning in Grimsby was hardly a festive occasion. For much of the year, icy winds swept across this bleak outpost of a once thriving fishing industry. Although fishing on a large scale had departed the town, visitors swore that the municipality continued to be permeated with the odour of stale fish, a slander vehemently denied by local residents. As the bells of Grimsby Minster beckoned the faithful to enter and face hypothermia, whilst singing about heavenly delights, Albert Hardcastle trudged homewards from his regular visit to the newsagent.

Come winter or summer, each Sabbath morn, Albert would make his pilgrimage to exchange greetings with Mr Khan, who many seasons previously had replaced Charlie Earnshaw as proprietor of the corner shop. Being fellow shopworkers, Charlie and Albert had much in common and would spend a good half-hour discussing football, local politics or nothing in particular. Mr Khan was less communicative than his predecessor, and as Albert's horizon hardly extended beyond the Lincolnshire boundary, and Mr Khan had yet to master the local dialect, there was little to talk about. Clutching his newspaper, Albert let himself back into the house where his wife was pouring herself a second cup of tea.

'Well, Albert,' she said as she slopped hot tea into the saucer and cooled it with blasts of air from her pursed lips, 'You're a free man now – and tomorrow and the day after that. What now?'

'What do you mean, luv?' asked Albert, opening his paper. 'Nowt's changed.'

'Nowt's changed?' repeated Alice incredulously. '*Nowt's changed*? Come on, Albert lad. If you think I'm going to put up with you sitting around all day gawking at the paper, then have another think. Have you seen the state of the kitchen? And take a look in the front room. If that doesn't need papering, then I'm Dutch. How long is it since we spoke about double-glazing? Come on Albert, how long?'

Albert sank deeper in his armchair, his depression increasing as he read the dismal results of Grimsby Town football team who had played the previous afternoon. His mood brightened slightly as he turned the page and gazed solemnly at a dusky maiden reclining on a tropical beach. Alice didn't wait for him to answer but slurped the remainder of her tea and vanished into the kitchen. Albert continued to peruse his newspaper as page after page extolled the delights of foreign travel, something that lay quite outside his limited experience of the world beyond Grimsby. He had visited London once to see the Co-op Brass Band compete in the Royal Albert Hall and had been to Chester when, as manager of the provision counter, he attended a Cheshire Cheese festival. Apart from that, Grimsby and Cleethorpes were his territory.

Albert was still miles away in deepest Borneo when his wife marched back into the living room.

'Come on, Albert,' she said. 'Now's the time for a bit of action. You can't decorate today, but you can get your old working suit ready to take to the cleaners. There's plenty of life in it yet and it will do for when we visit Cousin Pam in Cleethorpes. Come on now, lad. Make haste.'

Reluctantly Albert rose from the fireside and ascended the staircase. He removed the suit from its hanger and returned to the kitchen.

'Here you are, luv,' he said as he obediently handed the jacket and trousers to his wife.

'I don't suppose you've had the common sense to look in the pockets,' she said, as she removed a used handkerchief and a packet of cough sweets from his trousers.

'Hey up!' she exclaimed as she dug into the inside pocket of his jacket. 'What's this?' She removed a small sealed white envelope inscribed with his name.

'Eh luv,' said Albert, 'I'd quite forgotten. Just before I came home last night, Mary and Karen from the stockroom gave it to me. They said it was a surprise gift.'

'Well,' said Alice impatiently, 'better open it, eh?'

7

Albert carefully tore along the top of the packet and removed three small tickets.

'By go,' he said, 'lottery tickets!'

His wife gave a grunt. 'Some gift,' she said. 'Not a chance Albert. Not a bloomin' chance.'

Admiral Sir Benbow Harrington seated himself in his Captain's chair in front of a huge ornate desk. He claimed that it was made from the original timbers of Nelson's flagship, HMS *Vanguard*. This ship had a nasty accident when entering Plymouth in 1794 and had to be partly dismantled before being rebuilt. It was then that Benbow claimed some of the timbers were purloined for his desk, although this claim was treated with considerable scepticism by his wife. The desk was placed in front of a bow window from which there was a distant view of the English Channel. An ancient brass telescope on a tripod remained permanently trained on the ocean, although very little shipping ever passed by.

On the desk stood an empty in-tray complemented by an equally empty out-tray. Routine correspondence dealing with the business of Golden Oceans was dealt with by the Admiral's agent Harry Parkhurst, who was conveniently situated in South-end-on-Sea. Harry would occasionally telephone the Admiral if there was a matter that required an executive decision but, more often than not, he was left to manage the fleet - which was fortunate, as the Admiral was not the brightest beam on the light-house. The success of the company was largely due to Harry who, when he retired as a Chief Petty Officer in the Royal Navy, had gained a wealth of business experience managing a punting enterprise in Cambridge.

The Admiral had just opened his copy of *The Times* and was turning to the obituary page when the door of his study burst open and Lady Felicity blustered into the room.

'Benbow!' she cried. 'What have you been up to?'

The Admiral swivelled round in his chair and saw that his wife was carrying several items of mail.

'I don't think we have ever had this many letters since you announced your retirement from the Royal Navy!' she exclaimed. 'There must be at least seven here.' She planted them firmly on the desk.

Benbow gave a satisfied grunt.

'Ah!' he said. 'These will be the replies to my advertisement placed last week in the Nautical News.'

'Advertisement?' queried Lady Felicity. 'What advertisement?'

For the past few weeks, thoughts of expansion had been occupying the Admiral's active mind. It all began when Harry Parkhurst telephoned him with what he said was 'a real corker.' A friend of his, who ran a business transporting horses from England to

France, was about to retire and the vessel, which for the past twenty years had carried hundreds of these unfortunate animals to an uncertain future, was 'going for a snip.'

'It's a beauty, Admiral,' said Harry. 'With a bit of work it would make a lovely addition to the Line. My Cousin Ted in Chatham would do a bit of pre-fabricated work inside and we could tack on a few balconies - and bingo! Another cruise ship!'

The Admiral was greatly taken with the idea, especially as the ship could be leased at a sum easily paid for from the profits now coming in from the other Ships of the Line. Harry was given permission to 'Go full steam ahead.'

'Well, dear,' said Sir Benbow, 'I have been thinking of expanding Golden Oceans into what I believe will become the major cruising company of the British Isles. A luxury cruise ship has been drawn to Harry's attention and at this very moment is being refitted at Chatham.

We are now set fair for a significant expansion into the increasingly popular cruise market.'

Lady Felicity did not reply immediately. She was reflecting on the past when her husband had got carried away with some scheme or other that inevitably ended in disaster. There was the time when he sank his first command by being too enthusiastic in a naval exercise off Southend-on-Sea. To this day it remained a mystery to Lady Felicity how he managed such a calamity and, had her uncle not been First Sea Lord, he would have undoubtedly faced a Court Martial. As it was, he was speedily transferred to a shore station where the dangers of sinking the ship were negligible. Alas, there was trouble here also when he misplaced all the Service records of the ratings, who consequently did not get home leave for some twelve months. He seemed to have a propensity for misplacing documents, for when he was given promotion and a position with the War Office in London, he incinerated thousands of secret files in a misplaced attempt to reorganise the paperwork. It was then that he was promoted again and retired. However, she had to admit that since he had formed a partnership with Harry, things had gone remarkably well.

'Well dear, I hope you're right,' she said somewhat anxiously. 'We really don't want trouble at this stage in our lives. But you mentioned an advertisement, Benbow. What is that all about?'

'Well,' said the Admiral as he placed the unopened letters into his in-tray. 'As soon as this new ship is ready - and that will only be a matter of weeks - I intend to launch the first World Cruise for Golden Oceans. For that venture I shall need an experienced crew. These letters will be applications for the all-important post of Captain of the SS *Golden Handshake* for that is what I intend to call this proud new addition to the Golden Oceans Line.'

Lady Harrington held her tongue. Her face was impassive

but inwardly she could see dark clouds on the horizon. She left the room without uttering another word.

Albert Hardcastle, retired grocer and man of leisure, sat immobile in his chair in front of the fire. For once, his wife sat silently opposite him, too shaken to move.

'It can't be right, lad,' she muttered in a half-whisper when she had summoned enough strength to speak. 'It can't – can it?'

Albert picked up the paper as he had done several times in the last fifteen minutes. There, at the bottom of the page, was printed a series of numbers that exactly corresponded with the numbers on one of the tickets that he clutched tightly in his fist.

'It is luv,' he murmured. 'Six million, six hundred and sixty six thousand, six hundred and sixty-six pounds and six pence. It *is* right.'

For a brief moment silence reigned in the Hardcastle household. Finally Albert spoke.

'It's a lot of brass, Alice luv, a lot of brass. I might even buy a few decent racing pigeons now.'

For once in her life Alice was too stunned to think of anything to say. Albert picked up the paper which had dropped to the floor and stared yet again at the numbers.

'By go,' he said. 'By go.'

3

Rear Admiral (Retired) Sir Benbow Harrington picked one of the letters from the small stack in his in-tray and slit open the envelope with a silver letter-opener. He removed a single sheet of lined paper and unfolded it. The writer had written in block capitals in pencil.

DEER YOUR GRACE, it began unpromisingly.

MY NAME IS JEZ FARTHING AND I AM SKIPPER OF THE BRIDLINGTON STAR A FINE LITTLE SHIP I MUST SAY. I AM LOOKING FOR A KNEW CHAL-LANGE AND IF THE MONEE IS RIGHT I AM YOUR MAN. TO SAVE MONNEY I AM STAYING WITH THE SALLY ANN BETWEEN TRIPS SO

RIGHT ME THERE PLEESE.

HOPING TO BE YOUR SHIPMATE

CAPTAIN JEZ

The Admiral threw the letter directly into the leather wastepaper basket beautifully embossed with a naval coat-of-arms.

'Bloody illiterate,' he muttered to himself. 'What the hell this country is coming to I don't know.' The Admiral, being a religious man, was not given to using strong language, but on occasion the common parlance of the mariners entered into his vocabulary.

The next three or four letters he opened were of the same standard of English as Eric's epistle and gave him a variety of designations, ranging from that of a royal personage to the Mayor of an English provincial town. As he reasoned that the Captain of a World Cruise would have to have a reasonable social awareness, as well as being proficient in English and with a working knowledge of other languages, they too were discarded.

With a heart that grew increasingly despondent he applied the opener to the final letter from the in-tray. At first sight this appeared promising. It was neatly typed on quarto paper and bore the address:

At Sea. From the cabin of Captain Peché Sparda.

Sir,

It is with respect that I write to you Admiral Sir. My name is Sparda and for many years I have been Captain of the Ferry travelling the most dangerous currents of the world. This is Sir, between the Italian mainland and Sicily. Many fine ladies and gentlemen have travelled on my ship Sir and have been entertained by my Cousin Pedro who knows many old Sicilian songs.

I was born in Catania Sir but lived many year in England in the fine town of Deptford when I was Captain of a ship on the great river Sir. My spoken English is good Sir but my written English not good and so my sister Rosetta, who is cooking for the Sisters of the Star of the Thames in Deptford, is writing this letter for me. My good wife Lilian is an English lady Sir and now lives with me in Sicily with little visits to England. My relatives care for her very much Sir and they also care for my little ship. Sorry Sir but my ship has now been taken by government and I do not know why. My cousins will help me Sir. Now I need new job and so I like to work with you Admiral. The sea is my blood Sir.

Please write to me at the Convent in Deptford where my sister Rosetta will give me your kind reply.

With many salutes Sir,
Captain Peché Sparda

Benbow read this letter through several times and the more he read it the more convinced he became that he ought to see this man. Captain Sparda seemed to be experienced – had, he assumed, a Master's Ticket – and possessed some written and spoken English. There and then he picked up the candlestick telephone that adorned his desk and instructed Harry Parkhurst to arrange an interview without delay.

It was exactly two o'clock when Admiral Harrington pulled into the car park of the Vacation Inn at Southend. The building itself was unimpressive, having been built of pre-fabricated units bolted together and faced with a yellowish brick. Harry Parkhurst had reserved a room in this establishment in order to interview Captain Sparda and also another candidate who had come forward to be interviewed for the position of Cruise Director. Enzo Bigatoni hailed from Southern Italy but had lived in the United Kingdom for many years, working as a Bingo caller at various holiday camps. He was friendly with Captain Sparda and on occasions had spent several days on the Messina ferry meeting and greeting passengers. Captain Sparda assured the Admiral that there was no better person in the whole of the Cruise industry to fill the vacant position on board the *Handshake*. Apart from his skill at number calling, he had a phenomenal memory for faces. Apparently he never forgot a face (even though he could never remember where he had previously seen that face, nor the name of its owner). The Admiral thought this to be an excellent quality as he believed that passengers loved to be remembered, even if their name was not immediately identified. That could easily be checked by a quick glance at the passenger list.

Harry was waiting in the tiny entrance hall to greet the Admiral.

'I thought we would interview at this hotel,' he said half-apologetically. 'It's a bit on the downmarket side but it does mean we can interview our candidates without being spotted by our rivals who have agents in all the large hotels in Southend. We can't afford to lose such promising candidates to Canard Cruises or the Silver Salver Line. They are always on the lookout, and I know for a fact would snap up the two men we are seeing this afternoon.'

The Admiral nodded in agreement and they both approached a glass screen behind which sat a blonde teenager busily occupied with staring at herself in a small hand mirror. Harry rapped smartly on the glass. The girl made not a movement. He rapped again and this time bellowed in stentorian tones: 'Admiral Harrington and Mr Harry Parkhurst who have reserved a suite for the afternoon.'

This time the girl stirred. 'Navy, eh? We've had enough trouble with the Navy here. Last time they wrecked three bathrooms and scared the life out of our cleaning lady. No Navy here, shipmates.'

The Admiral took a step backwards in surprise at this unexpected outburst.

'Madam,' said Harry with all the dignity he could muster, 'this gentleman is an Admiral and is not to be confused with the common rank and file who appear to have caused you such distress. If you check your reservations you will note that Mr Harry

Parkhurst has reserved a suite for the purpose of interviewing candidates for a most important role in shipping.'

The girl tossed her head. 'Huh!' she exclaimed. 'I can guess what *that* is. Well, let me tell you this is a respectable establishment, and if there is the slightest sign of trouble, our security officer will be onto the case immediately.'

With that, she pushed a key under the glass and resumed her staring.

Harry and the Admiral ascended the bare concrete stairway and navigated their way along a narrow corridor until they arrived at the reserved 'suite.' Harry inserted the key in the lock and entered the room. It was pitch dark and there was a distinct odour of stale beer and cigarettes. He flung back the curtains and light flooded into the room. Outside there was an uninterrupted view of a flat roof and an oversized air-conditioning unit. Two single beds took up the main part of the 'suite' together with a single upright chair and a dressing-table. The Admiral frowned.

'Not much of a suite, Harry,' he said. 'This will hardly convey the impression of a first-rate Cruise Line, will it?'

'No problem, Admiral,' said Harry confidently. 'Once I explain the security situation they will understand.'

He had hardly finished speaking when the Bakelite telephone by the side of one of the beds began to ring. Harry picked it up.

'Mr Pankhurst?' queried a female voice on the line.

'Parkhurst!' bellowed Harry, angry at the misreading of his name.

'Oh sorry,' replied the caller. 'I didn't want the prison, I wanted Mr Pankhurst at the Vacation Inn!'

Harry let out an expletive. 'I don't know who you are, but this is Mr Harry Parkhurst and this is the Vacation Inn suite number 11201.'

'Oh, good afternoon, Mr Parkhurst. This is Lilian Sparda, wife of Captain Sparda. He asked me to phone you as his new Sat Nav took him in the wrong direction and both he and Mr Bigatoni may be rather late.'

This news did not amuse Harry in the slightest. 'Where in goodness are they?' he shouted down the phone.

'Well,' said the messenger who, had she been in close proximity to Harry, would have been in real danger of being shot, 'they are circulating the M25 for the second time and are now held up because the road has been closed. They hope to be with you as soon as they can.'

At this juncture Harry became speechless and slammed the phone down with such force that a leg on the small table collapsed, sending the cheap bedside light crashing to the floor along with the telephone receiver. Immediately there was a sharp rap on the door, which burst open revealing a very large black individual dressed from head to toe in a blue military-style uniform and sporting a long baton.

'I thought as much,' he shouted. 'Tracy on the desk warned me about you two Naval types. Out. Out now. Pronto. *Out*.'

It was useless to try and explain. The Admiral picked up his small leather case from the bed and Harry slung his knapsack over his back. The two men were rudely shoved along the corridor and down the concrete stairs back into the reception area.

'Credit Card,' barked the guard.

Harry produced a Visa card, which was promptly snatched by Tracy, who glowered at them from behind the safety of the glass.

'That'll be one hundred pounds for damage,' she said 'and you do *not* get your deposit back. Sign here and good afternoon.'

Harry duly signed and the two shipping magnates stepped outside into a fine drizzle and plodded towards their respective cars.

'I'll meet you at the first service station we come to,' said the Admiral, 'so that we can decide what to do now.'

'No problem,' said Harry, having resumed his customary cheerfulness. 'I'll phone Peché and call the interview off for today. We will have to meet him and Enzo at some other place and at a later date. Leave it to me, Admiral. All will be well, let me assure you.'

'Right you are, Harry,' said the weary sailor. 'Another time. I'll leave the interviewing to you, and if you think they are up to the job, hire them right away.'

With that, the Admiral climbed into his car and set off for Frinton and the relative peace of the Essex coast.

4

For the first time in his life Albert Hardcastle had been invited to meet the manager of his local bank for lunch. Earlier in the week he had received notice that the sum of six million, six hundred and sixty six thousand, six hundred and sixty-six pounds and six pence. would be deposited in the Grimsby North branch of the Yorkshire Prudent Bank. Albert had refused all publicity and turned down offers of help from lottery officials.

'I know how to spend my own brass,' he said, 'and I don't want some toffee-nosed adviser from London poking around in my affairs.'

His wife agreed with him completely and the money was duly dispatched to the joint current account of Mr and Mrs Albert Hardcastle.

On the morning of the lunch Alice took what she now called 'The Lottery Suit' from the wardrobe and gave it a quick once-over with the iron. It was rather worn, having seen many years of service since Albert had bought it in a sale from the Grimsby branch of Messrs Burtons, but both he, and his wife, reckoned that it had plenty of wear left in it yet.

'No sense in throwing money away on new clothes when there is a perfectly good woollen suit in the wardrobe,' said Alice, echoing the thrift that had been with her for years. 'It's good for another ten years at least!'

Although Grimsby was in Lincolnshire it was permeated with the values that made Yorkshire great, and thrift was not the least of them.

Promptly at midday Albert adjusted the golden watch-chain that adorned his waistcoat and then slipped on his greatcoat and football scarf.

'By gum, Albert,' said Alice. 'Folks won't half stare when they see you walking out like that on a weekday.'

Albert said nothing but, with a nod, stepped into the street and headed in the direction of the Prudent Bank. En route he wondered if he ought to call in and announce his good fortune to the stockroom girls who had presented him with the winning ticket. He was still puzzled as to what to do about this. At some point they were bound to ask him how he had fared. On the other hand, if he kept quiet they might assume nothing at all had happened - unless of course they had taken a note of the numbers, which he very much doubted. He decided he would walk on the pavement opposite the Co-op to reduce his chances of meeting anyone and thus facing awkward questions.

As luck would have it, just as he was passing on the opposite side looking resolutely ahead, he heard someone call out his name.

'Albert, you old bugger, are you not calling in to see us?'

Of all people it had to be Jason Smith who had taken Albert's former position as guardian of the trolleys and baskets.

'Do you know,' Albert had said in his final briefing before leaving, 'do you know that each time a trolley goes missing, that costs the Co-op at least two hundred quid. That's a lot of divi.' Jason had since reflected on this wisdom. It *was* a lot of money – and in his time he must have seen at least eight hundred quids' worth semi-submerged in a nearby waterway. Albert decided that if he called in the shop this morning the subject of the tickets would be bound to come up and Alice would be furious if he gave the slightest hint that he might have won.

'Sorry, Jason,' he shouted, 'another time! I'm almost late as it is.' He plodded on.

On arrival at the portals of the Prudent Bank, Albert stopped for a moment and gazed at the solid stone pillars on each side of the doorway. Many was the time when, as a young married man, he had crossed this threshold with a deep sense of foreboding to face an irate clerk urging him to 'take more care with your outgoings'. In later life he hardly visited, but on the infrequent occasions when he did, despite the fact that his account was a safe sanctuary for moths, the clerk was all sweetness and light and urged him to borrow as much as he could carry – and more besides.

Albert stepped inside and before he could utter a word, Darren Worthington, the head clerk, was by his side offering to help him off with his coat.

'We saw you approaching on the security cameras,' said Darren, tugging at the Yorkshire twill. 'We're all terribly excited you're visiting us today.'

Darren Worthington had recently relocated to Grimsby from a branch somewhere in Surrey and Arthur thought it was typical of a nancy boy Southerner to get excited about nowt.

'Mr Havergill is expecting you and has asked me to show you immediately into his office,' crooned Darren, totally captivated by the occasion. He pressed several numbers on a side door which swung open, revealing a short corridor along which they both walked. Before them was another door, this time adorned with a sign which read *Mr Bernard Havergill JP. Manager*. Worthington gently tapped on the door and was greeted with a deafening 'Come in!' Albert was ushered into the room and the head clerk discreetly disappeared. There, behind a desk totally clear of any documents or writing implements, but containing one half-empty glass, sat a florid-faced man with ginger hair. He was perspiring profusely, even though the outside temperature was equivalent to that in the Arctic.

'Ah, Mr Hardcastle. What a delight it is to see you. I don't think we have had the pleasure. My name is Havergill and I am the Manager of this establishment and of several other branches in the Grimsby region. I know you have been a customer of ours for years, and it is always my very great pleasure to make the acquaintance of our long-standing and faithful account-holders. You are most welcome. Please take a seat and let me get you a drink. Gin and tonic? Whisky?' Mr Havergill replenished the glass on his desk from a crystal dispenser and went to get Albert a glass.

'Hold on,' said Albert. 'I usually drink Brown Ale.'

'Brown Ale,' repeated Havergill. 'Brown Ale . . . Is that what they drink up here?' He took another gulp of his gin and pressed a button situated underneath the desk. 'Bring in a Brown Ale for our esteemed friend Mr Hardcastle!' he bellowed, seemingly at no one in particular.

From somewhere in the room a loudspeaker crackled into life.

'Certainly, Mr Havergill, sir. I think we may have to go to the Co-op to get one.'

'Bring several,' boomed the Manager, 'and while you are at it, bring another bottle of Gordon's. The last one seems to have evaporated.'

Albert had seen some topers in his time, but sitting before him was surely one of Grimsby's best. Several minutes passed before there was a tap on the door and Darren Worthington staggered in with a crate of Brown Ale and a litre of Gordon's Gin.

'Well done, Washington,' slurred the Manager. 'Pour Mr

Albert an ale and take one yourself and then clear off.'

Darren poured the ale as requested, and ignoring the generous offer of the Manager to help himself, he quickly left the room.

'Well,' said Mr Havergill. 'This is all very homely, isn't it?'

He slurped more gin and went to open another bottle of tonic water. 'All very homely isn't it'?

Albert reflected that it was like no home he had ever known, and despite the generosity of the Manager the atmosphere did not seem to be either relaxed or homely. However, he held his tongue.

'Well, well, well,' uttered Havergill. 'Well, well, well.'

Albert was at a loss as to what to say, since he had no idea what Mr Havergill was referring to.

'Well, well, well. It is, isn't it?'

By now the gin was beginning to take over the Manager's ability to speak and reason clearly. For no apparent reason he pressed the button on his desk again, and within a moment Worthington appeared. Havergill fixed him with a glassy stare.

'Warburton,' he began. 'You know what I like about you?'

Darren Worthington said nothing but bowed his head slightly.

'Nothing!' the Manager exclaimed. 'Absolutely nothing. Get out.'

Darren disappeared immediately and Albert took a sip of his

Brown Ale.

'I think we ought to get down to business,' he said, conscious of the fact that time was slipping by and soon all luncheon establishments in the immediate area would be closing. 'I understand the lottery folk have paid money into my account and I would like to know exactly how much and what interest I will be getting if I leave it with the bank?'

Mr Havergill took another swig at his gin and once again replenished his glass. He slouched in his chair and appeared to have considerable difficulty in not slipping to the floor.

'Account?' he muttered. 'Account? By all accounts you have an account. We have accounts in banks, you know, old boy. Accounts. Oh yes, by George. Accounts.'

'Well,' said Albert, now beginning to lose patience. 'I'm talking about my account, Mr Havergill. I would like to see MY account.'

Havergill rolled his eyes, closed one and fixed Albert with a glassy stare.

'You can't see my account, old boy. Private. Secret, you know.' Here he touched the side of his nose with his forefinger and shook his head.

'I want to see MY account, Mr Havergill. MY account, not yours'. Albert was now running out of patience and not a little apprehensive. The prospect of lunch seemed to be receding by the minute, and as for his account - he seemed to be making no progress whatsoever.

'Call Withington, old boy,' mumbled Havergill. 'Withington is just like Jeeves. He knows everything. Withington?' he bawled. 'Wallington, where the hell are you when needed? *Wiverington*.'

Once again the door opened and Darren reappeared.

Mr Havergill turned in his chair, and this time missed his balance and fell under the desk. Both Albert and Darren rushed across the room and helped him back. When he was seated, he shook himself rather like a dog emerging from a pond. He straightened his tie and cleared his throat.

'Mr Jeeves,' he began. 'Mr Hardacre wants to see his account.' With that, he placed his head between his arms on the desk and began to snore loudly.

'I really must apologise to you, Mr Hardcastle,' said Darren, clearly disturbed by the events of the last hour. 'I was hoping Mr Havergill would break the news to you himself. It is rather alarming, I must admit. I'm afraid The Manager seems to have lost your account. There is no record whatsoever of you ever having an account with this bank, and no record at all of any money being received from the National Lottery.'

Albert dropped his half-empty glass of Brown Ale onto the beige carpet.

'My God!' he uttered. 'That's terrible. No record whatsoever?'

'I'm afraid not, Sir.' We were searching the computer records all night long, and first thing this morning we contacted the Lottery to see if they could throw any light on the problem. All they know is that the money was paid in here two days ago and that it has gone out of their Lottery account.'

Albert collapsed into the nearest chair and stared at the expanding brown stain on the carpet.

'No record,' he muttered. 'No record?'

'Please try not to upset yourself, Mr Hardcastle. I'm sure that once Mr Havergill is feeling himself again, all will be well.'

'What about Head Office?' asked Albert. 'What do *they* say about all this?

'Well, the truth is that they don't know at the moment.'

Darren paused as Mr Havergill gave a low groan, followed by an exceptionally loud snort. He continued: 'Mr Havergill was hoping that something might turn up before he was obliged to let them know. As soon as he is well again, he will start another search. Of that I'm certain.'

Albert got to his feet. 'That's it then. I'd better be off.'

Darren helped him on with his coat and handed him his scarf before opening the door. Albert followed him down the corridor and back into the customer area. As he made his way to the exit, the counter clerk gave him a wan smile.

'Good afternoon, Mr Hardcastle.'

Albert nodded and stepped into the street. A light snow was

falling and with a heavy heart and feeling somewhat hungry he set course for home.

As he approached his former workplace, to his surprise he noted that the blinds were drawn across the windows and the main entrance appeared to be closed. He stopped for a moment, fumbled inside his coat and consulted his pocket watch - 2.45. He couldn't understand it. It wasn't a public holiday. No Royal Personage had died, as far as he knew. Why was the Co-op not open for business? As he stood by the entrance he could hear sounds of laughter inside and he was sure that he heard one of the girls from the stockroom shouting, 'Good old Jason.' He was just about to resume his journey when the door was flung open, and who should appear but Jason himself.

'Albert, come on in and join the party. No work today, nor ever again for that matter!' exclaimed Jason, somewhat flushed in the face. Increasingly puzzled, Albert crossed the familiar threshold and the door was firmly secured behind him. Littered around the floor were several empty bottles which had once contained the Co-op's finest champagne. A large iced cake from the display cabinet had been attacked and it seemed as though all the pork pies had gone from the provision counter. A glass was thrust into his hand and was immediately filled from a freshly opened bottle of champagne.

'An amazing story,' gurgled Jason as he gulped the sparkling beverage, like water. 'I only wish Heather was here to celebrate with us instead of being with her ailing mother in the Outer Hebrides.'

'What on earth are you talking about, Jason?' asked an increasingly mystified Albert. 'What is going on?'

'Well,' said the jovial trolley-keeper, 'each week my wife buys a couple of lottery tickets. She checks the numbers and I don't pay much attention, for we never win. Today I went home for lunch as usual and there was the mail with our joint account statement from the Prudent Bank - and guess what? I looked at it and saw that we had been credited with six million, six hundred and sixty six thousand, six hundred and sixty-six pounds and six pence. Six million quid! Heather must have checked the tickets, got in touch with the Lottery folks - and bingo. There is the lovely cash in our account. That's why I am treating everyone, see? Drink up, lad. There's more where that came from.'

Albert could literally feel the colour drain from his cheeks.

So that explained it, he said to himself. That drunken old fool of a Bank Manager had credited Jason and Heather Smith with his legitimate winnings. The situation would have to be put right, but there was bound to be trouble.

'Drink up, Albert,' said Jason as he flung an empty bottle across the room, narrowly missing the Co-op cat and striking a pile of biscuit tins.

'Hold on, lad,' said Albert. 'You can't damage the place.'

'Oh yes, I can,' said the increasingly inebriated trolley man.

'I've telephoned the office and told them what to do with their rotten job. I'll pay for the party today and for any accidental damage that might be caused. Have a pie Albert.'

By now Albert was ravenous, having missed his lunch, so he accepted a Melton Mowbray special and bit into it gratefully. What on earth was he to do? The shop looked as though a tornado had hit it and the staff would have done credit to pre-Lent festivities in Munich.

Albert was still trying to work out in his mind how this appalling mix-up was going to be resolved when there was a loud ringing on the shop's telephone. As he was the only sober person present, he picked it up and answered it. Immediately he recognised the soft lilting tones of Heather Smith.

'Hello, is that the Grimsby Co-op?' she asked.

'It is,' said Albert, just as there was a mighty crash and a display of baked beans went cascading across the floor.

'Goodness, what's that?' asked Heather. 'And to whom am I speaking? I need to speak to Jason, please.'

'It's me - Albert. The cat's just knocked some tins over, nothing to worry about. I'll get Jason for you.'

Jason lurched out of the back room, champagne bottle in one hand and pork pie in the other.

'It's Heather' said Albert in a stage whisper. 'For God's sake, sober up!'

Jason dropped the pie and grabbed the receiver.

'Heather chuck. My dream girl. My angel. You are wonderful. Well done my sweetie. Well done.'

He dropped the phone with another crash, picked it up and resumed his monologue. He was quickly cut short by Heather.

'Jason, are you all right? Whatever is the matter? And what's all that noise? You don't sound at all well, my dear. What is it? I hope you *are* well, as I am ringing to ask you to collect me from the station at six this evening.'

'No problem, my honeybun. No problem whatsoever. I'll have a car meet you. Do you prefer a Rolls or a Bentley?'

'What *are* you talking about, Jason?' asked Heather, now becoming seriously alarmed at her husband's telephone manner.

'The lottery, my pet. Why didn't you tell me earlier we had won? You are a real little tease, of that there is no doubt.'

'Lottery?' queried Heather. 'Won? Jason, I haven't done the lottery for the past two weeks, as it's not at all easy to get tickets up here in the wilds of Scotland.'

Jason froze and for once that afternoon was speechless. He gently put the champagne bottle down and looked directly into Albert's eyes.

'Bloody hell,' he said, and collapsed in a heap on the floor.

5

Admiral Sir Benbow Harrington was in a jovial mood as he tucked into his breakfast kipper. 'Delicious, my dear,' he remarked to his wife as she poured him another cup of coffee. 'Do you realise, Felicity, that there is only one genuine smokehouse left in the Isle of Man? I once stayed with Jumbo Chessington the Governor, and he was seriously alarmed at the state of affairs on the Island. Oak chips are what are needed. Oak chips.'

Felicity, whose knowledge of smoking fish was limited, simply nodded her head in agreement.

'Well,' continued the Admiral, helping himself to a liberal spoonful of thick-cut marmalade, 'today is the big day. If it's fine I will meet the team in the garden where we should be able to have an uninterrupted briefing before the launch. Harry assures me that the sea trials have gone better than expected. He took the ship along the route he knows so well in Southern Italy, and apart from some difficulty in strong currents with the rudder, all seemed to be well.'

'I hope he's right, dear,' Lady Harrington replied with a

somewhat worried look. 'A World Cruise is an ambitious venture, Benbow, and you can't afford to have too many problems.'

'All will be well, dear, don't concern yourself. With my long experience in the Navy and Harry's extensive knowledge of choppy waters, plus a seasoned Captain in Sparda, we don't have a worry in the world.'

Lady Harrington reflected silently on how frequently she had heard these self-same sentiments uttered by her husband across the years, and she shuddered slightly.

The Admiral folded his napkin, picked up his daily copy of The Times and made for his study. He had only been gone a few moments when Lady Harrington heard her husband cry out.

'Felicity, dear! Felicity, come here this instant. Make haste.'

She rushed along the hallway to the study where the Admiral was seated with the Travel Section of *The Times* open before him.

'Just look at this,' he chortled in delight.

Harry Parkhurst had certainly not wasted any time following the trials, for there was a half-page advertisement announcing the Inaugural World Cruise of the SS *Golden Handshake*.

Rear Admiral Sir Benbow Harrington (Rtd)
Owner of the Golden Oceans Cruise Line
proudly announces the First World Cruise of a
brand new addition to the company's fleet

the SS *Golden Handshake*.

The *Golden Handshake* now sails alongside
the *Golden Guinea*, the *Golden Crown* and the *Golden Sovereign*
and is the Flagship of the Line.

Applications are invited now
for a place on what will be a unique experience.
Tickets will be issued strictly on a
'First come, first served' basis.

The Admiral picked up the receiver of the candlestick telephone and dialled Harry's number.

'Splendid work,' he congratulated him. Today's *The Times* is excellent. Well done.'

Harry was duly modest in his reply.

'My old friend at Carnard was helpful in drafting the text and we have been able to get a mention in all the local papers around the country. Just watch the applications roll in. We will certainly be oversubscribed.'

The Admiral replaced the receiver and resumed staring at the newspaper. He remained at his desk throughout the morning - a happy and contented man.

Back in Grimsby things were less tranquil. Albert hauled Jason up from the floor and poured a glass of cold water over his head. News of the disaster had yet to reach the party-goers in the staff-room, and unfortunately Albert was the one who had to bring it.

He gingerly opened the door to a scene of complete chaos. Mary Ellsworth, late of the stockroom, was performing what she considered to be a Spanish dance on the table. Crystal Weathergate, previously in charge of the drinks department, was surrounded by bottles from that said department, the majority of which were empty.

'Albert, old pal' cried Andy Pink, one of the van drivers. 'Where have you been all my life. Come in, old friend. Take a pew. In fact take anything you like.'

'Shut up, Andy,' said Albert sternly. 'Shut up, the lot of you.'

A silence descended on the room as they all stared at him in amazement.

'Come on, mate,' said someone. 'It's not often we have a party.'

'No,' said Albert, 'and unless you sober up and clear up pretty quickly, this will be the last party you will have for many a year. And your last job!'

He began to explain how it seemed as though there had been a ghastly mistake, and it appeared that Jason's wife had *not* won the lottery, after all. Looks of amazement crossed the flushed faces of the once-jovial revellers, to be quickly replaced by expressions of panic and despair.

'Hell's Bells,' said Andy. 'Who's going to pay for all this lot if Jason can't?'

Albert did not answer directly.

'If I were you,' he said, 'I would clear this mess up and get the shop opened pretty quickly. You can worry about payment later. Come on, the lot of you. I'll help.'

Jason, who was too far gone to take part in any activity other than sleep, was left in the staffroom while the remainder of the staff set about clearing away the debris and piling up the cans of beans. An hour later, the shop was reopened for a final hour of trading and Albert departed for home sober, starving and not a little relieved that his fortune now seemed to be secure.

6

Rear Admiral Benbow Harrington glanced at the brass ship's clock in his study. It had been salvaged from the first ship he had commanded – the very vessel which unfortunately had sunk during a naval exercise off Southend-on-Sea. The fact that the maiden cruise of the SS *Golden Handshake* was due to take place in several days' time from Southend Pier had caused the Admiral to pause and wonder if he might be tempting fate. However, he dismissed such thoughts from his mind and turned his attention to the meeting shortly due to take place with several of his senior staff members.

Harry, the invaluable Harry, would be there, of course, for he had been responsible for the recruiting of most of the ship's company. The Admiral was looking forward to making the acquaintance of Captain Peché Sparda, recently retired from long and distinguished service as Master of the Messina ferry and soon to be Captain of the flagship of the Golden Oceans Line. He was due to arrive at three that afternoon, along with his friend Enzo Bigatoni, the newly appointed Cruise Director. The irritation that the Admiral felt when these two senior officers failed to master their Satellite Navigation system on the M25 had long since passed, for like many senior Naval Officers the Admiral was a religious man with a forgiving nature.

A new person on the scene was also expected that afternoon - a certain Mr Radley Duvet (pronounced like the bedding) who also had been recruited by Harry and who would occupy the all-important role of Hotel Manager. For many years Mr Duvet had assisted his wife in the running of a Bed and Breakfast establishment in Scarborough and on occasions had taken a summer job running the canteen on the Dover-Calais ferry. Harry was convinced that he would have all the necessary skills to ensure that the ship was adequately provisioned and the passengers made to feel at home.

At exactly ten minutes to three o'clock the Admiral heard a motor vehicle crunching its way along the gravel driveway in front of the house. He peered through the window of his study and observed a large black car which, for all the world, looked like the sort of transport that followed the hearse in a funeral procession. The doorbell issued its nautical chime and within a few moments, Lady Harrington was ushering a party of four into the study.

'I'm sure you would like some tea,' she said when the introductions were over and the party was seated. Without waiting for an answer she left the room and the Admiral took command.

'Now gentlemen,' he began, 'today is an historic day. A day

that will go down in the annals of the Golden Oceans Line. You gentlemen compose the heart and soul of the *Golden Handshake* and we are meeting for the first time to agree our plan of action. For this unique and historic voyage I intend to sail with you, but I shall not interfere. You have responsibility for your own area of work and for the overall welfare of the ship and her company. Captain Sparda!'

The Captain, who had been attempting to decipher a large nautical map hanging on the wall, visible jumped.

'I have not had the pleasure of your company previously. Perhaps you will report on the recent sea trials.'

The Captain, a diminutive man of no more than five feet four inches, rose to his feet.

'Sit down, Captain,' ordered the Admiral. 'This is all very informal today, although once on board we shall have a little more discipline and order than that which is usually found on cruise ships. Today we can relax.'

'Thank you Admiral, sir', Sparda began. 'The engine was a little rusty and made quite a lot of noise but, once we had insulated it with thick cardboard, it seemed well - although the insulation must be changed every other day. The balconies, six in all, were riveted outside the six top-grade suites. Alas, there was not the time to fit balcony doors, but the portholes are reasonably large and most passengers should have no difficulty in squeezing through. The former stables have been converted into very handsome, pre-fabricated suites, and the old cattle trough has been kept for sentimental reasons but also to provide a pool where passengers can sit with their feet in the water. It will remind them of seaside holidays.'

'Capital, Captain,' boomed the Admiral. 'Quite excellent. We want our clients to have a new experience and yet to feel secure in memories from the past, evoked by the ship's artefacts. What about the rudder?'

Here a cloud seemed to pass across the face of the good Captain, but it was gone as quickly as it appeared.

'A few problems at first,' he said. 'Initially it had the unfortunate habit of sticking in one position so that for several hours we went round and round in circles. I think the ship is seaworthy now.'

'Well,' said the Admiral, always quick to turn a misadventure into an opportunity, 'if that happens on the voyage, it will give our passengers a three hundred and sixty-degree view of the territory they are exploring. Thank you, Captain. Most satisfactory.'

The Admiral made several notes in his *Missions to Seamen* diary and turned towards Mr Bigatoni.

'Now sir, what are your plans?'

For the past several weeks Enzo had been perusing the London Telephone Directory in a vain attempt to remember lists of names. Faces? No problem, but where he had seen the face and to whom it belonged defeated him. He produced a simple paper-covered book from his pocket.

'This, sir,' he said, 'will provide us with the highlight of the cruise.' He handed the Admiral a volume entitled *A Visitor's Guide to the French Language*.

'I have similar volumes in Italian, German, Spanish and Albanian. Each morning at the prime time of eleven I intend to conduct a language class, when I shall read a word to the passengers and they will repeat it back to me. We want there to be an educational element to the cruise, Admiral, and I am sure that my classes will provide just what is needed.

'We have also been fortunate to secure the services of two world-renowned lecturers. Sir Horace Beanstalk will talk at six o'clock each evening in the space available before dinner at seven. He will address the passengers on the flora and fauna of the Isle of Man. The attendance may not be too great at this hour, but I have asked Sir Horace to have cyclostyled copies of his text available, and that, together with a set of Magic Lantern slides, will be available in the library. The other lecturer, Dr Ludwig Bernstein, will speak at ten thirty each evening on the music of Stockhausen.'

'This gets better and better,' said the Admiral, beaming brightly. 'I can't wait to listen to these two esteemed gentlemen. What about a quiz, Mr Bigatoni? Passengers love that sort of thing.'

'Ah.' said Enzo, with obvious delight. 'I have already thought of that.' He produced a very large box labelled *Piddling Pursuits*. 'This box, Admiral, contains five thousand questions, together with answers - and I alone have the key to it! Each day at a prime time in the afternoon I intend to have a team quiz with prizes for those who complete the course.'

The Admiral nodded in satisfaction at the innovative skills of his new team. Harry had certainly chosen well.

'Now, Mr Duvet, your turn. What have you to report?'

If the truth were known, Mr Duvet's purchasing experience was rather limited. He had in the past made a bi-weekly journey to the local supermarket in Scarborough to purchase breakfast cereals and the ingredients for a Full English Breakfast, and on the Cross-Channel ferry all he had to do was to pop a cheese or ham sandwich under the grill. But he had spoken with a friend who at one time served in the Army Catering Corps and was now in charge of catering at Durham Jail, and had received invaluable advice.

'Think big' was the gist of it. Mr Duvet did just that and ordered massive tins of baked beans and sacks of powdered milk. He was able to buy at a reduced price some out-of-date provisions from a charity food store and dozens of cases of powdered egg. For the cabins he obtained a huge quantity of Army-surplus blankets.

'The kitchen is equipped,' Mr Duvet said, 'and the larder is virtually ready. As for the cabins, as I speak an army of volunteers are assembling some excellent flat-pack furniture from a well-known store that recently went into liquidation. All I need now is a quick visit to France to collect some duty-free wine – and I shall buy a lot as I know our passengers love a drink – and of course there will be a vast mark-up for the company.'

'Gentlemen,' declared the Admiral, 'I am proud of you all. You have certainly got the situation well under control and there is not the slightest doubt in my mind that we will enjoy a cruise that will be an unforgettable experience for all who take part.'

He stretched out his hand and grasped hold of a small rope, hanging beneath a polished brass bell. He tugged it, sending a deafening noise throughout the study.

'Onward ever!' he cried. 'And now for some tea.'

7

For the second time in a week Albert Hardcastle found himself in the private office of the Manager of the Yorkshire Prudent Bank - Grimsby branch. This time the Manager's chair was occupied by none other than Darren Worthington who, following the rapid departure of his predecessor to unknown territory, had received swift promotion.

'I am delighted to see you again, Mr Hardcastle, and under much happier circumstances. I should inform you immediately that the lottery money is now safely in your joint account, and a cash sum has been transferred to Mr Jason Smith to ease any inconvenience he may have suffered as a result of the bank's error. Of course we have asked him to keep this whole matter confidential, and Mr Smith has no idea that the money belonged to you. We are strict on confidence at the Prudent Bank, Mr Hardcastle, very strict.'

'Well, thank the Lord for that,' said Albert. 'You gave me and the missus a nervous moment, I can tell you. Do you know that Jason Smith, thinking he had won millions, actually phoned the Head Office and told them what to do with his job? Had he not had a drink or two which befuddled his reasoning, he would have been in real trouble. As it was, he mistakenly got through to the Co-op Funeral Department, who thought someone was ringing to arrange Jason's funeral. His wife herself nearly died when the Funeral Director called round with his little black book.'

Mr Worthington maintained a discreet silence and jotted something down on a pad before him. He looked up and addressed Albert once again.

'I well understand you wanting to keep the fact that you have won a substantial sum of money secret, Mr Hardcastle. As we are all aware, this whole affair has caused so much speculation in Grimsby that I would advise you to say nothing further and to keep your head down. Perhaps get away with your wife for a week or so. After all, you have now retired and no one would think anything of it if you went on an extended holiday. As it might cause comment if we were seen lunching together, I have taken the liberty of ordering a light lunch here in the office. Some smoked salmon and just a glass of champagne.'

'Very considerate, I'm sure, but I would prefer Brown Ale,' said Albert, unwilling to change the habits of a lifetime.

'Brown Ale it shall be,' said the ever-tactful Manager - and smoked salmon and Brown Ale it was!

Albert arrived home that afternoon after what he considered to be a most insubstantial lunch. He had no love for brown bread at the best of times, especially when it was cut so thinly that the slightest draught would have blown it off the plate. As for the salmon, it tasted like no salmon *he* had ever come across. Often his wife would open a tin of sockeye red and that, together with lettuce, radishes and sliced hard-boiled eggs was the sort of high tea he knew. That was real salmon, not the uncooked muck he was obliged to swallow at the bank. However, it was a kindly gesture even if, throughout the meal, Mr Worthington made several attempts to get him to transfer the six or so million pounds out of his current account into 'something more suitable for such a large sum'. Albert was having none of it. The money stayed where it was and he would draw on it whenever he might need it.

Alice was doing the ironing when he entered the kitchen through the back door.

'Wipe your feet, Albert!' she cried. 'I've just swabbed the floor and I don't want you messing it up with your great clod-hoppers.'

Albert did as he was bid, wandered into the living room and sat in his chair by the fire. Casually he picked up a copy of the *Grimsby Soapbox*, a newspaper he had known since he was a lad. Clearly they were struggling to find fresh news for this edition. The story of a local MP, who in an attempt to gain popularity took on 'Bruiser Barlow' in a local fairground and had still not recovered consciousness three days after the bout, continued to run. Otherwise fish, or the shortage thereof, dominated the columns.

Turning the pages, he could not fail to see a large advertisement headed by the picture of a Naval Officer in full ceremonial rig.

Golden Oceans, he read. First World Cruise. See the world in luxury. First come, first pleased! For Albert, whose horizons were limited indeed, this was heady stuff. A chance to see the world. A chance to see for himself what this world had to offer. The wonderful thing was that he had the cash. The sum required to pay for two on this exotic journey of a lifetime would hardly make a dent in his six million.

'Alice,' he called out. 'Come here, luv.'

His wife appeared from the kitchen.

'Have you seen this?' he asked, holding out the newspaper.

'Of course I haven't,' she replied indignantly. 'Do you think I've nothing better to do than gawk at the paper? It's a rag anyway. I hear Jimmy Ockshott is still unconscious. As he spent most of his time in Parliament asleep, it ought not to make much difference to him anyway.'

She took the newspaper from his outstretched hand, adding, 'Well, what's so important?'

'Look,' he urged. 'The World Cruise.'

'World Cruise,' she repeated. 'World Cruise. Who in their

right mind would want to spend God knows how much being seasick and eating foreign muck?'

'I think this might be different,' said Albert hopefully. 'If you read on, it says that there will be traditional British home cooking and that the modern ship is equipped with all the latest devices they can afford. They even have balconies.'

Alice read on. 'Aye,' she murmured. 'They do make some claims, of that there's no doubt.'

Her husband cut her short.

'If we went, Alice, we could visit Cousin George in Australia.' He was getting more enthusiastic by the moment. 'We've not seen him since he left on a ten-pound passage years ago. He were but a lad then.'

'It's a lot of brass, Albert,' Alice said with her customary Northern caution. 'A lot of brass.'

'Against six million it's nowt,' replied Albert. 'Nowt but a trifle.'

To make such an assertion indicated a major move in his thinking. Within twenty-four hours, Albert and Alice Hardcastle had sent off for a brochure containing complete details of the journey of a lifetime.

8

Harry Parkhurst was a happy man. Since placing the advertisement in *The Times* and having had it picked up by virtually every local paper in the British Isles, applications for brochures had flooded in. He was especially gratified when a travel piece he had written, under the pen name of Bryson Paxman, appeared in a popular magazine. He deliberately chose the surnames of two well-known personalities in the hope that members of the public might think that the piece had been written by one or other of these two discerning gentlemen and thus have *gravitas*.

What could be more delightful, began the blurb, *than to relax on the balcony of your suite, under a tropical sky with a refreshing drink in hand. A gourmet dinner awaits, followed by the best entertainment money can buy. All this and more with Golden Oceans, the Line everyone is talking about.*

The piece went on to describe the new Flagship of the Line, and to make special mention of the fact that the company enjoyed the expert direction of a retired Naval Officer, of the most senior rank, whose experience of matters nautical was unrivalled.

Captain Sparda, 'a jovial and seasoned sailor' was praised for his hospitality on board and his skill when facing the elements.

During the sea trials of the Golden Handshake, wrote the spectral Bryson Paxman, *I had the pleasure of dining at the Captain's Table. An honour indeed and one that will be accorded to all passengers who book a Balcony Suite. Never have I experienced such charming and wise company. Alas, the occasion went far too quickly. It was an evening to remember. A magical evening.*

Judging by the number of applications received for Balcony Suites following the publication of this piece, there were plenty of prospective passengers who desired to dine with the former Master of the Messina ferry. Harry was delighted. Bryson and Paxman had done them proud.

9

Down in Southend-on-Sea, Radley Duvet was feverishly provisioning the ship for the first leg of the World Cruise. He seemed to have acquired an extraordinary quantity of baked beans and milk powder, but had been assured by his ex-Army friend that he would never regret having these two faithful standbys in his locker.

'Everyone likes baked beans,' he was informed. 'As for milk powder, it is invaluable when mixed with dried egg to form scrambled eggs. Cheap, nourishing, and served with a sprig of parsley it is very appealing.'

The *Golden Handshake* was moored at the end of the pier reputed to be the longest pier of its kind in the British Isles. Harry, with the permission of the local Council, had pitched a reception marquee on the promenade and had been able to staff it with several elderly ladies who always volunteered for anything and everything in Southend. Several years previously they had named themselves 'The Southend Sea Belles' and their prime mission in life was to be helpful to everyone and anyone who visited the town. They were determined to correct the erroneous image of 'Essex Girls' and replace it with a positive picture which more accurately reflected the true character of this delightful county.

Enzo Bigatoni, the fledgling Cruise Director, had written to, or emailed, each person who had booked for the voyage and asked them to send him a passport-sized photograph. He felt that if he could see the face of the individual then it would be a relatively easy matter to match it to a name. What he failed to take into account was the vanity that afflicts most of the human species. Almost without exception, the photographs he received were totally useless. A seventy-year-old passenger sent in a faded picture taken at a formal dance sometime in the nineteen nineties! Since then he had increased in weight considerably, and his now wrinkled face bore little resemblance to the individual posing next to all Master of Hounds. Another showed a Mr Robert Jones, now aged eighty-six, dressed in a cricket blazer at a match he had played in 1979. The Brylcreemed hair he then possessed had now departed, leaving his head as smooth as a billiard ball. Enzo silently cursed the vanity of the cruising public and resumed the arduous task of attempting to commit to memory the passenger list.

During the last few days before departure, Captain Sparda, the Master of the *Handshake* was nowhere to be seen, having been locked in urgent discussions with the Chief Engineer. The two of them spent the better part of each day in the engine room. The engineer appeared at odd intervals when he was seen frantically ordering large quantities of engine oil, which was swallowed up as soon as it arrived. A fisherman, enjoying an afternoon's sport at the end of the pier, swore that he witnessed Captain Sparda leap over the stern of the ship and spend at least half an hour wrestling with the rudder. This assertion was vehemently denied by the Captain but, when he developed a very heavy cold, suspicions were aroused.

Meanwhile, Admiral Benbow Harrington had visited the Naval outfitters in town and ordered a full set of whites for each of his senior crew.

'My little gift for you all,' he had said. The gesture was much appreciated, even though some alterations were required as the Admiral had, in fact, bought a job lot which had been ordered by the Navy of a far-away country where the largest sailor was barely five feet tall!

'Thank God for the Southend Sea Belles,' said the Admiral, as he handed across several dozen whites for alteration. These were quickly converted from long white trousers into shorts by the ever-helpful Belles.

On the day before departure the Admiral and Lady Harrington arrived in Southend where they had booked a room at a leading hotel. Lady Harrington had wisely decided that she would not join her husband on this voyage; her past experiences of life at sea had completely cured her of any desire she might have once had to see more of the world.

That evening, there was to be a pre-cruise reception, to which local dignitaries had been invited. The Admiral had hoped that a royal personage might attend the reception but, as the Princess Royal was visiting a cat-food factory in Liverpool and the younger members of the Royal Family were busy shooting up bad men in far-flung parts of the world, or more domestically, changing nappies at home, it was left to the Chairman of a nearby local Council to do the honours. Councillor Paddy Patterson and his partner Bernie Bollinger were duly booked. The Band of the Royal Marines were invited to play but, alas, cuts in the Defence Budget prevented this and so the Featherthorpe Secondary School Brass Ensemble under the direction of Rodney Stope MA stepped into the breach. Specially invited passengers were to attend the reception, and the main body of travellers would arrive the following morning ready for an afternoon departure.

The evening went pleasantly enough. As the Admiral had instructed that whites would be worn for the reception, he was the only person to arrive in long trousers. The other senior staff turned up wearing shorts, which caused some comment as spring had not yet arrived and the evening was a little chilly, to say the least. Unfortunately, due to the Education Secretary ordering Featherthorpe Secondary School to convert into a night school, most pupils were occupied with their studies and only three members of the Ensemble were able to be present, a trombonist, a tuba player and a percussionist who was learning to play the triangle. The latter was not always heard above the general chatter of guests and the playing of the brass, but he did well enough and was roundly applauded at the conclusion of the evening. Rodney Stope, who had missed his bus, arrived much to his disappointment just as the guests were departing. However, the Admiral promised him a free cruise around Poole Harbour, which somewhat compensated him. The Chairman of the Council made an unusual speech about the merits of Gay Marriage, which greatly angered the Admiral and Lady Harrington, who did their best to try and cancel his appearance at the departure the following morning. Alas, there was nothing they could do at such a late juncture and so the arrangements went ahead.

Dawn broke and Harry arrived at the marquee before the town was stirring for the day. Exactly at six in the morning the first group of the Southend Belles arrived and began to lay white cloths over the wooden trestle tables. One of their number appeared with a box of plastic cards which were to act as identification for the passengers and also as electronic door keys for the cabins and suites.

Radley Duvet dragged in a large cardboard box full of plastic beakers and placed them next to a sizeable container holding a suspicious-looking orange liquid which he claimed was fresh orange juice. As earlier, one of the Belles had seen him empty a packet of crystals into the container, he was given little credibility for accuracy. Unfortunately, the cable linking the tent to the mains electricity supply had mysteriously disappeared during the night and so it was impossible to play recorded music as was originally intended. The problem was soon resolved when one of the Belles went home and returned with an ancient gramophone and a plentiful supply of 78 records which she played throughout the morning. The Admiral was not too happy with the selection, as they did not exactly convey the modern image he so wanted to display, but 'retro' was all the rage these days, thank goodness.

A local Scout troop had been hired to collect the passengers' luggage on arrival and transport it along the pier to the ship - a distance of over a mile! Radley was in charge of this operation and briefed the lads as soon as they appeared at eight o'clock. He had borrowed several wheelbarrows from the Southend Gardening Club, which he thought might be of considerable help to the boys, who were willing, but could not possibly manage some of the heavy luggage which was to come their way.

'Where is Enzo Bigatoni?' shouted an irate Harry as the clock approached nine. 'That man has the one and only passenger-list, without which we cannot let anyone board.'

One of the Scouts was dispatched to a nearby boarding-house where the Cruise Director had been accommodated for the night. A bleary-eyed Director finally arrived at nine thirty, *without the list*, which he had left behind in his haste to get to the ship. He had spent most of the night attempting to memorise the names of passengers and attach them to faces, but the task defeated him. He was in very low spirits indeed when he finally took up his position behind the first trestle table.

By ten o'clock the Admiral, the General Manager, the Hotel Manager and the Cruise Director were all assembled in the tent ready for the first passengers to arrive.

'Where is Captain Sparda?' the Admiral asked irritably. 'He ought to be here to greet the first of the passengers on this all-important occasion.'

Enquiries were made and it seemed that he had last been seen the previous evening making his way to the ship when the reception broke up. The Admiral trained his telescope on the distant vessel moored to the end of the pier and observed a figure clambering over the side and jumping onto the jetty. It was none other than Captain Sparda . . . and he presented a sorry sight. His white shorts, so carefully tailored by the good ladies of Southend, were streaked with grease and oil. His hair was dishevelled and it was clear that he had not shaved.

'Good heavens!' exclaimed the Admiral. 'What on earth has Sparda been up to?'

The unfortunate Captain eventually staggered into the tent and was immediately handed a cup of orange liquid by Duvet, which, after taking one gulp, he promptly spat out.

It transpired that the worthy man had spent the whole night with the Chief Engineer, pouring gallon after gallon of oil into the engine and attempting to get the rudder to operate correctly. He assured the Admiral that everything now seemed well. As it was too far to go to the hotel to get cleaned up, he was escorted to a local Public Convenience where he did his best to make himself presentable for the first guests.

At exactly eleven that morning, all was in place. The Scouts were lined up at the entrance to the tent, each lad with a wheel-barrow. Captain Sparda had been able to borrow a pair of clean tennis shorts from one of the Belles and, providing he stood behind one of the trestle tables, he looked presentable as only his top half was visible.

Enzo, who guarded the entrance to the tent from unwelcome visitors, kept an anxious eye open for the first passengers to arrive. Suddenly he heard the clip-clop of horses' hooves and a landau rolled into sight, pulled by two rather tired-looking carthorses. It stopped by the entrance and the coachman leaned over and addressed Enzo.

'Hey, you mate. Is this where folks enlist?'

Enzo looked shocked. 'What do you mean, Sir?' he replied haughtily. 'This is where passengers embark for the World

Cruise on the *Golden Handshake*, if that is your meaning.'

'Oh,' said the coachman, glancing at the Scouts. 'I thought it was Bob-A-Job week.'

Enzo went to open the passenger door.

'Watch out mate,' said the driver. 'It's liable to come off its hinges if you ain't careful.'

Enzo cautiously opened the rickety door to none other than Mr and Mrs Albert Hardcastle. Mrs Hardcastle wore an enormous hat decorated with a selection of what appeared to be tropical fruit. Her husband sported a black overcoat and a flat cap. Since deciding to go on the cruise, Albert thought that he ought to do things in style for once in his life. He had visited a local gentleman's outfitter and bought himself a new suit. Well, quite new. It had been returned the previous week and only required minor alteration to fit him, and of course it was a very reasonable price. His wife's wardrobe was largely made up from items bought from a Grimsby departmental store when they went into liquidation, and from a Marks and Spencer's sale, along with a variety of homemade summer dresses. She had fashioned the hat herself and was immensely proud of it.

It was Albert's idea to arrive in this fashion. He reasoned that, as they were miles away from Grimsby, he and Alice could get away with a little flamboyant behaviour, hence the coach and horses. Enzo assisted the first passengers down from their equine transport and Mrs Hardcastle, being kindly disposed towards animals, went to pat one of the horses. Before the coachman could issue a warning, the animal took one large snap at the delicacies displayed on the hat and in a trice had munched through them all.

'My God, Albert!' she cried. 'Me hat - me lovely hat. He's bloody well eaten it all.'

Quick to act in any crisis, Enzo took Mrs Hardcastle by the arm, and followed by Albert, the party were ushered into the tent where Radley was waiting to thrust a plastic beaker into their hands. One of the Belles, who had witnessed the whole unfortunate episode from a peephole in the canvas, ushered the distraught Alice Hardcastle to a chair.

'Never mind, dear,' she said soothingly. 'There are plenty of fresh bananas on board and I am quite sure the handicraft instructor will be able to repair the damage done to your lovely hat.'

Mrs Hardcastle dabbed her eyes with a violet handkerchief and Albert looked uncomfortable. By now other passengers were arriving and the boarding operation was swinging into action. The World Cruise was almost - not quite but almost - ready to go.

10

Considering all the things that might have gone wrong, the boarding itself went reasonably well. There was a nervous moment when the Belle responsible for checking the names of passengers and handing them their plastic identification card, got hopelessly muddled due to the fact that she had left her reading glasses at home and was operating with a mixture of guesswork and assistance from Radley Duvet and Enzo Bigatoni, both of whom confused the situation considerably. Enzo, who for practice had attempted to memorise names from the London Telephone Directory before the passenger-list was known, now found that the telephone-list was all that he could remember! Radley simply did not have a clue and eventually it fell to Harry to take over the operation and relieve a senior Scout from luggage duties to deal out the cards.

When passengers had walked well over a mile from the tent to the ship, a further complication occurred as the deckhand assigned to operate the onboard check-in system found that none of the cards would work. Apparently Radley had left his new iPad on top of the box of plastic, with the result that they had all been neutralised by the magnet in the computer. A fresh supply of cards would have to be ordered, and as that would take several hours, passengers boarded with no electronic identification. Names were scribbled on a writing pad by an Indian crew member whose command of English was limited. Throughout the voyage, therefore, some passengers were never properly identified.

Given that Mrs Alice Hardcastle had experienced such an upset on alighting from her carriage the Admiral, gallant to the last, secured a place for her and her husband on the little train that ran the length of the pier, and so the couple were able to ride in state to occupy their suite. This caused a slight disturbance among other passengers who were required to walk, and an occasional scuffle broke out as tired cruisers attempted to secure a seat on the crowded transport.

The arrival of Councillor Paddy Patterson and his life-partner, Bernie Bollinger, was treated with the respect that it certainly deserved. The Scouts and the Belles were lined up on the Promenade, and just inside the tent the senior staff members were assembled in their white dress uniforms. As Captain Sparda had not yet retrieved his trousers, he had to remain partially hidden behind a trestle table, but he was now well accustomed to this. Regrettably it meant that he could not be with the Admiral outside to be one of the first to welcome the distinguished visitors as the tennis shorts, whilst respectable, were not entirely in keeping with such an event.

The Admiral, with Lady Felicity by his side, took up his position, and waited. Eventually, some twenty minutes after the expected time of arrival, an ancient motor vehicle pulled up and from out of the rear seat emerged the civic partnership, accompanied by a reverend gentleman whom they identified as Justin Longparish their chaplain. Councillor Paddy had donned his pinstriped suit and best purple shirt for the occasion, and alongside the cleric might well have been mis-identified as a Bishop. In fact, he was referred to as 'My Lord,' by the Captain, when the introductions were taking place, which flattered him considerably. Bernie wore a bright pink shirt and a canary yellow bow-tie along with a rowing blazer of kaleidoscopic hue. The two made a delightful couple and greatly impressed the Belles.

Once the tent party had been introduced, the Admiral led the newcomers towards the train, where they were introduced to the driver. As the engine-driver had been at school with Bernie and Paddy, and had a low regard for both, this meeting was rather abrupt. They were ushered by the Admiral into a minute compartment within which the Belles had thoughtfully placed several plump velvet cushions which, when sat on, elevated the party to a dangerous height. Had there been any bends on the line, the whole group would have been in grave danger of being tipped out. In this style they made their ceremonial way to the gangway.

There were very few people indeed who were privy to the fact that the *Golden Handshake* had previously been a cattle and horse transporter. Visitors had remarked on occasions that there seemed to be a slight odour of the equine kingdom, but this was brushed aside by Harry, who informed them that the ship had transported members of the Olympic Equestrian Team and that leather saddles, and other items of equipment carried by the competitors, tended to leave behind their own aroma.

Once safely up the gangway, the two guests were both seen to wrinkle their noses and glance at each other. The Admiral quickly moved them on into what had been the cattle-holding area and was now converted into a ballroom. A stage had been erected at one end and on it was a lectern and microphone. Hanging from the rather low ceiling was a banner which read: *Golden Handshake World Cruise - Welcome.*

The room was nearly full of passengers, some of whom had managed to find a seat. Most stood around clutching yet another beaker of coloured liquid supplied by the ever-thoughtful Hotel Director. When the stage party entered, consisting of the Admiral and Lady Harrington, Paddy Patterson, Bernie Bollinger, Mr Harry Parkhurst, Captain Peché Sparda (now thankfully reunited with a new pair of trousers), Enzo Bigatoni and last, but certainly not least, Mr Radley Duvet, the whole room stood as though it was a school assembly.

As Cruise Director it was Enzo responsibility to host the

proceedings. He stepped carefully towards the lectern and it appeared as though he was speaking, although not a sound emanated from the equipment in the room.

'Can't hear!' cried a voice from the floor. 'Speak up!' urged another.

Enzo tried the time-honoured technique of tapping the microphone with his forefinger, to no avail. A technician appeared in the wings and began a crouched run towards the centre of the stage. Why he crouched no one knew as he was not obscuring the vision of anyone, but again technicians always do a crouched run when having to take the stage in an emergency and he was simply following tradition. He produced a large screwdriver and there was a sharp retort when sparks flew from Enzo hand-mike, which he promptly dropped. Another crouching technician appeared from the opposite side carrying a megaphone which he thrust into the empty hands of Enzo and left the stage.

'Welcome everybody,' began the Cruise Director, bellowing down the ship's hailer. 'Welcome to the World Cruise of the *Golden Handshake*.'

This was to be the cue for one of the technical staff to start a gramophone record of the Band of the Royal Marines playing the National Anthem. Unfortunately, everyone had forgotten that the said gramophone had been pressed into urgent service the previous evening at the reception - and no one had thought to bring it to the ship. There was an awkward pause before the Admiral started to sing and everyone else joined in. At the end of the first verse several began to launch into the next stanza, but Enzo brought them to a ragged halt by holding one hand high in the air and waving it furiously.

'Golden Cruisers,' he intoned, 'may I present to you the Commandant of the Fleet and the Owner of the Company, Rear Admiral Benbow Harrington, Retired, accompanied by his charming wife Lady Felicity Harrington.'

The Admiral stepped forward and was handed the hailer by Enzo. His speech, which detailed the history of the company and the excellent safety record of the ships, was long. The passengers, many of whom had travelled a great distance and had had to walk the length of the pier, in addition showed signs of flagging. Most of them had yet to be shown to their Suites, and many were worried about being reunited with their luggage. All they wanted was a cup of tea and a period of calm. Finally he concluded his opening words and introduced his honoured guest, Councillor Paddy Patterson, who, he said, would give the official speech inaugurating the World Cruise.

Councillor Paddy rose from his seat and, as he did so, received a whispered word of encouragement from his consort Bernie, he of the pink shirt and yellow dickie bow. He was just about to begin speaking when there was a slight commotion from the wings and a somewhat dishevelled clerical figure appeared. As the Councillors' chaplain had not been introduced, few people had the slightest idea who he was and what he was doing on the platform. It transpired that he had been taken on a tour of the ship and had been busy placing religious tracts in each cabin. He would have liked to have deposited Bibles but, as he was single-handed, he could not manage the weight and so contented himself with a document which invited the reader to become a Sunbeam for Jesus. Alas, the chaplain had strayed into the crew's quarters and was apprehended whilst inserting a document in the bedside drawer of the chief greaser. Thinking that he was being robbed, the greaser set about the unfortunate cleric and locked him in the oil storage room where he languished until he was released when it was noticed by one of the Councillors' party that he was missing.

Councillor Paddy gave him a long hard stare then turned his attention to the megaphone.

'We are delighted to be here today. It is an honour for me to be invited to inaugurate this great world cruise. It is an honour for Southend and for my Council in the County. Er, it is an honour indeed ... Um, an honour ... Uh, indeed ... Yes, it is ... An honour.'

Consort Bernie glanced at his partner with a worried look on his face. This was not going as smoothly as it had this morning when they had rehearsed the speech in front of the bathroom mirror. Perhaps dear Paddy had mixed up the pages of his notes as he did occasionally. Bernie half-stood and, adopting the standard crouching position, edged towards the lectern. He held out his hand for Paddy's notes, grabbed hold of them and did a quick shuffle before returning them.

That did the trick.

'We are living in days when equality is important,' Paddy resumed. 'Why, you tell me, why ought a ship be referred to as "she"?' From the corner of his eye he could see the Admiral flinch. 'It is nothing but discrimination and ought to be banned by law,' he went on. 'By law, I say.'

Here he thumped the lectern with such force that the Admiral not only flinched, he visibly jumped.

'Why is a floating marine device referred to as a lifebuoy? Do you know? Is it not another example of sexism? Why are we instructed to shout "Man overboard" and not "Person overboard"? The country is riddled with sexism. Riddled, I tell you. Through and through.'

At this juncture the platform party were getting distinctly restless and passengers were beginning to drift out of the arena. The Admiral glanced at his watch and passed a written note to Enzo, who looked pained. He half-stood but the Councillor motioned him to sit down.

'I have not yet finished,' he said, peering round at the bemused gathering on the platform.

Just then, a crew member appeared at the doorway and

with sweeping theatrical gestures caught the Admiral's eye and pointed at his watch. Still Councillor Paddy continued to expound his case. Another crew member appeared with a large blackboard on which he had scrawled *Tide rapidly going out. Grave danger of not sailing.*

No sooner had this vital message been received by the Admiral than the ship gave a sudden lurch and Councillor Paddy was thrown violently into the auditorium, together with the supporting cast. Panic ensued. The dispenser of what passed for orange juice discharged its contents across the floor, drenching several passengers in the process. Captain Sparda extracted himself from under the mighty bulk of Bollinger and made haste for the bridge. Lady Harrington swooned and the Admiral, a gentleman to the last, dragged her to the nearest exit and deposited her on a couch before leaping towards the bridge after the Captain.

The ship was now leaning at an angle of some 25 degrees, and in the storeroom sacks of powdered milk had burst, creating a scene reminiscent of Scott of the Antarctic.

Eventually the problem was identified. The initial proceedings had gone way over time during which the tide had receded to such an extent that the keel of the *Handshake* was left resting on the seabed. Had it not been for secure mooring ropes, it would have capsized completely. The Admiral, Captain Sparda and several officers balanced themselves precariously on the bridge and attempted to make a plan of action. The Pier Master had now appeared and was shouting incomprehensibly at the bridge from his position of safety at the end of the pier. It seemed as though he was advising that the *Golden Handshake* be evacuated immediately. Although lifeboat drill had not yet been conducted on board, crew members had rounded up as many passengers as possible and were instructing them how to don their lifebelts.

Albert and Alice Hardcastle were considerably shaken by the events of the last hour. They had not managed to get to their cabin but had found a seat in the assembly hall. Albert fell asleep and was dreaming of exotic beaches in sub-tropical climes when it seemed as though an earthquake struck. He awoke to a scene of pandemonium. Alice was clutching him with a grip of iron and all around him people were shouting and screaming.

Gradually they both slithered across the floor to an exit and found themselves on deck peering down at the sea.

'By go,' said Albert to no one in particular, 'this is a rum do. Of that there's no doubt.'

Alice remained speechless until she finally succumbed and, following the example of Lady Harrington, fell into a deep swoon.

The Pier Master was nothing if not efficient. He quickly rigged up a bosun's chair and, one by one, the passengers were hoisted ashore ready to begin the long trek back to dry land.

To this day it remains unclear what happened to the two

worthy Councillors. Someone claimed to see them clambering over the side and stepping into a pedalo, from whence they proceeded to pedal furiously towards the nearest shore. Their chaplain seemed to have disappeared completely, and the mystery of his disappearance was not resolved until the ship was under way. Lady Harrington was winched ashore as soon as she recovered and immediately set out for Frinton, having had all her worst fears confirmed.

The good citizens of Southend-on-Sea rallied to the occasion and, with the ready help of the Belles, arrangements were made for passengers to spend the night in local homes. The very next day at high tide the *Golden Handshake* took leave of Southend to tumultuous cheers from many local residents. And so began the first leg of the World Cruise.

11

Albert and Alice spent a fairly comfortable night in the home of a retired bank manager and his wife, Mr and Mrs Arnold Robinson. As Albert did not wish to be reminded of his earlier encounter with the bank at home, he steered clear of discussing Mr Robinson's career, which had taken him as far afield as Brighton and for relief duties to Bournemouth. The Robinsons had never taken a world cruise, and urged the Hardcastles to send plenty of postcards and give a full report on their return, as they themselves might want to take one, one day. This Alice promised to do.

Early the next morning, the kindly Robinsons packed Albert and Alice into the back of their ancient Ford Anglia.

'A treasure,' said Arnold; 'a dream to drive and so cheap to run,' and drove them to the pier where, after fond farewells and promises of everlasting friendship, the couple set off once again on the long trek to the boat. The tent had been dismantled, as Golden Oceans only had a one-day permit from the council, and so they were received by a crew member with an umbrella who pointed them in the direction of the end of the pier.

Once on board there seemed to be some semblance of order. Although the Admiral had retired at three in the morning, the senior staff and crew members had worked feverishly throughout the night to make the ship ready to receive the passengers for the second time in twenty-four hours. At the top of the gangway their names were ticked off a list by a crew security officer. The plastic cards were still not working properly and only ever part-functioned throughout the whole of the cruise. A helpful young man in a white jacket escorted them across the ballroom floor, along a corridor and up several sets of stairs.

'My word,' puffed Alice. 'It's a climb.'

It was indeed a climb to one of the six Balcony Suites that the Hardcastles had reserved.

The young man inserted the plastic in the door handle but the red light continued to glow. He performed the operation several times without success. Finally, in desperation, he put his shoulder against the door and with a crash it flew open, plummeting the steward headlong into the suite. He picked himself up with a smile, since he had been instructed always to smile. If asked by passengers 'How are you?' he was always to answer, 'Excellent.' If asked where he came from, as he would be, he was always to answer, 'India,' and not to be any more specific.

When he had smoothed himself down he addressed the fledgling cruisers.

'I am your personal butler and my name is Udi. If you require anything, rapidly turn the handle on the telephone on the desk and ask for me. I am at your service, sir,' he smiled broadly, then turned politely to Alice. 'Madam.'

Alice did not know what to say, never having had butler service before, so she simply replied, 'Very nice, thank you, I'm sure.'

Albert looked around. 'Eh lad,' he said, somewhat surprised. 'I thought we had a balcony.'

'But, sir, you do,' said the ever-obliging Udi. 'Through there.' He pointed upwards at a porthole secured by heavy wing-nuts. 'Sir, I have to tell you sir that Health and Safety would not allow balcony doors, sir. Too dangerous, sir. Seawater might enter, sir.'

Albert pushed his cap back and scratched his head.

'Well, how the Devil are we supposed to sit on it, lad?' he asked, somewhat annoyed.

'No problem, sir, very easy, sir. You call me on telephone, sir'. Udi opened a small cupboard and produced a set of steps. 'I undo porthole and help you up steps. You go through and enjoy. I bring you drinks. Very nice, sir. Very nice, madam. Very private for sunbath, madam.'

Udi, still continuing his introduction to the suite, picked up a paper from the flimsy-looking dressing table.

'You like drink, sir?' he asked.

Albert replied that he was partial to a Brown Ale and Alice

had been known to have a sweet sherry on a Sunday and a small gin at Christmas.

'Very good, sir. Very nice drink, sir. Very fine drink, madam. Today, no drink on ship. Tomorrow we get drink on ship in France.' He handed Albert the printed list which read:

We understand
that our passengers are on holiday
and that they might like to have a refreshing beverage
at intervals during the cruise,
especially at mealtimes.
In order to make sure
that our esteemed passengers get the best possible value
we have arranged for the international Duty Free Emporium,
Vin Bon Marché
to give a generous discount at their store in Calais.
On arrival in Calais
passengers will be escorted to the
Vin Bon Marché warehouse
and will be able to make their own selection from
the huge range available.
On production of your Cruise-card you will receive
a 5% reduction if you carry your purchases back to the ship
yourself.
If you have them delivered, the reduction will be 3%.

Please indicate below your requirements.
After Calais
there will not be another opportunity to purchase beverages
until we reach the port of Cochin in India,
noted for its excellent whisky,
so we advise all passengers to consider their requirements carefully.

Albert read the list with a pained look on his face.

'I thought the brochure said booze would be free,' he said to Udi.

'Duty-free,' replied the butler. 'All duty-free, sir. Very good bargain, sir.'

After asking if the occupants of the Balcony Suite required anything further and being told, 'Not now, lad,' Udi withdrew and only managed to close the door by pulling it violently and causing a picture of Westminster Pier, the home of one of the other Ships of the Line, to crash to the floor. Albert picked it up and laid it on the bed.

'Well, luv,' he said to Alice, who was gazing incredulously at the upper porthole, 'at last we're on our way.'

As if by some miracle, their suitcases had been delivered to their Suite and Alice set about unpacking and arranging their clothes in the very modest wardrobe. As she was engaged in this task, her husband climbed the steps and gazed out of the porthole.

'We seem to be moving,' he called down. 'Although not very fast.' From his vantage-point he could not see the sea but he had an excellent view of the clouds, and this told him that the ship might be moving through the water. There was also the *thump thump* from the engine, but this was an unreliable guide to movement as the Chief Engineer often tested the machinery when in port and had advised the passengers that from time to time the engine might make a little more noise than usual.

Albert was just stowing the suitcase beneath the bed when a slip of paper appeared under the door. He picked it up.

It read:

Dear Balcony Suite Guest
During the course of the voyage
important announcements will be made over the
Public Address system.
It is important that you listen to them carefully.
Three minutes before an announcement is due
a buzzer will sound in your cabin.
When you hear this you should immediately leave your cabin
and walk briskly along
the corridor (see diagram).
Ascend the first steps you come to
and at the top you will see a marker which clearly says

PUBLIC INFORMATION POINT.
Stand as close to this marker as possible and you will hear the message clearly.
Thank you for your kind attention.
Enzo Bigatoni Cruise Director.

No sooner had Albert read the information through to Alice when a loud buzzing noise was heard in the cabin. 'That's it, luv,' he said to Alice. 'Let's get moving'.

They tugged at the door, which reluctantly opened onto the corridor, along which several other couples were hurrying. With considerable effort they climbed the stairs and arrived at the Information Point, around which a large group of passengers had collected. There was a crackling noise and a small loud-speaker, fastened high on the wall, came to life.

'This is Enzo your Cruise Director speaking with an impor-tant message,' said the disembodied voice. 'Please listen care-fully.'

'Can't hear,' said an anxious voice from somewhere in the crowd.

'Shut up,' said another, 'otherwise none of us will hear.'

'This morning at the prime time of eleven o'clock, and every morning at this same time, there will be a language class con-ducted by myself. In ten minute's time I shall expect to see as many of you as possible in the Friesian Lounge, where I shall introduce you to the French language. If you intend to go ashore this afternoon to collect your beverages, then it is of supreme importance that you have a basic grasp of French. Later in the cruise I shall be introducing you to other languages, all of which I speak fluently. Thank you for your kind attention and have a wonderful day.'

'Damn waste of time,' said Albert as they made their way back to the suite. 'Who the hell needs French to order Brown Ale.'

No sooner had they got back to the cabin than the buzzer sounded again.

'Good Lord,' said Alice. 'Is there no peace?'

Once again they joined the throng and made their weary way back to the loudspeaker. This time there were not quite so many people, as the more infirm of the group were still returning to their cabins following the first call. A few moments passed and the loudspeaker burst into life. Now it was Captain Sparda.

'Good morning, ladies and gentlemen. It's a lovely morning and we are well on our way. It is mandatory that at the start of every cruise there be a lifeboat drill. Yesterday, due to events beyond our control, we could not have the drill and so it will take place this afternoon, following the short visit to Calais. Please read the lifeboat instructions fastened to your bathroom door. Thank you ladies and gentleman. Happy sailing.'

'Why the hell can't they co-ordinate these announcements?'

said a disgruntled Albert. 'We will spend all day running up and down the ship. I came for a cruise, not marathon training.'

Again Alice said nothing as her feet were hurting and she was beginning to feel a little queasy due to the slight motion of the ship. As it was almost eleven, instead of returning to their suite they found the Friesian Lounge where a largish group of passengers had assembled. Enzo made his entry and perched himself on a stool, whilst the class sat around him.

'First,' he said, 'you will divide into groups. Each group will be tested after I have instructed you all. Points will be given for correct answers. At the end of the cruise you will not only have mastered several languages, but will have earned points to win wonderful prizes.'

He produced a book within which he had written a list of French words.

'Right,' he said, 'repeat after me. Thank you - - - *Merci*.'

The passengers obediently repeated the word.

'Isn't he wonderful?' whispered a passenger seated next to Alice. 'He never forgets a face and has a total command of thirty-six languages.'

Alice held her counsel.

'Wine - - - vin,' he continued, and added a dozen or so other words which he regarded as essential.

Suddenly he pointed towards Albert. 'Wine?' he commanded. 'Quick.'

Albert blinked. 'I don't want wine,' he said. 'I want Brown Ale.'

'No points for one,' said Enzo with obvious satisfaction.

'What the hell was all that about?' asked Albert when the class was over.

'That's it for me. Leave French to the Frogs, is what I say.'

Lunchtime approached and Alice had no appetite whatsoever. In order not to leave her on the first day, Albert considerately decided to order room service from the list in the suite.

'What's "De Jour" soup?' he queried as he read down the list.

'Sounds French to me,' replied Alice. 'Best not have that.'

He read further.

'Pommes Frites,' he said. 'That sounds like an Aussie concoction. Don't think I want that.' Finally he settled for a corned-beef sandwich with pickle and a Brown Ale on the side.

Although Albert did not know it, he had made a fortunate choice as Radley Duvet had ordered a very large number of tins of corned beef which he reckoned could be used in many different ways. Many other items on the menu were regrettably off and would remain off for a considerable period of time. The Brown Ale did not arrive as the ship had yet to dock in France where alcoholic supplies were due to be purchased by the passengers. Albert had to content himself with a Dandelion and Burdock.

After lunch, Albert suggested that Alice might rest for

an hour or so and he would do the same. Alas, due to the fact that the Daily Programme, normally circulated to each suite, had been delayed, frequent announcements were made by the Cruise Director, which meant that Albert found himself in a constant state of motion between the Information Post and his cabin. Shortly before four in the afternoon, he was summoned yet again to be told that the ship would dock soon after five and would depart about seven that evening. All wanting to go ashore to sample the delights of the town, or to collect their drinks for the cruise, were told to assemble in the main ballroom. The drinks party would not have a courtesy coach as there was a strike at the port, but the Hotel Director had made special arrangements and there was no need for anyone to worry.

Albert left Alice sleeping and arrived in the ballroom promptly at four. The drinks party was by far the largest group; the majority of them were clutching small pieces of paper and mouthing the French words they had learned that very morning. Radley, still very tired, addressed them. He said that they would proceed ashore in crocodile fashion with himself at the head and the Cruise Director bringing up the rear. Earlier, this assignment had almost caused a fight between these two senior men as Enzo wanted to take the lead. Radley, quite rightly, resisted this suggestion with the argument that it was his show and he would lead it.

When it appeared that the party was complete, Radley

instructed his charges to hold onto the waist of the person in front of them and not to let go. They proceeded to the security desk where the crew member on duty threw up his hands in despair at the sight of so many passengers about to leave at once, so he simply waved them all on. They moved uneasily down the gangplank and stepped onto French soil, continuing to hold tightly on to each other. As 'Vin Bon Marché' was only, according to Radley, a short walk away, they proceeded at a gentle pace. On they proceeded along the dock front and into what seemed to be a waste area, still keeping crocodile formation.

They had just reached a collection of pre-fabricated buildings when there suddenly appeared two *gendarmes* on huge motorcycles. The impressive-looking policemen pulled up in front of Radley and brought the whole procession to a halt. Speaking rapidly in French, they fired several questions at him and he, not having attended the morning class so ably conducted by Enzo, was mystified. A message was passed down the crocodile and Enzo was summoned. He arrived, somewhat bad-tempered, saying that he ought to have led the procession all along as one never knew what might happen on foreign soil.

The senior officer addressed him in rapid French. Enzo did not reply but produced a small notebook from his pocket which he consulted. The other policeman now addressed him, in what seemed to be a more angry manner. Enzo frantically turned the pages of his little book but continued to remain silent. Finally, the senior policeman produced a radio and within moments several other police motor cyclists appeared, together with three police vans.

A man in plainclothes jumped out of one of the vans and questioned Radley. 'What is the meaning of this demonstration?' He had very passable English, even if he was angry. 'Today there is a strike, and demonstrations are forbidden. Yes. You understand? Forbidden.' He wagged his finger at both Enzo and Radley, who recoiled in shock, then turned to Enzo and hissed, 'You are in France, old man. Why do you not speak French? Why do you come with English rabble to strike?'

Enzo remained speechless. Although he would never admit it, his command of French only extended to a few pages of the 'Vin Bon Marché' guide to buying wine. After that, he was as much at sea as any of the others. Also, to be called an 'old man' greatly insulted his dignity. He turned on his heel and prepared to walk away, but the policeman was having none of it.

'So,' he said, 'we will see what you English are made of,' and with that he snapped a pair of cuffs on the unfortunate Cruise Director and led him towards the van, where he pushed him inside and slammed the door.

Returning to the crocodile once more, he challenged Radley, who explained the situation to him as best he could. The English-speaking policeman defended his actions by saying that the English were acting in a most suspicious manner and there was to be no more of it. He concluded by saying that if they wanted their *vin* they had better make haste as 'Vin Bon Marché' closed in twenty minutes' time. And so the crocodile resumed its journey, albeit in a different and less suspicious formation and at a much faster pace, leaving Enzo to work his own way out of trouble.

The group of intrepid travellers arrived at 'Vin Bon Marché' just as the staff were preparing to leave for home. The staff were not in the best of moods, given that the majority of their fellow workers in the vicinity were on strike and able to enjoy an extra holiday. Throughout the day they had had to endure the taunts of some strikers who castigated them for not coming out in sympathy, but had they done so, 'Vin Bon Marché' would have sacked them all on the spot. So, they remained at their posts disgruntled and unhappy. When they observed a large group of strange-looking individuals approaching the store, they imagined that they were about to be attacked by angry strikers and so immediately closed and bolted the doors. This incensed the passengers, who pointed at their watches and made threatening gestures. One or two of the more aggressive banged on the door demanding to be let in.

By now it was two minutes to closing time and there was no hope whatsoever of being able to buy supplies. More passengers showed their wrath by marching to the rear of the store and peering through the windows where they tried to catch the attention of the frightened assistants. Radley did his single-handed best to try and restore order, but he met with little success. Although it was now past closing time, those inside the building were too terrified to leave, and one of the passengers looking through a window noted a Vin Bon Marché employee speaking on the telephone. As the passenger turned around, to his alarm he further noted the two police motorcyclists approaching at a rapid pace, their sirens blazing. Enzo, who had obviously been released from custody, was seen sprinting furiously back towards the safety of the ship.

At the sight of the *gendarmes* the group scattered. Gone was the orderly crocodile. In fact, gone was any semblance of order. It was every passenger for himself.

The *gendarmes* sounded their sirens and blew their whistles. On board, Captain Sparda, thinking he was being acknowledged by the authorities, gave three merry toots on the ship's whistle. This further terrified the passengers, who imagined that this was the sign that the ship was about to depart and so ran even faster towards the gangplank. The old tradition of 'women and children first' never crossed the mind of any of the party. The elderly stumbled along; the infirm wheezed and groaned, and the minority who had reasonable health were the first to enjoy the sanctuary of the *Golden Handshake*. The last person to stagger up the gangway was Albert. On stepping aboard he turned around to see the quay swarming with French cops and military types toting automatic weapons.

'Funny country, France,' he said to himself as he plodded to his cabin without a bottle of Brown Ale to his name. 'Very bloomin' funny.'

Back in the safety of his cabin, Enzo reflected on the events of the afternoon. By any stretch of the imagination, it could not have been described as a success. How was he to know that there was a strike in port here? The French police had behaved dreadfully, and because of their rough tactics with the handcuffs, his wrists hurt terribly. He poured himself a very small tot of Pussers Naval Rum and rested for a few moments. Now he had to face Lifeboat Drill - a regular happening which he hated, as he believed that most of the passengers would never remember what to do if there was a real emergency, as they hardly ever listened to the instructions given by the crew. He remembered reading somewhere about a crew-member of the Titanic who was believed to have said to an embarking passenger, 'God himself could not sink this ship.' He smiled as he pulled his lifejacket out of the locker. Anything can happen at sea, he thought - anything.

By comparison with the events of the afternoon, the drill was a model of precision - well almost. The exclusive Balcony Passengers met by the Information Post and, as they had trodden that way numerous times to listen to messages, they assembled without difficulty. One or two misunderstood the directions given on the cabin card and, instead of bringing with them a warm wrap and essential medicines, came loaded with heavy suitcases, into which they had thrown all their possessions. The ever-patient crew politely told them that such action was not required in future, but they complained that if the ship were to go down they would lose everything they possessed - a statement which the crew took with a pinch of salt, but extreme politeness. When all was completed, Enzo breathed a sigh of relief and returned to his cabin, to prepare himself for the first formal evening on board the SS *Golden Handshake*.

12

Albert and Alice returned to their Suite, and after much banging and shoving, managed to get the faulty door to admit them.
It had proved rather expensive for the ship to equip each Suite
with the modern-style lifejacket, and so life-belts had been supplied which the wearer had to step into and secure around their
waist. They had carried these bulky objects to the drill, where
they had been instructed to put them on. The return to the
Suite was difficult, as both Albert and Alice when wearing the
belt occupied the whole width of the corridor. It proved impossible for them to enter the narrow doorway to the Suite with the
belts in place, but they managed to squeeze out of them - causing a major hold-up to others wanting also to get back to their
Suites. Several passengers remarked that in the event of a disaster, it might prove difficult enough to pass through the corridor,
let alone join a lifeboat.

'You know,' said Albert as he unlaced his boots in preparation for the evening's attractions, 'there's not a lot of spare time
on this ship. No sooner are we back here than it's off again to
some other damn thing.'

Alice picked up the daily programme which had been delivered to their Suite.

'Better get changed quick,' she said abruptly. 'It's Captain's Reception in twenty minutes, and then we have a dinner. It says formal here, so you'd better spruce up, lad.'

Albert groaned inwardly as he recollected the shopping expedition he had been forced to make before the cruise. Never having owned a dinner jacket in his life, he was more than reluctant to splash out now, but Alice had insisted. They were going on a world cruise and he would need a decent outfit; she too would need dresses for the gala occasions that were forecast in the brochure. In the Boss Brothers branch in Grimsby, he had examined the evening suits. No matter what Alice said, he was not bending. They were far too costly to be used for one cruise only.

'Well,' said Alice, 'we might take another cruise. What then?'

'We're not made of brass,' he replied. 'Come on, let's see what they have in the second-hand depot.'

They left Boss Brothers and walked to one of the many charity shops that enlivened the dying high street. Alice pushed Albert, past the bric-à-brac and straw hats, past the neatly ordered books and the ladies' cast-offs until they came to a rail at the rear of the establishment. It was full of very dull shirts and even duller ties. An elderly assistant was sorting through a box of the most unsaleable-looking objects and Alice addressed her.

'We are looking for an elegant dinner suit for my husband. As he has recently put on a little weight, the ones he has do not exactly fit, but he will return to his normal weight - I shall see to that. But now, as we have some very important functions to attend, we would like to see what you have. It's not worth buying new, is it?' She gave a coy little laugh and stretched out her hand to feel the quality of a miserable-looking shirt on the rail.

'Well,' said the assistant, 'you're in luck. Only half an hour ago, a very nice outfit came in. It's not priced yet but it might be just the thing. Hold on.'

She disappeared into a back room as Alice surveyed a shelf of figurines for sale at twenty pence each.

'Ooh, aren't these lovely?' she said.

Albert grunted and said nothing. Within a few moments the assistant returned bearing a jacket and trousers on a wire coat-hanger. Albert was ushered into a small cubical and struggled into the clothing. To his great alarm it seemed to fit, after a fashion. He emerged and Alice immediately seized him, turned him round, pulled at the jacket and announced that it would do splendidly if the trousers were turned up an inch and providing he put on no more weight. A price of ten pounds was agreed and the items were carefully folded and placed in an old supermarket plastic bag.

'Oh,' said Alice. 'As we are here we might as well get you a new dickie bow.' She had noted several amongst the ties and selected a large velvet bow.

'I think we can let you have that,' said the kindly lady as she popped it into the bag.

Alice was duly appreciative and, with her husband in tow, she walked out of the shop and into a world of dinner parties and elegant occasions.

Albert felt awkward in his new second-hand acquisition. Although the fit was passable, the jacket did make him appear somewhat like an elderly 'Teddy-boy' and as for the bow-tie - well, it was unusual to say the least. Alice wore her peach-coloured outfit which she had bought from British Home Stores. Frankly, it was not the most suitable colour for her as it made her look even heavier than she was, but she liked it and that was that. The time allowed to get to the reception was far too short, and there was a great deal of bad temper displayed as Alice tried to smarten Albert up and struggle into the peach costume at the same time.

Ten minutes after the appointed time they appeared at the entrance to the reception area where there was a long queue of expectant cruisers waiting to be greeted by the Captain and, most importantly, be photographed with him. This experience was new to the Captain. True, he had welcomed people aboard the Messina ferry, but the welcome then was highly informal and certainly no photographer was ever present. Alice eyed the other

ladies and was panic-struck when she noticed that the majority
were wearing long evening dresses and she was in a peach costume. She took Albert's arm and quickly propelled him out of
the line.

'Albert, dear,' she said, 'would you be so kind as to escort me
back to our Suite?'

She emphasised 'Suite' so that lesser mortals in lower cabins would recognise that she and Albert were amongst the elite.
Albert looked startled.

'But - - - ' he began, but before he could utter another syllable he was being propelled back along the corridor to the Balcony Suite.

'This is terrible,' Alice wailed, 'just terrible. Did you notice,
Albert?'

Her husband was nonplussed. He had noticed that his braces
were not secure enough and he had to keep hitching up his trousers, but that was about all he had noticed.

'I can't go to dinner, Albert. I just can't.'

Albert, who was now feeling distinctly peckish after the
exertions of the afternoon, looked startled.

'Eh up,' he said. 'Come on, luv. We've got to eat, we've paid
for it.'

'It's the costume, Albert. Did you see what the others were
wearing?'

Albert had certainly noticed some rather startling outfits but he paid little attention and certainly did not understand at all that there might be some dresses that were appropriate and others that were not.

Alice rummaged through her wardrobe. 'I've brought all the wrong clothes,' she wailed.

By now she was virtually in tears.

'The fox-fur cape won't do, neither will the summer fruits outfit.' When waiting for the photograph, Alice had noticed one or two ladies wearing trousers with some form of coloured top. She found a pair of black trousers which Albert unhelpfully remarked 'looked like a pair of pyjamas' and together with a decorative top, prepared to set off yet again. Albert hitched up his trousers and resumed the trek.

Alas, by the time they had reappeared at the entrance to the dining room, the photographer had disappeared and the Captain had gone to host his table. The Maitre D' greeted them then checked their names from a list in front of him.

'Mr and Mrs Hardcastle,' he intoned.

'Balcony Suite,' added Alice.

'Indeed,' he replied smoothly. 'Tonight I have placed you with two other Balcony Suite guests, - Sir Archibald and Lady Willoughby. They are both long-term cruisers, but of course are sailing with us for the first time.'

Albert glanced nervously around the dining area where Filipino waiters were busy serving the first course. On their way to the table Alice noted a passenger sitting alone and with whom she had exchanged some words at the lifeboat drill. The lady stopped Alice for a moment to pass, or ask for, some item of information and Albert, oblivious that he was walking alone to the table, continued on his way.

He stopped at their assigned table number four, where an elegant gentleman and a slightly less elegant lady were seated. They had started their meal. Albert hovered, now conscious of the fact that he was alone and uncertain as to whether he should sit or wait for Alice. The gentleman at the table looked up, saw Albert and without a moment's hesitation said that the first course was delicious and he could now bring the pasta as soon as he wished.

The lady added in an accent, totally strange to Albert, 'And make soup really hot next time.'

Albert shuffled uneasily, totally at a loss as to what to say when, fortunately, Alice appeared and addressed the table.

'I do apologise for our lateness,' she said in her best Northern accent. 'We were unavoidably detained in our suite. A Balcony Suite, you know.'

She sat down and Albert followed her lead.

'Oh I say,' said the gentleman, 'I do apologise, my dear chap. My eyesight is not what it was, you know. By George, I can see now you're nothing like these foreign johnnies running around. My name's Archibald Willoughby, Sir Archie if you like, and this is my lady wife Veronika. It is spelt with a 'k' in Russia, you know. She was well-named as it means 'bringer of victory' - and she's always been a fighter!

Lady Willoughby gave a frosty look at her dinner companions and uttered an incomprehensible monosyllable.

'I'm afraid Veronika does not speak much English, old boy. She spent much of her life in deepest Siberia and we met quite recently when I was hunting for the great Mongolian Elephant. Only three known of this species left in the world, you know. If I had been lucky, that would have made four. As it was, the blighter proved to be totally elusive. Never saw a thing, old fellow. Veronika grew up in that part of the world and told me they used to slaughter them to make soup to last the villagers through the icy winter. That's where they have all gone - Siberian soup. A great shame. Ever been to Siberia, old boy? Oh I say, I don't have your name. Call me Sir Archie but don't call me before breakfast.'

He laughed uproariously at his feeble humour and looked through his fading eyes at Albert. As one eye was slightly off-centre, Albert could not tell if Sir Archie was looking at him or surveying the room. He found it distinctly off-putting.

'My name is Alice Hardcastle,' Alice said before Albert could say anything to embarrass her. 'I am the first daughter of the late Bernard Alsop, formerly of Bradford. This is my husband Albert. We are taking the whole world cruise in a Balcony

Suite, you know. My father called me Alice as the name means 'noble'.' Albert stared at his wife in amazement, but remained quiet.

'Jolly good show, what?' replied their jovial companion. 'Good show, eh, Veronika'?

Lady Willoughby nodded and continued with her meal.

'Well, don't let me hold you up, old boy. Order what you want. What about some vino, hmm? Nothing like it for gladdening the heart, what? I always bring my own drink with me on world cruises. Here, try this. It's a Rothschild '72. Damn good year, I say.'

Out of politeness Albert did not like to refuse and so held out a beaker for Sir Archie to fill.

'Hold on, my dear fellow,' said Sir Archie. 'I know this wine is first-rate, but I have not yet taken to drinking it out of a tumbler!'

He seized a wine glass from the side of Albert's place and proceeded to half-fill it. Albert took a gulp and decided there and then that Brown Ale was, and would remain, his drink. From the look on his face, Sir Archie saw that the wine was not entirely to his fellow passenger's taste.

'No matter!' he exclaimed. 'Veronika won't drink the poison either. All she will take is yak's milk, or vodka.'

He went to pour some wine in Alice's glass but she politely declined.

'Jolly good,' said Sir Archie cheerfully, not at all put out. 'All the more for me.' And he filled his glass to the brim.

13

Meanwhile, back in his tiny office, Enzo Bigatoni, Cruise Director, was feeling totally exhausted. He had not been able to sleep the previous night due to the fact that the ship had to be prepared to sail first thing the following morning. He had had to turn his hand to some hard manual work, to which he was not accustomed. As soon as the clearing up tasks were completed, he had to 'meet and greet' passengers for the second time, and this duty was followed by endless announcements as the ship sailed.

The first port of call, Calais, had been a total disaster and a very frightening experience. He seemed to have spent hours locked in the back of a police van, after which he was questioned endlessly in both French and English. Given that he had lost his little French phrase book in the mêlée, he answered everything in English, and the French policeman, who had been told that Enzo was a language teacher on board, thought that he was obstructing the police in the course of their duty and became increasingly furious. Eventually, having been released from the van with a warning to never *ever* again come to France to support a strike, he had had to run for his life when the police arrived the second time and chased the passengers back to the ship.

Now there was more trouble, this time with lecturers. The Admiral insisted that there must be lecturers on board as they were extremely popular with the guests. Enzo had to acquiesce but secretly he resented their inclusion in the programme as their sessions got in the way of his language classes. The Admiral believed that during a cruise there were many passengers who would like to improve their education and, taking a leaf from the book of other companies, he ordered Harry to engage several lecturers.

'Get a mixed bunch,' said the Admiral one day. 'Music, the Arts, Geography, what have you. See if you can get hold of some well-known names.'

Harry spent many hours attempting to secure the services of eminent speakers. He would be able to offer a free cruise, but there could not be a fee, of course, as the cruise would be very expensive if the lecturer had to pay for it himself. He did not take into account the fact that many lecturers of renown were not particularly interested in just cruising but required payment to keep body and soul together. Eventually he found several individuals who fancied what they thought might be a cheap holiday, and promptly engaged them.

The first two lecturers engaged, Sir Horace Beanstalk and Dr Ludwig Bernstein, had been due to join the ship in Southend-on-Sea, and it was thought they were on board. Due to the initial confusion and the failure of the plastic card checking system to work, no one had any idea who was on board or who was not. After repeated calls over the loudspeaker system, which had passengers scuttling to the Information Posts every few minutes, Sir Horace appeared in the Cruise Director's Office ready for duty. Dr Bernstein, an authority on the music of Stockhausen, was nowhere to be seen. Eventually it transpired that the Admiral, not altogether familiar with classical music, had thought of doing a little preparatory work and had purchased a CD of Stockhausen's music. The sounds that emanated from his player at home not only frightened the dog but caused Lady Felicity to threaten to disable the equipment if such a din continued. The Admiral, being a man of action, immediately cancelled the appearance of Ludwig Bernstein who, understandably, was most upset. He had been looking forward to taking his audience through the world of modern music, culminating in a step-by-step analysis of the symphony in which not a single note was played. The Admiral thought that this latter work would certainly be preferable to Stockhausen, but nevertheless the series was cancelled.

Neither Harry nor the Cruise Director had been informed by the Admiral of this cancellation, and consequently were left to fill the gap in the programme. As always, the resourceful Harry came up with a solution. He had heard that there was a certain Toby Troy (British Empire Medal) who, when he was in foreign parts attempting to sell Bibles to Hezbollah, had been captured and had spent many years in solitary confinement. Newspaper reports said that it was Mr Troy's own silly fault that he got caught as he would keep pestering Hezbollah, and eventually they got so tired of him appearing at their secret headquarters with a cartload of Bibles and hymnbooks, that they took him inside and kept him out of harm's way for several years.

Harry had been informed that Mr Troy, now a firm disbeliever, was always willing to jump up and speak for hours about his exciting life, and so he was engaged. Mr Troy, it was hoped, would join the ship somewhere in Spain.

It was late when Enzo put the finishing touches to the programme for the first sea day when they would be crossing the Bay of Biscay. There was no time for the poor man to join the passengers for the Gala Dinner that evening. Wearily he sent the events sheet to the print shop, ordered a sandwich, and then retired for what he hoped would be a restful night.

'Golfo de Vizcaya,' muttered Captain Sparda as he studied a chart. 'Where the hell is that?'

This was the Captain's first venture into the mighty oceans of the world, and he was not totally conversant with charts, especially as the one he was studying was in Spanish. Fortunately the Staff Captain was more familiar with the wide world beyond Italy, having served on a banana boat for many years.

'Bay of Biscay, Captain,' he replied promptly.

The Captain fixed his gaze on the document before him. 'It doesn't seem too bad,' he replied. 'We should arrive in Bilbao on time.'

The leg they were now starting began in Calais and would take two nights and one day to complete, providing the weather held up.

'It can get pretty rough around here,' warned the Staff. 'It's been a graveyard for many vessels, but at the moment we seem to be doing OK.'

'We can only hope the rudder holds up,' the Captain remarked. 'It ought to be fine - but who knows'.

The helmsman remained mute whilst the two senior officers engaged in this discussion. He was not at all sanguine about the steering gear. From time to time the wheel would act as if it had a mind of it's own, and it took him all his strength to keep the ship on the set course.

The Captain had gone directly to the bridge from the dining room where he had hosted his first table of the voyage. This again was a new experience for him and it had had its trying moments. First, the welcoming of passengers and photographs at the entrance to the dining room was a bore once he had greeted the first dozen or so guests. His social hostess, Angela Fairweather, had stood in for Enzo the Cruise Director and she had a problem sorting out who was who as the passenger-list was by no means complete. Several dozen passengers corrected Angela as to their true identity, which she then whispered to the Captain who, being a little hard of hearing, frequently misunderstood and got the names wrong again. The photographer had set up an enormous flash unit, which blinded the Captain each time a picture was taken, so that for much of the time he was both blind and deaf. It was with some relief that he greeted the last of the passengers, after which Angela was able to guide him towards their table.

Once seated, he again faced the task of attempting to remember with whom he was dining. Eventually he decided to forget names altogether and just get on with the evening.

'Lovely to see you, Captain,' said a rather overdressed lady. 'This is my fifteenth World Cruise but I don't suppose it is anything like as many as you have done Captain.'

As this was Sparda's first circumnavigation he evaded answering directly but simply said he had spent most of his life at sea.

'A very unfortunate beginning to this cruise,' remarked another diner. 'I can't say that I've undergone anything like that before.'

Captain Sparda replied that it was a most unusual beginning and indeed most unfortunate. He was grateful to have such an experienced crew and he could assure passengers that all would be well for the remainder of the cruise.

'How is Admiral Harrington?' asked another diner. 'I thought he might be hosting our table tonight.'

Here Captain Sparda had to answer very carefully indeed.

'When on board,' he said, 'I am in command and the Admiral takes a back seat. Tonight he is otherwise occupied but I have no doubt that from time to time he will be at a table in this very dining room.'

What the Captain omitted to say was that, at that very moment, Rear Admiral Benbow Harrington was fuming in Calais, having missed the ship. Unaware of the strike, he had set out at a brisk pace to visit the town, but could not get hold of a taxi to take him back to the ship, and therefore was left stranded. Due to the non-functioning card system he was not missed until the radio operator received an extremely irate message ordering the *Handshake* to return immediately and collect him. As turning the ship in strange waters and with a suspect rudder did not appeal to the Captain, it was decided that the Admiral would catch the Bilbao ferry and join the cruise in that Spanish port.

The meal dragged on. Only those known to be very wealthy were invited to join the Captain for dinner, and one or two of these, who were cruising for the first time, demonstrated their ignorance of matters nautical by asking such questions as: 'Where do the crew go at night, Captain?' or 'From where does the ship get its electricity supply?'

Sparda answered with great patience, but he could see that

after several meals of this kind his patience would be drawn very thinly indeed. The cheese was about to be served when a steward approached Captain Sparda and whispered something in his ear.

'Eh?' queried the Captain, 'speak up, *ragazzo*.'

The steward increased the volume, upon which curious diners overheard the word 'chaplain' and 'distress' but that is all they gleaned.

'Please excuse me,' said Sparda, not at all sorry to be called away. 'Angela will look after you. *Buonanotte*.' With that he hastened away towards the reception area where he was met by Radley Duvet, the Hotel Manager.

'Rather serious news, I'm afraid, Captain,' said the anxious-looking Duvet. 'I would not have involved you, had the chaplain not asked to see you urgently.'

'Where is the man?' Sparda queried. 'I have not seen him since the very first day of the cruise.'

'He's in the sickbay,' said Duvet glumly, 'and he won't rest until he's seen you.'

Captain Sparda descended into the lower regions of the ship where there was still a distinct equine odour - a reminder of many previous voyages taken with very different passengers.

The chaplain lay strapped in a small cot. He was as pale as the freshly painted walls of the former cattle stall and he was mumbling to himself.

'*Buona sera, padre*,' said Sparda cheerfully. 'Not feeling too good eh?'

The chaplain opened one eye and closed it quickly. Sparda turned to the young attendant. 'What is the matter?'he asked. 'Is he dying?'

'That's what he thinks, sir,' the fellow replied. 'It seems that he left the platform party to attend to a call of nature in the heads. He had just entered the cubicle when the ship lurched, he hit his head against the wall, and the door was completely jammed. He remained there until he was discovered half an hour ago. He believes he is dying, and as you, sir, perform all religious duties when there is no chaplain on board, he wants you to hear his confession.'

'Crazy nonsense - *tutto pazzo*,' said Sparda as he aimed a kick at the cot. 'Undo those straps and sit the man up. Tell him to report to me tomorrow.'

'As you say, Captain, but he's not the ship's chaplain. He was simply accompanying the Chairman of the Council. He really ought not to be on this ship.'

'Too bad for him,' said Sparda unsympathetically. 'We will ship him ashore in Spain.'

The chaplain now opened both eyes and gave another groan.

'Has the doc seen him?' queried Sparda.

'We can't find the doctor,' said the attendant. 'He may have also got left behind in Calais.'

Sparda thought for a moment.

'I'll have a look at the *Medical Guide for Ships' Captains*, and if I come across Locked in the Heads syndrome I'll let you know how to deal with it. In this fellow's case he has been locked *in* the heads, knocked *on* the head and consequently has gone daft *in* the head. That's my diagnosis.'

With that he turned on his heel and made for the bridge.

At midnight Captain Sparda left the bridge and retired to his small cabin located just a few paces away. The radio was playing up again, and instead of receiving regular weather reports, the bridge party were treated to loud bursts of Classic FM playing soothing music throughout the night.

'It's blowing up a bit,' said the Staff Captain, 'and from what little I can gather, the wind might get stronger as the night goes on.'

'Well, don't disturb me,' said Sparda. 'The last few days have been stormy enough. I need some sleep.'

And so he departed, leaving his juniors to deal with the terrors of the night.

The least said about the Bay of Biscay the better. Suffice to record that it was rough. Very rough. Albert and Alice clung, for all they were worth, to the handrail at the head of their double bed. Albert was thrown out twice and Alice felt so ill that she managed to stagger to the tiny bathroom, where she spent the remainder of the night. When the storm had subsided somewhat and Albert was able to get to the bathroom himself, he found Alice wedged in the tiny bathtub sleeping fitfully.

'Some bloomin' holiday this is,' he said ruefully. 'By go, if I'd known this was to happen I'd have gone to Butlin's instead.'

'We've paid for it, and we're not packing up now,' said the resilient Alice, still feeling the effects of a night in the bathtub.

'Ee our Alice,' said Albert, in an attempt to inject some humour into the situation, 'when I saw you in the bath, it gave a whole new meaning to "Knights of the Bath". Night *in* the bath, more likely.'

'Don't be so silly, Albert Hardcastle,' snapped Alice. 'That's a very poor joke and not at all funny.'

Neither felt like going down to breakfast and so they called for Udi who brought them tea and a medicine that he swore would prevent seasickness. The ship was still pitching sharply and it took all their best efforts to sip the beverage.

'Very terrible weather, sir.' said Udi as he collected the cups. 'One day on ship grand piano thrown upside down. Chairs on deck overboard. Sea very terrible, sir, I promise you. You very strong lady. You very strong sir.'

The last thing Albert required was a promise of more terrible seas and so he thanked Udi for the tea and after wrestling once again with the door, let him out into the corridor.

On the bridge there was relief all round that the ailing rudder had withstood the storm. For most of the night they had pressed on without weather reports and had become so exasperated with constantly being told to relax to soothing classics that they turned off the radio completely and navigated as best they could. And so, twenty-four hours later, the SS *Golden Handshake* steamed slowly into Bilbao harbour and moored directly by the Guggenheim Museum.

14

Rear Admiral Harrington was feeling distinctly annoyed. The journey of a lifetime that he had planned and worked for so carefully had got off to a terrible start and now, to cap it all, he was stranded in Calais. He had telephoned his wife back in Frinton and she was most unsympathetic.

'I never had a lot of faith in this venture, Benbow,' she said unhelpfully. 'Quite frankly, your whole career has been littered with what you like to call "unfortunate incidents". I would call them something different. I can only hope you manage to find your ship eventually.' And with that she hung up.

These remarks increased Benbow's depression even further. Years of separation had resulted in both of them developing an independence of mind, but there were times when the Admiral would have welcomed a little more empathetic understanding. In times of difficulty he had learned to lean on the ever-supportive Harry, but even this prop was denied him now as, try as he might, he could not make contact with the ship nor with Harry. He had retired to a nearby bar to work out what to do when a dejected-looking character entered. He wore a distinctly worried expression on his face and the Admiral heard him order, in English, a brandy - even though it was only ten in the morning.

'Mind if I share your table?' said the forlorn character, who wandered over from the bar clutching his glass.

'Of course not,' said the Admiral, glad to have some company.

The visitor downed his brandy in one gulp and signalled to the attendant for another.

'The truth is,' he said to the Admiral before they had introduced themselves, 'the truth is that I have got mixed up with one of the most damn-fool operations I have ever come across.'

The Admiral listened sympathetically.

'Ever heard of Golden Oceans?' the man queried.

At this juncture the Admiral decided to say nothing. He simply nodded.

'Well, let me tell you, it's a real cowboy operation. It's supposed to be a world-class cruising company. They couldn't navigate the Serpentine, I can tell you. I was hired as Ship's Doctor for the World Cruise, as I had some spare time due to leaving my practice prematurely. All very unfortunate. These days, one only has to make a simple mistake and out you go. I'm not proud to admit that I diagnosed a case of smallpox as measles, and the whole town was afflicted. It's a mistake anyone could make, don't you agree?'

The Admiral ordered another strong black coffee and nodded. Good Lord, he thought to himself, we have hired this man.

If the Admiral had only known that his companion was relating but a fraction of his colourful past, which included being struck off the medical register in the Congo (a feat that very few members of the medical profession have ever achieved), plus failing to get a job as a counter assistant in Boots the Chemist, he would have been even more concerned.

'Very unfortunate indeed,' said Benbow, desperately trying to think what to say next. 'What do you intend to do now? I would have thought it best for you to make your way back to England, wouldn't you?'

'Not on your life,' replied the medic. 'What can I do there? After another drink I'm going to hitchhike to Spain, where I hope to find the ship. I gather that it's going to be there for a while. No one thought to give me a contact number in Calais so I am on my own.'

Even having heard only a tiny part of the past history of the doctor, the Admiral was not at all keen for him to join the ship. He couldn't imagine how he had slipped past Harry, but it seemed that he had - and further, it seemed as though he was determined to get to Spain.

The Admiral quickly swallowed his coffee.

'I must be off,' he said. 'The best of luck to you, doctor. I still think you might be better returning to England, you know.'

After a quick handshake he left the café and followed the signs to the main railway station. He arrived to be greeted with scenes of confusion. It seemed as though every school in the vicinity had planned to travel by train that day and the station was crowded with noisy French children, and their harassed teachers, all trying to board different trains. The Admiral fought his way to the information office and to his dismay discovered that to travel from Calais to Bilbao by train would be a very difficult journey indeed and the clerk doubted that he would arrive in Bilbao at the time he wished to be there.

'Do you have much baggage?' enquired the clerk.

The Admiral said that he had no luggage whatsoever as he had left his ship merely to take a stroll. He was too embarrassed to say that the ship left without him so he said that he was unavoidably detained and left it at that.

The clerk gave him a long knowing look and winked.

'The quick way to get to your ship is with my cousin who can help you. If you have no baggage he can give you first-class transport right to the ship, no problem. You pay for the outward journey and for the return journey of my cousin. *Oui?*'

'That is most kind,' said the Admiral, quite taken aback. 'Thank you very much indeed.'

He was more than glad to have a guarantee that he would arrive in time to catch the sailing. The clerk asked him to wait at a certain point outside the station and Cousin Jacques would meet him with a sign bearing the word *Admiral*.

Admiral Benbow went to the appointed location and waited. Numerous taxis slowed down and invited his custom. He rejected them all. He was feeling increasingly anxious when he noticed an elderly man wearing what appeared to be a flying suit and a leather flying helmet approaching him, holding aloft a card with *Admiral* written on it. Benbow went up to him and in appalling French introduced himself. Fortunately the individual replied in perfect English that he was Cousin Jacques and would now transport the Admiral to Bilbao.

'I confess to being a bit surprised that we are to fly,' said Benbow.

Jacques looked startled. 'Fly, *monsieur*? *Non*, you will travel in my speedy land transport. Come.'

He rounded the corner and there was an ancient Royal Enfield motor cycle, complete with sidecar. Jacques handed the Admiral a leather helmet identical to the one he was wearing.

'This will be good for the wind,' he said. 'Please make yourself comfortable in the sidecar.'

It was too late for the Admiral to back out now, but he had genuine apprehension about this mode of transport, which had come as a total surprise to him. A large pair of goggles were on the seat and he placed them around the top of his head.

'You'll find a scarf on the floor,' said the ever-helpful Jacques. 'Use it if you like.'

The Admiral found a coloured woollen scarf and wrapped it around his neck. The Enfield took a little persuasion to get started and only did so after the Admiral had been politely requested to get out and push. Having struggled to get into the sidecar, he now had to struggle to get out. After a hundred paces or so, which completely winded the Admiral, the engine came to life but hardly with a roar. To his ear it sounded as though it needed a complete service but now was not the time for this procedure. He somehow got back into the narrow seat and off they set.

The first part of the long journey was uneventful, aside from one unfortunate incident. They were passing through a French village, totally unknown to the Admiral, when a raw egg shattered on the tiny windscreen of the sidecar. This was followed by several more, one of which caught the top of the flying helmet. The Admiral, well versed in military tactics, observed immediately that the missiles were being thrown from a passing car, the occupants of which were shouting and gesticulating as only the French can.

'Go home!' they shouted (in French, of course).

They continued their invective with increasing vehemence until Jacques was well outside the village boundary and they had turned off the road.

'What was all *that* about?' shouted the Admiral, wiping egg off his helmet as best he could.

119

It transpired that the scarf worn by the Admiral was a rugby scarf with the colours of a club that had soundly beaten the village through which they were passing. Naturally they were not too well pleased to see the colours that reminded them of their humiliation the previous week, and so had launched the attack. The Admiral folded the offending garment and placed it on the floor of the sidecar.

'Drive on,' he said to Jacques. 'Time is at a premium.'

About three quarters of the way on this uncomfortable, and not altogether speedy, journey, Jacques shouted across at his passenger, 'I think we ought to take a short break for coffee.'

Although time was going all too quickly, the Admiral agreed and they spluttered into a small petrol station with a wooden hut attached which seemed to be some sort of establishment where refreshments might be bought. Benbow once again eased his aching bones out of the sidecar and with Jacques leading the way, entered the shack.

Jacques went over to the counter and the Admiral was just about to sit down when he froze. There, sitting at a table, was the doctor with what appeared to be a large brandy before him. Always quick thinking, Benbow pulled the goggles down over his eyes, turned on his heel and marched smartly out of the room. He heard Jacques cry out, 'Hey!' but that was all he heard.

Not knowing what to do, he hid himself behind the shed, keeping the motorcycle in view so that when Jacques emerged he could rush over and they could leave. As it was, the intrepid Jacques came out immediately, looked around and began to shout: 'Admiral. Where are you?'

Benbow rushed across to the bike, goggles firmly in place.

'Quick!' he shouted to the startled motorcyclist. 'I just realised I got the tides wrong. The ship leaves earlier than I expected. Start her up, we must be away.'

A puzzled coffee-less Jacques did as he was bid, the bike was kicked into life and the Admiral, seated as low down in his seat as he could manage, set off once again in the direction of the Spanish coast.

As they bowled along at a steady pace, the Admiral reflected on the situation facing him. The determined doctor had clearly been in luck with his hitchhiking and it looked as though he might get to the ship, after all. On the other hand, hitchhiking was a risky business and there was no guarantee that he would make it. If the doctor *did* get to the ship and boarded, then there would be acute embarrassment for both of them. In the end Sir Benbow decided that he would face the situation if and when it occurred – and not worry unduly about it. Doing his best to settle back in his seat, he once again pushed the goggles up across the top of his head as they got rather hot if he wore them constantly.

Suddenly he heard a loud tooting on a car horn. Jacques

looked agitated. 'Damn drivers,' he shouted. 'He knows it's not safe to pass here.'

The Admiral glanced behind and saw a little MG sports car bearing up on them. Suddenly, it pulled out and there, sitting next to the driver, was none other than the hitchhiking doctor. Once again the Admiral snatched at the goggles and pulled them firmly over his eyes. As the car drew alongside, the doctor put his thumb to his nose and gave a rude sign before the car accelerated and disappeared into the distance.

A road sign appeared. *Bilbao Port 25 kilometres.* The Admiral groaned, the bike spluttered and Jacques continued on his merry way, determined to get his charge to the ship before low tide.

15

Back on board, Captain Sparda, having enjoyed a refreshing sleep whilst crossing the Bay of Biscay and also a relaxing day in port, was preparing the ship for departure. After the nightmare of Calais, Bilbao had proved to be tranquillity itself. This time, Radley and the Cruise Director had organised the passengers into groups of ten, who were then escorted ashore to a duty-free establishment where they could purchase their supplies for the journey. The ever-helpful Spanish, anxious to offload their cheap brandy, were more than delighted to arrange transport to and from the ship and provided two mini-coaches, Radley being in charge of one and Enzo the other. These coaches went back and forth with the duty-free carried in a trailer hitched behind the coach.

There was a minor problem on the Cruise Director's transport when the driver gave the passengers a running commentary as they passed through the dock area. Enzo, who was acknowledged on board ship as a language specialist, insisted on correcting the English of the driver, to the considerable annoyance of the same. Minor fisticuffs might have occurred but were averted when the irate driver stopped the coach halfway between the ship and the liquor store and walked away! Fortunately, a passenger who had experience of driving a milk float, took the wheel and the passengers were able to get their supplies - with one exception. Albert. He did not want wine or spirits but a few cases of good old Brown Ale, a beverage he had drunk for fifty years or more. Unfortunately Brown Ale was unknown to the vintners of Bilbao. They could find a few cans of lager which rudely Albert referred to as 'gnat's piss', and as there was nothing further to offer him, he reluctantly bought six cans.

Before noon, Captain Sparda again trekked down to the sickbay where the previous day he had visited the Councillor's chaplain and made an instant diagnosis of his condition. The patient was now sitting up in his cot sipping a hot lemon tea and looking distinctly better.

'Ah Padre,' said Sparda in his usual hearty fashion. 'I see you are well on the road to a complete recovery. Get dressed and prepare to disembark - we are due to sail this evening.'

The chaplain looked startled.

'But Captain,' he mumbled, 'I am totally stranded. I only came on board to accompany the official party. Where are we?'

'Spain,' roared Sparda. 'Espagna! You can find your way back to Southend from here, surely.'

'But Captain, my head still hurts and I don't have any money on me. All I have are a few Sainsbury's petrol vouchers and my passport, which I needed to get on board.'

Sparda snorted. 'You could hitchhike, padre. That clerical collar might get an undertaker to stop for you.' He laughed at his own joke.

'Captain,' bleated the poor unfortunate. 'Please, I can't get off in this state.'

'Well, let me think. This is a World Cruise and we do have one or two religious types on board. I could sign you on as Chaplain, but I can't promise to pay you. Understand that. You can have your meals and we'll find a bunk for you somewhere or other. That's the best I can do.' With that, and without waiting for an answer, Sparda returned to the bridge assuming, correctly as it happened, that the offer had been accepted and the *Golden Handshake* now boasted a chaplain.

'Where's the Admiral?' bawled Sparda when he returned to the bridge. 'And has anyone seen the doctor?'

As the card security system continued to be non-functional, there was no means of checking who was or was not on board, and so no correct answer could be given concerning the two missing individuals. It was rumoured that one or two passengers, after the confrontation with the police in France, had returned home, and that several others, after sampling the Bay of Biscay, had also decided to call it a day - but no one knew for certain.

'We can't delay,' Sparda said. 'We've experienced enough

nonsense since we set out. Now on this ship, what I say goes.' He was certainly getting into his stride as Captain of the *Golden Handshake*, making it clear that he was the boss and intended to act the part throughout.

Departure time drew closer. The hardworking crew had arranged the deck so that a 'sail-away party' might be organised. To compensate for the troubles endured by passengers during the first part of the cruise, a small quantity of cheap Spanish wine had been purchased by the ship in order to make Sangria which would to be served gratis during the departure. The final mini-bus of the day returned and the grateful passengers climbed the gangway with their supplies for the voyage. Once everyone was settled, the Cruise Director sounded the beeps throughout the cabins and passengers hurried to the Listening Posts to be told about the party, and that the ship would be sailing directly.

The party got under way and the Sangria flowed. The partygoers, glasses in hand, gazed over the side and watched the mooring ropes being discarded and preparations being made for the removal of the gangplank. Suddenly, an ancient motorcycle and sidecar were spotted racing towards the ship. A figure in the sidecar, dressed for all the world as one of the magnificent men in their flying machines, was seen to be standing rather dangerously and waving furiously.

'Holy Mother!' remarked Sparda from the bridge, as he

peered through his telescope. 'It looks like one of Rommel's men chasing us.'

The helmeted passenger leaped from the sidecar and raced towards the gangplank, reaching it literally seconds before it was withdrawn and the ship prepared to move. Loud clapping broke out amongst the passengers and yet more sangria went down the hatch.

Once on board the Admiral felt an enormous sense of relief at having caught the ship. He made his way to the bridge to inform the Captain of his arrival, and was just exchanging pleasantries and telling of his adventures, when their attention was drawn to what appeared to be yet another late arrival. Speeding towards the ship came a pony and trap, within which was an individual who was waving frantically at the ship. By now the gangplank had been stowed and the lines cast off. Captain Sparda examined the new late arrival through his telescope.

'*Dio Mio!*' he exclaimed as the figure came into focus. 'It's the *medico* turned up at last. Hold the ship! He must get aboard.'

The Admiral felt a deep sense of foreboding.

'I don't think so, Captain,' he said, as sternly as he could command. 'We had better leave immediately. We can't afford further delays. Port fees, you know. Very costly.'

'To hell with the fees,' argued Sparda. 'Compared to this ship, a Saga cruise would seem to be a rave party. Some old folks are bound to die and I have no desire to be an undertaker. We need him.'

'I still think we should leave now, Captain Sparda,' intoned the Admiral.

Sparda ignored him and stepped outside the bridge to shout down at the deckhands.

'Throw Dr Hackett a hawser!' he bellowed.

To the great delight and amusement of the passengers, a line was thrown over the side and was ably caught by the doctor. He hung on for grim death and gradually, to much applause and shouts of encouragement from the partygoers and crew, Dr Stuart Hackett M.D. was slowly hauled aboard.

The Admiral swiftly retired to his cabin. This cruise was proving to be a little more complicated to run than the others of the Golden Oceans Line. Being a religious man he uttered a small prayer, followed by an oath, then laid his aching head on the pillow.

What next? he thought. Dear Lord, what next?

16

It was not normally the practice of Enzo Bigatoni, the Cruise Director, to have staff meetings with the lecturers and their fellow entertainers. All he needed to know about them was that they were willing to speak and would do so as and when he arranged. By no means did he want them interfering with his language classes or taking passengers away from Piddling Pursuits, both of which activities were the highlights of the cruise as far as he was concerned. However, on this cruise he was asked by Radley Duvet, the Hotel Director, and the immediate superior of Enzo, to get them all together for a brief chat. As the next leg of the adventure would take two days before the port serving Seville was reached, there was time to meet with the group.

They were assembled after dinner on the first night of the voyage to Seville. Sir Horace Beanstalk was the first to arrive in the tiny office of the Cruise Director, quickly followed by the former captive Mr Toby Troy, who in turn was followed by the chaplain, now well on the road to recovery. The World Ludo Champions had been invited to join the cruise to instruct in the art of Ludo and to run several championships, and a certain Mr

Terry Waite

Fennington Barley, a retired dairy farmer from Northern Ireland, had been hired to act as a gentleman host. Mr Barley had taken up dancing on his retirement and now spent most of the year flitting from ship to ship, dancing with single elderly ladies to whom he had to be unfailingly charming. That was his job. To be charming to all and sundry. Mr Barley was not paid for his invaluable services; in fact, *he* had to pay, albeit at a reduced rate, for the privilege of entertaining his dancing partners. The final individual to join the party was a former AA Patrol man, Fred Batty, who had been hired as a Destinations lecturer. Batty had spent his entire adult life visiting different destinations in the British Isles and so, it was reasoned by Harry, he ought to be able to quickly get a grasp of destinations on the world cruise.

Enzo got off to an unfortunate start as, although he knew the faces of those assembled, he could not put a name to them.

'Good to see you, Mr Speed,' he said to the chaplain, who looked up with a start.

'I think you – ' began the chaplain, but was cut short by Enzo who, quickly realising his mistake, decided that he would not address anyone directly.

'I must explain,' he said, 'that you are here as both passengers and crew.'

Toby Troy looked puzzled. 'What does that mean?' he asked.

Before Enzo could answer, Sir Horace, a veteran of the lecturing world, jumped in.

130

'It means,' he said, 'that if the passengers get free handouts you pay because you are crew. If the crew get special treatment you don't because you are a passenger.'

Everyone looked at Enzo for his reply but there was none as he chose to ignore the explanation given. Rather he continued with his introduction.

'Remember,' he said, 'that passengers come first. If there is not enough ice cream, then you must go without. We do not have the facilities to video record your lectures, but still photographs will be taken of you as you lecture and they will be available for the passengers to view in the library. From time to time local entertainers will be brought on board and will require the use of the stage for rehearsals. You may find your lecture time cut short on such occasions. You will be rated by the passengers, of course, and unless you get ten out of ten for two out of three lectures, you will not be back with Golden Oceans again. Ever. Any questions?'

The assembled company looked glum. It didn't seem to be such a good holiday, after all, but they remained silent as they had no wish to upset anyone at this stage of the cruise.

'Now, chaplain,' said Enzo, waking the good man from his meditation. 'What are your plans, as I have no information at all about you, since you are a late entrant.'

The chaplain blushed. 'The Captain has kindly invited me to stay on board and be in attendance for spiritual duties. Each

131

day I propose to teach the passengers who volunteer to come to my group to sing some little songs,' he said innocently.

'Such as?' queried Enzo.

'Well, "Jesus Wants Me for a Sunbeam" is very nice. 'I am sure they might enjoy singing that. I intend to form a Golden Glory Group and they will sing at the service on Sundays.'

Enzo nodded, while Toby Troy, the former Bible-puncher turned apostate, snorted. Sir Horace, a devout Anglican, expressed the hope that the 1662 *Book of Common Prayer* would be the one and only book used on a Sunday, and the Ludo Champions said that as Ludo would be played all day and every day, they would not have the time to attend any other activities. To be an expert Ludo player required hours of practice, and they dare not miss one single moment of one day.

Fred Batty said nothing as he was a nominal Roman Catholic, for whom there seemed to be no provision on board. It remained to Fennington Barley from Ulster to declare that he suspected the Captain and 'certain other senior staff members' were those who gave their allegiance to the Pope in Rome and that his motto would be 'No Pope here' - at which point Patrol Man Batty was heard to whisper under his breath, 'Lucky Pope.'

Sensing possible conflict, Radley Duvet, who had remained quietly in the background, rose to his feet.

'That's about it,' he said. 'You will all be informed twenty minutes before you are due to perform, so always be ready. By the way, the Golden Chopsticks Restaurant is not open for the use of entertainers and lecturers unless you are invited by a guest. That restaurant is reserved for passengers occupying Balcony Suites and Grade One accommodation. Good night, ladies and gentlemen.'

The assembled party rose and made their way back to their cabins, duly instructed.

17

Another sea day dawned as the good ship *Handshake* ploughed her way to the next port of call, Seville. It was a big day for former AA Patrol Man Fred Batty as he was due to deliver the Destination lecture, the first of a series that would take him right around the world. He had never visited Spain before, let alone Seville, as his route back in England only covered Basingstoke and the surrounding area, but Fred was an enterprising chap, as all AA patrol men have to be. Before leaving home he had spent days in the local library consulting the internet and Wikipedia in particular. He was able to copy reams of information about the places the ship was due to visit and, with a little touching up, they were easily converted into what he considered to be an instructive and erudite lecture. He had also been able to assemble a set of slides, many of which he had picked up at a local boot sale. It took him hours of careful study to look at a slide of, say, Seville Cathedral and then check it against a picture of the Cathedral drawn from the internet. Eventually he thought he might have got things right, but also reasoned that if everything was not totally correct, no one would ever know.

Albert and Alice, also new to Spain, decided that they might attend Fred's peroration but were a little put out when they discovered that it was scheduled for eight in the morning, a time when they would normally be having breakfast. It was arranged at this hour by Enzo so as not to interfere with his language classes, and also the Ludo champions, who were a formidable couple, had promised to create real difficulty if other events clashed with their session. This was difficult as their classes continued from nine each morning until late afternoon.

Fred had been up very early studying his notes and adding last-minute touches. Although he was a casual dresser when out of his AA uniform, he decided that he ought to display a touch of sophistication on the ship and so he had come equipped with a velveteen purple bow-tie and a maroon smoking jacket. The tie and the jacket nicely contrasted with each other and made him more visible to his audience at the rear of the auditorium.

Albert and Alice were waiting outside the breakfast area at seven thirty and as soon as the doors opened they went in and rushed through their meal. They arrived at the auditorium at a few minutes to eight o'clock, and to their surprise there were only three other people present, one of whom was Sir Horace Beanstalk. He was the one lecturer on board who had considerable experience of cruise lines, and often attended other lectures mainly to see if they got more people to attend than he did. An eminent botanist, he was reputed to have the largest collection of coloured slides of any other living person.

Fred Batty hovered nervously at the entrance, waiting to be fitted with a lapel mike. The technician emerged seemingly from nowhere and placed the device in the inside pocket of Fred's jacket and the miniature mike on his lapel. By now another couple had arrived and Fred stepped towards the lectern. He then waited for Enzo to arrive to introduce him and was still waiting when he heard the technician shout out, 'OK, mate. Start now.'

Fred straightened his notes and looked out at the gathering. He was somewhat disappointed at the turnout, but thought things might get better as the cruise got into its stride.

'Good morning, ladies and gentlemen,' he began. 'May I welcome you to the first of many lectures about the places we are going to visit. When this series is over you will be very well informed, believe you me. Today our next port is called Seville.'

After this cursory introduction, he then turned to his notes, copied verbatim from the Internet and which he proceeded to intone.

'Seville is the capital and largest city of the autonomous community of Andalusia and the province of Seville, Spain. It is situated on the plain of the River Guadalquivir. The inhabitants of the city are known as sevillanos (feminine form: sevillanas) or hispalenses, after the Roman name of the city, Hispalis.'

Fred Batty stumbled along and had quite forgotten how difficult some of the words were to pronounce. In his cabin the previous night he seemed to have managed well, but this morning it was an effort. He came to the end of the first page and looked up at his audience. Sir Horace who was sitting directly in front of him, appeared to be sleeping, but the two or three others whom he could make out in the gloom were still conscious.

'Now for my first slide,' he said, uttering the pre-agreed cue to the technical officer stationed in a booth at the back of the room.

He waited and nothing happened.

'Now is the time for the first slide,' he repeated in a louder voice.

Still nothing happened.

'My slide!' he shouted. 'Can you please show my slide of Seville Cathedral?'

The shouting awoke Sir Horace, who had been dreaming that he was lecturing on the flora and fauna of the Isle of Man. He stumbled to his feet and turning towards the booth, shouted, 'Not Seville, you fool. The Isle of Man. Flora.'

The technician, who had also lost consciousness with the world for a moment, heard the request from Sir Horace and was puzzled. The only flora he knew was 'Interflora' who sent flowers around the world. He shouted back, 'If you want Interflora you can get hold of them via the internet after the lecture. I can't do anything now.'

Fred, still on stage and increasingly confused, repeated his request for his first slide. The technical officer, who had now found some holiday pictures taken when one of the passengers had visited Kew Gardens, inserted one into the Magic Lantern and the audience were treated to an elderly lady in a mackintosh standing by the side of a bed of tulips.

In desperation Fred turned to his notes in an attempt to resume his commentary. To his utter horror, when he turned the page he revealed the dinner menu for that night which was always left in the cabin the previous evening. Somehow he had picked this up and left his notes behind. Quick-thinking and as resourceful as ever, he decided to cut his losses. 'Well, ladies and gentlemen,' he said, 'that's all for this morning. Before I leave, let me read to you what your choices at dinner will be this evening.'

He slowly read through the menu and then with a small bow left the platform.

'Funny do,' said Albert as he and Alice left the room. 'I shan't miss me breakfast for that again.'

The day in Seville was uneventful. Albert had gleaned nothing from the lecture and both he and Alice spent the day looking in shop windows for the only thing they knew about Seville, which was marmalade.

'Not a jar to be seen anywhere,' grumbled a disappointed Alice. 'I so wanted to take a pot of the real stuff back to Cousin

Pam in Cleethorpes, but I can't even find Golden Shred, let alone Seville.'

On their return to the ship, at long last the electronic card system was working and they were able to check in without difficulty. It appeared that now, the teething problems of the *Golden Handshake* were over and everyone could relax and look forward to visiting that home from home, Gibraltar.

18

After the start of the cruise, which no one could pretend had been a total success, the past few days at sea had given Harry Parkhurst some respite. As always, he had been thinking ahead and now he was occupied with attempting to engage some local entertainers to come on board for a short period and provide an evening show or two. The ship, having been a former cattle-boat, presented a challenge in that the main place where enter-tainment could be held was the former holding-pen for cows and horses. However, it had been tastefully adapted and pro-vided a sizeable space within which to stage a show.

Harry had seen many performances at sea. *Hits from the Shows* constantly did the rounds, but it took a largish group of young singers and dancers to perform it and frankly, it was a bit tired no matter how many changes of costume the leading lady managed in an evening. Fortunately, it was not too difficult to secure the services of a multi-talented musician who would play anything from a tin whistle to a tuba, and a pianist who could thump out popular classics, and no doubt at some time during the voyage such individuals would find a place on the programme. However, Harry wanted the first show on the ship to be really unusual, and unlike the sort of thing one would normally see on a World Cruise. He spent a lot of time talking to an associate in Gibraltar and learned that there was a totally unique act that would be available for boarding once the ship arrived in Eilat. Keeping this information to himself, Harry booked the show there and then without informing the other members of staff. It was to be a surprise for everyone.

On the bridge, Captain Sparda was well pleased with the performance of his command. He was now in complete charge. The Admiral had made it clear from the start that he would take a back seat, and since sailing from Bilbao he had hardly put in an appearance. He took his meals in his little cabin and was only seen at night, when he came out for some fresh air. No one knew that he was attempting to evade the doctor until he could think of some way of dealing with what might be a very embarrassing situation. Captain Sparda was, by now, utterly fed up with hosting his own table and was now given to asking the Staff Captain to sit in for him while he, the Captain, remained on the bridge.

Enzo Bigatoni was disappointed with the attendance at his language classes. Unfortunately, word had got round the ship that his language ability was zero due to his less than creditable performance in Calais. At the last class, only three passengers had turned up, two of whom came from China and apart from a very few words of English, spoke only in Mandarin. The phrasebook they carried everywhere was infinitely better than the one used by Enzo for instruction, much to his annoyance. They made no progress with him whatsoever. The third pupil was Lady Veronika Willoughby, who hailed from deepest Siberia and who was far from communicative at the best of times. She took an instant dislike to Enzo, but this was hardly surprising as she took an instant dislike to most people. She insisted on bringing into the class a large glass of yak's milk at which she sipped constantly as Enzo was attempting to to get one word through to the Chinese. Lady Veronika had brought her own supply of yak's milk with her on board; it was kept frozen and she hoped to be able to top it up on shore from time to time during the voyage.

Enzo was at a loss to know how to increase numbers at his class and spent many a long hour worrying about this.

Due to the turbulent weather experienced during the first days of the cruise, the Hotel Manager, Radley Duvet, had not been under too much pressure from passengers regarding food, as few had been eating. He had received several angry visits from Mike Tucker, the Head Chef, who complained at the lack of variety in the store. Beans there were aplenty, and Mike, who formerly ran a café in the Old Kent Road, knew a thing or two about beans. On this cruise he had served them on toast, curried them, made them into a chilli, filled out a shepherds pie, introduced them into wraps – but his stock never seemed to diminish. The Head Chef insisted that in Gibraltar he would have to go ashore and put the stores in some sort of order, as the fool who had stocked the ship in Southend had no idea what he was doing. Radley took great exception to this slur on his reputation, and the problem was only resolved when Mike produced a large cleaver and chased him out of the galley.

Down in the bowels of the ship, where the Medical Department was located, the doctor lay low. He had managed to stuff one bottle of brandy into his pocket before he was hauled aboard in Bilbao, but to his everlasting regret he had left two further bottles behind in the pony and trap in his haste to catch the ship. Now the bottle he had brought with him was dangerously low and he was informed that all drinks on the ship had to be brought on by passengers as the ship had a very limited stock of alcohol. He was waiting anxiously for the first patient to arrive when there might be a chance of accepting a bottle in return for a reduction on their medical bill. Meanwhile he took small nips of the beverage to keep his spirits up.

Little did the doctor know, that in the small sickbay was a member of the senior staff, the chaplain - added at the last moment by the Captain. The latter was given to making decisions without consulting his shipmates. Consequently there was no cabin allocated to the Padre. Following his accident in the heads he had languished in the sickbay under the care of a medical attendant, believing that he would be put ashore at the first available opportunity. He had then been taken on by the Captain but remained cabin-less in the sickbay, where he was discovered when the doctor made his first appearance.

'Hello, Johnny,' said the doctor cheerfully when he stumbled across the chaplain making up his tiny cot in preparation for the night. 'Sit down, put your tongue out and say *ah*.' The chaplain did as he was told.

'Ummm,' murmured the doctor. 'Ummm . . . ' He turned to the attendant.

'Tubular Pie-aka,' he said. 'Never seen such a clear case. Only water for forty-eight hours and after that lemon juice for forty-eight hours.'

The chaplain tried to say something but was cut short.

'Dangerous to speak, Johnny old boy. You'll ruin your vocals if you do. Total silence for forty-eight hours, after which four words per hour for another forty-eight hours. By the way, before you do go silent, you don't happen to have any brandy, do you?'

The chaplain shook his head.

'Well, too bad,' said the ever hopeful doctor, regretting that his first patient had proved to be so disappointing. 'Next time perhaps. Off to bed now.' And with that he left the cubicle and returned to his office, leaving the dismayed chaplain under the ever-watchful eye of the attendant.

Back on the bridge everything appeared shipshape. Rounding the Rock of Gibraltar had been slightly turbulent, but the

Golden Handshake had behaved beautifully and Captain Spada was delighted with her performance.

'A fine little ship,' he commented to Roger Hallworthy, the Staff Captain, who was somewhat miffed that he had been usurped on the bridge by Sparda.

Having previously served as Captain of a dredger he found hosting tables rather a strain, especially as it seemed that he was now required to do so each evening. When questioned by passengers about his previous sea-going experience he simply said that he had spent much of his life clearing some of the major waterways of the world, which gave the passengers the impression that he was some sort of security expert - and he did nothing to disillusion them.

As Gibraltar hove into sight, Captain Sparda instructed Enzo to suggest, via the address system, that passengers might wish to come out on deck where they would get a splendid view of their destination and perhaps see some interesting shipping also.

A large group gathered and the ever-helpful crew served beakers of the orange-coloured liquid and small pieces of toast and Marmite for refreshments. Captain Sparda went to the microphone on the bridge.

'Ladies and gentlemen, we are approaching Gibraltar which, as you know, is more British than Britain herself. We have many British passengers on board and many of us have lived in the

United Kingdom, so we are always attracted by this charming location.'

One of the bridge officers who hailed from Spain glowered angrily but kept his peace.

'Enjoy the magnificent view from the ship. Thank you. *Gracias*.' He signed off and, picking up his telescope, surveyed the land.

Suddenly, for no apparent reason, the ship began to turn around completely and head back towards the Rock. The helmsman wrestled with the wheel - but to no avail - as Sparda gave order after order and frantically cut the engines. After much heaving the ship was turned around and, to the relief of all, resumed its proper course. It seemed as though the faulty rudder was playing up once more.

Sparda again addressed the passengers.

'You will have noted,' he said rather breathlessly, 'that we did a little circuit in order to give you all a better view of Gibraltar. Now, if you look towards the starboard side, you will see approaching us one of the greatest ships ever to sail the oceans - the QE2!'

In the middle distance passengers gazed at this massive ship which was rapidly coming towards them and would soon pass by. The QE2 drew nearer . . . when once again, without warning, the helmsman had to start wrestling with the wheel. The *Golden Handshake* was veering to starboard, and heading directly across the bows of the mighty *Queen*! At first, the passengers thought that good Captain Sparda was doing this to give them all a better view, and took out their cameras and snapped away. Some applauded and waved their thanks to the bridge. Their jubilation was short-lived, however, when it appeared that unless the *Handshake* moved with greater speed she would be hit side-on by the larger vessel. Captain Perkins, the officer in command of the *Queen*, did his level best to slow his ship down, but realised that this was an impossible task. He sounded the whistle repeatedly and instructed his crew to stand by the lifeboats in case there was a collision.

On the bridge of the *Golden Handshake* there was panic. Sparda was issuing orders in both English and Italian. The helmsman continued in combat with an unresponsive wheel. Various other bridge officers ran up and down, not knowing what to do.

The passengers had now scattered in confusion. Several clambered into a lifeboat and hid under a tarpaulin. Others ran to collect their valuables from the cabin. It was a scene of utter pandemonium. By nothing short of the grace of God, a collision was avoided and the mighty *Queen* of the ocean sailed by, leaving the *Golden Handshake* bobbing like a cork in the turbulent waters. A large wave sloshed over the deck, drenching any passenger who had not sought shelter. Captain Perkins, normally a mild-mannered Christian man, came on the radio to Captain

Sparda, and his remarks are not printable. Eventually order was restored and the *Golden Handshake*, complete with a very traumatised group of passengers and crew, sailed into Gibraltar.

Gibraltar came as a rude shock to many passengers who had been persuaded to buy their liquor in Seville, for here in Little Britain real bargains were to be obtained. The only two people to be delighted were Albert, who was able to purchase a reasonable supply of Brown Ale, and the doctor, who found enough brandy to last even him for a week or so. The remainder complained that they had been ripped off in Spain and that they ought to have been warned, but their complaining got them nowhere and reluctantly they bought more supplies in Gibraltar to last them even further into the cruise.

Albert and Alice were doubly delighted for, in Gibraltar, they found that they could enjoy fish and chips just like the fish and chips back home in Grimsby. Albert ordered two portions and declared Gibraltar to be 'a grand little town'. There was a slight delay to the departure of the ship as an inspection party had to be summoned to check the rudder. This time Captain Sparda did not venture underwater but contented himself with the report which said that no problem could be found but a proper investigation could only take place in dry dock. As such a move would mean cancelling the cruise, the Captain ruled it out and decided to continue to chance his arm.

There was only one minor incident that caused some alarm to a few passengers. They had decided to take a break from a diet of beans and have a meal in a restaurant situated high up on the Rock, with superb views over the ocean. The group sat at an outside table and were perusing the menu when one of their number turned to give his order to the waiter, and to his alarm, rather than a black-coated attendant, he was confronted by some sort of ape. At first he wondered if the vino he had been consuming was stronger than usual, but when the ape cuffed him across the ear and took several slices of bread from the table, he realised that the animal was real enough.

All the table panicked and began to run towards the covered part of the restaurant, chased by this formidable and hungry native of Gibraltar. A waiter rushed from the kitchen with a water pistol, which he proceeded to fire off, but as he was no marksman, instead of hitting the ape, he drenched several passengers.

The only person to be pleased by this event was of course the doctor, as two or three of the party suffered from minor cuts and bruises obtained when they stumbled when fleeing from their assailant, and one had a very sore ear. The doctor now had his brandy, which was good, but he reckoned that a few fees would also be very acceptable - and he welcomed his patients with open arms.

19

It was Sunday morning and the ship was bowling along at a merry pace towards the super-rich territory of Monaco. The Admiral was not happy about this port of call for, as a religious man, he was firmly against gambling in all its forms and regarded Monaco as one of the gambling capitals of the world. Harry was insistent that the venue be included as he reasoned that many of the passengers would love to see the Casino and even perhaps risk staking a euro or two. The Captain was not bothered in the slightest. If Monaco was on the list he would go there. If not, no matter. Monaco was included and so on a lovely sunny morning, the good ship *Golden Handshake*, set sail for the Principality.

As it was a Sunday morning, the Reverend Justin Longparish was due to take centre-stage and conduct morning worship. If there was no Chaplain on board a British Registered ship, then the Captain of the vessel took Divine Service. Because the *Handshake*, thanks to an unfortunate incident, *did* have an official cleric on board, now was the time for him to perform.

The Admiral was faced with a dilemma. His conscience told him that he must attend Sunday worship, but he had not yet determined how he was going to deal with the situation when he came face to face with the doctor. He decided that worship should come first, and knowing what he did about the doctor, he doubted that the man would turn up to sing any hymns. Of course, he thought, if the doctor had been consuming his normal intake of brandy he might be more than happy to sing about angels, sunbeams or anything else one might care to name.

At ten o'clock the Admiral, Captain and senior officers, plus the Hotel Manager and the Cruise Director, gathered in the auditorium. Harry Parkhurst was seated at the piano which was somewhat out of tune, but passable if he played loudly enough. Angela Fairweather stood at the door with a bundle of hymn sheets that Harry had been able to obtain from the Salvation Army in Huddersfield. She handed one to each passenger as she bade them a cheery good morning.

Eleven o'clock approached and the Captain became agitated.

'Where is that damn man?' he whispered to the Staff Captain, who was beside him. 'And where is the Golden Glory Choir? He said he was going to have them in top form for today. I know Harry obtained some old curtain material which he said could easily be adapted into the most attractive vestments for them. Surely they would be glad to show off.'

As the minutes ticked by without any sign of the chaplain, Enzo the Cruise Director became more and more worried for, unless the service started soon, people would be late for his

Albanian language class at eleven. Enzo was not the only one to be concerned. By now the Captain was furious. He turned to the Admiral.

'You start the service and I'll go and hunt for the man.'

Although small in stature, Captain Sparda was most agile. He leaped from the stage and proceeded at the double towards the Medical Centre.

The ever-dutiful attendant flinched when the Captain burst in and shouted, 'Where is he? Doesn't he know the time?'

The attendant, thinking that the Captain required the doctor, pointed towards the medic's small cabin.

'I think he's asleep, Captain,' he stuttered.

'Asleep?' roared Sparda. '*Asleep?* I'll put him to sleep for good when I see him.' With that he threw open the door and revealed a supine doctor fast asleep clutching an empty brandy bottle.

'What in God's name is this?' Sparda seethed. 'This isn't the chaplain.'

The terrified attendant remained mute.

'Come on, fellow, stir yourself. For the last time, where is the damn chaplain?'

The attendant pointed a trembling finger towards the tiny sickbay and without more ado the Captain entered to reveal the chaplain, attired in a dressing-gown and seated at a small table.

'What do you think you're playing at?' he roared, as only little men can roar. 'Stand up, man. Well, explain!'

The chaplain stood as he was commanded, but remained mute, which increased the Captain's fury.

'Are you a total *imbecille?*' he shouted, using the forceful Italian word. ' Explain. E - S - P - L - I - N - E'.

He spelled out the letters of the word one by one.

Still not replying, the chaplain fumbled in a drawer and produced a pencil and paper on which he scrawled: *I have a very serious throat condition. I am forbidden to speak. Tomorrow I am allowed four words per hour.*

'*Diavolo!*' cursed the Captain as he aimed a kick at the chair on which the chaplain had once again sat. 'As soon as your quota of words increases, report to me.'

And with that he stormed out of the sickbay to resume Divine Worship.

When Captain Sparda returned to the service, it was almost over. The Admiral had managed to make things up as he went along but, due to the fact that they had been depending on the chaplain to provide the readings and prayers, it was impossible to arrange these at such short notice and so he filled in with hymns. When Sparda entered, the congregation were on their tenth hymn and approaching exhaustion. Captain Sparda took his place on the stage as the worthy passengers were singing about golden corn waving in some far-off land. He signalled to Harry to bring the hymn to a halt and introduced the final hymn

- the 'sailor's hymn' as he described it: 'Eternal Father, Strong to Save'.

'After this hymn,' he announced, 'there will be a collection for Mrs Hubbard's Fund for Shipwrecked Sailors. Please be generous.'

The weary congregation waded through the restless waves, contributed generously so that Mrs Hubbard did not lose face, and then speedily hastened towards their cabins for a drink and a rest.

'Thank you all,' said Sparda to the stage party. 'The chaplain is currently indisposed, but will be back on full duty shortly.'

The moment the congregation had gone, Enzo scurried off to explore Albanian lexicography; Radley went to the kitchen to make his peace with Chef Tucker; Harry went to the bar area which now had a limited stock of drinks and where he was due to play the piano during the hour before lunch, and Captain Sparda returned to the bridge, leaving the poor old Staff Captain to escort the eighty-year-old twin sisters from New Zealand who were celebrating their birthday in the Golden Chopsticks restaurant with a plate of noodles and perhaps a slice of date pie with custard.

The remainder of the sea day passed tranquilly enough. During the afternoon, a game of deck quoits was arranged, but so many quoits were lost over the side that the game was brought to a premature halt. At the Sunday-evening dinner, Mike Tucker and his team excelled themselves, having bought extra supplies in Gibraltar. After several days of beans in various disguises, some fresh fish or a beef steak were much appreciated by the travellers, who warmly applauded Mike when he appeared in the dining room wearing his traditional Chef's gear. Prior to this evening he had remained well out of sight for fear of being attacked by irate passengers.

Another member of the ship's company who continued to remain in hiding was the owner of the Line, Admiral Benbow Harrington. He still could not puzzle out how he was going to deal with the problem of the doctor. He had requested that Captain Sparda monitor his performance and get passengers who visited him to fill out an evaluation sheet. If there was rampant displeasure with the man, then this would give grounds for putting the fellow ashore. What was clear was that he, the Admiral and shipping magnate, could not remain in hiding on his own ship simply because he was embarrassed by a rogue medico. He determined that the following day he would confront the fellow and have things out with him once and for all.

That evening, the Admiral, as usual, had dinner alone and later on, when the ship was quiet and there was only the sound of the ancient engine throbbing its weary way through the water, he took his customary stroll around the deck. He was just about to return to his cabin when he caught his foot in a deck quoit which had been left behind following the abandonment of the game that afternoon. He went down with an almighty crash, hitting his head on some object or other and immediately lapsed into unconsciousness. Some twenty minutes later, he was discovered by a deck-hand who sounded the alert. A stretcher-party arrived and the poor man was bundled through the narrow corridors of the ship and down to the Medical Centre.

The same weary attendant was on duty and he suggested that the stretcher be laid out across a table so that the doctor might examine the patient. The attendant, who had had too many nervous encounters with his superiors on the ship, paled visibly when he was informed that the figure lying prone on the stretcher was none other than Admiral Benbow Harrington, the owner of the Line. He said that he would summon the doctor immediately and disappeared.

It was the practice on the ship not to broadcast emergency messages across the information system so as not to cause unnecessary alarm. However, coded messages were relayed. The doctor had been given a code name 'Fairylight 42' and 'Fairylight 42' was requested to make his way to to his post immediately. That evening, the doctor had been for dinner with several passengers and had greatly appreciated their hospitality, especially their willingness to share with him some of their spoils gained from a visit to Gibraltar. Several bottles of wine were dispatched, and had not the host, an elderly gentleman from

Godalming, become alarmed at the rapid rate at which his precious stock was diminishing, most of the table would have finished up on the dining-room floor.

After a most convivial dinner, the doctor withdrew to the library where he accepted a very large cigar and engaged two or three of his dinner companions in a game of pontoon. Some rather cheap brandy, which a passenger had bought in Seville, was produced and the evening progressed nicely. The library was one of the places on the ship with a loudspeaker and, at a particularly tense point in the bidding, the said speaker sprang into life.

'What the hell can that be?' queried the doctor. There was much laughter as the appeal went out for 'Fairylight 42'.

'Perhaps it's approaching Christmas,' said one wit, 'and they want to decorate the tree.'

More laughter followed as the appeal was repeated.

The doctor was too far gone to recognise his code-name, even if he had remembered it - which he hadn't. When the message was repeated a fourth time, he looked up and threw a solid glass ashtray at the speaker, which fell silent at the very same moment as it fell off the wall.

The merry group resumed their game and 'Fairylight 42' continued to do damage to the brandy bottle on the table. Half an hour later, the door of the library burst open and the worried medical attendant entered. He took one look around, spotted the doctor and moved to his side.

'Sir,' he began.

The doctor waved his hand at him, saying, 'Sit down, laddie. We'll deal you in next time.'

The attendant did not sit down but tugged at the man's sleeve.

'Sir,' he pleaded. 'You are urgently needed.'

'I know *that*,' the Doctor said dismissively. 'A doctor is always needed on board a ship.'

'Sir,' repeated the boy with increasing anxiety. '*Now* sir. Please – come with me.'

One of the group, a certain Mr Coles who had been more moderate in his imbibing that evening, stepped in.

'I think he wants you to go with him immediately,' he said. 'Perhaps there is an emergency?' It took all the persuasive power of the attendant and Mr Coles to get the doctor to his feet and propel him in the direction of the Medical Centre where he arrived some very considerable time after the Admiral had been carried in.

Never has anyone in the living memory of drinkers across the ages sobered up so quickly as the doctor did that evening. He entered the room, took one look at the semi-conscious figure on the table and cried out, 'My God in heaven, who is that?'

The attendant explained that it was Admiral Benbow Harrington, the owner of the Line and a considerable shipping magnate. To the consternation of all present, the doctor immediately rushed into his own quarters and slammed the door. The attendant and his little band of helpers looked on in bewilderment, not knowing what to do. After a moment or so, the attendant rapped on the doctor's door. He could hear the sound of splashing water. Several more moments elapsed and the door opened to reveal the doctor wearing a surgical mask which completely covered his face, topped with a plastic head-covering normally used by surgeons and operating room attendants. He approached the stretcher and immediately started to work on the Admiral.

The gash on the forehead was not half as bad as it appeared and was soon attended to. What concerned the doctor was the fact that the patient had been lying on the deck for some time before being found and had lapsed in and out of consciousness. He ordered a cot to be made up in the room next to the chaplain and for the Admiral to be kept there under close supervision for the next twenty-four hours.

To his great credit, the doctor rose to the occasion. That night he did not sleep a wink but every hour he went into the small cubicle and checked his patient's condition. Each time he entered he wore the mask, for he was quite certain that once he was recognised he would be off the boat before he could turn round. For his part, the Admiral reflected on the situation as best he could. His head no longer hurt too much and sleep, that great restorer, gradually made him feel much better. The doctor, thought the Admiral, was clearly a compassionate man at heart. Yes, he had his weaknesses, but then so did they all. A model patient, the Admiral, did exactly as he was told and slept a good part of the night and much of the following day.

Late in the afternoon, the doctor appeared, once again still completely masked.

'Tell me,' said the Admiral mischievously, 'is my condition so contagious that you have always to appear in that fashion?'

The doctor mumbled something incomprehensible and produced his stethoscope.

'Come on, old chap,' the Admiral said, 'the game's up. You can take off that disguise right now.'

Visibly startled, the doctor shrugged and removed the gauze from around his face.

'I'll pack my bags,' he said, 'and get off in Monaco. Sorry, Admiral, but I have been a bit of a fool at certain times in my life.'

The Admiral wan't sure, but he thought he saw a small tear appear in the eye of the medic.

'You'll do no such thing,' said Admiral Harrington in his best commanding voice. 'We can all make mistakes. That's human. I've made my fair share although I'm not prepared to reveal them now. Get me out of here and continue with your duties. I think you'll make a very good ship's doctor.'

For once in his life, Doctor Stuart Hackett was speechless.

All he could say was: 'Thank you, sir,' before stepping backwards and nearly knocking himself out on the low doorway.

'Hold on, old chap,' said the Admiral. 'We need you, you know.'

And they did – but that's a story for later in the voyage.

20

The Admiral made a full and complete recovery from his unfortunate encounter with the deck quoit and was now able to leave behind cabin service and resume dining in the main dining room with the other passengers. This was a considerable relief to Roger Hallworthy, the Staff Captain, who had been landed with hosting the Captain's Table night after night. Naturally, once the Admiral was back on the scene, passengers were falling over themselves to dine at his table.

The main bonus of the accident was that the Admiral now had completely resolved the issue with the doctor and Harry was relieved of the responsibility of finding another medic to replace him. Doctor Hackett seemed to have moderated his habits since being reprieved and, although the Admiral was under no illusion whatsoever that the man's personal problems were resolved, he was reasonably confident that things would not be as bad as he had formerly feared.

Albert and Alice had now begun to settle into the cruise, despite the challenges they had encountered. As they had nothing to compare the cruise with, having hardly set foot outside

Grimsby for most of their life, they imagined that all cruise ships experienced similar issues, and that these were just a normal hazard facing those who chose to holiday on the sea. To a certain extent they were right. All cruise ships *did* face problems - and the Public Relations departments of most of the Lines were active much of the time, attempting to keep stories out of the news rather than the other way round.

Fred Batty, despite an inauspicious start to his destination lecture series, continued to be cheerful. His long solitary years spent on an AA motorcycle had made him very resilient, and having come up against every possible problem that could ever affect an internal combustion engine - and dealt with them using an ordinary set of tools - he had developed considerable innovative skills. Immediately after his first lecture, when the technician had made such a pig's ear of the slides, he had gone into the control booth and sorted it out using only his brain and a screwdriver.

Never having been a gambling man, nor super-rich for that matter, Monaco held little interest for Fred, but he had to swot up on the Casino and on the government of the Principality. To add interest to his lecture he recorded a verse or so from the ditty 'The Man Who Broke the Bank in Monte Carlo', and planned to play this at the start of his talk. He was frustrated at having his lectures put on the programme at eight in the morning but, as he was told that the timetable was not negotiable once they had set sail, he accepted the situation with reasonable equanimity.

There were slightly more people at his lecture on 'Monte C' as he called it, partly because he had buttonholed one or two people and offered them the points he might win at the quiz conducted each afternoon by the Cruise Director. Passengers were told that there would be a glittering array of prizes available for them at the conclusion of the cruise, but exactly what these prizes were was known only to the Cruise Director. At this early stage of the voyage, Enzo himself had no idea what they might be, but the thought of a prize was sufficient to add to Fred's disciples.

Captain Sparda was slightly worried. Not that the recent events had unduly disturbed him. His days on the Messina ferry had equipped him to deal with all eventualities, and as for working with awkward customers – well, he had had to knock along for years with his 'insurers' from Sicily. What worried the good man was that since fresh supplies had been taken aboard in Gibraltar, he was beginning to put on weight. A daily diet of beans, although monotonous, had 'kept him regular' as the saying goes, but now that bacon and black pudding had made their appearance, even in a couple of short days he had noticed an increase in weight. For an Italian this would be a curious diet, but the Captain was married to an English wife who had instructed him in the correct way to eat breakfast! It would not have been dignified for him to be seen jogging around the deck in his ex-Italian army shorts – 'Bombay Bloomers' as ex-Indian Army regulars called them – so he took to doing isometric exercises on the bridge. He would frequently startle the Staff Captain by suddenly falling to the floor and doing several quick press-ups, or when speaking to the helmsman, clench and unclench his fists in what the helmsman first thought was a threatening manner.

It was when he suddenly dropped to the floor one evening in the dining room, having temporarily forgotten where he was, that the Admiral suggested he must take a little more control of himself, otherwise the passengers would become unduly alarmed. In fact, that very same evening when he had clenched his fists in the presence of the Maitre D' he was fortunate not to receive a straight left to the head from one who had been a boxer during his days in the Army Catering Corps.

Weight problems aside, the good ship *Handshake* was now set on course for Monaco, home of the rich and famous, and playground for the playboys of the world.

The Staff Captain was in command, and Captain Sparda trotted here, there and everywhere, frequently scanning the horizon with his telescope. Eventually Monaco was sighted.

'My heavens,' said Sparda. 'Just look at those yachts.'

The crew on the bridge duly noted the most amazing-looking vessels moored against the quay. One in particular was cruising in a haphazard fashion as the owner attempted to impress the bevy of young women gathered around him at the helm.

'Some of those private vessels are as big as this ship!' exclaimed Roger.

'My God. Look at that fellow'. A gleaming white monster bearing the name '*Petersburg Pride*' was racing towards them. Seemingly, it was under the command of a swarthy-looking individual chomping on a cigar and wearing a nautical cap positioned in a rakish manner on his head. He was surrounded by several bikini-clad maidens who were laughing and giggling at the antics of their hero. The Staff Captain attempted to change course and managed to do so, but not before the *Petersburg Pride* had caught the fenders of the *Handshake* leaving a long black mark along the side of the errant sailor's yacht. Immediately the cigar was removed from the mouth of the oligarch and he began to shout across at the crew. He wasn't speaking in any language that the bridge party recognised, but they guessed it might be Russian.

This whole scene had been witnessed by a group of cruise passengers who had, as was their custom, gathered on deck to watch the arrival of their ship in port. Sir Archibald Willoughby and his formidable wife happened to be amongst the group. They had an apartment in Monaco and also many business interests there. The *Petersburg Pride* was now directly alongside the *Handshake* and the shouting and threatening gestures continued unabated.

Suddenly, a voice from the deck of the *Golden Handshake* pierced across the bows of the *Pride*. It was that of Lady Veronika. Although she had confined herself to monosyllables on the *Handshake*, now she showed the extent of her vocabulary in a long stream of incomprehensible invective. Not content with mere words, to the amazement of all, she leaped from the *Golden Handshake* onto the deck of the *Pride*, ran towards the abusive helmsman and smacked him soundly across the head. The startled fellow fell backwards down the stairs and Lady Veronika was seen following him, as the bikini-clad beauties scattered screaming. This resulted in a loud burst of applause from the observers on the *Handshake*, mingled with shouts of 'Well done!' and 'That's put him in his place.'

A few moments later, Lady Veronika appeared on deck and with another leap returned to the safety of her ship, this time to tumultuous applause from more passengers who had gathered to view this unique spectacle.

The Staff Captain gently eased the vessel forward, leaving the *Pride* motionless in the water. Thus they entered Monaco harbour.

'This is a damn hilly place,' muttered Albert to Alice, as they struggled upwards from the ship to the town.

They had yet to discover the system of escalators which connected one level to another, and so were obliged to do what he described as 'mountaineering'. At the time the *Golden Handshake* called into port, Monaco was in the process of being torn down and rebuilt. Some of the charming old buildings were being demolished in favour of new build and, although in some instances the facade of the old building was kept, it felt to many that the town lacked character.

'Someone is getting backhanders for all this,' said Albert sagely as they walked past a half-demolished building.

The only thing Alice wanted to see was the Radio Monaco building for, as a youngster in the 1960s, she had listened to this station under the bedclothes, along with Radio Luxembourg and Radio Caroline. The couple had been directed to the site, only to find like so many others before them that the building was gone – replaced by a modern hotel. They wandered on past some apartments curiously named 'La Shakespeare' and wondered why it was that the English bard had got a block of flats named after him.

'Damn Frogs,' said Albert, grumpy after so much climbing. 'They'll ruddy well pinch anything.'

'If you had been listening to Mr Batty this morning,' Alice reproved him, 'you will have heard him stress that the residents of this place are *not* French but Mohicans.'

Albert laughed, although he did not know that Alice had got the name completely wrong.

'Indians then,' he quipped. 'Come on lass. Let's get back to the ship before they raid us, eh'.

Only a few hours were left in port and Captain Sparda was not keen to linger as he feared that the evil-looking foreigner with whom Lady Veronika had dealt in such a satisfactory manner would be seeking revenge. When news of the illegal boarding of the Russian yacht reached the Admiral, he was gravely alarmed and immediately sought Harry for his wisdom. Harry suggested that they should leave as quickly as possible, but as passengers had disembarked and been told to be back at the ship at a certain time, they could not leave before then. The hours ticked by and nothing was heard from the authorities. In the late afternoon, about an hour before the last returning passenger was due to board, Captain Sparda was informed that three foreign-looking gentlemen were anxious to see him and that they were waiting at the foot of the gangway.

Before inviting them on board, Captain Sparda conveyed the intelligence to Harry. Fortunately, Admiral Benbow was on board and immediately came to join the Captain in a small room off the reception area. Within a few moments three muscular-looking types appeared in the doorway. Even though it was a mild afternoon they wore long black coats and broad-brimmed black hats pulled well down over their foreheads. Captain Sparda invited them in. To his alarm, two entered but the third stationed himself in the doorway, completely blocking it. The

Admiral looked nervously at Sparda as the two giants refused a seat.

'Good afternoon,' began Sir Benbow politely. 'To what do we owe the pleasure of this visit?'

The pair did not answer but fixed a glassy stare on the two cruise specialists.

'Will you have a drink?' enquired the Captain. 'Tea perhaps, or something stronger?'

Once again there was no answer.

Finally, one of the pair spoke.

'The woman. Where she? Bring here. Now.'

Captain Sparda pretended to look puzzled. Although he knew immediately that they were looking for Lady Veronika he denied that he knew what they were talking about.

'Bring woman now!' shouted the bear and banged an over-sized fist on the little table. 'Now, or I eat you.'

Captain Sparda was not sure whether the giant said 'beat' or 'eat', but neither prospect appealed. He gave a wan smile and picked up the telephone. Outside the office he could hear the sound of passengers returning and realised that in a very short time indeed, the vessel was due to leave Monaco.

'Harry,' said the Captain as the ultimate fixer picked up the phone. 'Three gentlemen are here with me and the Admiral in the reception office. They say they want me to bring them a woman. Do you have any idea what they are talking about?'

Harry knew only too well what they were talking about. He had had dealings with Russian thugs before - and not all the encounters were pleasant.

'I think I do, Captain,' he said calmly. 'Kindly ask them to come to my office and all will be well.'

The Captain replaced the receiver. 'My executive agent says he knows just what you require, and if you will come with me to his office he will meet you there.'

The bruisers looked at each other and then nodded.

'OK, go,' said the vocal visitor. 'Quick.'

Subject to the curious stares of the returning tourists, Captain Sparda and Admiral Harrington moved swiftly along the corridor in formation. One bruiser led the way and received directions from Sparda behind him, who was walking alongside Harrington. Both were followed by the two remaining evil-looking types. Harry Parkhurst was waiting at his office door and immediately ushered the party in.

'Gentlemen,' he said, 'I do understand what you require, and as we have to leave Monaco in a few moments I think we ought to say what we have to say quickly. We cannot apologise enough for the misdeeds of one of our spirited passengers. So perhaps you had better meet her and deal with the situation in your own way.'

As he said these latter words, a side door in the office opened and out jumped several men sporting hand-guns and shouting in Italian. The giants looked around and there were several more sharpshooters stationed behind them.

'Down!' the armed men cried. 'On the floor - *pronto.*'

The Russian heavyweights were sat upon and efficiently frisked for weapons. Several weapons were found and immediately thrown out of the door, to be collected by yet another Italian who had appeared from nowhere. Within a few moments the three Russian visitors were frog-marched down the gangway and into waiting black Mercedes cars. Once inside the vehicles one of the Italian group waved at the ship and then the vehicles departed without a further word.

'Great Scott. What was *that*'? said a stunned Admiral.

'The Captain's insurers, Admiral,' said Harry smoothly. 'They don't like to receive too many claims.'

And with that, the ship cast off.

21

'You know, Harry,' said the Admiral the next morning when they were having a coffee together, 'I am not too happy about the events of last night.'

Harry said nothing, merely sipped at his espresso.

'It was an alarming happening, you must admit.'

'It *was* all very dramatic,' Harry agreed, 'but that was the only way we could sort out the problem. For a woman to insult the dignity of a Russian mobster - well, that's no small matter.'

'As for the Captain's insurers,' continued the Admiral, 'it was disturbing that they carried firearms. I can guess who they were, but how deeply is Sparda involved with them?'

Harry got up and fetched them another coffee each from the ancient espresso machine, recently restored to life by the ship's engineer. He returned to the table.

'As you know, Sparda is married to an English wife, and as you have seen, he speaks English fluently, although his written skills are only average. He was brought up in the South of Italy and comes from a large family who have many "involvements" both in Sicily and across the country. There is nothing he can do about that. He is an honest man – you know that – but he does have to pay his dues. I would be surprised if he had not declared this to you before you offered him the job.'

'Yes,' said the Admiral, recollecting the somewhat amusing letter of application he had received from Sparda some months earlier. 'Yes to be fair, he was clear from the start that he had his friends as he put it.'

'I knew he would,' replied Harry. 'As for last night, I think we have seen the last of that problem. Although the Russians are vicious fighters, they won't want to take on our people. The thugs who came to the ship last night were pretty low-level operators. The real bosses were in fact getting together with the Italians for a joint business meeting in Monaco. It's not in their interests to take this any further, so we can forget about it.'

This conversation considerably eased the Admiral's mind. He got up to leave.

'Naples next,' he said. 'I dread to think what awaits us there.'

The Hardcastles had witnessed the Admiral and the Captain marching resolutely along the corridor in the company of the three visitors, and at the time thought it rather odd, for when Albert said a cheery, 'Ow do, Captain,' instead of a warm smile and effusive reply, all he received was a stern look.

'What's up with him then?' Albert asked his wife.

Other passengers had witnessed the procession and rumours

circulated the ship. It was being impounded for non-payment of port fees. The Captain had been arrested for shop-lifting and, worst of all, the ship was being inspected by health and safety officials! Lady Veronika had also seen the procession and had immediately identified one of the black-hatted thugs as Boris Boroneski of the Siberian Secret Service. He was a member of the Siberian criminal underworld and was known for travelling everywhere in an ornate sledge pulled by several Husky dogs. Later, when he advanced in the criminal world, he was given charge of the sledge rental business, a lucrative operation which hired out sledges throughout Siberia.

She had lost track of him when he moved to Moscow. As soon as she spotted him, she informed Harry and then went to hide in a linen cupboard, knowing that Harry would resolve the problem – which of course he did.

It was a lovely fresh morning and Albert and his wife had had their breakfast on the veranda, a tiny space just outside the main dining room with only space for two tables. Well, they tried to have breakfast there. As the warmer weather approached there would be a rush for these places, but it was usually possible to get one if you appeared early enough. This morning, Alice lost several napkins over the side (Albert refused to use them, describing them as being for 'sissies') and when her cornflakes were blown completely out of the dish due to a sudden gust of wind, the couple decided enough was enough and sought refuge inside.

'By gum,' said Alice, as she poured herself a cup of tea. 'This stuff is nothing like we get at home.'

Albert agreed. This was the first time ever they had used tea bags and they were not impressed. They shunned the coffee completely, describing it succinctly as 'poison'. Alice made a face as she sipped the weak liquid in her cup.

'I think today we ought to go to the Italian Language Class,' she told her husband, 'as we might want to do a little exploring by ourselves.'

For their stay in Naples, the Tour Manager had organised a series of visits to some of the noted classical sites, such as Pompeii, Herculaneum and Paestum. Albert had taken one look at the cost and there and then decided he did not want to 'pay that to visit a pile of old stones'. Alice agreed that it was all rather expensive and besides, why pay for an extra lunch on shore when there was a perfectly good meal on board. They had spoken with a passenger who had visited Italy before and who suggested to them that they might hire a car for the day. He assured them that a small Fiat Cinquecento could be hired for next to nothing at the dockside, and, once they had got used to driving on the wrong side of the road, they would have a carefree experience.

Albert was most reluctant. The thought of driving on the wrong side did not appeal to him in the slightest, and he had no idea where they would drive to. Alice's confidence had grown since the start of the cruise and, as often was the case, she won the day. They would have an early lunch on board and then hire a car. As the ship was not due to sail until eleven that night, there was plenty of time to explore the surroundings and, providing they had some knowledge of Italian, all should be well. Albert remained unconvinced, but as domestic harmony was important, given that they were sharing a suite with limited space, he acquiesced.

At the prime time of eleven that morning, Enzo stood at the door of the lecture area ready to welcome his students.

'Good morning, Mr and Mrs Hardcastle,' he said, for once accurately connecting faces and names. 'Welcome to the Italian class.'

'Not many here,' commented Albert, looking around and noting the many empty seats.

'We tend to be a select group,' Enzo replied. 'Those who attend these important sessions are the ones who want to get as much as they can from the experience of being at sea. They also want to *take home* something of the experience. What could be better than returning with an understanding of several languages?'

Albert and Alice sat down and other select passengers seated themselves at points around the auditorium.

Enzo began.

'I am going to teach you this morning everything you will need to converse with the local people in a way that will ensure you have excellent relations with them. They like nothing more than a foreigner who makes the effort to speak to them in their own language.' At this point he produced a small booklet. 'I shall read out a word in Italian and its English meaning. You will repeat it after me,' he told them.

'*Buongiorno* – good morning.'

The group intoned the words.

'Good, excellent,' enthused their instructor. 'You are making amazing progress.' And now to: '*Buonasera* – good evening,' he continued.

Once again a few voices around the room repeated the words.

'Oh well done,' beamed Enzo.' You have the accent perfectly.'

The lesson continued as he went through numbers from one to ten, taught them how to say *pizza* and *pasta* and one or two other simple words.

'This is bloody boring,' Albert muttered as the lesson droned on.

'Quiet!' snapped his wife. 'This will be invaluable tomorrow when we will need to speak Italian.'

After half an hour the lesson was brought to a close with Enzo congratulating his students once again and suggesting that they might wish to come and learn Albanian at the next class.

'Not on your nelly,' said Albert to himself. 'One lingo is enough for me.'

Following the Italian class the day passed peacefully enough. As the weather was beginning to get warmer Albert was able to dispense with his waistcoat, but he continued to wear his cap whenever he went out on deck. The Balcony Suites, being the exclusive accommodation on the ship, were equipped with small safes hidden in a dark corner of the wardrobe.

'Put yer gold watch in there,' said Alice, as Albert hung up his waistcoat. 'You never know.'

Albert fiddled with the safe. The instructions as to how to lock it were on a printed sheet fixed to the wall adjacent to the safe, but as the room was dark, and Albert's eyes were not as good as they once were, he could not read them clearly. Finally, with Alice's help, he was able to work out that he had to select a four-digit number which he then had to enter, and when the door closed, the safe would lock immediately. Before closing the door they selected other valuable items that they had with them and put them alongside the watch.

'Right,' said Alice. 'Close the door.'

Albert jumbled the numbers and closed the door. They heard the sound of the bolts moving across, thus locking it securely.

'I think we ought to see if it works properly,' said the ever-cautious Alice. 'Put the numbers in, luv, and see if it opens.'

'What are they?' he asked, looking at her.

'What do you mean?' she said. '*I* don't know. *You* put them in.'

'I thought you made a note of them,' he replied, now somewhat alarmed.

'How could I?' she asked. 'I couldn't see the blessed things for a start.'

Albert tugged at the door then spun the dials. The door remained firmly closed.

'It's hopeless!' he cried. 'Totally hopeless. Why they make such daft devices I don't know.'

'Here, let me try,' said Alice. She pushed Albert aside. 'Have you any idea what numbers you might have chosen?'

Albert had no idea whatsoever. After several vain attempts, she gave up.

'This is a fine mess, Albert Hardcastle. We have all our money in there, as well as your driving licence and goodness knows what else. How are we going to see Naples tomorrow?'

'I don't give a damn about Naples,' said Albert. 'What we need is that daft safe opened. It's a good job I've got my Swiss Army knife with me as I might be able to unscrew it off the wall and get in through the back. There must be some way of getting in.'

Albert rummaged in his luggage and produced his Swiss knife given to him by his Uncle Charlie many years previously.

'This gets you out of all sorts of difficulties,' he said and disappeared into the wardrobe. For the next half-hour, much banging and cursing emanated from the small dark cubbyhole. Alice remained silent, having learned over the years not to disturb her husband when he was engaged in an important task. Suddenly there was a loud crash. Albert emerged from the gloom clutching one leg and shouting, 'Ow, my foot! The damn thing fell on my foot?'

As he was hopping around the floor, the cabin doorbell rang. It had been Radley's idea to have a different tune for each doorbell of the Balcony Suites. Albert and Alice's played the first bars of 'You Tak the High Road', a good old Scottish melody. From time to time the bell stuck and that, along with the sticking door, was the cause of much irritation during the voyage. Alice heaved at the door, which eventually opened to reveal their neighbour from the next cabin.

'I do apologise for disturbing you, Mrs Hardcastle,' the woman said politely, 'but I am afraid that in the last half-hour there has been so much banging from your cabin that all the pictures on our wall have fallen off and now a hole has appeared so that we can see directly into your changing room.'

She glanced at Albert, who had now stopped dancing around the room and was sitting with his foot held high and a very pained expression on his face.

'Is anything wrong?' their neighbour enquired.

Alice gave a nervous laugh. 'Oh, nothing too serious,' she

replied. 'A small difficulty with the coat-hangers, but my husband will attend to it. He's very handy, you know.'

'But what about the hole?' said the anxious neighbour. 'That is more serious, is it not?'

'Don't worry,' replied Alice soothingly. 'We'll hang a coat over it and then get the ship to deal with it. So sorry to have disturbed you.'

She forced the door to and returned to the room, seething.

'Albert Hardcastle, how dare you embarrass me like that. Sitting with your bare feet in the air like a loony. Whatever will our neighbours think?'

Albert was just about to reply in a way that was bound to cause further trouble when 'You Tak the High Road' pealed out again. It was the Indian cabin steward, Udi.

'Oh sir, madam,' he said. 'You have problem with coat-hanger. You have bad feet, sir?' noting Albert's swollen toe.

Albert, not in any way wanting to lose face on the ship, thought quickly.

'Look, Udi,' he began. 'We don't want to cause any alarm or any trouble on this cruise.' Udi nodded. 'Very good, sir. You no trouble. You good man, sir. You good lady.'

Albert lowered his voice and beckoned Udi to come closer. He spoke in a half-whisper. 'Udi, someone has tried to steal our safe with all our valuables inside.'

Alice stared incredulously at Albert.

'We arrived back at our Suite and had trouble like we always do in getting the door open. When we got in, I went to put my cap in the wardrobe and stubbed my toe on something. The safe was on the floor and I could see into the next Suite.'

'Goodness gracious,' said the startled attendant. 'This very serious, sir. I must report it.'

Albert waved his hand for Udi to be quiet.

'When he heard us entering, the thief must have hid under the bed and escaped when we ran into the corridor to see if we could see anyone.'

Udi peered under the bed. 'Not here now, sir,' he said.

'Udi, I don't want any fuss. This must be treated with great discretion. We don't want to cause alarm on the ship. Get the safe opened and replaced, and we will forget all about the matter, OK?'

'OK, sir, very good, sir. Thank you, sir. Nothing stolen, sir.'

Udi looked from the heavy safe on the floor to the hole in the wall. As he peered at it, he noted the occupant of the next cabin staring curiously at him. Quickly he hung a coat over the gap and retreated.

'No worry, sir. I get engineer, sir,' and with that he left.

'Udi!' shouted Albert as the attendant scuttled down the corridor. 'When he's here, get him to fix the door, please. The wife and I are going on deck for some air.'

When they returned one hour later, the Suite door opened

so quickly that Albert was catapulted into the room. He looked into the wardrobe where there was a new safe with the door swinging open. On the table was a message.

Sir, madam. If you call at Reception the precious things from your safe are in plastic bag. Happy to help sir. Udi.

'Damn good ship, this,' said Albert as he hobbled back across the room. 'Damn good ship. But from now on we put our valuables under the bed, luv.'

Alice nodded, and the ship with her valuable cargo of contented cruisers continued on her way to Naples.

22

It was part of the job description of the Security Officer to keep a low profile and Arthur Chub did just that. Arthur had been recruited for the *Golden Handshake* by Harry. He had had a career in the Royal Military Police and for a year or so after leaving the Service had worked as a security officer at Wigan Gasworks. This post he found to be both poorly paid and unsatisfactory, as all he had to do was wear an ill-fitting uniform and check those who entered and those who left the premises.

In his new post at sea he was responsible for the total security of the ship and had a small team of loyal workers reporting to him. He stressed that every suspicious activity must be reported, no matter how slight. The initial difficulties with the card system had caused him tremendous headaches, and he was still not happy with the passenger-list, even though they had been at sea for several days.

When the alarming news of the attempt to steal Albert's safe reached him, he immediately suspected that there was a stowaway on board and ordered a discreet search of all the lifeboats. No one was found, but Arthur remained unsatisfied. He wondered if he ought to visit the scene of the crime, but he did not want to go against the express wishes of a Balcony Suite passenger so he kept his distance. Unfortunately, when the problem was first reported to the engineer by the cabin attendant, Arthur had been fast asleep after sitting up late in yet another fruitless attempt to work out who was and who was not on board. By the time the report of the attempted theft reached his desk, the safe had been replaced and the scene of the crime considerably disturbed.

Once again he issued a confidential circular saying that he must be contacted personally, the moment any suspicious activity was discovered or reported. He was totally unaware of the visit to the ship by the Russian gangsters and the Italian 'insurers'. The Captain and the Admiral had kept this whole matter very quiet, and that was how it would remain. As for Lady Veronika - well, Chub had written her off as a complete lunatic of the kind one often finds on cruise ships. He would have been greatly intrigued had he known of her colourful past, spent in the wilds of Siberia.

Naples, known to him as a place where crime was not totally unknown, caused him concern, and he had asked Fred Batty to slip in a few words of caution to passengers who would be going ashore. Even so, someone was bound to have a wallet or handbag stolen. He was thankful that passports were securely held on the ship, as trying to replace those documents was a total nightmare.

So, Arthur Chub, ex-military, ex-gasworks, sat in his tiny cabin awaiting Napoli and struggling with incomplete passenger-lists whilst, out on the deck, carefree passengers played deck quoits (now resumed again as a fresh stock of quoits had been unearthed), and leaned over the rail as they had seen people do in brochures, or just dozed in their cabins, happy to be sailing towards a romantic location so frequently eulogised in verse and song.

The next morning, Alice woke early and did her best to remember the Italian language she had learned the previous day. It was strange, but before retiring last night she seemed to be quite good at it, but this morning her mind was a blank. As for Albert, it wasn't worth asking him anything as he paid no attention at all when the charming Enzo was conducting his class. She consulted the notes she had made on the back of waste paper that Enzo had handed out for note taking. She had scribbled *pizza* and *pasta*. Those words were familiar as she had used them often enough in Grimsby, but never had she said 'Ow do in Italian to her neighbours.

Getting ashore was not too difficult, but as the couple were checking themselves out of the ship they were approached by a uniformed man they had not seen before.

'Mr and Mrs Hardcastle,' he said genially. 'A very good morning to you.'

'Aye,' said Albert. 'It's a grand day, of that there's no doubt.'

187

'I assume everything is well with you both?' the man then asked.

'As well as can be expected,' said Alice. 'Although I don't care for the tea much.'

'Ah,' he replied. 'It might be the water. Water affects the taste of tea very much.'

'It's those damn tea packets,' Albert stated. 'Useless, totally useless.'

'Is all well with your suite - a Balcony Suite, I believe?'

'Yes,' Alice answered, 'we like to travel that way. So much more comfortable, you know.'

'It is indeed,' rejoined the officer. 'If one does not mind the little extra climb then one is well rewarded with great comfort.'

The officer seemed reluctant to let them go. 'Is everything working well in the Suite?' was his next question.

'Aye,' Albert said impatiently. 'Come on, Alice, we will have no time to see around if we continue to linger here.'

The officer smiled politely. 'Have a lovely day,' he said, secretly irritated at not having been able to extract some details of the alleged attempted theft from the Suite.

At the car-hire booth neither Albert nor Alice needed to have had the slightest concern about language problems. The couple ahead of them were conversing with the clerk in faultless English. They approached the desk with confidence.

'We want a car,' said Albert.

'That is what we are here for, sir,' replied the desk clerk. 'Would you like a Mercedes? A lovely car and most suitable for cruise passengers.'

They examined the price-list and the car offered was about twelve times the cost of the Cinquecento they had been advised to hire.

'Well, we are Balcony Suite passengers,' said Alice, 'and normally we would hire a car and a driver.'

Quick as a flash the clerk jumped in.

'Oh, we can arrange that without any difficulty,' he replied. 'In fact, I would drive you myself.'

'Very kind, I'm sure,' said Alice. 'But today my husband insists that we hire a car he drove when he was a young man - a Cinquecento.'

Albert looked startled. It was only two days ago that he had first heard of the vehicle, let alone driven one.

'Ah, I see,' the man replied, slightly crestfallen. 'We have just the thing for you.' He completed the formalities and directed them to a park outside.

'*Numero Venti,*' he said, forgetting his English for a moment.

'Eh?' queried Albert.

'Oh, my apologies, sir. Number Twenty, Vehicle Number Twenty.'

Outside, a very large number of cars were parked. After much searching they found Vehicle Twenty, a minute vehicle which Albert immediately likened to one of the dodgem cars that he had seen at the fairground in Grimsby.

'Thee were right, Alice,' he said. 'I did drive this sort of contraption when I was a lad.'

They squeezed in and tried to understand the controls, which were nothing like the controls on Albert's car in Grimsby, nor one of the dodgem cars for that matter.

'See what the manual says luv,' said Albert as he looked for the ignition.

'It's all in a foreign language,' she told him as she thumbed through the glossy document. 'I don't see one word we learned from Enzo yesterday. Not one word.'

After half an hour of precious time had elapsed, Alice returned to the booth which was now closed. Back at the car, she noted a youngish man in a sharp suit unlocking a Cinquecento parked nearby.

'Bon afternoon,' she said politely.

He stared at her. '*Non capisco.*'

'Bon journal,' she tried next, thinking that she might have got the first greeting wrong.

'Speak English?' he enquired, to Alice's relief.

She said that she did, and within a moment or so the car was started and they were on their way.

It would be kind to the reader of this book to pass over the details of Albert's venture onto the highways of Naples. Apart from having to be constantly reminded by Alice to keep to the right, which he just about managed to do most of the time, he was constantly alarmed by vehicles darting in front of him, and drivers gesticulating – and not least by his unfamiliarity with the controls of the vehicle. They were both so occupied in attempting to preserve their lives that the scenery around them went totally unobserved.

'Remember where we are going,' said Albert as they left the city behind them. 'We have to get back, you know.'

Obediently, Alice did her best to scribble notes on the scrap paper she had brought along but, as the car was bumping up and down, and also as every sign was in Italian, which she had difficulty in recording, her directions were not altogether legible. They approached a high point overlooking the bay and a totally exhausted Albert suggested that they call a halt and take a breather. They pulled off the roadway by a small path that led towards a viewing-point.

'While we are here we might as well walk up there,' said his wife. 'After that we can go back to the ship. I've had enough.'

They secured the car and set off toward the summit.

It was a lovely view. Below them was the town, which looked strangely attractive from this height and, of course, there was the bay with the sparkling waters of the Mediterranean to complete the picture.

'Now that *is* nice,' said Albert as he surveyed the scene below him. 'Very nice indeed.'

'Best be getting back,' said Alice after a while. 'I dread the journey, don't you? They are like madmen on the roads here.'

Near to where the car was parked was a small café and, had their language skills been greater, they would have stopped in for a drink. As it was, they decided against this and proceeded towards the hire vehicle. As they approached, Albert stopped in his tracks.

'Is that our car?' he queried.

As it was the only car in the area, and in the place where they had left it, Alice replied that it was very likely their car.

'Then look at it,' said Albert with a pained expression on his face.

'My God!' cried Alice. 'It's got no wheels.'

They rushed towards it and clearly on the windscreen was a small sticker with the number Twenty visible.

'What in God's name has happened here?' asked Albert. He looked around desperately. Some distance away, a family group were picnicking. Sitting at tables outside the café, several more people sipped drinks. Albert felt panic approaching.

'Alice,' he said, 'as you speak Italian, try and explain the problem to the chap in the café. He might be able to help. I'll guard the car.'

Alice, as near to tears as she had been for many a year, and clutching her scrap of paper with her Italian words written on it, went into the bar. An elderly man stood behind a gleaming espresso machine which made a furious noise as he prepared a coffee for a patron.

'Bon Bon,' she said, completely forgetting the customary form of greeting in Italian.

The assistant didn't reply but turned around, took a packet of confectionary from off the shelf and handed it to her. She stared at the packet of sweets and handed them back.

'No, non,' she stumbled. 'My car no wheels. I need four wheels.'

Not knowing what the Italian was for wheels she drew four circles in the air with her hands.

'Wheels, round like pizza,' she said. 'Quantro.'

She had almost got the Italian word for 'four' right but not quite.

The waiter seemed delighted and his face lit up. He gestured to her that she should sit outside and he would bring the order across. Alice rejoined Albert.

'It's all right now, luv,' she said soothingly. 'He will bring four wheels for the car in a moment.'

Albert puzzled as to how a café in Italy would have four car wheels in stock, but there was no telling what these foreigners would get up to so he said nothing. Fifteen minutes went by and then they saw the waiter approaching.

'I can't see the wheels,' he said anxiously.

The waiter came closer and beamed at them both before placing before them four pizzas and a full bottle of Cointreau. Albert and Alice gawped at him in disbelief.

'What's this?' asked Albert as he examined the bottle. 'What have you done, Alice? We can't run the car on booze and pizza.'

The waiter presented them with a bill and reluctantly Albert paid it with the money he had changed on board that morning.

'This is a right carry-on,' he mumbled as he took a bite from one of the pizzas. 'What on earth do we do now?'

There are times in life when guardian angels seem to take pity on the poor mortals whom they are charged to protect and, for Albert and Alice, such a moment had arrived. For who should pull up in front of them on a scooter but the very officer with whom they had spoken on leaving the ship. He recognised them instantly.

'Ah, Mr and Mrs Hardcastle,' he said. 'Enjoying some light refreshments, I see.'

Immediately they poured out their troubles to him, and who better to listen to those troubles than the ship's Security Officer. In no time at all he had contacted the car-hire company and arranged for the sorry couple to be driven back to the *Golden Handshake*.

'I always said this was a damn fine ship,' said Albert that evening, now safely back on the ship and ensconced in the safety of the Balcony Suite.

'Aye,' said Alice, as she packed the unwanted bottle of Cointreau into a suitcase.

'It's not bad, Albert. It's not bad. But as for Naples . . . '

She said no more and neither did her husband.

23

On the bridge, all was sweetness and light. The Captain and the Staff Captain quipped with each other as the *Golden Handshake* cut a fine figure through the water on course for Messina in Southern Italy, or as many preferred to emphasise, Sicily.

'The cattle didn't know how lucky they were when they sailed in this ship,' said Sparda. 'Sheer luxury.'

The Staff Captain was a little more cautious with his enthusiasm as he was receiving frequent reports about the poor functioning of the steering gear. However, he had to say that since the problems experienced in Gibraltar had been dealt with, the ship had performed reasonably well.

Sparda was looking forward to meeting his wife for a few brief hours. Lilian Sparda had been born in the United Kingdom and was known there as Lilian Foster until she met and married Sparda in Deptford. He had been doing a temporary job dredging the Thames and had lodged with the Foster family, many of whom had connections with shipping in one form or another. It had taken Lilian some time to settle in Messina, but certain of the changes were easy enough. She left the closeness of a London family, where relatives lived around every corner, for the closeness of an Italian matriarchy where relatives lived in every corner of the house! Peché, her husband, was very accustomed to English ways, and with his support she was able to develop a degree of independence. Some of the relatives, especially those who lived in Catania, rather frightened her, but thankfully they did not visit too frequently and she had little occasion to visit this inland Sicilian town.

The chaplain continued to languish in his limited quarters in the sickbay. The doctor had declared him completely cured of the throat condition, but had warned him in no uncertain terms that he must not, under any circumstances, sing hymns too loudly, and any sermon he delivered must be limited to three minutes. This was because the doctor knew that as a senior staff member, he would be required to attend Divine Service and he could not tolerate clerical sermonising.

The chaplain took this warning seriously, but as there had not yet been a Sunday which was a sea day, he had not been called on for duty. Neither had he been able to see the Captain, as Sparda had requested. Each time he tried to get an appointment, he was fobbed off with one excuse or another. Finally, as the ship headed towards Southern Italy, Sparda came out of the bridge into his own small cabin.

'Come in,' he boomed as he heard a timid knock on the door.

The chaplain had put on his only clerical suit for the occasion and this, together with a very broad clerical collar, made him look for all the world like Mr Slope, the Trollopian character. The chaplain entered and the Captain gave him the once-over,

'Off to a funeral, are we?' said Sparda merrily. 'Who's died then?'

'No one that I am aware of, Captain,' the man replied softly.

'Speak up, young man,' said Sparda. 'I can't hear a word you say.'

The chaplain cautiously cleared his throat and tried once again. This time apprehension got the better of him and not a sound emerged from his quivering lips.

'Look, lad,' said Sparda impatiently, 'I got a fine education, but lipreading was not on the curriculum. Speak up or get out.'

By now the chaplain had forgotten what he meant to say and so once again remained mute.

'By sainted George of England you're a queer fish. Well, I'll do the talking then. This Sunday is all yours. There will be Divine Service at ten o'clock, and you,' at this juncture he prodded the chaplain in the chest with his forefinger so that the other man nearly fell over, '*you*,' emphasized Sparda, 'will be responsible for the service. Understand?'

The chaplain nodded.

'Furthermore,' continued Sparda, 'I like good rousing

hymns and better still, a full-blown sermon. I don't consider that I have been to church unless there is a sermon of twenty-five minutes at least. Understood?'

Remembering the doctor's instructions, the poor chaplain began to tremble again.

'But . . . ' he began, this time in a half-audible whisper.

'No buts,' boomed the Captain. 'You have to work your passage on this ship. Now, back to your quarters and get stuck into that sermon.'

The chaplain did not think it opportune to raise the question of his quarters and so he resigned himself to returning to his little room in the sickbay.

'Good day, Padre,' said Sparda in farewell. 'Don't tax your tonsils too much. You'll need them on Sunday.'

And with that the chaplain left the cabin and returned to the bowels of the ship.

In another part of the ship altogether, Mr Toby Troy, former hostage turned lecturer, was working on his lecture series. The unfortunate fellow had been detained by Hezbollah, mainly because he had irritated them and, alas, he had not lost the ability to irritate all who came into contact with him. Although he had long ago abandoned his fiercely held religious beliefs, he had simply transferred his energy into promoting the activities of 'The Society for Exposing Anything'. The Society had been founded by Assad Wikiwhats who, as a market trader in Swindon, laboured under a heavy sense of injustice. Why should he, a simple seller of fruit and vegetables, be denied access to global secrets? Brave Assad threw caution to the wind and set up the Society, and from day one never looked back. He met Toby Troy at an antique gun fair in Bristol, and they had worked together ever since. Their first major coup consisted of exposing an MP for paying too much tax.

'He cannot be diligent,' trumpeted Troy, 'if he pays too much tax. He must go.' And go he did.

The next triumph was for exposing a well-known retailer for selling bent bananas when European Economic Community regulations clearly stated they must be straight.

'There are too many lawbreakers,' thundered the Society, 'and the country is going to the dogs because of them.'

The retailer was fined a considerable sum and banned from selling fruit for twelve months. Troy also took it upon himself to 'doorstep' individuals whom he considered needed exposing. He visited a home in Sevenoaks which had appeared on a television commercial. The lady of the house, a Mrs Liza Goodrich, had held before the camera a shirt and had both said and sung 'Washo washes whiter'. When visited by Mr Wikiwhats and asked, 'Whiter than what?' she was stuck for an answer and admitted, on camera, that she had held up a new shirt that had never been previously washed. This caused massive unrest across the British Isles and resulted in the Company of Detergent Operatives completely revising their code of practice. Clearly Toby Troy, partner of Assad Wikiwhats, was a dangerous man to have on board.

24

Enzo Bigatoni, Cruise Director extraordinaire, and master of the game 'Piddling Pursuits,' was a happy man. So far on the cruise his quiz session in the afternoons had attracted very satisfactory numbers, largely because no other event ever clashed with this slot. He had spent hours collecting obscure and unusual facts which he carefully noted in his little red book. Black books were for his language classes and red books for quiz questions.

The game was simple. Passengers were divided into teams and collected points, which were named 'carats', for correct answers. At first passengers thought they were being awarded vegetables, which caused much innocent laughter, until it dawned that this was a clever play on the 'golden' theme and stood for a measurement of gold. From time to time he would announce a special session of Pursuits during which he asked a series of difficult questions - twenty-four in all - all related to the same theme. In the most unlikely event of anyone getting every single question correct, (i.e. reaching pure gold) he was able to tempt them with a very special prize - a shore excursion for two with lunch and all the trimmings, the total value of which would not exceed five hundred pounds. As he never believed that any one person would ever win such a difficult quiz, he had not thought it necessary to get authorisation from the Hotel Manager for such a huge prize.

Sir Archie, a simple good-natured man, was a regular attender at Pursuits, although his solitary wife did not go along. Behind her brooding exterior lay a fierce intelligence and she would have undoubtedly been able to collect a massive number of carats, had she so wished. Mr Toby Troy had gone to each session of the game and had succeeded in irritating his team members by boasting about his unique knowledge of the world and, on most occasions, failing to get the correct answers and thus bring glory to the team. Albert and Alice had gone to one session, after which Albert declared it 'totally daft' and they avoided it thereafter.

On the sea day, when the happy ship was steaming full speed ahead for Messina, Enzo summoned passengers to rush from their suites and cabins for an important announcement. They gathered expectantly around the Information Points and the familiar voice of their Cruise Director came over the loudspeakers.

'Good morning, ladies and gentlemen. This is your Cruise Director, Enzo, announcing a very special event today. Piddling Pursuits this morning at eleven o'clock will be the Speciality

Session with an enormous prize worth five hundred pounds going to the winner. There will be only one or two Speciality Sessions each cruise, so do come along. See you around the ship and have a wonderful day.'

At the appointed time, rather more passengers than usual made their way to the venue and were given a paper and pencil by Angela Fairweather, the social hostess. Sir Archie was amazed that Lady Veronika decided to accompany him that morning. Normally she disdained the game, but there was no telling with his unpredictable wife and so, wearing her distinctive Mongolian knitted jacket, she made her first appearance.

A beaming Enzo greeted the assembled competitors. He instructed them that as this was a session with so much at stake, the rules would be strictly enforced and his word was final.

The group waited anxiously to see what the speciality subject would be, and when he announced it was 'yaks' a huge groan went up around the room. One or two passengers got up at that point and left, but the majority stayed behind although they realised that they were probably doomed from the start. Sir Archie could not believe it. He knew of his wife's Intelligence background, of course, and marvelled that in some way or another she had been able to discover the subject for this demanding quiz. His respect for her ability increased dramatically.

Enzo called for absolute silence and produced his little red book.

'Question one,' he announced solemnly.

'How high can a yak climb without experiencing any problems?'

There were various wild guesses. Toby Troy, who claimed to have visited the habitat of yaks many times in his life, did a few quick calculations in his head and scribbled a number on his paper. Lady Veronika, impassive as ever, noted something down.

'Question two,' he declared. 'What is the name given to the cross between a yak and a bison?'

'A bloody freak!' shouted some wit from one of the groups.

Enzo looked sternly at him. 'Remember the huge prize on offer,' he said, 'and please try to take this seriously.'

By the time Enzo had arrived at the final question, deep gloom had settled on the group. Apart from the subject being so specialised, the questions were obscure in the extreme and it would be nothing short of a miracle if all the correct answers were given by one person.

'Question twenty-four,' said Enzo with a confident air. 'What is the connection between Chinese Opera and yaks?'

'Their tiny feet are frozen,' shouted the same comedian who had interrupted before.   Enzo ignored him. 'Kindly fold your papers and hand them to Angela, please,' he said. She will mark each one, and in a few moments we will see if there is a winner.'

Confident that no one would ever get twenty-four correct

answers, Enzo strutted around the room smiling at passengers whose names he had yet to remember, but whom he recognised. He was talking pleasantly to an elderly lady who was telling him of her life as a missionary in India, when Angela beckoned him over. She looked concerned.

'Someone has won,' she muttered in a half-whisper. 'They have all twenty-four questions correct.'

Enzo sat down heavily on a bar stool.

'What?' he gulped. 'Impossible. Give me the papers.'

Angela duly handed them across and Enzo, peering through his bifocals, studied them carefully. He went pale.

'This is correct, he muttered. A yak can indeed climb to 20,000 feet. How could a passenger know that? She even knew that the hairs from a yak's tail are used to make beards in Chinese opera. What a situation! Five hundred pounds and I didn't clear this with the Hotel Manager.'

Angela remained silent.

Enzo pulled himself to his feet and, summoning all his strength, put on his best Cruise Director's smile and said, 'Wonderful news. Lady Veronika Willoughby has got twenty-four carats and thus has won the magnificent prize. Well done, Lady Veronika.'

As a final intervention, the budding comedian brayed like a donkey, which again engendered much merriment. Lady Veronika glowered from behind her tortoiseshell spectacles as

Sir Archie applauded loudly, to be sportingly joined by others in the room, while Enzo reluctantly departed for what would be, at some point, a tricky meeting with the Hotel Manager.

Messina, sometimes called 'the gateway to Sicily', hove into sight. Captain Sparda felt a wave of nostalgia sweep over him as he viewed Villa San Giovanni on the port bow and Messina on the other. These were the treacherous waters he had sailed for many years, and a host of memories returned as on his new command he sailed them yet again. It was here that the legend of Scylla and Charybdis originated, Scylla on the Italian side being an outcrop of rock and Charybdis off the Sicilian coast a treacherous whirlpool. The waters were notoriously difficult to navigate and the saying 'Between a Rock and a Hard Place' originated from this very spot.

The Captain scanned the harbour with his brass telescope and could just about make out a group of people who were waving in his direction. He was too far off to distinguish them, but he imagined that it would be his family, who had promised to be there to meet him when he called in at his home for the first time on the *Golden Handshake*.

They approached the dock and Sparda could now clearly make out his wife and family who, to his surprise, had been supplemented by Lilian's family from London. He had not known that there would be such a large party to greet him. By now he could hear their shouts of welcome in Italian from one group and English from the other. Suddenly the helmsman began to struggle with the wheel and, without warning, the ship turned around 180 degrees and began heading away from the dock. He could hear cries of dismay from the shore.

'Hey, come back!' they cried. '*Tornare indietro.*'

The helmsman was doing his level best to return to the set course, but it seemed as though the ship had a mind of her own and was determined to head for the rocks on the Italian side. Then it happened again. The helmsman was once more taken by surprise when exactly the same thing took place and the ship began to head back towards the port. On deck, Fred Batty who, in his latest lecture, had spoken of how the Black Death was supposed to have come into Europe from here, now said to nearby passengers that the Captain was simply giving everyone an excellent view of this fascinating part of the world and that was why he was circling. The devoted family party had produced some flags, and as the ship headed back towards them they cheered even louder than before and furiously waved the banners. The melodic tones of Cousin Pedro, the tenor, floated across the water and sure enough, Uncle Giovanni could be heard playing his ancient piano accordion.

Captain Sparda could not believe it when yet again the ship spun round and once more made for the mainland. By now, family patience was running out and Sparda could hear what he thought was his uncle from Catania shouting, ' *Stupido*' and '*Dove stai andando?*' (where are you going?). This was becoming ridiculous and, determined to sort the matter out, Captain Sparda ordered the helmsman away from the wheel and took it over himself. He managed to get the ship back facing towards Sicily, ordered the helmsman to return to his post, commanded the Staff Captain to take over, and rushed outside to greet his family. To shouts of: '*Bravo*' and '*Non andare via di nuovo*' (don't go away again) the good ship *Handshake* finally docked.

The Admiral had suggested that all the Sicilian members of the ship's company take shore leave for a few hours, and they took little persuading. Mr Fennington Barley, not a Sicilian but someone who had had plenty of free time up to this point, was a gentleman host whose prime responsibility was to dance with any lady who required a dancing partner. He had heard that the International Clog Dancing team were paying a visit to Sicily, and as dancing on board the ship was his speciality, he decided to track them down. Up to this point Mr Barley, or 'Pearl' as he was sometimes rudely named by some of the more macho members of the crew, had not been at all busy as there was no band on the ship and the piano was so out of tune that it was virtually unplayable. He was promised that musicians would embark in Messina for several days and that a piano-tuner would come on board and do the necessary.

Mr Barley was a retired farmer and all his life had had a

longing to take up dancing; between milking and bringing in the sheaves, however, he had never had the time to even begin to learn the first elementary steps. When retirement came and the farm was sold, he enrolled at the local dancing academy and quickly became a star pupil as he had a natural ability. Never having travelled, he heard through the academy that, if he was to make a small payment, he could be taken on by a cruise line and be able to dance his way around the world. His job required extreme tact. He was instructed not to enter into any romantic liaison with any of his dancing partners; not to be seen to be dancing too frequently with any one lady; always to compliment the lady on her grace and skill on the dance floor and never ever run the ship down to a passenger. Given that times had changed since ships introduced Gentlemen Hosts, he asked his mentor at the academy what ought he to do if a single male approached him on board ship and requested a dance. Unfortunately he did not get an answer as his teacher had to leave quickly to catch a bus, but the question was always in the back of his mind, and if the occasion arose he wondered what he would do.

It seemed as though Mr Barley would be kept busy after Messina because the Cruise Director had informed him that the Captain's Uncle Giovanni would be joining the ship to play the piano accordion, together with a Signor Marko Contoni, who would play the clarinet. Once tuned, the piano would be played by a crew member who normally worked in the kitchen but could be released between shifts to 'tinkle the ivories' as the Cruise Director nauseatingly put it.

Mr Barley spent one of his last free afternoons clog dancing his way through the streets of Messina with the international team, who had joined forces with the Mad Maypole Men, on a tour arranged through the good offices of the British Council. It was a great success and later in the year the clog master was awarded a knighthood for his outstanding work in promoting international relations through the arts.

Lilian Sparda greeted her husband warmly and, together, they were swept away for a few hours to the family residence where an enormous meal had been prepared. Following the meal, Uncle Giovanni played along with Signor Marko, who had been especially invited to join the party. Cousin Pedro tuned his vocals and led the party in singing a selection of Sicilian favourites, which delighted everyone. Sparda was so impressed that there and then he invited Pedro to join the two others and come on board for some days to entertain the passengers. Pedro, who normally sang in the streets, was overjoyed and agreed immediately.

The evening grew late and Sparda was just about to say a fond farewell to his wife when one of his half-cousins from Catania sidled up to him and, in Italian, asked if before the ship sailed he might board to conduct a small inspection, 'for insurance purposes'. Although the good Captain would have been overjoyed to take his family on a tour of the *Golden Handshake*, time was limited and he knew that one or two of the more distant cousins might want to take some advantage of boarding a ship bound for foreign parts. So, his decision was to keep them all ashore.

'You remember, Peché, of the help you had in Monaco?' whispered the Catanian. 'I think you owe us a little inspection, don't you? You don't have to come with me, Peché. Just inform Security that your dear cousin will be coming on board for a few moments so that he can assure all the family that you are really comfortable.'

Sparda remained silent. He had no idea what mischief his half-cousin might be up to, but he was certain that something was afoot.

'I shall be leaving in half an hour,' said the Captain. 'When I arrive at the ship I expect you will have departed for home so I shall say goodnight now. Goodnight, Cousin.'

With that Captain Peché Sparda left to say farewell to his wife.

Whilst the Captain was occupied with his family, and various other members of the ship's company were on shore, or fulfilling their duties, on board Harry Parkhurst had not been idle. Gradually he felt the cruise was falling into place. Some of the teething troubles had been attended to, but he was not sanguine and by no means were they through the proverbial woods yet. However, he was reasonably satisfied. The visit to Messina had caused him some concern, for he knew from what he had learned in Monaco that there would be an interest taken by the Insurers in the *Golden Handshake* and that this interest might result in disaster not only for his dear friend Sparda, but for the Admiral and the whole of the Golden Oceans Empire. As the Insurers tended to spend much time in the South of Italy, and some of them were actually related to Sparda, he was sure they would attempt something or other when the ship was in Messina. What, he knew not. He had had a confidential word with Arthur Chub, the Security Officer, and warned him to be especially vigilant and to keep a close lookout for anyone seeking to gain entry to the ship. When intelligence reached Harry of the impending visit of Sparda's cousin, his anxiety increased.

'Mr Chub,' he said urgently, when he called to see the Security Officer who was on duty at the gangway. 'As you know, the Captain will not be bringing his family aboard this time. I believe, however, that a cousin of the Captain will come on board this evening just before we sail. He has known the Captain since they were together in the Sea Scouts, and out of loving concern for our Captain he wants to be personally assured that all is well on board. Although he is a relative, Mr Chub, I want you to screen him thoroughly. As we are bound for Libya, we cannot afford to take the slightest risk.'

213

Mr Chub, who occasionally had to search people before they were allowed into the gasworks, understood perfectly.

'Please treat him with the greatest courtesy, Mr Chub, and warn him that he must be off the ship before eleven this evening, when we sail.'s

Arthur Chub nodded enthusiastically. His job was to keep the ship safe and he would do just that.

The security staff were kept reasonably busy checking in revellers that evening and, as it was mandatory that all crew members must be on board one hour before sailing time, the hour before sailing was relatively quiet. Chub dismissed all but the card inspection team and stationed himself by the gangway. Exactly half an hour before the time to depart he saw a solitary figure approach the gangway, look around to see if he was being observed and then begin to ascend the steps. When he reached the top, Chub stepped out of the shadows.

'Good evening, sir,' he said politely. 'Can I be of help to you?'

'*Io sono il cugino del capitano,*' muttered the visitor.

Chub, who was more proficient in Italian than the Cruise Director would ever be, understood that this was the Captain's cousin. Welcoming him profusely, he apologised that regulations insisted that everyone, the Captain included, must be searched before entering the ship. The cousin nodded and Chub gave him a thorough going over. Satisfied that he was bringing nothing on board except a greasy comb, he released him, and after pointing out directions to the bridge, warned him that he had twenty minutes before he had to be back on shore.

The cousin padded in the direction of the bridge and Chub waited for him to return. As the main purpose of this visit was for the visitor to get an idea of the layout of the ship for future insurance purposes, once he had found the steps leading to the bridge he prowled around the deck and then descended into the lower regions of the vessel. As by now activities for the day had closed down, not all areas of the ship were lighted. The cousin felt his way along a narrow corridor and suddenly, to his horror, felt himself falling. He landed with a tremendous crash, severely twisting an ankle as he landed. When, with some difficulty, he picked himself up, he discovered, as luck would have it, that he had landed directly outside a door marked *Medical Centre*. He hopped to the door and turned the handle, which revealed a brightly lit reception area with several doors leading off it. Tottering into the room he called out - in Italian, of course: 'Anyone at home? Medical emergency!'

After a moment or so a willowy-looking fellow, wearing a clinical nightshirt, emerged from a side room. As the nightshirt was one of the kind that is slipped on, leaving a gap at the rear, the wearer of this garment kept his back pressed against the wall as though he was edging along a narrow cliff-top pathway.

'Ah, Doctor,' said the wounded visitor. 'I need my foot strapping up quickly as I must leave the ship in ten minutes.'

Little did the cousin know that he was in fact addressing the poor unfortunate chaplain, who had been awakened from his slumbers by the sound of the fall and had been scared out of his wits. As the visitor addressed him in Italian, the chaplain had no idea what he was talking about except that, when he heard the word '*Medico*', he assumed the visitor wanted to see the doctor.

Unfortunately, the doctor had taken the night off and was sharing it with a brandy bottle either on shore or somewhere on the ship. The chaplain, having gained a First Aid Certificate when on the East Cheam Ordination Course, recognised that the foot was the problem and motioned for the visitor to take a seat on a low bench. Edging further along the wall and twisting awkwardly, he managed to fill an electric kettle which he promptly switched on.

The patient shouted at his helper: '*Non. Io non voglio una bevanda calda. Non c'è tempo!*' Although the injured man had said that he did not want a hot drink because there was no time, the chaplain, when he heard the word 'calda' – hot – thought that the word meant cold, and assured him that it was not a cold drink he was getting but some hot water to soothe the pain. The kettle boiled and gingerly the chaplain poured the scalding water into a deep bowl which stood nearby. Grasping the bowl with both hands and keeping his back against the wall, he edged further around the room. He was just passing in front of the doorway when it opened with a terrific crash, sending the chaplain flying and tipping the boiling water over the poor unfortunate cousin. He let out a scream, the chaplain in vain attempted to protect his modesty, and who should enter the room at that moment but none other than Captain Sparda.

It is best to pass over the next few moments, but a short description needs to be given. Sparda had been told that his cousin was on board, and as sailing time was approaching, had gone to find him. Knowing that some members of his family were well versed in pharmaceutical products, the first place he thought of looking was the Medical Centre. Even the Captain was dumbfounded when he discovered a half-naked chaplain lying flat on the floor with his cousin hopping around the room. Aiming a kick at the cleric and missing by a fraction, Sparda grabbed hold of his cousin and, throwing him over his shoulder in a fireman's lift, he hauled him out into the corridor and up the companionway. Here, the wounded man was quickly wrapped in a blanket and dispatched down the gangway into the hands of waiting relatives, who bundled him into a car and set off at a frantic pace, holding white handkerchiefs out of the window and sounding the car horn repeatedly to signify an emergency. Thus the *Golden Handshake* sailed away from Messina and made for the ancient Roman town of Sabrata in Libya, where further adventures awaited them.

25

Next morning, Arthur Chub took his usual early stroll around the deck. He took the opportunity of these moments alone to contemplate the doings of the past twenty-four hours and to plan what, if anything, needed to be attended to, to ensure peace, tranquillity and safety on board. As he did his third and final circuit he thought he saw the tarpaulin covering one of the lifeboats move slightly. He stopped and fixed his gaze on the boat, wondering if he had seen correctly. Sure enough, it moved once again. Silently approaching the boat, he stopped directly at the spot where he had noted the disturbance. Listening carefully, he was sure that he could hear the sound of heavy breathing, even though the wind and the waves were quite noisy.

At last, he thought to himself. A stowaway. This will be the fellow who attempted to take the safe from out of one of the Balcony Suites.

Looking around, he saw a wooden paddle attached to a post by the boat. He unfastened it and, intending to give the individual inside a nasty surprise, he raised the paddle in the air and brought it down with a whack on the taut tarpaulin cover.

Immediately there was a loud shout from within, followed by several low moans.

'Got you, you rascal,' said a triumphant Arthur. 'Come out now. This moment!'

The corner of the cover was raised slightly, and to Arthur's horror he recognised the somewhat bleary features of the doctor. He took a step back in surprise.

'Oh my sainted aunt!' he exclaimed. 'What on earth are you doing there, Doctor? I am so sorry.'

The doctor was too bruised to reply, but simply moaned further as he attempted to struggle out of his resting place.

'Oh,' he cried. 'Oh, my back. What the hell happened? Who are you?'

Arthur thought it prudent not to reveal his identity at this juncture but took the doctor's shaking hand and guided him onto the deck.

'Take it gently, sir,' he instructed. 'You seem to have had an accident of some kind. I'll help you back to your quarters right away.'

Almost bent double, the aching medic was guided by Arthur into the lower reaches of the ship where the Medical Centre was situated. With the doctor on his arm, Arthur pushed the door open and they both entered. Without a moment's warning, no sooner had they taken one step across the room than their feet went from under them and they both went crashing to the ground. The spilled water from the previous evening had yet to be wiped up.

'Ye gods, the place is flooded,' lamented the doctor as he attempted to assist the now injured Arthur to his feet.

As he was doing so, a side door opened to reveal the chaplain, who gazed in amazement at the two unexpected visitors. This time he was fully dressed and wearing his broad clerical collar.

'Good morning, gentlemen,' he said meekly. 'Can I be of any assistance?'

The doctor sat down heavily on a bench and Arthur sat opposite him.

'Make us some hot tea, will you, with plenty of sugar,' Arthur said breathlessly. 'We've both had a bit of a shock.'

Remembering the events with the hot water the previous evening, the chaplain began to tremble.

'I'm not too good at making tea,' he said. 'And the ship is pitching a little. It might be dangerous.'

'Well, dammit, change some water into wine then,' said the irate doctor. He stood up, opened another door leading to his quarters, and limped inside. A few moments later he reappeared with two Bloody Marys.

'Drink this,' he ordered Arthur. 'This is a cure-all, believe you me.' He swallowed his drink in one gulp and went back for another.

After a couple more drinks, Arthur and the doctor became much calmer. It transpired that, after a convivial evening with the distilled fruit of the grape, the doctor could not find his way home and so took his repose in one of the lifeboats, where Arthur had discovered him. As they drank together, Arthur said that Doctor Hackett had taken a very sensible course of action and he could not think what had given him such a rude awakening. However, no harm was done that could not be put right by another drink, which they took and enjoyed, parting good friends. As they conversed, the poor chaplain retreated into his cell and sat on the edge of his tiny cot.

'This is a most extraordinary way of life I have entered,' he said to himself as he turned his thoughts to his forthcoming sermon. 'Most extraordinary.'

'It's a sea day today, dear' said Alice as she perused the daily events sheet. She studied the sheet avidly each morning and particularly enjoyed reading the potted biographical details of those who were prominent on the ship. Today she had been reading about the Captain's Cousin Pedro.

'*He always enjoyed singing,*' she read. '*When he was a little boy in Sicily he charmed his loving parents by singing to them before sleeping each night. He has sung all over the world, normally at open-air concerts and with the world's leading orchestras and is greatly looking forward to entertaining on* the Golden Handshake'.

The bio omitted to mention that the open-air concerts took place as he was singing in the streets of Messina and in the London Underground. The greatest orchestras accompanied him via a tape-recorder. No matter. Pedro was undoubtedly a treat in store for that evening.

'As it's a sea day,' Alice continued, 'and as the weather is getting warmer, we ought to rest a little today on our balcony. It would be nice to spend some time enjoying the privacy of our Balcony Suite. Albert, can you please ask our butler to come in and assist us.'

Albert noticed that, as the days went by, Alice was developing a taste for the good things of life and was adapting very quickly to life in the Balcony Suite. He turned the handle on the telephone and got through to Udi.

'Can you come in, lad, and fix the balcony?' Albert requested

Udi said he would be around immediately and good as his word, a few minutes later 'You Tak the High Road' played on the doorbell. Udi entered carrying an oversized spanner clearly marked, *Balcony Suites*, together with a small pair of folding steps.

'Good morning, sir, good morning, madam,' he said, following his customary lines.

When they had been assured that he was 'excellent', he began his instructions.

'Madam, may I suggest madam that you put bathing costume on *before* going on balcony. Also you, sir.'

'I'm not putting on trunks for no one,' said Albert indignantly. 'The missus can, but not me.'

'Very good, sir, no problem, sir. You want balcony now, madam?'

Mrs Hardcastle said that she would like to take the morning air on her balcony and so Udi said he would withdraw and return in ten minutes when she had changed. He disappeared and then Alice too disappeared into the confines of the cubbyhole.

After much bumping and banging, which caused the next-door occupants to question if another attempted burglary was taking place, Alice emerged in an outfit that was probably designed when Noah's wife took swimming lessons. She wore a floral bath-cap as she did not wish to damage her hair with too much sunlight, and had painted all exposed parts of her anatomy with what, at first appearance, looked like lard. The suggestion regarding the High Road pealed out yet again and Udi was admitted. He carefully unfolded the small steps and, carrying the spanner, ascended them and began to try and turn the heavy wing nuts that secured the porthole. After a great deal of effort the nuts were released and the porthole swung open, sending a blast of cool air through the cabin.

'It might be a bit chilly outside,' said Alice. 'I shall need you

223

to pass me some things, Albert, so don't go away.'

'Now,' said Udi. 'Madam, if you go up the steps, place foot on this little ledge and I hold you as you put foot first through window.'

Albert was amazed that Alice would consider such a manoeuvre but, knowing that she was determined to get full value from the Suite, his surprise was not total. Alice gingerly put a foot on the first step of the ladder and held onto Udi. Slowly and deliberately she went higher as Albert stood to one side.

'Now, madam,' said Udi, 'you very good. Now put foot through window.'

With considerable effort Alice managed to get one foot and then a leg through the porthole.

'Very good, madam. Now other foot.'

As Udi held her from behind she lifted the other foot and put it through the space, resting her ample rear end on the ledge of the porthole. She was now half in the suite and half out.

'Now, madam, move forward and land on balcony.'

Alas, Udi had not taken into account the fact that Alice Hardcastle was somewhat broad around the waist. She pushed, but totally failed to move forward even though she was greased like a Channel swimmer.

'Push, madam,' said Udi, betraying some concern in his voice. 'Push hard, madam.'

Try as she might, she could not move an inch forward, and

to her alarm could now not move backwards either.

'Please help, sir,' said Udi to Albert, who was standing scratching his head.

Albert got a chair and stepped on it. With Udi on the steps, and Albert on the chair, they both pushed for all they were worth until there was a cry and a noise like a shot from a gun as Alice disappeared from view.

'My God,' said Albert, somewhat alarmed. 'She's gone!'

He quickly moved Udi out of the way and ascended the steps. Being of slimmer build to his wife, Albert was able to lean out of the porthole where he could see his wife sitting with a pained expression on her face on the floor of the balcony.

'Are you OK, luv?' he cried.

Alice, conscious of her dignity as a Balcony Suite passenger, replied immediately.

'Of course I'm all right, but there's no chair.'

'There's no chair,' repeated Albert to Udi.

'No problem, sir. I have chair.'

He left the suite and returned a few moments later with two folding camping chairs clearly marked *Balcony Suite*. He passed these through the porthole and Alice seized them.

'Some towels, Albert,' she demanded.

'You can't swim from there, luv,' he said.

'Don't be daft, Albert Hardcastle. Pass me some towels.'

Albert raided the bathroom and handed over the towels.

'Let me know when you want to come back inside,' said Albert, 'and I'll get Udi and we'll haul you aboard.'

Udi politely withdrew and Albert settled down for a short nap.

Approximately five minutes elapsed when Albert heard a cry from the balcony. He climbed the small steps and looked out.

'It's not as warm out here as I thought,' Alice told him. 'I think I had better come back in.'

'Righto,' said her husband, disappointed that he was not to get a longer period of peace. 'I'll call Udi.'

Udi duly appeared and climbed the steps.

'Madam,' he said, 'you now come back other way. Head first.' Alice tried to pull herself up towards the porthole, but the task was too much for her.

'Stand on chair, madam,' advised the ever-helpful butler. Alice did just that and now appeared at the porthole.

'Now, madam, come through.'

Alice put two arms through the gap and managed to get her shoulders through, but that was all. Despite the fact that both Albert and Udi pulled and pulled, there was no moving her. Finally they all had to admit defeat and Alice sank from view, back onto the balcony. 'Oh dear,' said Udi, shaking his head. 'Oh dear, oh dear.'

Albert climbed the steps once again and saw that Alice was sitting forlornly on the little camping stool, swathed in towels and shivering.

'Don't worry luv,' he said in his most soothing voice. 'We're going to get the top man on the ship to help you back inside. Would you like an orange?'

Alice exploded. 'No, I don't want any damn oranges, Albert Hardcastle. I want to get in where it's warm.'

Albert retreated and, grabbing a blanket, he stuffed it through the porthole. Unfortunately, the wind caught it and it blew away before Alice could catch it.

'Try again!' she shouted.

Albert fetched a duvet and Alice managed to keep hold of it this time.

'Hold on, luv. Won't be long,' said Albert hopefully.

As he was busy supplying Alice with necessities, Udi had rushed to get the Hotel Manager, Radley Duvet, who had the overall responsibility for Suites and allied services. He came running down the corridor and entered the Suite.

'What seems to be the problem, Mr Hardcastle?' he asked in the calmest voice he could muster.

Albert explained. Duvet climbed the ladder to make a personal inspection of the problem.

'Good morning, Mrs Hardcastle,' he called down to the figure below him wrapped from head to toe in bedding.

She looked up at him.

'I'm trapped,' she cried. 'Trapped.'

'Don't worry, Mrs Hardcastle. We will get you in eventually.'

Radley descended the steps and conferred with Albert. 'In your bathroom you will find some very good shampoo,' he said. 'It has rather a pleasant smell. If you could ask your wife to cover herself with this lotion, especially around the parts that will not go through the porthole, we might be able to slide her back inside.'

Albert got hold of the bottle from the bathroom and Udi went into the corridor to collect several more bottles from the service trolley that was parked there. They wrapped them all in a small towel and passed them through the porthole. Reluctantly, in order to grab hold of the package, Alice Hardcastle divested herself of the duvet, which promptly followed the blanket into the ocean.

'Oh my goodness,' she cried. 'This is terrible.'

One by one she opened the small bottles and applied the lubricant around her ample waist. She stepped onto the camping stool and inserted her head through the porthole. Mr Duvet recoiled at the sight of the flowered bath cap, but he stood his ground and, together with the two others, seized hold of Mrs Hardcastle's hands and tried to haul her inwards. After ten minutes of serious effort they had to admit defeat.

'She got out, she must come back,' said Albert.

'Um,' mused Duvet. 'It has been known for people to put on a couple of pounds in a few minutes. Don't ask me how it happens, but it does.'

'Then why didn't you think of that when you installed the balconies?' asked Albert with faultless logic.

Duvet explained that in a survey conducted by Fairground Cruises it was revealed that virtually all passengers would like a balcony, but those who had one used it very infrequently.

'Frankly,' he confessed, 'we didn't expect our Balcony Suite passengers would actually want to use the balcony.'

Albert looked increasingly perplexed.

'Well,' he said, 'this is a right carry-on. What now?'

'I think we had better call the Admiral,' said Duvet. 'He will know what to do for sure.'

Albert set about to tidy the Suite and Duvet operated the handle on the phone to get in touch with the owner of the Line.

The Admiral had been attending one of Enzo's language classes and quite frankly was not impressed. It was some relief to him when a steward tapped him on the shoulder and said that he was required urgently in one of the Balcony Suites. The Admiral made his way to the upper reaches of the ship and entered the Suite that was gradually filling up with interested parties. Albert introduced himself and explained as best he could what the problem was. Now it was the turn of the Admiral to climb the steps to observe a shivering Mrs Hardcastle covered from head to toe in a green liquid and smelling just like a high-class

229

hairdresser's shop in Mayfair.

'Mrs Hardcastle, Admiral Harrington here. How are you today? Enjoying the cruise, I trust?'

Harrington was never much good at rising to the occasion but today he excelled himself. Mrs Hardcastle took one look at him and threw an empty bottle of shampoo directly at his head. He recoiled and promptly fell off the ladder.

'Ah,' he said. 'Hmmm. Yes, I see. Well, carry on then, Duvet,' and with that he simply left.

Duvet looked at Albert in amazement but out of concern for his job said no more. Finally it was decided that Albert ought to go through the porthole to comfort his wife. The next morning when they docked in Libya, a ladder would be placed against the ship and the couple would be able to descend in perfect safety. Apart from her jumping into the sea in a lifebelt and being hauled out again at the stern of the vessel, Albert could think of no other way of resolving the problem and so he agreed to venture onto the balcony to join his fragrant wife. This he did. Ample warm clothing and bedding was passed to the couple, which they securely anchored, and this was followed by a complimentary bottle of Brown Ale for Albert and a flask of tea for Alice. The pair were assured that each hour, on the hour, someone would come to the porthole to make sure they were safe, and if they needed anything – anything at all – all they had to do was to ask. Thus they settled uncomfortably onto the airbed, which they had had to blow up after it was handed through to them, and prepared for the night.

In the distance, somewhere on the ship, they could hear the melodious tones of Cousin Pedro giving his first performance. Although it was uncomfortable in the extreme on the balcony, they had to admit there was a certain romance about the whole situation, had they been fifty years younger. As it was, it was pretty terrible. Around four in the morning they managed to catch a few moments of fitful sleep. At six o'clock the coastline of Libya was in view but, alas, the ordeal of Albert and Alice was not yet quite over.

That night, under cover of darkness, Alice had removed her swimming costume and reluctantly thrown it overboard. It was a one-piece outfit with a very pretty skirt around the bottom and she was attached to it. However, it had got covered in shampoo and had also been torn during the failed attempt to return to the cabin, so overboard it went. To save their own clothes, various items of heavy clothing had been passed to them for the night. Albert received a blue seaman's sweater with a thick pair of serge trousers, and Alice received a similar outfit. They both got a duffel coat, together with the inflatable mattress and plenty of blankets. Hot drinks were constantly supplied and Albert gratefully received a second bottle of Brown Ale.

As they approached Tripoli, they heard someone calling

them from the porthole. Albert struggled to his feet and saw that it was the Hotel Manager.

'Mr Hardcastle,' he said with a sheepish look on his face. 'This unfortunate happening has been most embarrassing for the Golden Oceans Company and for the *Golden Handshake* in particular. This morning we are due to dock immediately next to one of the cruise ships belonging to Fairground Cruises. If they see you climbing down from your balcony by means of a ladder, I am afraid that our Captain, and the whole Line, will be subject to much ridicule. If you could bear with us, we will stop at a spot just before our assigned dock and let you off there. Our Port Agent will pick you up in a car and take you immediately to a hotel where you can get some new clothing.'

'Well,' said Albert, 'if you say so. What do you say Alice?'

'All I want is to get off this balcony,' his wife said tearfully. The strain was now beginning to tell and she was very tired, having been on the balcony for at least twelve hours.

'Good,' said Radley. 'Then that's settled. Just await further instructions.'

The ship steamed slowly forward and they approached a dock. The ship drew to a halt. On the dockside they saw a small group of men in Arab dress with a long stepladder which, with much difficulty, they positioned so that it reached their balcony.

'It's a terrible long way down,' fretted Alice.

'Don't worry, luv. I'll go first,' replied Albert, not a little fearful himself. Udi had now appeared at the porthole and was peering through.

'Well done, sir. Well done, madam. You OK now.'

Below, there was a great deal of excited chatter in a language that was totally incomprehensible to both Balcony Suite passengers. Gestures were made from the dockside and Albert, understanding that they were now to leave, stepped over the side and put his foot on the first rung.

Meanwhile, in the Port Office, Libyan Immigration officers had assembled for their shift. Some were assigned clearance responsibilities at Passport Control. Others were put on undercover duties to keep a watch for suspicious activities. That morning, a senior undercover officer, Mr Zlitni, was required to wear plainclothes and patrol the dockside. He trained his binoculars on the *Golden Handshake* as she entered the harbour and scanned the ship. As far as he knew, it had never entered Libyan waters before and so he took a particular interest in her. To his surprise the ship stopped before her assigned station.

This is unusual, said Mr Zlitni to himself.

He kept his binoculars trained on the ship. Suddenly he observed a ladder being positioned against the side of the vessel, just by a balcony where two rough-looking characters in duffel coats were standing. The smaller of the two stepped over the balcony onto the ladder and was instantly followed by the stout one. Immediately Mr Zlitni pulled out his radio and contacted the mobile patrol car with the information that two illegal immigrants were leaving the *Golden Handshake* by stepladder and they were to be arrested immediately.

Albert and Alice continued gingerly down the ladder, frightened rather than encouraged by the shouting from the ground below. They felt immense relief when they both stepped onto dry land, even though they were surrounded by a group of chattering Arabs pushing and pulling to get a better view of the new entrants.

'I wish that car would hurry up,' said Albert. 'These trousers itch like mad.'

No sooner had he uttered these words than there was a wailing of sirens and two large black cars pulled up with a screeching of brakes. Several men in sharp suits leaped out.

'These must be the Port Agent's men,' said Albert cheerfully, and both he and Alice without needing any persuasion jumped into the back of the nearest vehicle. Another man got in beside them and they sped off at a tremendous pace. The man next to Albert addressed him but Albert could not understand a word. Albert mumbled something about not understanding and the man gave a dismissive laugh but refrained from asking more questions.

'Is the hotel far?' Albert asked innocently, after about twenty minutes.

Both the driver and the man in the back thought this question extremely funny and laughed loudly but did not reply. Another ten or so minutes passed and they pulled up outside a low brick building with armed policemen at the door.

'Funny hotel this,' said Albert, 'but I suppose it's an exclusive place and they have to guard their customers.'

The door of the car was flung open and the couple were pulled out, rather roughly, Albert thought.

'Hold on,' he said, 'we can manage. You don't have to grip our arms like that.'

No notice was taken of their protests and they were marched inside, into a room that did not look like any hotel Albert or his wife had ever seen. Uniformed men strolled around and on a bench sat a group of dejected-looking characters wearing chains.

'Funny way to dress,' said Albert, 'but one can never tell what these foreigners get up to.'

After a moment or so, a man in a very smart dark suit with an open-neck white shirt appeared and beckoned to them to follow him. They did as they were told and entered a small room where they were motioned to sit on a bench. The man in the suit sat behind a desk.

'I suppose this is their way of checking in,' said Albert to Alice.

'Quiet!' barked the suit. Alice jumped and Albert looked surprised.

'Passport,' demanded the suit.

'Well, it's like this . . . ' began Albert.

'*Passport!*' bellowed the suit in an even louder voice. Both Balcony Suite passengers looked vacant. Their passports were with the ship, as were all their possessions. Albert spread his hands to indicate they had no documents with them. The suit wrote down something on a pad and then looked up at Alice.

'You, Mister. Name.'

Alice was completely taken aback. Never in her whole life in Grimsby had she been called Mister. Mister, indeed. She stood up and thumped the desk.

'I'll have you know I am Alice Hardcastle from Grimsby and I am a Balcony Suite passenger and this is my husband Albert.'

The suit appeared surprised at the violence of the reply and stood also. He pressed a bell on his desk and two armed policemen entered. He motioned towards the Balcony passengers.

'Take away,' he said, and with those two words Albert and Alice were led to the cells.

Back on the ship, rumours circulated quicker than the waters at Messina.

The British Secret Service had landed two agents in Libya, went one.

Two Balcony Suite passengers had frozen to death on their balcony, went another.

The loyal crew refrained from telling passengers what had actually happened but precautions were taken and Captain Sparda confiscated the large spanner marked *Balcony Suites* so that no one would now be able to actually get onto their balcony. They would still, however, have the prestige attached to the fact that their suites were Balcony Suites at the very top of the ship and that, reasoned the Hotel Manager, was what was important.

Down in the depths of the ship, the poor chaplain continued to struggle with his sermon in the cramped conditions of the sickbay. He seemed to have had nothing but difficulties since he was persuaded to stay on board and, frankly, he was fed up. He hardly knew anyone apart from the Captain and the doctor, and they did not seem to have much time for him. As for the passengers, they had no idea that he was on board to assist them with their spiritual needs. He had no clothes, apart from his clerical suit and a pile of disposable nightshirts. No one had thought to tell him where the ship was going and when or where the ship docked. Fortunately, in order to board the ship with the Councillors' party, he had had to bring identification and thus was in possession of his passport, so he could leave the ship and go home if he could find enough money for the fare. He was feeling very sorry for himself when the doctor breezed in.

'Hello, old man,' he greeted him. 'Said your prayers yet'?

The chaplain managed a weak smile and continued to study a sheet of paper on which he had written some notes for his sermon.

'This is a cruise and a half,' the doctor continued. 'Rumour has it that a couple of Balcony types tried to jump ship to avoid their bar bills and have landed in prison.'

The chaplain looked up. 'Where are we?' he enquired.

'The land of liberty,' replied the doctor. 'Libya, old boy. Just the place to land in jail, what?'

Libya rang a bell with the chaplain. When he was studying at the East Cheam Ordination Course, a fellow student, Guy Raleigh, tried to get him interested in sailing. As East Cheam was hardly the centre of the yachting world he went with Guy to Norfolk, where the bitter winds and dampness put him off sailing for life. The chaplain had little interest, and even less flair, for the activity and so that was that. Years later, it came as no surprise to him to hear that Guy had joined the ranks of the Society for the Protection of Underprivileged Fisherfolk and Ancient Mariners, and had been sent to man their outpost in Libya. He mentioned to the doctor that he actually had a clerical friend in Libya, but Doctor Hackett made no reply and so the chaplain did not explain further.

The doctor continued to sort out a pile of prescriptions on his desk.

'These damn ships,' he muttered. 'Colds, flu, Novovirus. It's like a zoo for ailments. Every disease known to man resides here, with one man to deal with them all. Me.'

Here he threw the papers into a tray and reached in the drawer for a snifter.

'Join me?' he offered generously.

The chaplain shook his head and the doctor poured himself a liberal measure.

'This keeps the germs away,' he said as he quaffed the beverage.

The chaplain made a face even though he was getting accustomed to the doctor's drinking habits.

'You said we are in Libya?' he queried as the doctor returned to his paperwork.

'That's the place,' he replied. 'For some reason the anchorage we were due to take and where cruise ships normally call had been declared a prohibited zone, and so we are in what seems to be a vast oil terminal alongside a floating monster belonging to Fairground Cruises. The *Merrygoround*, I think it is. I bet their passengers are having a jolly time visiting the petroleum works.'

'What about our two passengers?' queried the chaplain. 'Will we have to leave them here?'

'Quite likely,' said Hackett. 'Silly fools. Fancy jumping ship in Libya of all places. Gibraltar perhaps, but Libya!'

He replaced a bottle and glass in the side drawer and made to leave.

'Look, old man, you have spent too much time down here. My guess is that we will be here for a couple of days. Cruise ships have the curious habit of overnighting in the most unpromising of places. Why not get some air, perhaps visit your holy fishing friends who live here. Rather them than me.'

With that, he got up and left.

The chaplain thought that it might be a very good idea to get away from the ship for an hour or so, and an even better one to visit an old companion. Fortunately he never went anywhere without his SPUDFAM (Society for the Protection of Under-privileged Fishermen and Ancient Mariners) diary, and he quickly consulted it. There, printed prominently in the front, was a list of all the stations around the world where the Society was at work, together with the names and telephone numbers of the Societies' chaplains. Sure enough, the Reverend Guy Raleigh MBE was listed as being resident in Libya. The chaplain, acting boldly for a change, went across to the doctor's desk and asked Reception to put him through to the number he had before him. Within a few moments he was talking to a surprised and delighted Guy Raleigh.

Deep below ground, somewhere in Libya, the two Balcony Suite passengers languished. Still wearing their duffel coats and grey bobble hats, they sat on the floor. Alice was in tears and Albert did his best to comfort her.

'It's all my fault,' she wailed. 'This would never have happened if I hadn't gone sunbathing.'

'There, there,' Albert replied soothingly. 'They must have mistaken us for someone else. We will be back on board soon.'

Every so often, a dirty bearded fellow, wearing what seemed to Albert like a long nightshirt, came and peered at them through the bars. At each appearance Albert tried to ask him a question but the only reply he ever got was 'Inshallah', which meant not a thing to the two travellers from Grimsby. Unknown to Albert and Alice, upstairs in the reception area Harry Parkhurst had been conversing with the authorities and attempting to explain the unexplainable. Alas, Harry had got nowhere and was threatened with detention himself if he did not return immediately to the ship which, he was informed, was being impounded. As soon as Alice and Albert had been whisked away in the car and the group of Arabs with the ladder had been thrown into the back of a police van, Immigration Officers had boarded the ship in force and ordered that no one was to leave. Harry was given permission to visit the authorities but, as we have already heard, his journey was fruitless. He returned to the ship seriously worried.

Unknown to everyone on the ship, the chaplain, who had no idea what was happening, had arranged for the Reverend Guy to visit him, after which they would both return to the Mission House for a meal. Guy arrived at the dockside and saw the *Golden Handshake* moored alongside. Normally he walked directly on board any ship he cared to visit, but today his old friend Ali stopped him as he was walking to the gangway.

'Mr Guy, Sir.'

Guy responded by greeting Ali like the old friend that he was. Years ago, Guy had got Ali's son a job as a steward on one of the cruise lines and this cemented a relationship that would prove invaluable today.

'Ship full with bad men,' said Ali. 'You no go there.'

Guy looked surprised, as well he might.

'Plenty men on ship want to live Libya,' continued Ali. 'Plenty jump ship. Libya clever and catch bad men. More bad men on ship, sir. You no meet bad men, sir.'

'Ah,' said Guy, who had gained but a vague idea as to what was going on. 'My friend padre on ship.'

Ali's face lit up. 'Sir, your friend, my friend, sir. You get your friend, sir. No problem.'

The chaplain ascended the gangway and nodded to the two policemen on duty who made way for him. The reception area was buzzing with activity. Armed police and plainclothes men were seemingly everywhere. He spotted the chaplain standing alone by the reception desk looking somewhat dejected. When they caught each other's eyes, the chaplain's face lit up.

'Guy!' he enthused. 'How good to see you, but it's bad news, I'm afraid. I can't leave the ship.'

'Nonsense,' Guy replied. 'Follow me,' and together they descended the gangway, went through the Customs Hall and in no time at all were sitting together in the Mission House.

The Mission House was but a short distance from the port and provided simple facilities for visiting seamen such as a canteen, free wifi and a library. Guy lived on the premises and was regarded as part of the furniture in the port and with many of the ships, both cargo and passenger, that called at this somewhat depressing oil terminal. He was a natural communicator and knew everyone in town associated with shipping and Port affairs.

When they had caught up with the years that had passed since their college days, the chaplain explained how he came to be on board the *Golden Handshake* and what a terrible time he was having. Guy sympathised.

'Why is the ship impounded?' the chaplain asked. 'No one tells me anything.'

Guy said that he hadn't a clue but from what he had heard there might have been some kind of immigration problem. As they were puzzling out what might have happened, the phone rang and Guy answered it. He held his hand over the mouthpiece and whispered across to the chaplain, 'It's from your ship. A chap called Parkhurst.'

Guy removed his hand and listened, occasionally interjecting with a 'yes', or 'that's right', or 'how terrible'. The chaplain, as usual, was not able to make head nor tail as to what was being explained. Finally, the long monologue came to an end and Guy replied that he would see what could be done, and that as he had the chaplain from the *Handshake* with him, he would give him news to bring back to the ship that evening.

'He seemed very taken aback when he learned you were here,' Guy remarked. 'It seems there has been a colossal mix-up somewhere and two passengers are in the immigration lock-up. Come on - we'll go and visit them.'

Guy set out with the chaplain in tow, who was marvelling at the confidence, and seeming access to the whole of Libya, of his former college friend.

'Keep quiet,' Guy warned him when they approached a low brick building with armed guards on duty outside. 'Leave all the talking to me.'

The chaplain was more than happy to leave the talking to Guy as he still was totally at sea regarding the whole affair.

On entering the building, Guy greeted the staff in Arabic and proceeded to a large office where he had a long conversation in the same language with an official, who looked as though he might run Libya as well as the Immigration Department. They were served strong black coffee and sweet cakes, and there was much smiling and occasional outright laughter. When an hour or so had passed and the chaplain, as promised, had not uttered a word, they rose and the capo shook hands all round before handing them over to a deferential fellow with a large bunch of keys on his belt.

'Where are we off to now?' asked the chaplain in a whisper.

Guy motioned him to be quiet and just to follow. They descended some steps and went along a corridor. The deferential chap, who immediately on leaving the office had lost all signs of deference, unlocked a cell-type door and ushered them in.

When the chaplain had adjusted his eyes to the gloom, he saw two duffel-coated, bobble-hatted individuals sitting on the floor and staring at him. Looking closely at them, he thought he might have seen them before - but before he could say anything, the stouter of the two cried out, 'Good Lord, the last time I saw you, you were being pitched off the stage at the start of the cruise.'

Guy gave a quizzical glance in the chaplain's direction but said nothing.

'By gum,' said the slight fellow. 'If it isn't the padre.'

'Mr and Mrs Hardcastle,' said Guy.

'Right first time,' said the little chap, struggling to his feet.

The larger of the two piped up, 'We are Balcony Suite passengers on the *Golden Handshake*.'

'Good,' said Guy. Then he announced: 'Come on, you are off back to your Suite'.

After fond farewells were said in the upstairs lobby and assurances were given of eternal friendship, the little party were escorted to a car and this time Albert and Alice were gently ushered into the vehicle. They drove to the dockside, still uncertain what the events of the day had been all about, but were too tired to care. At the entrance to the Customs Hall Guy said that he had to leave quickly as he had to attend a prayer meeting. He bade farewell to the Hardcastles and promised to keep in touch with the chaplain. The party of three rejoined the car and were driven, in state, back to the *Golden Handshake*.

As the Hardcastles made their way up the gangway, followed by the chaplain, they heard the strains of music. It was Uncle Giovanni on the piano accordion and Mr Contoni on the clarinet, doing their best to play the tune 'See the Conquering Hero'. At the top of the steps stood the Admiral, the Captain, the Hotel Manager, the Cruise Director, Harry Parkhurst and even the doctor. The Head Chef, Mike Tucker, stood by with an enormous cake, fashioned like St Paul's Cathedral and bearing the words *Well done Padre*. Behind them stood the passengers, who applauded for all they were worth as Uncle Giovanni broke into 'For He's a Jolly Good Fellow.'

The Admiral slapped the chaplain on the back and handed him a glass of champagne.

'Well done, old fellow, well done. You're a credit to the cloth, of that there's no mistake. Congratulations.'

The chaplain sipped a little of his champagne and blushed, still wondering what he had done to warrant such a turnout.

All Albert could say was: 'It's a grand little ship this. A grand little ship.'

26

As the *Golden Handshake* sailed away from the oil terminal, beeps sounded in the Suites and cabins, and passengers gathered around the information points.

'This is your Cruise Director, Enzo,' began the message.

'I am afraid that following today's delay in Libya and the unfortunate closing of our normal ports of call, the next few days will be spent at sea. As soon as we have clearance for our next port, I shall let you know where it is. Meanwhile, we shall have the usual full programme of events for you to enjoy. There will be lectures, and the language classes will continue at eleven each morning. In the evenings we shall have special entertainment for your delight. Tonight, after the excitement of the day, I think we all need an early night. Thank you, ladies and gentlemen.'

Considerable problems faced Captain Sparda following the Libyan adventure. Although his ship was allowed to depart, and the passengers released, he had been warned to stay away from Libyan ports in future and not to even think of calling at the two Ancient Roman sites that were on the original itinerary. He was to consider himself lucky that his ship was not confiscated, and had it not been for the intervention of the great leader himself, who had a high regard for the clergyman, he would have lost his ship. The Captain thought that the clergyman referred to was the chaplain, not Guy, and his respect for him increased tremendously. The serious news concerning future visits was kept from the passengers, of course, and was known only to the Admiral, Sparda and Harry Parkhurst. Where was he to go now? Port fees were excessive these days and he had no desire to get caught up in troubles that might surround a visit to Egypt, although the country had to be encountered in one way or another as he wished to travel through the Suez Canal. So, he decided to cruise around for a bit and then make for the Suez and see what happened.

Back in the Balcony Suite, Albert and Alice were more than happy to be rid of their heavy clothing.

'That's the last time I use that balcony,' said Alice. 'The very last time.'

'They've all been closed,' replied Albert, 'but not to worry. Being in a Balcony Suite, we still get free laundry once a fortnight.'

'Aye,' his wife agreed, 'that's a great thing about this level of Suite. Not only do we get the washing done, but every Sunday afternoon we get a plate of biscuits brought to our Suite. Lower cabins don't get that, Albert.'

'No, they don't,' replied her husband. 'They certainly don't.'

When Captain Sparda had finished consulting with his senior staff about the route to be taken during the next few days, he went in search of the chaplain, who modestly had taken himself off to his cot in the sickbay. The poor man was exhausted and had gone to bed early, hoping to get some 'primetime sleep' as he had heard the doctor describe sleep before midnight.

Sparda entered the empty Medical Centre and shouted out, 'Chaplain, where are you?'

A door opened and this time, remembering the unfortunate episode with the surgical nightshirt, the chaplain had wrapped himself in a blanket before appearing.

'There you are,' said Sparda, gazing at the blanket-swathed cleric. 'Where's your chariot?' Try as he might, Sparda could not resist teasing the clergyman but today, following what everyone considered to be a remarkable achievement that had undoubtedly saved the World Cruise and perhaps 'Golden Oceans' itself, Sparda wanted to speak to the chaplain personally.

'Your brave actions today have been noted,' he began. 'All the senior staff are recommending you for one of the highest honours the company can bestow – The Golden Eagle Award.'

'But Captain . . .' stammered the chaplain,

'Enough, lad, I've not finished. In recognition of your calling we shall make a special one-off award to you personally, called the Golden Chalice Award. At some time during the cruise the Admiral himself will present you with your honour. Meanwhile, one of the Balcony Suite rooms has become available due to the fact that there was a slight problem with the wall, which was repaired quickly. As it was possible to see into the next Suite, the couple in there moved out and are happy with their new quarters. You, Chaplain, will now have superb accommodation - as you so richly deserve.'

The chaplain pulled the blanket further round his shoulders and was about to stammer a reply when the door burst open and in walked the doctor.

'Hello, hello, hello,' he said in his usual breezy manner. He stared at the blanket-wrapped cleric.

'Got the shivering habjabs, Chaplain? I know the remedy for that, for sure. Evening, Captain sir', he continued respectfully. 'I trust you are fighting fit.'

'Perfectly,' replied Sparda. 'I came to inform the Reverend Gentleman that he will be moving to a Suite and will be honoured by the Admiral.'

'Quite right,' said the cheery medic. 'This calls for a celebration.' He pulled up two chairs for the others and seated himself behind his desk. He opened a drawer and took out a bottle and three glasses.

'Oh, I forgot,' he said, looking at the chaplain. 'You only drink jungle juice don't you?' He poured a tonic into the chaplain's glass and two stiff measures of something from other tropical climes for himself and the Captain. Then he held his glass high.

'Here's to the Great Leader,' he cried, 'and more especially to his spiritual adviser, the chaplain.'

Glasses were raised and the toast was drunk by all three. It was the end of a perfect day!

When the ship was being fitted out in preparation for the World Cruise, Admiral Harrington had wanted the passengers to be able to keep in touch with their family and friends via the internet. He had investigated the possibility of installing wifi in every Suite and cabin, but, as the cost was prohibitive, he contented himself with equipping a small computer room with four screens which would be available to passengers and crew. He did not think it worthwhile to employ a full-time technician to be responsible for this facility, so the role was given to Mr Angus MacDonald, the Chief Engineer – 'Beefy', as he was aptly known to the crew. Angus was none too pleased to be given this additional charge as passengers were constantly complaining about the slowness of the service, and the vast majority had not the faintest idea how to use a computer, let alone send an email. A great deal of his time was spent sorting out internet problems when he already had enough worries with the rudder, which was still not totally fixed.

Angus had attempted to delegate his computing responsibilities to a junior crew member, but the lad was so inept that he caused the whole internet and the ship's navigation system to close down for three hours. This gave the navigator agonies as he quickly had to revert to pulling out old charts and sharpening his pencils, something he had not done for many a year. The computer room was originally open from ten in the morning until mid-day, but as the Cruise Director complained bitterly that this timing conflicted with his language classes, the times were changed from the morning slot to ten at night until midnight. This really upset Angus as it meant he had to be available at this late hour, something which, quite understandably, he did not like. It led to a fierce confrontation between the engineer and the Cruise Director. Had several crew members not stood between the huge Scot and the manipulative Enzo, the ship would have been like the proverbial village - short of an idiot! At least, that is what Angus said.

The day began well enough in the engine room, even though the engineer had no idea where they were making for. Captain Sparda had said that they would cruise around for a day or so before entering the Suez Canal, and so that is what they would do. Fortunately, they had been able to take fuel on board in Libya, which was the one and only blessing received from that port of call. The route took them along the coast of Libya then along the Egyptian coast until just beyond Cairo where they would arrive at the Canal.

Instead of proceeding in a direct route along the coast, the Captain, conscious that there was time to kill, manoeuvred the ship as one might manoeuvre a pleasure cruise around Poole Harbour. As he was in foreign waters he was careful to keep outside the twelve-mile territorial limit, especially now that the ship was not in the best of relations with Libya. What he had failed to remember was that some time previously, Libya had laid claim to the Gulf of Sidra and he was sailing merrily through disputed territory. It would not have been so bad had he not cruised up and down, and backwards and forwards, much to the annoyance of the engine room. The passengers appreciated it very much and there were cries of delight on deck when the Captain ordered another change of direction.

'I wish the wee fella would make up his mind,' complained Angus. 'One moment it's full speed ahead. Then it's slow. Then reverse. If this damn thing could sail underwater, we would be thirty fathoms down by now!'

Sparda had been enjoying himself doing a figure of eight motion and was about to set course again for Cairo when he noticed two vessels approaching at speed; one from the Libyan coast and the other from the direction of Egypt. Both were flashing signals at him which, due to the very bright sun, he was unable to understand. Alas, the communications on the ship had failed once again, due to a problem with the system which Angus had yet to resolve, and so there was a temporary loss of radio contact with the outside world. As the boats drew nearer, it could be seen that one bore the Libyan flag and the other was an American vessel. They both stood off some distance from the *Handshake* and began to call the ship through very powerful loudhailers. Unfortunately, at that very moment the rudder started to play up and the *Handshake* turned rapidly and began to head directly for the Libyan boat. Loud shouts in Arabic emanated from the vessel, which speedily moved away just as the *Golden Handshake* turned once more – and this time headed for the American boat. There were scenes of panic on the bridge as both Sparda and the Staff Captain attempted to gain control.

In the engine room the air was blue as the crew on duty, already worn out by the morning's sailing, now had to cope with a malfunctioning steering gear. Suddenly and without warning, the engine gave a huge shudder and stopped. The two motor boats, thinking that a deliberate attempt had been made to ram them, pulled some distance away but continued to hail the *Golden Handshake*. When they saw that the ship was now stationary in the water they cautiously approached yet again. The exchange that took place between the bridge and the boats is best left unrecorded. As it was conducted half in Arabic with the Libyan boat, which no one on the *Handshake* could understand, it meant that there was a total lack of effective communication. The American boat stood some way off, so there was no telling what they were saying.

At one point Enzo, the linguistic Cruise Director, was brought out to translate but he simply caused further misunderstanding, so much so that a crew member from the Libyan boat gestured that he should be thrown into the water, at which point the Captain ordered Enzo below decks. In the engine room, Angus and his team were working feverishly to re-start the engine and to steady the rudder. By a minor miracle they achieved this, and once the engine was started, sufficient rapport, albeit fragile, had been established with the visitors and enough understanding gained for the bridge to realise that the *Golden Handshake* would be escorted to the Canal with immediate effect. The Staff Captain was put back in charge and now was able to continue gently towards the Canal.

Harry took the Captain to one side and explained what might have been the cause of the events of the day.

It had been known, he said, for mysterious ships to collect huge quantities of arms from Libya and transport them to equally mysterious destinations. That is what might have attracted the attention of the Americans. As for the Libyans, well, they were probably simply laying claim to what they believed to be their territorial rights.

Sparda listened intently. Messina was tranquil compared to

this part of the world, he thought. And on this point he was right.

The approach of the two speedy motor boats naturally attracted the attention of the passengers, many of whom were on deck enjoying the sunshine and showing their appreciation of the Captain's nautical skills. As it became clear that the marine visitors wished to apprehend the *Golden Handshake*, the crew were ordered to instruct the passengers to go below into the main restaurant and lie on the floor in case shots were fired. This caused much excitement and not a little complaining from those who entered the air-conditioned interior in their bathing costumes. As they were prohibited at this time from returning to their cabins to change, they lay shivering on the floor until helpful waiters came and covered them with tablecloths.

Albert and Alice had by now dispensed with the warm clothing they had been given for their night on the balcony and had changed into clothes more suitable for warm weather. Alice wore a light floral dress which she had made herself from a pattern she found in a popular magazine, and Albert wore one of three pairs of elastic banded trousers he had bought from a bargain offer advertised in his Sunday newspaper. Those, together with three shirts purchased for six pounds each from the local supermarket, completed his summer wardrobe.

The couple had just put on their new lightweight outfits and had gone on deck for some sun when they were ordered below into the cold of the dining room.

'This is a queer do and no mistake,' said Albert as he lay shivering on the floor. 'I could do with me old duffel coat back now.'

'I don't understand this at all,' remarked Alice as she drew the tablecloth over her ample shoulders. 'They certainly provide plenty of variety on this boat.'

After what seemed an age the all-clear was announced and there was a general exodus from the room.

After the drama of the morning, once safely in the confines of the Suez Canal, calm reigned on board. Radio communications were restored and explanations given, and it was a relief to the Captain when the ship passed from the coast of Libya to travel along the coast of Egypt. At the entrance to the Suez Canal the escort, which by then was an American vessel, departed and they were on their own once more. The journey through the Canal was one of relentless dullness as there were only sand dunes and the occasional burned-out tank to view, and so the crew had to work especially hard to provide a variety of activities to pass the time away.

The prime-time language class at eleven in the morning faced disaster. Students had become completely disillusioned with simply repeating lists of foreign words, and the chronic inability of the so called 'language guru' to translate in a time of crisis failed to win new recruits. Enzo found himself reading out a list of German words to the oldest passenger on board, a ninety-two-year-old retired General, who had no idea what it was he was attending and frankly didn't care. Radley Duvet said that shortly he would have to take a look at the scheduling as he had received many complaints about lectures being put on either too early in the day or too late.

As the ship was passing through an area where there had been, and still was, conflict, Toby Troy was invited to take the stage and give the first lecture of his series. He had promised to deliver an anecdotal account of his life, which would include graphic descriptions of his meeting with some of the bad hats of this world. This caused some considerable interest amongst the passengers, and a presentable number gathered for lecture number one.

Had Mr Troy chosen another career, he could well have elected to act as the double for the famous British comedian, Ronnie Corbett. Mr Troy was exactly five feet one inch, wore spectacles and was slightly rotund. This is where the similarity ended. His dogmatic manner, which at first had been propelled by religious persuasion, continued but in a different guise. As an apostle of Professor Dickie Querk, the renowned atheist from the West Country, now he sought every opportunity to attack his former beliefs, which he had held with such apparent conviction. Latterly, as a devotee and partner of Assad Wikiwatts, he was out to expose all and sundry. It came as a great shock to him when he discovered that there was a chaplain on board who was being fêted by the ship for his negotiating skills. There and then he sent off a missive to the Admiral asking why there was not a wizard and a witch on board also. The Admiral replied that both a wizard and a witch would appear in the pantomime performed at Christmas and he would have to wait until then. This did not amuse Mr Troy in the slightest and he was determined to confront the chaplain as soon as an opportunity arose.

He climbed onto the platform that acted as a temporary stage and stood behind the lectern which had been borrowed for the occasion from the set of religious props held by the ship. It was in the shape of a massive eagle preparing to soar into the heavens and had been obtained from a redundant church by the Admiral's wife. Mr Troy spread his copious notes on the eagle's back and began.

'Good day to you all, ladies and gentlemen,' he squeaked.

Unfortunately, he did not have a commanding voice and he sounded somewhat like a *castrato* with a cold. Several hands were cupped to ears as he continued.

'Today, I shall . . . '

Before he could continue, a technician came running towards him. He jumped onto the platform with the agility of a tiger and adjusted the lapel mike of the diminutive lecturer.

'That should be good now,' he whispered and leaped back to his booth.

Mr Troy began again. 'Today, ladies and gentlemen . . . '

Now his squeaky falsetto was so amplified that the startled audience recoiled in their seats.

Once more the young tiger pounced and the mike was adjusted yet again. Mr Troy now looked flustered, as when the technician mounted the stage he brushed against the lectern, scattering the notes across the floor. Both lecturer and the sound operative got to their knees and began to collect up the scattered sheets. The young man handed a bundle of assorted papers to Mr Troy and hurried back to a place of safety. Troy looked confused as he had failed to number the sheets and now they were in a total mess.

'If you would forgive me, ladies and gentlemen,' he bleated, 'I need just a few moments to arrange my notes.'

Several members of the audience, when they saw the considerable number of notes Mr Troy was sorting, decided that they did not want to listen to a lengthy oration that would bear a close resemblance to a Chinese Opera, and so they got up to leave. Mr Troy spotted them.

'Wait!' he cried. 'I haven't begun yet.'

His protests fell on ears which had been deafened by the over-amplification of half a sentence. What a full lecture would do to their hearing did not bear thinking about and so they marched resolutely out.

'I am afraid that I cannot continue as planned at this precise moment,' Mr Troy squeaked. 'My notes have got out of order, but let me try and speak without them.'

The room fell silent and there was a definite air of expectancy. Mr Troy cleared his throat.

'I often think it is good to begin with a funny story,' he started. 'I had written one down but I am afraid I can't remember it, nor can I think of one with which to begin.'

Someone gave an audible groan. It was probably the comedian who had made interventions when Lady Veronika won the carats. His identity was confirmed when he shouted out, 'Did your mother give you lots of shortbread when you were a nipper?'

This caused much laughter in the room and Mr Troy looked increasingly flustered as he failed to understand the joke, which of course referred to his height.

'She did not,' he replied seriously, 'but I fail to see what is funny about that. Can someone enlighten me, please?'

The invitation was too much for the funny man in the audience, who quacked loudly and said that he understood there might be an epidemic of Ducks Disease about to afflict the ship. There was more laughter, which increased when the ship lurched and it appeared that the eagle was about to take off as it plunged off the stage. The Admiral, who had been sitting quietly at the back, immediately ran forward to retrieve his precious artefact. He collected it from the floor, and with the help of a steward, carried it to the back of the room. Mr Troy's notes were now scattered everywhere. He stood helplessly, totally lost for words. He did manage to squeak out that he would return later in the week, and with that he stumbled off the platform and scurried down into the safety of his cabin.

27

So far on this cruise the lectures had not been a total success. Fred Batty had got into difficulties with his slides, Toby Troy with his notes, and it was yet to be seen how Sir Horace would manage. He was not scheduled to speak until later in the voyage, and so he had ample time to learn from the experience of his colleagues. It was arranged that the three lecturers, who provided the intellectual backbone of the ship, should meet together one evening over dinner to discuss how things had gone so far.

Meanwhile Enzo, the Cruise Director, had not had an altogether successful cruise. His precious language classes had started off well enough but had failed to attract the numbers he had hoped for, and now he was threatened with having to move to a less favourable slot. Although Enzo normally commanded and controlled the programme of entertainments on board, the Hotel Manager could intervene - even though he was loath to do so. Enzo was also facing an uncomfortable encounter with his superior, in respect of the five hundred pounds he had given away to Lady Veronika in the form of a totally free excursion with wines and what-have-you. Never did he imagine that the prize would be won, given that he deliberately chose the most obscure subjects for the special quiz. Someone must have known that the lady had brought on board her own personal supply of yak's milk as it would have had to be kept in the freezer. That someone must have been the Hotel Manager, reasoned Enzo. It was with a mixture of apprehension and defiance that he entered Duvet's office.

Duvet was sitting at his desk and swearing under his breath at the computer screen before him. He didn't look up but spoke nevertheless.

'This damn system is awful,' he said as he thumped the keyboard. 'A flock of trained seagulls would do better than email. As for Head Office - well, I give up. When the Admiral or Harry are not there to keep them in order, they do exactly what they wish. They fail, totally fail, to understand life on board. We have an entertainer booked to get on in a stop or two. It seems as though they are flying him around Australia on some kangaroo airline to get him here. That will save them five quid if they are lucky. Totally mad, I tell you. Totally mad. He will arrive on his uppers, give two shows and depart no doubt via South America to join another ship in China.'

Enzo nodded sympathetically. 'Very troublesome,' he said. 'Very troublesome indeed.'

'Well,' Duvet sighed, hitting the keyboard with such force that the screen went blank, 'what's all this about your language classes? Come on Enzo, it's a bit of a con, isn't it - and you have been found out. Some of these passengers are not as dim as they look, you know. Who is going to want to attend a lecture before breakfast and again immediately before dinner? It's bloody daft, man. The lectures are pretty dire, I grant you, but if you put them on right after lunch, you will have one hundred per cent of the group asleep rather than the present fifty per cent. The only way is to share your prime time of eleven, Enzo, and that is what I am going to enforce.'

Enzo paled. His whole life was increasingly caught up with the ship. Over the past weeks he had come to regard himself as a paternal father who would guide and direct his children in the right way. He knew what was best for them.

'But . . .' he began.

'No buts, Enzo. That is how it will be.'

The Hotel Manager once again turned his attention to the errant computer, but Enzo did not leave.

'One more thing,' he said. 'I have a bone to pick with you.'

'Pick away,' Duvet replied as the screen flashed into life and then quickly went black.

'Why didn't you inform me that Lady Veronika was bringing her own personal supply of yak's milk on board?' Enzo said aggressively.

For the first time since the Cruise Director entered the office the Manager looked up, a look of utter amazement on his face.

'What?' he shouted. '*What?* Do you really expect me to go round all the staff informing them that Mr Jenkins has brought a pot of Silver Shred marmalade with him and that his wife has brought her own personal toast-rack? What in God's name does it matter to you what the old bat brings on board! Baboon steaks, for all I care. I think you need a lie-down Bigatoni.'

Enzo was unsure how to proceed after this outburst and his courage failed him.

'I see,' he said in the most indignant voice he could muster. 'Well, as a colleague, I have to say I expect a little more sharing of information on this ship. Thank you.'

He turned and left the office as the Hotel Director stared after him, totally bewildered.

A blind piano-tuner had come on board at Messina and done his best with the concert grand. At one time it had been an elegant instrument, but at a certain point in its history it had been painted white and subsequently had been kicked and scratched so it did not look its best. Fortunately the tuner could not see this but he certainly could tell that it had witnessed better days. He spent a considerable amount of time attempting to get it in working order but, when the time came for the ship to depart and he had to leave, he declared himself dissatisfied. To untuned ears it sounded magnificent, and as the unmusical were in the majority, and this was a democratic ship, they carried the day.

It was approved for service and the piano player, one Rod Saddleworth, was summoned from the kitchen for a rehearsal. The piano did not blend exactly with the piano accordion played with such gusto by Uncle Giovanni, but the clarinet, expertly handled by Marko Contoni, sounded lovely. At least, that is what Angela Fairweather, the Social Hostess, said - and she should know, having been trained in classical ballet and also having had a part in the chorus of her local pantomime in Durham.

It was Angela who suggested that there ought to be a 'Golden Evening' when there would be dancing to the 'Golden Oldies' and a special 'Golden Dinner' served. She had rather taken a shine to the chaplain whom she had barely seen but, as he had achieved hero status on board, she felt even more inclined in his direction. Again it was Angela who suggested that as a surprise, the chaplain could receive his Golden Award at the special Golden Dinner. This suggestion was received with enthusiasm by both the Hotel Director and the Admiral, and it was agreed that the presentation be kept quiet and only disclosed on a 'need to know' basis. When outline plans had been made, it was remembered that there was a gentleman host on board in the person of Mr Fennington Barley, and he also ought to be brought into the planning as he would certainly be required to dance that evening.

Much thought was given by Duvet and Mike Tucker to the menu for the dinner. It was decided that there would be a

'Golden' theme running through the event, and as a provisional try they devised the following.

Golden Sweetcorn served with Golden Pastures Butter

It was Harry who suggested this first course, mainly because he could think of nothing else. Duvet was not keen, as he regarded sweetcorn as being fit only for pigs but, as he could think of nothing else, corn it was.

Duvet mentioned goldfish but Mike thought they might be inedible, and passengers would not like the thought of eating pets and so they were dismissed. Finally, as a main course they came up with:

Golden Beer-Battered Fish with Fried Golden Yukon Potatoes

Golden Cloved Baked Ham

Golden Chicken

Curried Golden Roast Beets as a vegetarian option.

This latter item did not seem very appealing to the assembled, but as they were desperate for a Golden option for the 'veggies' on board, it was included.

Puddings were much easier and they had a very long list. Finally they decided on:

Golden Syrup Steamed Pudding

Golden Delicious Apple Dessert

Golden Shred Marmalade Pudding

The meal would conclude with:

Gold Blend Coffee and

Terry's Old Gold Chocolates

Satisfied with their work, Mike Tucker retired to the kitchen to swot up on one of his recipe books and Harry to his office to plan further for the great day, the date of which had yet to be arranged.

The evening being fine, and the seas calm, the deck was laid out for a barbecue. Small tables were quickly erected and the galley staff spent hours bringing up cooking utensils and crockery from the kitchen and dining room. There were no duplicate sets of tableware and so everything had to be fetched from below and returned again as soon as the meal was over. It was not possible to move the grand piano without a great deal of difficulty, which was fortunate for the galley as Rod Saddleworth, the musical cook, was urgently required for cookhouse duties. It was left to Uncle Giovanni and his accordion, along with Marko and his clarinet, to provide the music for the evening. Mr Fennington Barley was instructed by Harry Duvet to be on duty until the very end of the evening as no doubt many single ladies would require him to dance, and dance he must.

'That is why you are here,' Harry said when he delivered his instructions. 'The Cruise Director will be hosting the evening, of course, but I shall be keeping a close eye on events as we want this evening to be a total success. There have been too many unfortunate happenings of late. Tonight we must see the end of trouble and the start of a new and exciting phase of the cruise.'

Mr Barley had not been aware of too many problems, although he had not had an opportunity to dance yet and, as he rather liked dancing, he felt he had missed out on something. He promised to do his best and went off to change into his regular uniform of black trousers, dinner jacket and bow-tie.

Radley Duvet tidied his office and took a stroll on the deck. Everything seemed to be progressing nicely. Piles of plates and cutlery were still being hauled up from below and were now being supplemented by huge bowls of salad and other tasty morsels. Enzo had changed into his best purple evening jacket which at one time he could fasten but alas, no more. He was still feeling bruised from his encounter with the Hotel Manager, but he tried to put it to the back of his mind and concentrate on the evening before him. His duties were not arduous. All he had to do was 'to keep the show on the road' as Duvet once put it. He would chat to as many people as possible and, if there was an opportunity, perhaps sing. It was not widely known, but in the past Enzo had actually starred as an extra in several musical shows. He had had an ambition to make a career on the stage but he never got further than wearing a silly uniform and singing in the chorus of a Gilbert and Sullivan opera. He had taken these roles so often that almost all the works of these Victorian musicians were committed to his memory. As he tied his floppy bow-tie, he hummed several ditties to himself. This evening, he thought, he would have an opportunity to shine at last.

At about seven o'clock passengers began to assemble. They were greeted on deck by Angela, who had persuaded the chaplain to make an appearance and get to know one or two people. Angela had a kind heart and felt truly sorry for the poor man, who had found himself on board a ship that he did not really want to be on, and then was stuck for days in a cubbyhole in the sickbay. Now (much to his surprise) that he had achieved celebrity status, everyone wanted to speak to him and he would have to get accustomed to that. Angela thought that the barbecue evening would be a good first venture out for him. He was hesitant at first as he said that all he had was his rather plain clerical suit and collar, but Angela told him that this was totally appropriate for the evening. Later in the cruise, when they stopped in India, he could get a new outfit for a few pounds.

The Admiral felt in a party mood as he put on his mess kit for the evening. Anticipating an occasion on board when fancy dress might be required, he had brought along a cocked hat of the type Nelson used to wear. He placed this on his head and thought it looked remarkably fetching. As he had offered to serve passengers with their complimentary first glass of rum punch, he decided that he would wear the headgear for this job.

On deck, before the punch had arrived, waiters were doing their best to make sure that everything was secure. A sudden gust of wind had smashed several glasses, and orders were given that only plastic glasses were to be brought up. Waiters were seen chasing a couple of linen tablecloths which, unfortunately, disappeared overboard, along with a whole bowlful of salad greens, which scattered like leaves in autumn. Apart from these minor upsets, preparations were going well. Giovanni and Marko were tuning up. Marko played 'Stranger on the Shore' not once, but half a dozen times, and Giovanni played Sicilian melodies that few people had heard but most enjoyed.

The punch arrived, along with the Admiral who stood behind a gleaming silver bowl with a ladle in his hand, ready to serve. The aroma of roasting meat wafted across the deck as passengers took their free drinks to a table and chatted with each other. Enzo emerged from a side door and, to his immense satisfaction, received a small burst of applause from the three or four people who had attended his classes. When his elegant attire was noted, more joined in, and he bowed in acknowledgement before crossing to the microphone. He beamed before welcoming everyone to the barbecue evening. As the weather was calm, he could be heard perfectly as he said that everyone was to have a good time and he hoped that they were enjoying the excellent barbecue. He invited everyone to dance, at which point Giovanni and Marko struck up a lively polka and happy cruisers bounced up and down the deck.

The Admiral, his bar duties fulfilled but still wearing his

cocked hat, joined the Captain's table where, for the first time, sat Angus MacDonald who had been persuaded to leave the engine room for a while and join in the fun. Being of a somewhat dour disposition, he glowered at everyone from behind his beard and soon made his escape back to the world of nuts and bolts.

An hour into the proceedings, Fennington Barley was both hungry and exhausted. Never in his life had he danced so much and with such vigour. Elderly ladies, who looked as though they could not manage a shopping trolley, once the music started jigged around the floor like two year olds. He was constantly being prodded by the Cruise Director to dance with passengers so he never got an opportunity to even take a small bite of his steak. Finally, in desperation, he filled a plate and rushed out of a side door where he quickly swallowed what he could before returning to further gyrations. When plates had been cleared away and passengers were now blithely signing chits for more drinks, Enzo returned to the mike. He held up his hands and requested silence which remarkably, he got.

'By special request,' he exaggerated, 'this evening I intend to sing for you.'

There were cries of 'Well done!' from sycophants and 'I'm off!' from the more boisterous of the gathering.

Giovanni struck up some opening chords and Enzo began to intone a well-known ditty from Gilbert and Sullivan's *HMS Pinafore*, taking the part of Sir Joseph Porter, First Lord of the

Admiralty. To everyone's delight he sang the rousing song about how, as a young office boy and before reaching his present high status, he had 'polished up the handle of the big front door'.

This caused immediate delight to the assembled, who roared their approval and sang together: 'He polished up the handle of the big front door.'

Enzo strutted across the deck and sang on, explaining that he had polished up the handle 'so carefullee', he was now the 'Ruler of The Queen's navee!'

There was more good-natured laughter as the party-goers sang with even greater fervour.

It was now the Admiral's turn to join in the fun and, still wearing his cocked hat, he leaped to his feet in mock anger and shook his fist at Enzo.

'Away, you impostor,' he shouted. '*I'm* in charge!'

Enzo dismissed him with a lordly wave of the hand as he continued until the end when he concluded with the memorable words, 'A British sailor is a splendid fellow, Captain,' at which point both the Captain, an Italian, and the Admiral joined Enzo, and the three took a bow to tumultuous applause.

'That were grand tonight,' said Albert as he and Alice returned to their Balcony Suite. 'I've not heard better since the Hudders-field lot were on tour.'

Alice agreed that it had been a very good evening indeed

and, along with the rest of the ship that night, the Hardcastles slept the sleep of the just.

28

The chaplain greatly enjoyed his first involvement with passengers at the barbecue. Angela had hovered, making sure that he was not monopolised by any one individual or group and that he got to meet as many passengers as possible. When he had finished circulating, which frankly he found quite tiring, she whisked him away to a small table in a corner of the deck where she had reserved places for herself, Harry Parkhurst, and the Ludo champions, Norma and Graham Trotter. The Trotters had spent years at sea teaching Ludo and encouraging others to take it up. They were immersed in the game and could talk of little else. They told the party that some players believed the game originated in Pakistan or India, but they thought it was first recognised in England. As World Champions they had visited many parts of the Ludo world. The chaplain, who knew nothing whatsoever about the game, listened politely but, after a prolonged monologue from Graham on the last World Championships, even this patient man flagged. Afterwards Angela apologised; an apology which he brushed aside as he said she could not be held responsible for other people being boring and it was quite right for her to attempt to bring them more into the ship's life.

The Captain's cousin, Pedro, was full of excitement at being invited to join the ship. The previous evening he had listened to the Cruise Director give his impromptu rendering from *HMS Pinafore* and, although he had never heard of the piece or the composer, he enjoyed it. Enzo was naturally flattered when Pedro told him he had a fine voice and was a wonderful singer. It could have been that Pedro was slightly exaggerating as he wanted to keep on the right side of Enzo as he, too, was anxious to sing to the passengers.

'Perhaps we might have a short talk in my office,' Enzo suggested when they met near to the reception area.

They squeezed into the tiny room.

'Pedro,' began Enzo, 'you will be with us for several days – correct?'

Pedro nodded. He had not been given any specific length of time but the Captain had told him he would be their guest for a short while.

'Good,' said Enzo. 'Very good. We are just about to enter the Suez Canal,' he continued, leaving Pedro wondering what he wanted to say.

'It is boring, Pedro – boring, boring, boring. Sand, sand and more sand.'

Pedro nodded again. He gathered that there was a lot of sand.

'Sand everywhere,' droned on the Cruise Director, 'as far as the eye can see. The passengers are not Bedouin Arabs, Pedro. They don't mind a little sand, but . . . ' Here his voice trailed off as he glanced through his tiny porthole.

'*Mamma Mia!*' he exclaimed. 'We seem to have entered the Canal. I can *see* the sand.'

Pedro wondered if the Cruise Director had got too much sun and was about to suggest a cool drink, when Enzo started to speak again.

'Pedro, my dear friend, I love my job. I love the passengers. I have decided to make a great sacrifice. I want to cancel my language classes at eleven each day and today I would like you and me to sing together in a special concert at eleven.'

Pedro had not the slightest idea that Enzo had been ordered to cancel his classes, and was thrilled at the thought of appearing at such a prime time. For his part, Enzo was more than anxious to continue to be a star performer no matter what. He was sure that the Captain would be delighted that his relative was appearing on stage, and the Hotel Manager would have great difficulty in banishing Enzo to a mere organising role as he had had such a success at the barbecue.

'This is what we shall do,' said Enzo. 'I will introduce you and Giovanni. You will bring your mandolin, yes?'

Pedro nodded. He never sang without some stringed instrument or other.

'I will sit on a little seat at the side of the stage. After two or three songs you will invite me to sing and I shall sing two or three songs. We will finish with a duet. Good?'

'Very good,' said Pedro, his little eyes sparkling at the thought of such an opportunity.

'Right, you choose your songs, I will choose mine and I shall also select a duet. We don't have much time. I shall now warn the passengers and invite them to come to a very special concert at eleven this morning. You can get Giovanni - quick, we have little time.'

Meanwhile, unknown to Enzo, the Hotel Manager had spoken to the three rather disgruntled lecturers, Fred Batty, Toby Troy and Sir Horace Beanstalk. He had told them that the Cruise Director would be offering them a prime slot at eleven each morning and they would appear in sequence. He would like all three to have fifteen minutes each to introduce their respective subjects to a morning audience and, if they could make their way to the stage at eleven, a new beginning could be made.

When the three men heard Enzo announce the concert at eleven, they were puzzled to say the least. However, they assumed that Pedro would be giving them a short warm-up and then they would be able to go ahead and do their stuff. It seemed a clever move to get more people to attend. Meanwhile, Pedro collected Giovanni, who in turn collected his piano accordion, and together they went through some of their favourite melodies. Pedro was a versatile chap. He could sing in a fine clear tenor voice but he could also sing in the somewhat gruff and rasping tones of an Italian peasant. For the folksongs this morning he decided that was the voice he would adopt.

Enzo knew nothing but Gilbert and Sullivan, and so chose some of his favourites that he had firmly committed to memory. As for the duet, he would have to print out the words and the music for that, as almost certainly neither Giovanni nor Pedro would know the tune or the words. He switched on the computer and gave it its customary smack to get the screen to spring into life. After much delay he finally got through to the internet where, after another wait of several minutes, he was connected to a site offering lyrics from Gilbert and Sullivan. He searched frantically for something that would be suitable for an Italian street-singer and a self-taught accordionist to sing and play without rehearsal. He was perusing the lyrics from *The Mikado*, of 'Three Little Maids' when, horror of horrors, the screen froze. Try as he might he could not move it on, nor dare he switch off and start again as there was no guarantee he would ever get back to the site. Quickly he took a pencil and copied out the lyrics showing on the screen.

'This will have to do,' he muttered to himself as he scribbled frantically.

Fortunately the copier was working and eventually he held in his hand three legible copies of the words and music. Pedro and Giovanni were easily found as the sound of an accordion and the rough tones of Pedro rehearsing in his country voice were audible in the reception area. He handed them the scripts.

Pedro and Giovanni, who both spoke very passable English but understood no written English whatsoever, stared at the paper. Giovanni could read music, however, and he began to play the tune so familiar with light opera fans the world over.

'Excellent!' cried Enzo. 'Really wonderful. Well done, Giovanni.'

Giovanni grinned. When it came to the words, marks were not so high. It was at this point when Enzo needed all the language skills he could muster.

'Three little maids?' queried Pedro. 'What is that?'

'No matter,' replied Enzo. 'Just repeat after me.'

Both Giovanni and Pedro repeated the first verse after Enzo.

'A maid is a girl, eh?' said Pedro, when they had gone through the first verse.

Enzo said that a maid was indeed a girl.

'You want me, a Sicilian, to say I am a girl?'

'It's a song, Pedro,' said Enzo, beginning to sense a problem.

'In my songs I am not a girl,' Pedro stated defiantly.

'Please,' Enzo begged him. We have no time to change it now.'

'You must change song,' said Pedro, not at all willing to back down.

Increasingly desperate, Enzo took the scripts and changed all the little maids into little boys.

'How about that?' he said, proud of his instant transcription. Pedro grinned - and it was then that Enzo realised that neither Pedro nor Giovanni could read English and would never remember the words in time for the morning performance.

'Forget it, Pedro,' he decided. 'Giovanni, you play and both you and Pedro hum the tune. Right - are you ready?'

Giovanni struck up and, humming along with Pedro, Enzo managed to go through several verses. When it came to the line about life being a joke that had just begun, he smiled ruefully to himself.

He hoped the performance would not turn out to be a joke and that at long last he would appear on stage in a leading role rather than just as a member of the chorus, as had been his lot so far in life.

At ten forty-five, as the *Golden Handshake* moved gently through the Suez Canal, passengers who, as Enzo had correctly predicted, grew tired with viewing little else but sand began to look around for other attractions. With memories of the previous night fresh in their minds, and having heard Enzo's announcement, they made their way to the performing area. Messrs Batty,

Troy and Beanstalk had arrived early and sat themselves prominently in the front row awaiting further instructions. They were
immensely gratified at the large number of passengers who were
filling the room, and privately congratulated Enzo on his skill
and consideration in preparing for their appearance in such an
effective way.

At eleven o'clock exactly, Enzo appeared on stage. He was
dressed smartly in his 'Compère' suit, which was simply a white
jacket worn with black trousers.

'A very good morning to you, ladies and gentlemen,' he
began ebulliently. 'How wonderful to see you here this morning
for my show.'

Batty, Troy and Beanstalk glanced at each other.

'You are in for wonderful entertainment this morning. Let
me introduce to you two fellow performers who will also take
part. Mr Giovanni on the accordion and the world-famous
Sicilian folksinger *Pedro!*'

The two fellow musicians entered and the audience broke
into loud applause.

'First, Pedro accompanied by Giovanni will sing a selection
of traditional Sicilian folk melodies. Then I shall sing a selection
taken from the world of English Opera and finally a concluding
song when both Giovanni and Pedro will provide me with the
musical backing.'

Troy leaned across and whispered to Beanstalk, 'What is

going on? He's announcing a show, not a warm-up!'

Giovanni operated the squeezebox and Pedro began to sing in his local dialect with a deep rasping voice. He finished the first song to polite applause and announced another.

'Hell!' exclaimed Troy. 'There's more.'

When he announced the third song, Toby Troy could contain himself no longer. He got to his feet and approached Enzo, who was sitting at the side of the stage awaiting his turn to sing. He tugged at the sleeve of the white jacket. Enzo motioned him to go away but Troy persisted.

'When do *we* go on?' he asked in a voice that could be heard several rows back.

Enzo, who had not the faintest idea what he was talking about, shook him off.

'Go away,' he hissed. 'You are disrupting my show.'

'What do you mean, "your show"?' Troy said in an angry tone. 'All three of us are due on stage now, and we only have fifteen minutes each.'

Despite the exchange at the side of the stage, Giovanni continued to play. Pedro was well into a ditty that told of the agony of unrequited love when Troy tugged again at Enzo's sleeve and the unfortunate man fell from his chair with an enormous crash. By now Troy had been joined by Batty and a somewhat apprehensive Beanstalk. Batty, as a former AA man and accustomed to dealing with emergencies, helped Enzo to his feet. Pedro came to the end of his song and immediately Troy leaped forward and commandeered the mike. He was just about to announce his introduction when Enzo, who had recovered from his fall, rushed in Troy's direction and attempted to wrestle the mike from his hand. Completely bewildered, the audience did not know whether to laugh, applaud or intervene.

Batty now came forward and tried to separate the combatants, but simply succeeded in bringing them both to the ground, where they continued to fight like tigers. By now the audience were on their feet shouting and yelling. Several old ladies were in tears and tried to squeeze their way out of the room. Beanstalk simply gazed in despair at the scene before him.

The Hotel Manager, who was enjoying a morning coffee in his office, thought he heard an unusual noise coming from the direction of the performance area. He remembered that the three lecturers would be appearing today to introduce their series at the new time of eleven o'clock, and he wondered what could possibly be causing such excitement. As he proceeded towards the room to find out, he came across several elderly ladies walking away from the hall and dabbing their eyes.

'Good morning, Mrs Ellis,' he said to one veteran. 'Did you find the lecture upsetting?'

Mrs Ellis stared at him. 'What lecture?' she responded. 'There have been no lectures. Just singing and now fighting.'

'Fighting?' he queried. 'I don't believe that was on the programme.'

He pushed his way into the room past a largish group of people, some of whom were attempting to leave and others who were shoving to get a better view of the stage. Enzo and Troy continued to be locked in combat, and somehow Batty had got caught up with them so it looked as though a free-for-all wrestling match was taking place. Giovanni and Pedro had quietly left the stage when it seemed to them that there would be no more folksongs that morning. Perhaps a little folk behaviour, but definitely no folk tunes.

Radley forced his way through the shouting throng to the stage.

'*Stop!*', he commanded in the most authoritarian voice he could muster. 'Stop immediately.'

On hearing the order, the two combatants slowed down enough to enable Batty to drag them to their feet and position them, one on his left and the other on his right. Poor Enzo looked a sorry sight. One sleeve of his once-immaculate white jacket had been torn off and he had completely lost his bow-tie. As for the diminutive Toby Troy, a secret that he had guarded for many a year was revealed when he emerged from the floor without his toupee. Fred Batty was the only one of the three to appear intact. He continued to hold on to his charges as a referee might separate wrestlers at a fairground contest.

Radley Duvet, conscious of the fact that he was surrounded

by curious passengers, turned to address them.

'It would be a help if you could leave now, please. It is almost lunchtime and there will be no more lectures this morning. Perhaps, gentlemen,' he said, addressing the trio, 'you might join me in the office for a moment.'

With that he turned and walked out of the room.

News of the morning's entertainment flew round the ship like lightning. One story was that Enzo, a master of the martial arts, had challenged one of the lecturers to a demonstration of his skill and had been soundly defeated. Another said that a lecturer had become unhinged and had launched a savage attack on Enzo, as he was singing, and nearly killed him. The lecturer, it was said, was now safely locked away in one of the cabins. It was even suggested that a stowaway, driven crazy by lack of water, had gone berserk and was now being hunted across the ship.

Back in the Hotel Manager's tiny office, Duvet was attempting to discover what had taken place. Sir Horace Beanstalk, who had remained detached from the stage performance, was able to supply an accurate account. When Radley had digested this, he asked if the three lecturers might now withdraw in order for Enzo and himself to have a quiet conversation.

'Well,' said Radley, when the party had left. 'Well?'

Enzo remained mute, conscious of the fact that one of his

eyes was beginning to swell.

'I thought I made it crystal clear that you were *not* to occupy the morning slot and that it was to be reserved for lectures. I have no objection to entertainment, but that is not for eleven in the morning. Understand? NOT FOR ELEVEN.'

Enzo quailed at the force with which the sentence was uttered.

'But there is more,' Duvet continued. 'Angela tells me that you have been awarding prizes at your precious quiz sessions. Big prizes. Prizes of excursions worth five hundred pounds. Is that correct?'

Enzo nodded.

'It is?' responded Duvet. 'It *is*? Have you gone completely and utterly mad? Have you lost every brain cell that you ever possessed, and I guess that was not many from the start. You are an idiot. A total blithering idiot.'

Enzo tried to reply but failed. He stuttered several incomprehensible phrases and fiddled nervously with the torn sleeve of his jacket.

'Mr Bigatoni,' said the Manager. 'You have come very near to disaster today. Last night, you were very good indeed. I give you that. Today, you flatly went against my wishes - and as for the five hundred, well, I am speechless. You have one last chance. You will find the five hundred pounds from your own pocket. You will arrange lectures for eleven each sea day. You will do some sensible programming for a change. If you wish to sing, you can sing your heart out late at night or early in the morning. Understand?'

Enzo nodded sheepishly.

'As for that aggressive little fellow Trot, or Troy, or whatever he calls himself, he will be leaving this ship pretty pronto. Batty will stay, of course, and Jack Beanstalk seems innocent enough, so he will remain. That's all. Good day to you.'

And with that, the whole unfortunate episode was consigned to history.

During the afternoon of the Suez day, the sun shone brightly and many passengers took the opportunity to sit out on deck as the ship sailed through seemingly endless banks of sand. Enzo wisely disappeared for the day. Sir Horace suggested that Batty, Troy and himself ought to meet for a discussion. This they duly did. Sir Horace said that in all the years he had spent lecturing at sea, he had never witnessed anything remotely like the debacle of that morning.

'Mr Troy,' he said, 'I am afraid that I have to say that you were too impulsive.'

Troy dismissed the comment with a snort. 'Impulsive my foot,' he replied. 'That fellow deserved all he got and more besides.'

'We can't always get what we like in this world,' replied Sir

Horace. 'Sometimes we have to be patient and wait for the Good Lord to intervene.'

'Who?' said Troy in mock surprise. 'Is he the owner of this Line?'

'I don't think there is any cause to be blasphemous,' said Sir Horace, somewhat taken aback.

Troy was unrepentant. 'I suppose you're a religious loony, are you?' he said, looking directly at Sir Horace.

'As you ask,' replied the botanist stiffly, 'I am a sidesman at our local church and have been for many a year.'

Troy was not impressed and responded with a feeble joke.

'Does that mean you have the keys to the vicar's sideboard?' he said. 'Keeper of the clerical booze, eh? There's not much you can tell me about the church, believe me.'

'I think we had better move on,' said Fred Batty, who had been silent up to this point. 'May I suggest that, as it has now been confirmed that we take it in turns to lecture at eleven in the morning, we address ourselves to working out a rota and then we can conclude our meeting.'

He produced a pencil and paper.

'All we need is to work out the order in which we shall speak, and afterwards we can find out when there are sea days and when there are not.'

After a lengthy discussion it emerged that Toby Troy would open, followed by Fred, and Sir Horace would bring up the rear.

With that they disbanded, not knowing that they would never meet as such a group again.

29

To any individual keeping a diary of events on board the *Golden Handshake*, it would seem that they followed a circular process. At one moment the very heights of the good life were experienced before the ship, or at least some of its inhabitants, were plunged into the depths of despair. Alarm and despondency spread around the vessel, after the outbreak of fisticuffs, but they vanished as quickly as they appeared as the ship departed from the Canal and made for the port of Eilat. At first sight, a port full of containers failed to impress, but those who ventured ashore soon found beaches, restaurants and many other delights which so appealed to those who spent their lives in northern climes.

News of the disturbance between the lecturers and the Cruise Director quickly reached the Admiral and the Captain. Radley explained to them both and his actions were approved.

'When does that little squirt Troy get off?' asked Sparda, who had taken an instant dislike to the lecturer for no other reason than he did not like the look of him.

'India, I think,' said Radley.

'Well, God help the Indians!' exclaimed Sparda. 'The sooner he leaves my ship, the happier we will all be. It's a pity Enzo didn't lay him out once and for all!'

During the meeting, the Admiral kept somewhat quiet as he did not relish intervening in the disputes which sometimes occurred. It was best if his officers attended to these matters, although he liked to know what was going on.

'I think that is all for now,' he said.

'One further matter,' put in Radley. 'The passenger computer room has been opened at a most inconvenient hour for guests. I think we ought to revert to the original planned time of ten in the morning to midday.'

Everyone nodded and the meeting disbanded.

In his little cabin, somewhere in the crew's quarters, Enzo nursed his injuries. Although his eye hurt, it was his pride that had suffered the most. Because of the intervention of that terrible man, Troy, he never got the opportunity to sing to a packed house and what is more, was humiliated in front of the whole ship. He looked forlornly at his once immaculate jacket, now torn and ruined. His elegant bow-tie had disappeared altogether, perhaps collected by a member of the audience as a souvenir. As his eye was now quite swollen, he decided to make his way down to visit the doctor to see what relief might be offered. He entered the Medical Centre to find the doctor sitting behind his desk staring at a pile of papers.

'Too much paperwork these days,' he said without looking up. 'These people want to know everything. What I had for breakfast. What the name of my cat is. How many pork pies did I eat last year. Complete rubbish. No such thing as privacy these days.'

He looked up.

'Hello, old man,' he said in his usual cheerful manner. 'I say, nice one you've got there. Black the other one and you're halfway to getting a part in *The Black and White Minstrel Show*.'

Enzo didn't find that comment funny. In fact, he thought it bordered on being a racist remark but he refrained from responding.

'It's amazing on this ship,' continued the doctor, 'how many objects there are positioned exactly at eye-level. One can't avoid them. Sit down and let me look.'

Enzo sat down and the doctor got up and shone a small torch-beam into his eye.

'Mmmm,' he muttered. 'Seems quite empty inside to me.'

Enzo failed to understand the joke and expressed concern.

'I hope it's not serious, Doctor,' he said.

'Lie down on the trolley,' replied the doctor. 'We'll soon fix it and you'll be able to see the White Cliffs of Dover again.'

Enzo lay down.

'Wait here a moment, I just need to talk to Mike Tucker.'

Enzo lay still as the doctor disappeared into a side room. Within a few moments he returned, saying, 'Won't be a moment, old chap. The cure is on its way right now.'

Right on cue there was a tap on the door and a steward entered. 'For you, Doctor, sir, from the Chef.'

The doctor took a platter from the steward and told Enzo to close his eyes. Suddenly, Enzo felt something cold and damp slap across his bruised eye.

'What's that?' he cried in alarm.

'A steak,' the medic replied. Not horse-meat, let me assure you, but a real, old-fashioned, full of goodness steak. Stay there for half an hour and I'll be back.'

Enzo did as he was told and within half an hour the physician returned.

'Is it cooked yet?' he asked, as he removed the meat and dabbed the area with a clean tissue. 'OK, that's it. Now wear this for a week.' He handed Enzo a large black eye-patch, saying, 'Wear this and all the passengers will think you're rehearsing for your operatic part.'

Enzo slipped the patch over his eye and thanked the doctor for his attention.

'Now, back to paperwork,' the man sighed. 'Cheerio to you. See you on the *Pinafore*.'

Harry Chub, Security Officer, was now facing one of the more critical parts of the cruise. The journey from Egypt, through the Suez Canal to Israel and onwards to Yemen, was full of potential dangers. They were entering a part of the world where conflicts were rife and a passenger ship might well become a target for mischief-makers who wanted to cause alarm and distress and advance their cause.

Golden Oceans was too small a company to have its own, full-blown security department. Harry was the only man who was really experienced in dealing with security issues, having served in the military. On the other three ships of the line operating on the Thames, Frinton and Poole Harbour, security was the responsibility of one or two ex-traffic wardens whom Harry had personally trained. Pirates were infrequently encountered off Frinton, which was more than could be said for the Yemeni coast. Before beginning the cruise the Admiral had engaged the services of a private security firm called 'Zap', who would board the *Golden Handshake* at Eilat and disembark in India. In order not to cause undue alarm, only the senior staff on board had been informed of this move. Entertainers, lecturers, Uncle Giovanni and Pedro, were not briefed and of course the passengers knew nothing.

The visit to Eilat had been a great success and, as darkness fell, contented passengers returned to the ship tired after a day of sun and sand. After dinner, when most of the passengers had retired for the night and the ship was preparing to leave, a party of four men were quickly led up the gangway by Harry and taken into the bowels of the ship. Each man carried a largish holdall and wore a small backpack. Harry was under the impression that they had boarded unobserved, but he was mistaken, for taking a night stroll around the deck was none other than Toby Troy.

It has to be said here that Mr Troy was, quite frankly, a troublemaker. He had linked with Assad Wikiwatts as he claimed that he was passionate about truth and the right of the public to know the truth about everything. Wikiwatts was delighted to accept him as a partner.

Troy was just about to leave the deck when he observed several shadowy figures approach the gangway and quickly ascend it. They seemed to be in the company of an officer of the ship, whom he had not previously seen. Quickly he ran down the steps leading to the gangway entrance but, apart from the crew member on duty, there was no sign of another living soul. It was a puzzled Toby Troy who retired to his bed that night wondering if there were happenings on this ship about which he knew nothing. He was determined to find out.

Originally it had been proposed that the *Golden Handshake* would visit Yemen and call at the port of Al Hudaydah, where transport could be arranged for those who wished to visit the ancient city of Sanaa. Fred Batty had done some extensive research on this part of the world and had assembled a considerable collection of coloured slides. Sanaa itself looked like a setting for a huge production of *The Pirates of Penzance*, for every male shown in Fred's collection seemed to have a massive dagger thrust into his belt and carried some sort of firearm also, just in case. Fred mischievously thought that the one-eyed Enzo would be the ideal man to escort such an expedition. Alas, trouble was reported in the country and the Admiral decided that to visit Sanaa at this time would be unwise and so they sailed on towards India.

As there was an extra sea day, Enzo, who was now beginning to function as Cruise Director once again, decided that the lectures ought to recommence in earnest. With not a little sorrow in his heart, he advised Mr Toby Troy that he must be prepared to lecture for forty-five minutes at eleven o'clock the following morning. Troy was delighted. He informed the Cruise Director that he would not, in his first lecture, tell of the amazing resistance of Hezbollah to the Scriptures. Rather, he had more up-to-date information to impart. Enzo shrugged. He could lecture on whatever he liked for all he cared.

At a quarter to the hour, Toby Troy returned to the platform from which he had attempted to lecture previously. The eagle lectern had flown, to be replaced by a flimsy-looking music-stand upon which he placed his notes. He had taken the precaution of numbering each page, as he did not want a repeat of the fiasco of last time. At one minute to eleven Enzo made his appearance and stood at the front of the room. It gave him no pleasure at all to introduce Troy but, he reasoned, it was his job and so he would get on with it.

'Draughty keyholes they have on this ship,' uttered the resident comedian, glancing at Enzo's eye-patch. 'Watch out, mate, or Long John Silver will have your job.'

Although the remarks were issued in a stage whisper, Enzo heard them and was not amused. He did not feel in the slightest bit amused today, as so many of his carefully thought out plans had had to be cancelled. He looked around enviously at the auditorium. His language classes had attracted four people at the most. Today the room was very comfortably full.

'Ladies and gentlemen, good morning. This morning, Mr Toby Troy will be lecturing to you. Mr Troy has had a varied career. As a muscular Christian,' here he glanced at the diminutive Toby and gave him a thin smile, 'Mr Troy bravely attempted to get Hezbollah to leave their evil ways and follow the light. For his exceptional bravery he was awarded the British Empire Medal. Ladies and gentlemen, Mr Toby Troy!'

A beaming Toby Troy appeared on stage and stood behind the music-stand, his numbered notes before him.

'Ladies and gentlemen!' he squeaked. 'Today I have taken the liberty of departing from my script. I shall not begin by telling you of my sincere efforts to evangelise Hezbollah. I realise now, alas late in the day, the error of my ways. Many years ago,

I left that work and joined forces with one of the greatest men of our day - Mr Assad Wikiwatts. Both "Wiki", as he is known to his close friends, and myself, are passionate about truth. We believe that the public - you, your children, your grandchildren, your great-grandchildren, your aunts, your uncles, your friends, your fellow workers - in fact, everybody, has a right to know the truth about everything. *Everything.* Too many people are being kept in the dark, and that is a national disgrace. I have to tell you today, in all seriousness, that you, the very people sitting in this room, are being kept in the dark.'

Alas, as luck would have it, at that very moment, Enzo, who was creeping out of the room in an attempt to leave unobserved, tripped over a wire and fell to the ground with a tremendous crash. Having been injured in the room before, it was proving to be a dangerous place for him. The wire which brought him down was connected to the lighting, which was immediately extinguished. Several of the passengers thought that this special effect had been pre-arranged by Mr Troy and applauded gently. Enzo picked himself up, reconnected the plug and the lighting was resumed immediately. He crept slowly out and Troy resumed.

'As we have just observed,' Troy continued, finding for once that he might interject some humour into the proceedings, 'you will not be in the dark for long.'

He paused for laughter and applause, but none was forthcoming.

'Today I intend to inform you of what is really happening on this ship. The truth, ladies and gentlemen. The truth is what I shall speak. *The truth.*

'Ladies and gentlemen, the Captain of this ship is nothing short of reckless.'

There was an audible gasp from the floor.

'He is not only reckless, but he is deceiving you.'

Again he paused for effect. From the platform he saw an unidentified officer quickly leave the place where he had been standing and disappear through the main entrance.

'This Captain, ladies and gentlemen, has brought you deliberately through the most dangerous waters in the world. You should know that. You should know more. This ship is bristling with armed guards. These camouflaged figures are everywhere on the ship. When I walk at night I see them lurking in every corner. Fellow passengers, in the name of Wikiwatts, and in the name of liberty and freedom, I expose the Captain of this ship as deliberately withholding the truth from you. Of exposing you to extreme danger. Of . . .'

He got no further. The officer he had seen leaving had gone straight to inform the Captain. Sparda immediately left what he was doing and rushed to the theatre, entering by a side door. With one leap he landed on the stage and with a smart left hook laid Toby Troy flat on the deck.

Two fights in succession were more than the passengers had bargained for. They had witnessed what seemed to be an all-in wrestling bout involving the Cruise Director and a couple of lecturers. Now the Captain had entered the pugilistic entertainment. They did not know what to make of things. Enzo, on hearing some commotion in the theatre, rushed back, only to trip over the wire once more and again plunge the place into darkness. This time, it proved to be a fortunate accident, as it enabled a couple of crew members to drag Troy off the stage unobserved and for the Captain to retire quickly. As soon as he was outside, he summoned Harry Chub.

'That fool Troy,' he snapped. '*Scassacazzo!* (A pain in the backside.). He is off this ship right away. I don't care if you throw him overboard. Get hold of him and lock him up. Get the Zap people to guard him, and when they get off in India, he goes with them.'

Admiral Benbow Harrington, ex-Royal Navy, was none too pleased when he heard of the Captain's impulsive action. He, like Sparda, was appalled that Troy should deliberately seek to cause alarm amongst the passengers, especially when it was common practice for all ships these days to be properly protected. For the Captain to display his Italian temperament in the way that he did, well, it caused him some heartache. It was clear that he must now address the whole ship's company of crew and passengers, and restore the calm that they had all enjoyed so

303

much in the sunny port of Eilat. As that evening there was to be held the 'Golden Dinner', he would make a special announcement then. Meanwhile, a note would be sent to every passenger informing them of this and inviting them to the dinner, which would be a gala occasion.

30

Albert and Alice had failed to witness the first bout of fighting between the Cruise Director and Mr Toby Troy. They had got confused with the timing of events and as they understood eleven in the morning was for language instruction, they avoided it. They had, however, received what was claimed to be a first-hand account of the excitement from another passenger. They were told that the Cruise Director was in the middle of singing something written by a chap named Tosca when a rival musician, jealous that Enzo had the stage, rushed up and tried to knife him.

'Sounds like another crazed Italian to me,' said Albert when he heard the story. 'How the loony managed to get on board beats me. Poor old Enzo.'

Alice had heard a completely different version. She was informed by someone, who claimed to be present, that little Mr Troy was at the stand, concluding an excellent lecture, when Enzo went to congratulate him. The ship lurched and Enzo fell on the poor little chap, causing him extensive injury. She didn't contradict Albert's version but she did remark that there were a lot of different stories going around and it was difficult to know what the truth was.

Curiosity, however, did take them to Mr Troy's revelatory lecture and they witnessed for themselves the Captain's knock-out blow. This impressed Albert greatly.

'By gum,' he said afterwards, 'that's a great spirit that chap's got.'

'Well, he is the Captain,' replied Alice, 'and he has to keep order on his own ship.'

'He does that an' all,' nodded Albert. 'High-jackers had better steer clear of Sparda. He's a cracker.'

During the day they received a note from the Admiral along with a reminder of the Golden Dinner that evening.

'You're fortunate, Albert Hardcastle,' said Alice. 'You can wear your father's gold watch. What shall I wear?'

Albert had not a clue and said as such.

'You're no help at all,' she complained. 'No help at all. I do have my nice yellow floral dress. You know the one, Albert. The one with sunflowers on it.'

Albert had a vague memory of some rather large blooms on some dress or another but, as it mattered nothing to him what Alice wore, he could be of no further help and he said so.

'But you've been no help at all,' she scolded, 'never mind further help. I don't know why I bother to ask you anything, Albert Hardcastle.'

Eventually the sunflower creation was chosen and Alice remained calm for a while. Then: 'I wish I knew what other people were wearing tonight,' she fretted later in the afternoon. 'That would make it so much easier.'

'Well,' said Albert logically, 'if you want me to go and knock on Balcony Suite doors and ask, I could do so. You only have to say, Alice.'

'Don't be daft, Albert. I don't know why it is that you can never give serious thought to serious matters.'

The Golden Evening drew nigh. Albert complained about having to wear a suit and Alice struggled into the sunflower creation. That evening, as they were Balcony Suite passengers, they had been assigned a place at the doctor's table. It was customary on the *Golden Handshake* for senior members of the ship's company to host tables from time to time. Most of the officers found this a dreadful chore, but they had to show willing and answer the most banal questions for hour after hour.

The Hardcastles were the first to arrive at their assigned table, and when the Maitre D' had seated them he suggested that they might like a drink whilst they waited for the others to arrive. Alice said she would like a small sweet sherry and Albert asked for his customary Brown Ale. They looked around them in awe. Gold was everywhere. Balloons had been sprayed with gold paint. Streamers were coloured gold. On each table there was a gold-coloured charger. Unfortunately there was not enough in the budget to provide gold-coloured cutlery, but anything that could be touched up with gold was so treated.

Alice was sipping her sherry when she noticed the Maitre D' steering a couple in their direction.

'Heavens above Albert - just look! It's Mr and Mrs Potts, who were in the Suite next to us. I can't believe it! She's wearing exactly the same dress as myself.'

Albert looked up. 'Aye, very nice too,' he said. 'And Old Man Potts is wearing a suit just like me. We'll make a nice table.'

Alice glared at him and then turned her head and beamed brightly at the Potts.

'How very nice to see you again,' she lied. 'We have quite missed you since you moved out of the Balcony Suite.'

Christine Potts smiled weakly as she gazed in despair at Alice's dress. 'Yes, we have missed you both so much. So much, haven't we dear?'

Her husband nodded and greeted Albert. 'Have you finished the renovations in your cabin?' he enquired. 'I could manage the noise, but when you broke through and tried to extend to our cabin, that was it for me.'

'Suite, dear,' said Mrs Potts, who although she had been pretending not to hear, had been listening carefully. 'Balcony Suite, dear, not cabin.'

She returned her attention to Alice. 'When we moved from

the Balcony Suite which was so suitable for us, we moved to a lovely Suite with all the facilities we could want. Isn't that right, Thomas?' He nodded.

'You have no balcony, I take it,' said Alice, anxious to retain her position of superiority.

'Not exactly,' Mrs Potts replied, 'but because of the inconvenience we suffered, the Captain invited us to use the private balcony by the bridge. That is very private, you know, and most suitable for relaxing.'

Alice knew when she was beaten and changed the subject.

'I'm afraid that due to the work in our Balcony Suite, all my dresses had to be sent for cleaning. I had to find something, but all I could find was this old dress I am wearing tonight. It was such a pity that the dry cleaning is not quicker on this ship.'

Christine Potts was spared from having to think up a riposte for, at that very moment, the doctor arrived.

'Hello, hello, hello, shipmates!' he cried. 'Just back from the Chelsea Flower Show, are we?' He laughed heartily at his own joke and sat down. 'All hale and hearty, I take it,' he continued as he gazed at the dour features of Thomas Potts. 'Cheer up, old chap. Death can't be far away.'

Mrs Potts gazed at him in horror but quickly regained her composure and managed a sickly smile.

'Now,' he said, as he picked up the menu especially embossed in gold. 'What harm is old Tucker going to do us tonight?'

He perused the menu. 'I say, it's a good night for those who like pig food. I see we are starting with sweetcorn.' He paused. 'Porker again,' he continued as he noticed Golden Glazed Ham. 'Yum, yum, pig's bum, as we used to say at school. I guess the Security Officer is taking no chances and making doubly sure no Islamic johnnies slip in for a quick kebab, eh?'

Alice thought it prudent to try and change the subject but, for the life of her, could not think what to say. She was rescued by Mrs Potts, who attempted to make polite conversation.

'Doctor,' she began, 'have you been at sea long?'

Doctor Hackett took a gulp of the champagne he had arrived with and held up the flute for a refill.

'I've been at sea most of my life, Mrs Potts. Totally at sea.'

He returned his attention to the menu.

'I say, Golden Syrup!' he exclaimed. 'Out of the strong came forth sweetness and all that. And Golden Shred marma-lade pudding. You can tell old Mike Tucker never went to board-ing school. If he had, he would never serve this stuff. Come on, drink up. It'll soon be time for the corn.'

He placed his glass on the table and began to sing, 'Fair waved the golden corn. In Canaan's pleasant land . . . Lovely hymn that. Brings tears to my eyes.'

Both Albert Hardcastle and Thomas Potts remained silent. The speed at which the doctor conducted the conversation was too much for them. Fortunately there was no need for further exchange for, at that moment, a side door opened revealing Mike Tucker and his team all wearing tall golden chefs' headgear and bearing golden salvers. They marched into the room as Giovanni struck up the theme from *Goldfinger* on his accordion. A team member made his or her way to a table and planted a salver on it. When Mike shouted across the room, 'Open sesame!' the cover was smartly removed, revealing a stack of corn on the cob.

'Come on,' said the doctor, 'tuck in. No FHB (Family Hold Back) at this table.'

The two flowered ladies politely declined the first course, both saying that they were saving themselves for later.

'Quite right,' said the doctor as he jabbed a corn with a skewer. 'I bet your husbands can't wait.'

The ladies ignored this saucy remark and Albert made a face. He had never eaten sweetcorn before and wasn't quite sure how to tackle it. He tried cutting it with his knife and fork but the corn kept slithering around his plate and was too tough to cut through. Thomas on the other hand picked it up with his fingers but, as it was so hot, he promptly dropped it and it went sliding under the table. Thomas thought this was how the doctor was eating his but he had failed to notice the two skewers inserted into each end of the other man's portion. He decided enough was enough and it was left to the doctor to take what he wished.

'Pretty good considering,' he said as he wiped butter from around his mouth with his napkin. 'I can now understand why porkers look so contented. Stay around long enough, old boy,' he turned and addressed Thomas, 'and the secrets of the universe will be revealed. Mark my words. I knew a fellow once who ate nothing but carrots. Day in, day out, carrots. He turned bright orange. He didn't feel too good, but at least he looked bright.'

He laughed loudly at this and his guests had no idea if he was being serious or not. The waiter offered Albert another Brown Ale, which he gratefully accepted. Thomas took the red wine that was on offer and the ladies decided that a light white wine would be just the thing. The doctor continued on champagne and requested that the waiter leave the bottle on the table in case of emergency.

The doctor glanced at the second course on the menu and noted the vegetarian option of Curried Golden Beets.

'I say,' he chuckled, 'Farmer Giles has made a fortune selling his animal food to this ship. We've got more root veg here. Beetroot or some such stuff.'

No one at the table replied as they could not think of what to say. They continued to bury their heads in the menu. Albert surfaced first, saying, 'Fish and some sort of golden chips for me.' Thomas went along with that and the ladies decided on the chicken.

'It's the good old porker for me,' the doctor said with relish. 'And I might as well clear the farmyard by having a bit of chicken on the side. Can't have too many animals eating all those delicious golden beets.'

By now they were halfway through the meal and the doctor's guests had contributed virtually nothing to the conversation. All four found it very difficult indeed to know how to respond to the man's comments, or what subject to introduce for discussion. The indefatigable Christine Potts made a further attempt.

'You must be kept very busy on board, Doctor Hackett,' she said. 'Particularly as there are so many elderly passengers.'

The doctor finished chewing the crispy end of a chicken bone and looked at her.

'Not so busy as a ship I was once on,' he said as he stabbed at a roast golden potato. 'The folks on that old tub were well past it and they were dying like flies. Of course, we tried to keep deaths from the passengers but they always knew because they got extra ice cream at dinner!'

Mrs Potts and the other diners looked blankly at the medic.

'The fridge – you know, we had to make more room in the fridge.'

Mrs Potts made a dreadful face and uttered a low, 'Oh.' Albert grinned. Alice remained silent and Thomas Potts retained the same impassive expression he had worn throughout the evening.

'I think I have had enough to eat now" Mrs Potts said. 'One has to be so careful not to overeat, Doctor, don't you agree?'

'No problem on this ship, my dear,' he responded. 'I'm

going for the syrup pudding. I always liked those green tins with the picture of the lion on the front. Brought up on the stuff. My nanny used to sing about Daniel, you know, as she tucked me up at night.'

For the second time that evening he broke into song, this time about Daniel and the Den of Lions.

'We all need a bit of divine protection, eh, Mr Potts? Helps with the liver and the digestion.'

Mr Potts actually managed to change his expression for a brief moment and then returned his attention to his fish and chips.

Meanwhile, at another table, Angela Fairweather the Social Hostess, and the chaplain, were acting as hosts. Their guests, carefully selected by the Hotel Manager, were a couple who had a Grade One Suite (one up from a cabin and one down from a Balcony Suite), namely Edna and Felix de Barkley. Mr de Barkley had gained minor notoriety on board because of his very witty interjection at the lectures. His wife of forty years was always embarrassed by his behaviour, but now simply accepted it as she realised that there was no changing him. They were complemented at the table by the eighty-year-old twins Petra and Philippa Parkinson. These venerable ladies hailed from the Hawkes Bay area of New Zealand, where they had lived for the past seventy years. They had celebrated their birthday on board, in the company of the Staff Captain and Enzo whom they regarded with great affection and treated as the son neither of them had ever had.

The chaplain was greatly interested in the stories of New Zealand as related by the twins. They had lived for most of their lives on the banks of a river quaintly named the Tukituki and their father had owned acres of land which was given over to beef cattle and sheep.

'I went to New Zealand once,' said Mr de Barkley. 'I was nearly blown off my feet in Wellington. My word, the wind does blow in that city.'

'We don't go there much,' replied Philippa. 'We can get everything we need in Waipukurau.'

'Where?' queried Felix. 'That's a mouthful for a lad born in Cheshire.'

'Waipuk is a lovely little town,' chipped in Petra. 'If you ever go there, my brother's granddaughter will give you a very good haircut, Mr de Barkley.'

'A bit too far to go for a haircut alone,' he replied. 'She might have to throw in a shave as well to make it worthwhile.' All the table laughed and were contented that the evening was going so well.

As coffee was being served, Enzo stood and rattled a teaspoon against his wine glass. The room fell silent.

'Ladies and gentlemen, or should I at this stage in the voyage say "Friends"?'

Mrs de Barkley looked across at her husband and gave him a warning look. He remained silent.

'It is not often that any of us get an opportunity to take a maiden cruise. If we are fortunate enough to do so, then it is something we will remember for many a year.'

Mr de Barkley could restrain himself no longer and whispered to one of the twins, '*He'll* remember it for sure with a shiner like that!'

Enzo was still wearing the eye-patch which, in fact, enhanced his appearance and gave him a certain romantic air.

'Admiral Benbow Harrington has had a long and distinguished career in the Royal Navy and we are fortunate that he not only founded Golden Oceans but planned this very cruise himself. Friends, let me ask you to rise and offer a toast to "Golden Oceans".'

There was a clattering as diners struggled to their feet, raised glasses and mumbled something incomprehensible before sitting again.

The Admiral rose to his feet. He cut an impressive figure as, for this special evening, he had decked himself out in his finest gold braid complete with an array of medals that would have put a shooting gallery to shame.

'Fellow cruisers,' he began. 'What a wonderful evening. I am sure you will want to join me in thanking those responsible, especially our Head Chef Mike.'

Giovanni's accordion sounded out several triumphant chords and Mike appeared yet again. When the applause had died down, the Admiral resumed.

'Life has its high moments and its low episodes. I owe you an explanation. Some of you will have been alarmed by incorrect stories concerning the security of this ship. Let me say clearly, as an officer and a gentleman, that all ships which pass through this region have full security. *All* ships - and the *Golden Handshake* is no exception. You may sleep soundly in your bunks.' (Here he quickly recalled that he was addressing cruise passengers, not ratings of the Royal Navy and quickly altered bunks to Suites.)

'You may sleep soundly in your Suites and cabins, knowing that you have a Golden Guarantee of security. The gentleman who got too much sun, and therefore became over-excited during his lecture, will leave the ship in India. Now, let me hand you over to the Master of this great cruise liner. Your Captain and Friend, Captain Peché Sparda.'

The Admiral's moving little speech engendered tremendous applause. Guests banged their tables and rattled the glassware. Never in his life had the Admiral been so well acclaimed.

Now it was Captain Sparda's turn. During this cruise he had become increasingly confident and had grown into his role as Master of the *Golden Handshake*. The ship had faced more problems than he had ever anticipated but, so far, if Angus Mac-

Donald and his team could keep the steering gear under control, then all seemed set well. Gradually he was getting to know the abilities and shortcomings of his team. Duvet was competent and unemotional. Bigatoni had his heart in the right place but needed a firm hand to direct him. Angela was just lovely, unobtrusive and charming to all she met. Harry Parkhurst, not really a member of his team but under his command whilst he was Captain, was a trusted and wise adviser. The Staff Captain, Roger Hallworthy, was a seasoned sailor and able to take command at the drop of a hat. Head Chef Tucker knew his job and could come up with wholesome food, even if some passengers said it was not exciting. He, the Captain, didn't want his meals to be exciting. He wanted good nourishing food, or 'tucker' as he had heard the doctor refer to it once. As for Doctor Stuart Hackett, well he was unquestionably a one-off, but so far he hadn't killed anyone, at least so far as he knew - and most people seemed to like him. Arthur Chub remained in the background as his job demanded, and seemed an able security man. That brought him to the chaplain, the Reverend Justin Longparish. Sparda had begun with a very low opinion of the fellow, but had been completely taken by surprise in Libya by the cleric's ability to resolve a problem that would have defeated the greatest brains in the United Nations.

Captain Sparda got to his feet and Felix de Barklay, the comedian of the lecture theatre, unable to contain himself any further, shouted, 'Seconds out. Round one.'

This brought him a very disapproving stare from his wife, but the other passengers, emboldened by complimentary wine, enjoyed the joke and laughed heartily.

Sparda, always ready to rise to the occasion, adopted a defensive stance by clenching and raising both his fists, which again caused laughter.

'Dear Friends,' he started. 'Tonight is one of life's Golden Moments for us all.'

An audible groan echoed from the doctor's table but Sparda continued undeterred.

'This cruise has had its challenges, but life at sea is full of challenges. In all my years spent sailing the deep, I have encountered storm and tempest, fire and flood, but with the aid of my trusty crew we sailed on, confident that we would reach port.'

'Is he auditioning for a part at the Old Vic?' whispered the doctor.

His table companions ignored him as they were listening intently to the Captain.

'Tonight, I want to honour a very special and humble man.'

The doctor looked at Albert. 'What have you done, Mr Hardcastle?' he asked.

Albert looked flustered, but made no comment.

'That man is with us tonight. May I ask the Reverend Justin Longparish MA to kindly step forward.'

'Who the hell is that?' asked the doctor, genuinely surprised.

On Angela's table, the chaplain stirred uneasily. Angela took hold of his arm.

'It's you, Justin,' she said gently. 'He wants you to go forward.'

'Me?' he said. 'What for?'

'Just get up and join the Captain,' she said.

The chaplain got uneasily out of his seat, and to shouts of, 'Good one, Justin!' he walked slowly forward and stood alongside Sparda. The Admiral then rose and positioned himself on the other side of the chaplain so that it looked as if they were about to march him away to the brig.

'Chaplain, I know you are a modest man and I shall not embarrass you further,' said the Captain, 'but I have to say that you, and you alone, have saved this cruise and the good name of Golden Oceans. We now present you with the highest award this company can offer. This award, normally called "The Golden Eagle Award", has been specially renamed in your honour as "The Golden Chalice".'

The Admiral picked up a small case which he handed to the chaplain, and then all three posed whilst Harry Parkhurst took a photograph. Giovanni struck up 'For He's a Jolly Good Fellow' and the whole dining room stood up and sang along. When they had finished, cries of, 'Speech, speech!' resounded around the room.

The chaplain, totally lost for words, thanked everyone and declared that he could not think what he had done to receive such acclaim. He did not ever intend to come on a cruise but here he was. He had been very ill, but the doctor had been very good to him. He rambled on but no one was really listening and it did not matter what he said. Everyone was determined to honour a hero and honour him they would. When he started to talk about his curacy in Littlehampton and how much he owed to his mother, the Captain touched his arm and the chaplain stopped in mid-sentence and promptly sat down to further applause.

'I have never been so humiliated in my life,' Alice fumed to Albert after they had returned to their Suite following the dinner. 'How was I to know that Christine Potts would take the same paper pattern out of the *Ladies Friend* and make the same dress as myself?'

Albert had no answer to that question. It was way beyond his competence.

'It were a nice evening,' he yawned, 'but I wouldn't want to do it every week'. And with that he turned over and went to sleep.

Following the Golden Dinner, passengers faced several days at sea before they reached their next port of call, Cochin in South India. Enzo, now back with the responsibility of arranging the programme for entertainers and lecturers had been able to produce a more sensible schedule. In consultation with the Hotel Manager, an extra act had been brought onto the ship at Eilat. This was due to a brainwave of Harry's, who wanted to provide the passengers of the *Golden Handshake* with a very special experience. As far as he knew, there was no record of any cruise ship providing a circus for the entertainment of passengers.

Through one of his many contacts he had heard of a unique act involving animals - and he asked for more details. A full-blown circus was quite out of the question, but a discreet act, involving a few members of the animal kingdom, might go down very well indeed. Eventually the information came through to him and he was in luck. It seemed that a certain entertainer by the name of Rupert van der Loon had just been performing in Tel Aviv. He was due to fly home to England for a period of rest but could be available to sail with the ship for several days.

Although not quite what Harry had in mind, the act seemed to him to be most unusual and worth booking. Mr van der Loon was, by all accounts, a hypnotist who travelled with a parrot which he claimed was a mindreader. He also had a dog, Charlie, who could whistle! Harry would believe that when he saw it, but, as Mr van der Loon was going cheap he snapped him up and secreted him and his two travelling companions on board in Eilat. Although the dreadful Toby Troy had observed the security guards, he had missed van der Loon and his fellow performers, and no one, apart from Harry, Enzo and the Security Officer, knew that the trio were on board.

It had been a peaceful day for the doctor. He had spent an hour of so in his surgery dealing with the usual run of coughs, colds and heart murmurs. Rarely did anything of real interest come up, and he wasn't too sorry about that as it was a long time since he had had a medical refresher – and since that time, the world of medical science had undoubtedly moved on. His evening surgery was equally uninteresting, and it was with some relief that he went to the Golden Dinner. The table he had been given to host was dire, but he tried to liven things up a bit – without much success. He was fairly generous to himself with the beverages on offer and finally got to bed about one in the morning.

He always slept soundly, but at about 3 a.m. he was snatched from the world of dreams by the ringing of his bedside phone and a sharp knocking on his door. He stumbled out of bed, uncertain what to do next. Answer the phone or open the door? He decided to open the door. A worried-looking passenger stood there wrapped in a frayed dressing-gown and in the company of a steward.

'Can you come immediately, Doctor? It's my wife. A medical emergency.'

'Hold on a moment,' the doctor replied. 'The telephone.' He picked it up and it was Reception, asking him to go to a Bal-

323

cony Suite for an emergency call.

'Trouble always comes in threes,' he said cheerfully as he quickly slipped into a tracksuit. 'I expect a carrier pigeon will arrive in a moment with the same message.'

He trotted off behind the two messengers, down the corridor and up the steps to the top of the ship.

'I suppose you sing "Nearer My God to Thee" every night up here, do you?' he said to the Balcony Suite occupant. 'One can only hope that it is truly heavenly.'

The doctor and the dressing-gown entered the room, leaving the steward outside. Once inside, the doctor observed a lady in bed moaning to herself.

'It's my wife, Doctor,' said the dressing-gown. 'She was at the dinner tonight, and almost as soon as she got back here she complained of feeling terribly ill - nauseous and breathless. I should add that she is a diabetic.'

'Ah,' said the doctor. 'I thought you had been raiding the chef's fruit store. That explains the smell of over-ripe apples. Good evening, Ma'am,' he said politely to the patient. 'Tell me, did you fall foul to the culinary efforts of the great Chef Tucker?'

The patient moaned. 'I couldn't resist the Golden Syrup Pudding,' she said weakly. 'It was so good, and then I had the Golden Shred option also. Oh, I feel dreadful.'

'Ketones,' said the doctor confidently. 'That's what it is, ketones. Get me her kit,' he said to the dressing-gown. Then:

'No, man - not her clothes, her diabetic kit!'

He quickly did a blood test and then injected her with a top-up of insulin.

'No problem now,' he said reassuringly. 'Ketones often make the breath smell, you know.'

The woman looked startled. 'Really?' she said. 'I didn't know that. Is that right?'

'Oh yes,' said the doctor, 'It's quite common and very noticeable. People don't usually pass comment, but they know all right.'

'Well, blow me down,' said the husband, looking relieved. 'I never knew that.'

'Perhaps you have recently married,' said the doctor, 'and you haven't noticed. If ever this dear lady's blood sugar goes high again,' the doctor told him, 'get up close and it will be obvious.'

Both occupants of the Balcony Suite now looked even more confused.

'It's incredible,' said the patient groggily. 'How can an over-indulgence in Syrup Pudding possibly make my breasts swell so quickly? Put on weight eventually, perhaps, but an instant increase in the region you mention seems totally incredible. Are you a properly qualified doctor?'

'My dear lady,' the doctor said patiently, 'I said *breath* smell, not breasts swell. Here.' He pointed towards his mouth with his forefinger. 'Over-ripe apples. Here.'

He pointed again.

'*Breath*. Well, I must return to the Land of Nod. Watch your figure, young lady, and lay off the syrup otherwise you'll swell all over. Toodle pip, and I won't say sweet dreams, just happy ones.'

He left the suite laughing to himself. As he descended to the lower regions he could have sworn he heard a sound that he had not heard since his days in the Congo. Was that a parrot? He listened again, but all was silent.

Perhaps Bigatoni had got some extra props to go with his eye-patch, he thought and continued to his quarters. He was soon to learn otherwise.

31

Sunday morning dawned and the chaplain woke in his double bed in the Balcony Suite. The sun was streaming in through the porthole, filling the little room with warm beams of light. Compared to the cot in the Medical Centre this was heaven, although he felt rather guilty at having been so honoured by the ship when all he did was accompany the Port Chaplain on his delicate mission. Perhaps, he reasoned, he had played a part in providing moral support to his old college friend. It was best now to forget the past and get on with doing what he had been requested to do, and that was be the chaplain on board.

Last night at the Golden Dinner, he had been very embarrassed and, had it not been for the supportive presence of Angela, he would not have been able to go through with it. Everyone congratulated him on his speech, but it was terrible. He had had no idea what to say or how to say it. Sermonising had never been his strong point. He suddenly realised that tomorrow would be Sunday, and a sea day, and he was due to take the morning service. What was he to do? The doctor had warned him not to exceed three minutes for his sermon and the Captain wanted half an hour at least. He would consult Angela who had a good mind for planning and would surely be able to help him resolve this dilemma.

It was well known on the ship that the aggressive Mr Toby Troy, once honoured by the State for his great skill in dealing with complex foreign affairs, would be leaving the ship in India and would deliver no more lectures. The chaplain understood that the unfortunate man was now locked in the brig, waiting to be put ashore. As chaplain, he felt it was his duty to visit the captive and to offer him some comfort in his distress.

Later that morning, he approached Captain Sparda whom he caught in the reception area. 'Ah Padre,' said Sparda, in his jolly confident manner. 'Well done last night. Lovely evening and you were the star turn.'

The chaplain blushed, an unfortunate trait which had caused him much suffering at school.

'I was thinking of visiting Mr Troy today,' he said, 'and wondered if this would be acceptable to you.'

'It would be acceptable to me if you took the little fellow and threw him over the stern.' Sparda replied. 'Never have I seen such mischief contained within so small a frame. Visit him by all means. I'll ask Harry Chub to give you the keys.' The Captain strode away and the chaplain went in search of Harry.

When the ship was converted into a cruise liner, there had been much discussion as to whether there ought to be a special place in which to confine miscreants, or not. Some argued that they could be secured easily in a cabin. Others said that as there might be some individuals who, because of drink, had lost control, a secure cell or brig would be more appropriate. It was decided that there would be such a place, and a very small area was utilised, which had formerly been used to store potatoes. Harry escorted the chaplain to the brig, unlocked the door and left him. Troy was sitting on a low stool reading by the light of a lamp attached to the wall.

'May I come in, please?' the chaplain said politely.

'If you must,' said Troy. 'Oh, it's you,' he groaned. 'God's last hope for a fallen world.'

The chaplain entered and sat on a ledge attached to the wall.

'I am so sorry to find you here,' he began, but Troy responded before he could continue.

'Well, who did you expect to find? Sleeping Beauty? Aladdin?'

The chaplain was taken aback. 'Well no, of course not. That was just a figure of speech. I meant that I was sorry that you have been confined to this dungeon.'

'Well, let me tell you,' said Troy, in a voice filled with right-eous anger, 'I am not a *bit* sorry! Not one bit. As soon as I leave this ship, this whole floating outpost of MI6 will be exposed to the world. It is no coincidence that there is an Admiral on board. They say he is retired. Tripe! My guess is he is a serving officer of the security services and that his lackey, Sparda, had deliberately endangered the lives of innocent people by sailing into dangerous waters to spy!' He almost shouted the last word.

'This is clearly a spy ship, Mr Holy Chaplain, sir, and you are complicit in a huge espionage operation involving the Mafia, Mossad, MI6 and a dozen or more private operatives.'

'Really,' said the chaplain, 'how can you make such an assertion?'

'With ease,' said Troy confidently. 'Did not the Captain loiter off the coast of Libya until he was chased away? I have seen with my very own eyes armed men prowling through this ship after cover of darkness. I am not easily fooled, you know. I know Hezbollah and their ways. I understand Mossad. As for the spooks from MI6, they are under deep cover as passengers or crew members. Mark my words in red ink, and reflect on them long after I have exposed this whole outfit through Wikiwatts.'

The chaplain reflected on those whom he knew amongst the passengers and wondered who might be secret agents. Albert and Mrs Hardcastle? Thomas Potts? Never. It was possible, he supposed, that the New Zealand twins had worked at GCHQ and had continued their work across the generations. Possible, but he didn't think it likely as they had never once yet found their way back to their Suite without being directed by a crew member. If their memory was that bad, they could hardly be spies. Unless, of course, the forgetfulness was part of their cover.

'But,' said Troy, 'I don't want to waste my time on these issues, important as they are. There will be plenty of time to discuss this ship when the whole conspiracy is exposed – as it will be. By me!'

The chaplain did not know how to respond to this flood of accusations so he remained silent. As he was thinking what to say next, Troy continued on a different tack.

'Tomorrow is Sunday, right?'

The chaplain said that indeed it was.

'There will be a religious service on the ship, right?'

Once again the chaplain confirmed the statement.

'Can you tell me, in words of one syllable why you,' here he jabbed at the chaplain with his forefinger, 'why you,' another jab, 'should be given the special privilege of holding a religious service on this ship?'

The chaplain had been jabbed in such a way before, and he didn't like it. He was about to answer, but before he could open his mouth, Troy continued.

'Why should there be a religious service at all?'

The chaplain took a breath so that he would not stutter and replied, 'I think I read in the newspapers, Mr Troy, that once you were a promoter of the Holy Bible, and because of your work in trying to sell them to Hezbollah, you were thrown into a dungeon.'

'Correct in every detail, chaplain – if that is what you like to call yourself.'

Anxious not to get caught in the emotions generated by a discussion of religion, the chaplain tried to put the conversation into the academic realm.

'Chaplain is a very old designation, Mr Troy. It goes back to Middle English and probably comes from Medieval Latin *cappellanus*, someone who looked after the cloak of St Martin. You remember that the saint shared his cloak with a poor man.'

'It can be traced back to Middle Wallop for all I care,' snorted the little man. 'But if what you say is true and that's where it goes back to, why aren't you in the laundry pressing shirts and ironing the bedsheets? Let me tell you, Mr Cappuccino, or whatever you like to call yourself, with my good friend Professor Dickie Querk from none other than the University of Totnes, we will be exposing the whole religious monopoly on cruise ships and on this one in particular. I have always suspected a link between MI6 and the Church of England. And I shall expose you, sir, as being a key operative. Time in this dungeon has given me an opportunity to prepare my case.'

'I don't wish to argue with you, Mr Troy. Is there anything you want?'

'Certainly,' said Troy, jumping to his feet and startling the chaplain. 'Truth. Justice. An end to Religious Oppression. Secret dealings exposed. Oh yes. I want a great deal and I shall get it. Now I must attend to my case and leave you to continue to dupe the passengers on this ship. Good day.'

He motioned towards the door and the chaplain left after what was his first pastoral visit on board.

32

Enzo was excited. He and Harry had brought the new entertainer on board and had hidden him in a remote cabin on the
lower deck. Mr van der Loon had insisted that his parrot, Nelson, and his dog, Charlie, were to share his cabin and in return
he was told that none of them must emerge during the daytime,
so as not to be seen by passengers. His show was to be a surprise.
He could leave at night with the two other performers but, during the day, meals would be served in the cabin. Rehearsal presented something of a problem. In view of the secrecy required,
the act could not go out to the performance area before the
show itself. It was decided that a rehearsal would take place in
the cabin, before Enzo and Harry, who would take notes and
instruct the technicians accordingly.

After lunch the two officers descended to the cabin and
knocked on the door. Chiming bells were reserved for Balcony
Suite passengers.

'Clear off,' said a voice from within. Harry knocked again.

'Are you deaf as well as stupid?' uttered the same voice as the
door opened. Mr van der Loon appeared, dressed in a long silk

dressing-gown and smoking a cigarette held in an ivory holder.

'I do apologise for Nelson,' he said. 'This is his rest time, and he hates to be disturbed.'

Nelson, the mind-reading parrot, was perched on top of the dressing-table mirror, and as they entered he gave them the evil eye.

'I'm afraid there is no smoking on this ship,' said Harry.

'Thank God,' said Nelson from on high, giving Harry a wink and then closing his eyes again.

Van der Loon extinguished the cigarette and offered his visitors a seat. This accomplished entertainer was acknowledged, by those who had seen his performance, as one of the finest ventriloquists in the business. It was difficult, if not impossible, for onlookers to tell when it was that Nelson was repeating a word or phrase he had learned, or when van der Loon was exercising his ventriloquism. Both Enzo and Harry were immediately taken in.

Half under the bed, Enzo noticed what he imagined was Charlie, the musical dog. He too was fast asleep, and snoring quite loudly.

'This really is an inconvenient time for all of us, as we normally rest during the afternoon.' Van der Loon sat on the edge of the narrow bed. 'I'm not sure Charlie and Nelson will be all that co-operative.'

'It's the only time we have,' said Harry apologetically. 'We'll have to make the best of it.'

'I'm afraid that it won't be a dress rehearsal,' van der Loon told them. 'My silk suit is with the tailor, being repaired where Charlie took a piece out of it when he was in a bad temper.'

Enzo sat back in his seat and moved his feet further away from the dozing Charlie.

'Is he frequently bad-tempered?' he asked, somewhat nervously. He had never felt quite at ease with dogs since one had chased him when he was a boy.

'Frequently, these days,' van der Loon replied nonchalantly. 'I think he is tired of screen and stage, but to me he is irreplaceable.'

With that remark Charlie rolled over and opened one eye. A trick he had learned from the parrot. He stared at the two visitors, got slowly to his feet, and went to drink some water from a crystal bowl placed at the far end of the cabin.

'Charlie,' said van der Loon. 'Come on. Greet your visitors.'

Charlie ignored them and flopped to the floor.

'I think we should begin,' said Harry. 'Time is going by and we have a lot to get through before the show tonight.'

Van der Loon got to his feet and cleared his suitcase off the floor, making a small space.

'Nelson!' he cried. 'Come on - rehearsal. You're on first. Come on, Nelson. We have to rehearse.'

Nelson strutted across the top of the mirror, paused and

bent down to view his own reflection, and then continued to the far edge. When he reached the end he flapped his wings, flew a few paces and perched on the back of a chair alongside Mr van der Loon.

'Right,' said his owner. 'I begin the act by appearing on stage in my silk suit and singing "Talk to the Animals" like Rex Harrison in *Dr Dolittle*. I then invite the audience to fire a question at Nelson, who will respond. Are you ready, Nelson? Mr Parkhurst will ask the first question. By the way, don't forget, Nelson is the only clairvoyant parrot ever discovered. Right, Nelson.'

The bird remained mute as Harry tried to think of something to ask. 'What are two and two?' he asked eventually.

There was no immediate reply as Nelson looked at him as incredulously as a parrot can look. Finally his voice rang out.

'If you ask any more bloody silly questions like that, I'll ask Charlie to deal with you. For goodness sake, this isn't a Kindergarten.'

Harry nearly fell off his chair in surprise and Enzo laughed.

'Why are you laughing, you fat man?' the parrot went on. 'I've heard crocodiles sing better than you.'

Enzo stopped smiling immediately. 'You've never heard me sing,' he objected.

'You forget, Fatso, that I am a clairvoyant. The best in the business,' snapped Nelson, quick to respond.

Harry turned to van der Loon who appeared to be busy

manicuring his fingernails as the exchange took place.

'I do hope he will be more polite tonight,' Harry said. 'Some of our guests are very sensitive, you know.'

'I've seen them,' said Nelson, chipping in. 'The only time they are sensitive is when they have to pay for drinks.'

'Be quiet, Nelson,' said van der Loon, pretending to get irritated. 'I'm sorry, gentlemen, but I warned you that the afternoon was not good for a rehearsal. I think we had better ask Charlie to show you what he can do. Charlie, wake up.'

The dog growled and reluctantly got to his feet.

Van der Loon rummaged in a suitcase and produced a conical hat which he placed on Charlie's head, fastening it with an elastic band. He then went to the cupboard and brought out a stand to which were attached a row of small trumpets. He set this down before Charlie, who looked far from pleased.

'Damn silly hat,' said Nelson from the safety of his perch.

'Will you be quiet, Nelson,' said van der Loon. 'You really are getting out of hand these days. Now,' he went on, 'I play that lovely old melody on my saxophone, "How Much is That Doggy in the Window". Then I stop and Charlie plays the same tune by blowing into each of the trumpets in turn.'

He began filling the small cabin with the noise of his instrument. When he had finished, he turned and nodded towards Charlie who, instead of playing on the trumpets, trotted back to his position under the bed and crashed to the floor.

'Oh come on, Charlie. Come on, be reasonable.'

'Quite right too,' said Nelson from his position of safety back on the mirror. 'Sleep on, Charlie.'

'Oh really!' sighed van der Loon. 'These performers are so temperamental. I do apologise, but at least you have some idea of what will happen. Also, they are both upset at having been confined to their cabin all day.'

Enzo and Harry got up to leave.

'It wasn't quite what I expected,' said Enzo, somewhat disappointed. 'But I hope they will be better behaved tonight.'

'I sincerely hope so too,' said van der Loon. 'I have to confess they didn't want to come away at this time as Nelson likes to have a good laugh at David Attenborough on the television and Charlie didn't want to miss the Last Night of the Proms or some such thing. Well, they have to learn. They can't have it all their own way.'

Enzo and his immediate superior left the cabin and returned to the main body of the ship. They said little to each other but were lost in their own thoughts. At least, decided Enzo, life on board was never dull. Never.

When the visitors had left, Mr van der Loon lit another cigarette and sat down. Charlie had now emerged from under the bed and was gazing at a picture of the famous dog who, many years ago, was used to advertise HMV gramophone records. This dog was

339

portrayed listening to an old-fashioned horn gramophone with an expression of intense seriousness. It was this very picture that inspired Charlie, and van der Loon was obliged to take it with them everywhere. Nelson, quiet for a change, was perched by the porthole gazing out at the sea.

Van der Loon thought for a moment and then addressed his fellow performers.

'I am very cross with you both,' he said. 'You may be star performers but in this world you are only as good as your last show. You have just insulted two very important men and frankly, I am ashamed of you.'

As he spent so much time in the company of Nelson and Charlie, he frequently spoke to them, and when Nelson did not respond with a stock phase he had learned, van der Loon, the ventriloquist, responded for him!

Charlie got to his feet and returned to his position under the bed. Nelson remained silent.

'Well,' said Van Loon to Nelson. 'Have you nothing to say?'

There was a long silence broken only by the occasional crashing of a wave against the hull.

'Look, if you want to sulk, that's OK by me. But I warn you both - it had better be good tonight or I shall send you, Charlie, to Battersea and as for you, Nelson - well, I don't know where you could go. The London Zoo perhaps?'

With that Mr van der Loon put out his cigarette, removed

his dressing-gown and put on a sweater.

'I don't care about the restrictions on leaving the cabin,' he said. 'I need some air. I'll be back in about half an hour.'

With that he got up, leaving the two performers to their own devices.

'Silly old fool,' said Nelson, repeating a phrase he had often heard van der Loon use when referring to his agent. 'I need fresh air. Smoke gives me psittacosis.'

Van der Loon had spent hours teaching Nelson this phase, which he frequently used when performing in some of the working men's clubs in the UK.

Charlie emerged from under the bed and shook himself, only to dart quickly back as he heard a tap on the door. Both performers remained quiet. The door gently opened.

'Hello, room service,' said a voice. The room remained silent.

The steward pushed open the door, secured it with a rubber doorstop and disappeared into the bathroom to check the toiletries. Quick as a flash, Nelson flew down from on high, hopped onto Charlie's back and off they set down the corridor.

As it was late on Saturday afternoon and most passengers were in their Suites or cabins preparing for dinner, the ship was fairly deserted. It was more complicated to find their way around than the two creatures had expected. Charlie darted up numerous staircases and along various corridors, where they had to take evasive action several times when a steward or crewman suddenly appeared. By luck rather than judgement, they avoided detection, but try as they might could not find a way out which did not involve opening a heavy door which, of course, was beyond their ability.

In the upper reaches of the ship they observed a couple in evening dress, walking away from them. They now found themselves in a carpeted corridor with just a few doors on either side. They were resting for a moment in an alcove, trying to work out what to do next, when the door opposite opened. A man wearing a flat cap emerged.

'I shan't be long, luv,' he called behind him as he set off down the corridor. 'The shop should be open at this hour.'

Suddenly both Charlie and Nelson found themselves in acute danger. The alcove in which they were hiding was the entrance to the crew's staircase, and someone was attempting to open the door from the other side. At that precise moment, the door of the Suite opposite opened and a rather stout lady emerged, propped the door open and rushed down the corridor, shouting, 'Albert, you've left your card. You can't get the aspirins without the card.'

Like a shot, Charlie leaped forward, almost throwing Nelson onto the carpeted deck, and they entered the Suite at the speed of light. Nelson flew to the top of a large wardrobe and Charlie took his accustomed place under the double bed that dominated the room.

Within a few moments Nelson saw the stout lady return and close the door. She glanced furtively around the cabin, and then quickly opened the wardrobe. She rummaged inside and emerged with an enormous box of chocolates. Quick as a flash she popped one into her mouth, then another, and observed by the hidden onlookers, yet another. She quickly returned the box to its hiding place. Several minutes later the cabin was brought to life as the doorbell sounded out a familiar Scottish melody. Albert entered.

'Here you are, luv,' he said, as he handed the aspirins to his wife.

'We ought to get ready soon as I want to get to dinner early and see the show afterwards. It's said to be very special tonight.'

From his position on top of the wardrobe Nelson could see and hear perfectly, although he could not be seen from within the room. Apart from the psychic gifts attributed to him by van der Loon, Nelson was also a very talented mimic.

'I don't know what to wear tonight,' sighed Alice, repeating the words she said every night on the ship. Nelson watched as she produced several dresses and laid them out on the bed beneath him.

'Well, for God's sake don't wear that bloody awful floral dress,' said Nelson, mimicking Albert perfectly. By sheer coincidence, Nelson repeated a phase he had been taught when, some time ago, van der Loon appeared on stage with a lady assistant.

343

There was a stunned silence.

'What did you say, Albert Hardcastle? What did you just say?'

From under the bed Charlie heard Albert spluttering and trying to answer.

'I didn't say anything, dear,' he said when he finally managed to find his voice.

'I distinctly heard you, Albert. I heard you as clear as day.'

'Come off it,' said Nelson, warming to the conversation. 'You're getting fat!'

'How *dare* you, Albert Hardcastle!' shouted Alice, now really furious. She moved towards him and gave him a resounding crack across the head with the flat of her hand. 'How dare you be so insulting.'

Albert staggered back and fell onto the bed. Charlie, seeing a pair of ankles suddenly appear, was startled and took a nip at one. Albert leaped up as quickly as he had fallen.

'Help!' he cried. 'I've been bitten!' He crashed forward, landing on a chest of drawers which smashed into pieces.

It would be prudent to draw a veil over the remainder of the conversation that took place in the cabin. 'Conversation' would be too polite a word to describe it. Accusations and insults flew like arrows at Agincourt. When he had sufficiently recovered his composure, Albert got on all fours and looked under the bed, only to leap to his feet, exclaiming: 'There's some sort of wild animal under there.'

Charlie gave a low growl, at which both Albert and Alice made for the door and ran headlong down the corridor, calling for the steward. Seeing their chance, Charlie came out of hiding, Nelson resumed his place on his back and they set off at a pace in the opposite direction.

Miracles sometimes happen and today was the day when Mr van der Loon was the lucky recipient of such a blessing. On returning to his quarters, he was taken aback to find that both of his star performers had disappeared. Time was leaping forward and they were due on stage within a couple of hours. He didn't know if he ought to inform the Cruise Director but, being an optimist, decided that he would wait a while longer before raising the alarm.

When passengers were at dinner the attendant usually came round to turn down the bed and prepare their cabin for the night. Mr van der Loon did not go down to dinner as he never ate before a show and neither did his performers. He was beginning to think that he had been too hard on his two companions and that they had finally decided to leave him, when there was a knock on the door. It was the attendant whom he was about to send away when he thought better of it. The door was propped open, and as usual the cleaner went into the bathroom to change the towels. At that very moment, a compartment under the trolley opened and he saw the familiar features of Charlie.

'Hey, Charlie!' he shouted. 'In here.'

Charlie jumped out, Nelson gripping onto his furry back, just before the bathroom door opened again and the cleaner returned to the trolley.

'Don't worry, I'll fix the bed,' said van der Loon as he quickly closed the door. 'Well,' he went on, addressing the returned explorers. 'What on earth do you think you are both playing at? There's no time for explanations now. We must be off in a few moments.'

He collected the conical hat and trumpets; asked Charlie to jump into a large holdall which, together with his saxophone, he loaded onto a luggage trolley. With Nelson perched on his shoulder, the talented trio set off for their first performance on the *Golden Handshake*.

Enzo and Harry were having a quiet drink together following the show.

'I have never in my whole life seen anything like that,' said Harry, totally amazed at the evening's performance. 'When that parrot told the Potts that they had been moved from a Balcony Suite because they couldn't pay the supplement, I thought he had gone too far. But it was all laughed off.'

Enzo agreed that it had been a success for the performers and for the two of them.

'As for that dog, he's amazing. If he could talk I bet he would have a few tales to tell,' said Harry, still reliving the show in his mind.

'Old Mr Hardcastle from the Balcony Suites looked dead worried when the parrot picked him out to have his mind read,' recalled Enzo.

'I doubt he really was thinking that his wife was the most beautiful woman on the ship with the most elegant dresses, as the parrot said, but one never knows.'

They laughed again. The success of the evening had brought them together, and the difficulties they had experienced in the past were beginning to fade. Harry had set a course and Enzo was relaxing into his position on the ship.

'We might have time for one more show,' said Harry, 'if van der Loon is willing. He is due to transfer immediately to another ship once we arrive in Sri Lanka, which will take him back into Europe somewhere.' They both agreed another show might go down very well indeed.

Back in the Balcony Suite, Albert and Alice were talking excitedly about the performance they had just seen. Whilst they were away, the smashed furniture had been replaced and the cabin tidied.

'How that parrot and the dog got into this Suite beats me,' puffed Albert, as he unlaced his boots. 'It must have been that dog Charlie that bit me. As for the parrot, he takes the biscuit.'

'If I hadn't discovered it was the bird mimicking you, Albert Hardcastle, I would never have forgiven you,' said Alice.

They both laughed. Alice made sure the chocolates remained hidden at the bottom of the wardrobe and they climbed into bed.

'Thank you, Albert, for thinking such nice thoughts tonight during the show, ' she said.

He grinned and sighed happily. 'It's been a right good evening,' he murmured. 'A right good evening.'

33

It was Sunday morning and the chaplain was sitting at his small table in his Balcony Suite putting the finishing touches to his sermon. He had consulted Angela about the time he ought to allow and she said that twelve minutes would be ideal. It was clear, she said, that the doctor wanted to get away as quickly as possible and therefore had tried to get the sermon cut right down, if not right out! As for the Captain, well, no sensible person would want to listen to a sermon lasting half an hour and the Captain must know that. Apart from anything else, Angela said, that as the chaplain was without question in the Captain's good books, whatever he did during the service would be accepted. Justin Longparish was greatly reassured by this advice and determined to follow it.

Today he found it difficult to concentrate. His mind was full of other things. First there was the curious business of Toby Troy. What had happened, to turn him from a Bible Puncher into an out and out opponent of religion? He understood that this was a not uncommon occurrence and that dogmatic believers frequently became dogmatic disbelievers when something

349

occurred that shifted the focus of their dogmatism. What was that event for Troy? He had no idea. Then there was the show he had seen last night. Both animals were remarkable, but the parrot was incredible. Was van der Loon a very slick ventriloquist? If so, he would have to be very clever indeed to put on a show as he did. Finally, Angela had the habit of frequently entering his thoughts. She was such a help to him, and he had to confess that he was so pleased when he had been invited to her table at the Golden Dinner. He would not have survived had he been dining elsewhere. All the experiences of the past week were more than he had ever dreamed of, as chaplain to Councillor Paddy Patterson and his partner Bernie Bollinger. They seemed miles away, as indeed they were, and the chaplain wondered if he would ever see them again.

He returned his thoughts to the sermon. He had written it out line by line, but when he read it through, it didn't seem quite right. It was a good plan, he thought, to speak about fishers of men and casting nets and other illustrations to do with the sea, but no doubt these themes would have been done to death by countless preachers before him. However, that was what he had written and it would have to stay. Angus MacDonald had been hauled out of the engine room to read a lesson and Angela had agreed to read some prayers. Rod Saddleworth was excused from basting the Sunday Roast to play the harmonium, and the Captain would introduce the proceedings by announcing the

National Anthem. All seemed in order. Senior officers, including the doctor, had been instructed by Captain Sparda to wear tropical whites, and at the very end of the service the Admiral would make a brief appeal for contributions to the Society for the Protection of Underprivileged Fisherfolk and Ancient Mariners. Being a humble man, and also a sidesman at his local church, the Admiral had insisted that the only other role he would play would be to take up the collection at the conclusion of the service.

The morning was cloudless and the sea tranquillity itself. After breakfast, some passengers walked around the deck. Others sat in the warm sun and enjoyed cruising at its very best. At a quarter to eleven, Enzo summoned passengers to the Information Stations for an announcement, which was that Divine Service, according to the rites and practices of the Church of England, would commence at eleven o'clock. All were invited no matter what allegiance they claimed, as the Church of England embraced all and sundry.

There were no clerical robes on board and as the chaplain still only had his clerical suit (he was planning to get clothes in Cochin), the ship's tailor had run him up a cassock of sorts and adapted one of the Captain's white nightshirts into a surplice. Mr van der Loon had been instructed to keep both Charlie and Nelson well away from the service as it would be most inappropriate if either caused a disturbance, as they might well do.

The story of their visit to the Balcony Suite had leaked out and caused some alarm, especially to the New Zealand twins.

Exactly at eleven, the senior officers marched in and the chaplain brought up the rear. Captain Sparda, although an Italian by birth, had over the years become more British than the majority of the inhabitants of Deptford, and thus it was with a deep sense of pride that he welcomed people to the service and asked them to stand for the National Anthem. This they duly did and the Captain launched forth in a deep baritone, with the officers doing their best to equal him. It had often been the custom for the National Anthem to be sung at the conclusion of Divine Service, but Sparda wanted it made clear from the outset that this was a British ship, loyal to Her Majesty, and so the anthem would be the very first item on the Divine agenda.

The service progressed smoothy enough. The first hymn, 'Eternal Father Strong to Save' brought tears to the eyes of many, but they were soon brought back to reality when Angus began to read the first lesson. To the vast majority he was incomprehensible. His broad Scottish accent, as thick as oatmeal porridge, echoed around the room. He thundered through the story of Noah and his trials on the water, with only the occasional word understood by the most astute. By contrast, Angela had a gentle and clear speaking voice and her prayers for Her Britannic Majesty and all the Royal Family, from oldest to very youngest, received a loud 'Amen'.

Now it was the chaplain's turn to deliver the sermon. He shuffled towards the Golden Eagle, at last put to its correct use, and placed his notes there. The congregation looked at him expectantly. What pearls of wisdom would he cast before them this morning? He had just opened his mouth to announce his text when there was one almighty explosion and the door of the assembly area flew open, revealing Arthur Chub, the Security Officer, accompanied by two individuals wearing balaclavas and toting machine guns.

'Down!' shouted Arthur. 'Down on the floor, everyone.'

For a moment no one moved as they were so surprised. It seemed that one of the perils they were singing about, and hoping to avoid, had actually arrived.

'Not again,' objected someone from the floor. 'This is the second time on this voyage we have done this.'

'This is for real,' bawled Arthur. 'Face down on the floor *now* - everybody!'

As soon as Arthur had appeared, Captain Sparda leaped from the platform and was quickly followed by his officers. The chaplain was left standing at the lectern with his unread sermon before him and a congregation seemingly in a position of Islamic devotion.

'We are being chased by a speedy motor boat,' said Arthur. 'We are not sure who they are, but the two gentlemen you see with me are here for your security. There is no need to panic.

The ship is well protected. Remain here until further notice.'

With that he left, and the two sinister characters took up position at the exit. Suddenly the ship began to swerve, first to port and then immediately to starboard. This caused so much disturbance that waves crashed against the portholes and passengers were rolled from one side of the room to the other. Out on deck, several more balaclavas had appeared and had taken up their positions. Sparda could see a very fast boat trailing them, rocking violently in the turbulence caused by the manoeuvring of the *Golden Handshake*.

'It's your friends, Bigatoni,' he said. 'Pirates.'

The Cruise Director, who was still wearing his eye-patch, did not find this amusing and hid behind a lifeboat. Up to this point no shots had been fired, although it was observed that the crew of the little boat were all waving what appeared to be machine guns and shouting at the ship.

'We'll fix 'em,' said Sparda confidently.

He went to the stern where two of the masked guards had slipped a steel hawser over the side and left it trailing just below the surface. They disappeared from view and Sparda hailed the brigands, motioning them to come closer to the ship. They edged nearer and nearer until there was a terrible sound of metal hitting metal. The small boat stopped dead in the water as the hidden steel cable caught their propellor and snapped it in pieces. Captain Sparda gave the pirates the thumbs-up sign and quickly made for the bridge, where the Staff Captain sounded the all clear on the ship's whistle.

'Your sermon went with a bang this morning,' Sparda commented to the chaplain when they met after lunch. 'I shall have to wait until the next Sunday to discover what happened to that grand old sea dog Noah, mentioned in the first reading. I guess you will tell us about him then. Can't wait, chaplain, can't wait.'

'The attack on the ship was an alarming experience, Captain,' responded the chaplain, changing the subject. 'Not one that I want to have repeated.'

'Pity,' said Sparda, with a mischievous look in his eye, 'we normally lay it on every Sunday Sea Day! Next week I shall ask Enzo to scare them off by singing from *The Pirates of Penzance*. We can then dispense with the guards!'

He laughed at his own wit and the chaplain smiled too.

The day passed pleasantly enough. Everyone was full of praise for the way in which the ship had been handled during the crisis. Not a shot had been fired and not one single person had been injured, apart from those who suffered minor bruising when they rolled across the lecture-room floor. Naturally there was much chatter about the events of the morning. Some passengers attempted to guess the identities of the men in balaclavas.

'I am sure one was Mr van der Loon,' said one of the New

Zealand twins. 'He had exactly the same way of walking.'

Her sister poured scorn on the suggestion. 'Of course it wasn't,' she said authoritatively. 'They were a trained team of frogmen who swim alongside the ship as it sails through troublesome waters.' She was not quite as sharp as she had been during her days as a codebreaker.

Following the excitement, the special security team retired to their hiding places greatly satisfied with their day's work. In one more day they would disembark in Cochin, ready to make the return journey to their home port on yet another vessel.

Down in the dungeon, as he called it, Toby Troy found himself thrown about as the ship swerved from side to side, when it was attempting to evade the pursuers. He had no idea what was taking place and no one thought to inform him. Once all was calm again he returned to the exposé he was writing to be placed on the World Wide Web.

Cruise Ship Deliberately Endangers Passengers would be the headline. He would tell the world the truth. He would expose the deception which was rife aboard this ship. Golden Oceans, indeed. He would turn the gold to dross and in double-quick time.

When all was calm again, Arthur Chub visited him.

'Not long now,' he said, 'and you will soon be back on dry land. Sorry about the turbulence earlier. Do you want anything?'

'Nothing at all except the truth,' said Troy aggressively. 'I fully intend to expose this vessel as a spy ship, you know. It's criminal to use innocent passengers in this way. They are just cover for agents of death!'

'The only agents of death I knew were in the galley,' said Chub cheerfully, 'and we got rid of them some time ago.'

'Ah, so you admit it,' shouted Troy, totally failing to see the joke. 'They *were* on this ship. I shall note what you just said, Mr Chub. I shall note it very carefully.'

'Let me know if you require anything, Mr Troy. I'm off now. I have an important meeting with MI6, Mossad, the CIA and two old ladies who are the official code-breakers for the ship.'

On that businesslike note Arthur Chub left his charge scribbling madly on a large yellow pad.

34

The remainder of the passage to India passed quietly enough. Fred Batty gave his lecture which informed passengers that Kerala was the only State in India to freely elect a Communist government and that it was a highly literate place, with more graduates per square mile than any other part of the world. At least, that is what he read on the Web and he hoped it was correct. If it wasn't, who was to know? He was sure that there was a tiny Jewish community with a small synagogue, and he had a picture to prove it. Also, there were a considerable number of Christians belonging to different traditions there, including one of the oldest Christian churches in the world, the Syrian Ortho-dox. He had collected so many facts from the internet about this part of the world that he overran his time and only stopped when Enzo frantically signalled to him from the back of the room.

Once docked and cleared by customs, passengers went ashore and the Captain, accompanied by Arthur Chub, met offi-cials from the both the British and Indian authorities for a full debriefing on the attempted highjacking. The security guards slipped ashore as unobtrusively as they had boarded, and Mr

Toby Troy BEM found himself on the quayside with a suitcase and a bus ticket to get him to Mumbai, some eight hundred miles or so distant, from whence he would get a cheapo flight home.

Radley Duvet, Hotel Manager of the *Golden Handshake,* had been exceptionally busy. Kerala, so he believed, was a magical place totally different from other parts of the sub-continent. As the ship was spending a night in port, he had arranged an evening on shore for Balcony Suite and Grade One Passengers, when they would be invited to a typical local meal and be entertained with singing and dancing. Not all the elite elected to accept this invitation, as some were acutely afraid of contacting some indescribable disease which might lay them low or lay them out completely! Albert and Alice, anxious to get the best possible value from the cruise, were persuaded to attend, as were Mr and Mrs Potts, and Petra and Philippa Parkinson, the eighty-year-old twins. Sir Archibald and Lady Willoughby declined the invitation as they had a private engagement on shore and, at the last moment, that master of the impromptu intervention, Mr Felix de Barkley and his disapproving wife, Edna, booked a place.

The group assembled by the gangway in the early evening, covered from head to foot in insect repellent. Radley had very kindly issued them with an evil-smelling potion which he claimed would not only keep mosquitos away, but would prevent unwelcome attention from other inhabitants of the region. Not that the ladies of the party had a great deal to fear. He previously had instructed them that they would be going to a home where they would be given a meal and entertained. They all clambered into a mini-bus just large enough for eight, plus Radley and the driver. All the group held on tightly as once outside the port area the driver put his foot down. They had become accustomed to rapid movement on the ship, but this experience was even more dramatic than that. The driver, singing to himself in Malayalam, whizzed past pedestrians, cyclists, motorbikes, autos and handcarts, and brought several chickens to within an inch of the cooking pot.

Before they had gone half a mile, Mr Potts, who was a retired plumber from Dartford in Kent, expressed regret at leaving the ship. His wife told him to, 'Be quiet, Thomas,' in a tone of voice that would have caused ice to appear on the windscreen had she been in the front of the vehicle.

Felix de Barkley, never one to hold back, addressed the driver. 'Being chased, are we, squire? Done a bank robbery or something?'

The driver, totally failing to understand British irony, smiled broadly. 'Very good, sir. I like English, sir. You live in Billericay, sir? I have sister in Billericay. Very lovely, sir. I like drive in Billericay, sir. I see you in Billericay, sir?'

'You won't see me for dust,' said de Barkley, holding on tightly.'

'Very good, sir,' said the driver.

They continued at breakneck speed along a very dusty road until, to the relief of all, with the possible exception of the twin sisters, they arrived at their destination. The Parkinson twins were clearly made of very stern stuff.

'What a lovely journey,' said Petra sweetly to the driver.

'So lovely,' echoed Philippa. 'I do hope you will be taking us home,' she continued, as the driver helped her down from the bus.

'At the rate he was going, we'll all finish up in the eternal home,' de Barkley muttered.

His wife pushed him towards a small welcoming party who stood with garlands in their hands, ready to drape them around the necks of their visitors.

Albert, who after much persuasion was wearing an Hawaiian coloured shirt along with his flat cloth cap, stood rigid as a young sari-clad lady placed the string of coloured flowers around his neck. It was slightly damp as it had been refreshed prior to the girl bringing it out of the house, and Albert felt a slow trickle of water running down his back.

'After a while you may remove them,' said Radley, 'but on no account leave them behind. That would be very rude.'

The party, now all welcomed and adorned, moved onwards through to what seemed to be a coconut grove. Suddenly Albert felt an insect that had crawled out of its fragrant home biting his neck, already made sore by sunburn. He made to remove the garland but Radley waved his hand and whispered, 'Too early - later.'

'Oh, do be still!' snapped Alice, as he continued to fidget with the garland. 'It's impossible to go anywhere with you, Albert Hardcastle.'

As she spoke she smiled broadly, just in case Mrs Potts was watching. Old Man Potts remained as morose as ever and meekly followed his wife. Years of squeezing under sinks and dealing with bathroom leaks had accustomed him to water and outwardly at least he remained untroubled by the irrigation of his flowers.

'Our hosts would like us to sit,' said Radley, once they were in the grove.

'Looks as though the bailiffs have called,' said de Barkley, unable to keep quiet for a moment. 'Not a stick of furniture to be seen, is there?'

'Oh, Mr Barkley, do you really think so?' asked Petra, with concern in her voice. 'How good of them to give us a meal when facing such hardships themselves.'

Some coverings had been laid on the ground and with much effort the party sat down.

Their host, a stocky man with a dark face that shone and glistened by the lights of the coloured bulbs that had been draped over a rough wooden structure, gave a small speech of welcome.

He said that he was honoured, his family were honoured, the whole village was honoured, and they would all remember this evening for many a year. Now some of his eleven children would sing a song of welcome which said how honoured they all were.

'This part of the world must dominate the New Year's Honours List,' quipped de Barkley, but no one was listening. All eyes were focused on several young men clutching hand microphones, and two or three young women in saris who appeared from the house.

One of the party, a youth clad like his father in a long white cloth which wrapped around the body like a skirt, began to sing and was soon accompanied by the others. The words made no sense whatsoever to the visitors, and the tune was one that was certainly not played regularly in the Hardcastle household. They listened politely as the ancient loudspeakers did their best to relay the welcoming message. When that was over, the young men sat down and the girls put a large banana leaf in front of the visitors.

'Ye gods,' quipped de Barkley. 'The bailiffs have taken the crockery as well!'

Each visitor was handed a small glass and this was filled with a milky-looking liquid by one of the young women.

'Toddy,' said the host. 'Very good toddy. Drink, please.'

Radley whispered that the drink was fermented coconut milk, and if they didn't want it then there would be bottled soft drinks available later. The twin sisters were the only members of the party to quaff their beverage immediately, and to accept more when it was offered. The host was delighted and filled their glasses for a third time, much to the alarm of Radley, who motioned to their host behind their back that enough was enough. The girls then came along and, after pouring water over the hands of the diners, began to serve the first course, which was a lentil puree and vegetables served directly onto the leaf.

'Sambar very good,' said their host, as he scooped a portion up in his hand and transferred it to his mouth.

The only time Albert had eaten with his hands was fish and chips from a newspaper, but they were a bit easier to manage than the hot red fish curry which came next. To say that it was hot was to underestimate the temperature. It was raging hot. Fighting hot - and those brave enough to attempt it, in desperation, downed their previously undrunk toddy and pleaded for soft drinks. Whilst they were still reeling from the effects of the toddy and curry combined, several more individuals appeared carrying drums and stringed instruments and began to play loudly.

The sisters, now well into the swing of things, were merrily waving their toddy glasses in the air and attempting to sing along. Mr and Mrs Potts looked stunned and were sweating profusely. Albert had removed his garland and handed it to Alice, who slipped it around her own ample neck. De Barkley seemed to have slipped into a coma, for he had his eyes closed and an expression of acute pain on his face. His wife, smiled and nodded at Alice, who smiled back. It was indeed an evening to remember. The music came to as abrupt an end as it had started, and some very sweet sticky rice was served, which managed to get all over Albert's shirt, much to Alice's annoyance. Frankly, it was a terrible struggle for the party to get to their feet - all except for the sisters, that is, who had been dancing around, much to the delight and amusement of their hosts.

Fond farewells were said and promises of everlasting friendship were made. The Hotel Manager slipped a brown envelope into the hand of the beaming host, and the Balcony Suite passengers returned to the safety and comfort of the *Golden Handshake*.

Back on board, the chaplain reflected on one of the happiest days he had spent in a long time. He had been given an address where he would be able to get some clothes made before the ship sailed the following day but, being somewhat shy and not having much of an idea as to what to order, he was apprehensive. He was conversant with the history of Christians in Kerala, a history which stretched back to the second century, and he was also aware of the ancient synagogue which he wanted to visit. He was contemplating all this over breakfast when Angela approached him.

'Hello, Justin,' she said. 'May I join you?' He agreed immediately and, in his shyness at the unexpected visit, knocked his tomato juice over the clean white tablecloth. The mess was soon cleared, however, and they sat down together.

'I wondered if you were busy today?' she asked as she started on her cereal. 'I was thinking of going ashore and if you were free, we might go together.'

He couldn't believe his luck. Angela was so friendly and helpful, and she would surely give him advice on the clothing he needed to buy. It was agreed that they would meet at the gangway at ten and go ashore then. Angela had insisted that he order three collarless shirts suitable to be worn with a clerical stock, a linen suit and two sports shirts – and a new dark suit as, she said, the one he was wearing had seen much better days. Shoes and other items, such as socks and underwear, could be purchased elsewhere in town.

When he expressed apprehension at the cost of this wardrobe, she astounded him by saying that the passengers had had a collection and, in her estimation, there was more than enough to buy what he needed.

'It is no good protesting,' she beamed. 'I have the money here and, as we have no record of who gave what, it can't be returned. So, you must use it.'

The day had been a resounding success. The tailor was found without difficulty. He measured the chaplain and promised that all the goods would be delivered to the ship before she sailed.

On a less cheerful note he had visited Toby Troy again, before Troy left the ship. The man's enforced detention had steeled his resolve to intensify his battle against all, that in his opinion, he considered oppressive. The chaplain had offered to accompany Troy to the bus station, but Troy had replied by saying that he didn't want a cleric at his funeral and he certainly didn't want one trailing him on his pathway through life. It had been his misfortune previously to have got caught up with religion and he had been duped by the clever rhetoric of religious propagandists when he was too young to make a proper judgement. As far as he was concerned, the clergy were parasites, feeding on a mesmerised public, and he could do without parasites, thank you *very* much!

So Mr Toby Troy, once the darling of the Bible Pugilists, went alone to the station to prepare himself for battle of a different kind.

That night, the chaplain laid his head on the pillow and sighed contentedly. It had been a full and almost completely happy day. Life at sea, despite its many hazards, was not so bad at all.

On the final day in Cochin, several tours had been arranged. Fred Batty, who had never been to India before but had done intensive research on the internet, was due to take a small group

367

around the sights in the city of 'Kochi'.

Enzo, who did not normally lead tours, had volunteered to take a party from the ship on the backwaters. He had heard a great deal about these waterways running through the State, and desired to see them. As the journey involved travel by road of almost two hours in each direction, those who had previously experienced road travel in Kerala decided that enough was enough. The exception to this was the New Zealand sisters, who had thoroughly enjoyed the minibus ride they had taken to the dinner and immediately put themselves down for the marathon to the backwaters. Harry Parkhurst was also keen to take this particular outing, as were Sir Archibald and his wife Lady Veronika. Various other passengers from the Grade One cabins and lower berths made up the remainder of the party.

Enzo assembled the group at the foot of the gangway. He had with him a huge yellow and black umbrella which he held aloft in the style of countless tour guides throughout the world. Harry discreetly remained in the background: his job was to keep count of the group in order to make sure that no one got lost or left behind. This was not an easy task as individuals would lag behind or wander off the main track. He was constantly counting and checking.

As near to the departure time as could be expected, a group of fifteen from the ship waited patiently for their bus. It was interesting for the locals for observe the manner in which the visitors dressed. Sir Archie had obtained from somewhere a toupee which, he insisted, was totally appropriate for India as the word was derived from the Hindi word 'topi' meaning hat. Harry suggested gently that it might stimulate memories of the old Raj, to which Sir Archie replied that if that was true, then so much the better. People should not forget their heritage otherwise they would become lost.

Lady Veronika had decked herself out in a very broadbrimmed white hat of the type often seen in China. It was so broad that anyone walking by her side was in danger of being struck by the brim and thus had to keep several paces distant. This may have been the purpose of such a hat as Lady Veronika had no time whatsoever for small talk.

Enzo had chosen what he called his 'Desert Hat'. This was green in colour with a peak, and protection at the back and sides from the sun. It was the sort of hat that he had seen Peter O'Toole wearing when he portrayed Lawrence of Arabia. It was certainly distinctive and, together with the guide's golden umbrella, he cut an unusual figure.

It was up to Harry to sport the faithful imitation of the Tilley hat which he called an 'Alpine' and was the sort of hat one might see in Australia rather than on the ski slopes of Switzerland.

It was for the New Zealand sisters to take first prize for the most distinctive headgear, although it must be said no one had suggested a contest. Back home in the lush valley of the Tukituki

River, they kept bees. They reasoned, with their flawless logic, that in a country like India, where flying insects were as numerous as people, there was only one suitable hat. So, they emerged, each wearing a beekeeper's straw hat with their faces completely shielded by opaque netting. Had de Barkley been on the tour he would undoubtedly have passed some comment which involved female followers of the Prophet, but as he was not, the group were spared his asides.

In case anyone did not have a sun hat, Enzo had brought with him enough paper hats to go round. They were not to everyone's taste, as they were inscribed *I'm a Golden Oldie*, a slogan which he had thought up all by himself and of which he was quite rightly proud. Only one member of the group – a solo passenger from an inside cabin somewhere near the engine room – took one, and insisted on wearing it back to front, much to Enzo's annoyance.

The mini-bus pulled up exactly three quarters of an hour late. The driver was the same one who had driven the small party to the dinner the previous evening. Now he drove a larger, but more ancient vehicle.

'Anyone for Billericay?' he shouted as he pulled up.

All but the twins were puzzled by this remark but one of the ladies from behind the net explained, 'He takes his holidays in Essex, you know. He loves the fresh air.'

Once settled and having been informed how to operate the

370

individual air conditioning, (open the window nearest to your seat), he crashed the antique trolley into gear and they were away. Enzo kept his eyes tightly closed for much of the journey to Alleppey. He was sitting in the front of the coach in a little jump seat next to the driver, and no matter how much he pleaded, the driver refused to slow down.

'If I slow, sir, many people get angry. They try takeover me, sir'.

Enzo understood him to mean 'overtake' but he did not trouble to say so.

The inevitable happened about one hour into the journey. They rounded a bend at breakneck speed as a trader, pushing a cart full of coconuts, veered just a little too far into the road - with the result that the cart went flying and coconuts flew in all directions like cannon balls. Several onlookers were winded by flying coconuts, and one poor fellow was completely knocked out as a nut caught him squarely on the head. The trader avoided injury by performing a leap that would have won him a Gold Medal at the Olympics. The small crowd applauded his agility. Unsurprisingly, he was not appeased by the acclaim and made a rush for the driver, who had stepped from the coach to inspect the damage.

Enzo, who had opened his eyes when he heard the impact and immediately closed them again, now opened them once more and motioned to the passengers to remain in their seats.

The coach was now surrounded by curious villagers, some of whom pressed close against the window, pointing and laughing at the exhibits inside. The twin sisters in particular were the subjects of considerable attention and caused a minor commotion when Petra, wearing her veiled beekeeping hat, opened a window to get a better view and caused a group of young boys to recoil in alarm at her appearance.

'Please stay in your seats and close all windows,' repeated Enzo. 'This matter has to be sorted out by the people themselves. We cannot be involved.'

A good half-hour passed and the coach grew increasingly hot. Harry passed around some semi-cool drinks whilst the driver continued to bargain with the trader. Finally, the matter was resolved and they were on their way again to waves and shouts from the onlookers.

'All OK, sir,' said the driver to Enzo as he resumed his former speed. 'No worry, sir. You get to boat, sir.'

Despite his anxiety, the heat proved too much for Enzo and he fell into a gentle slumber. He awoke to find that the coach was drawing to a halt and several armed men in military uniform were approaching the vehicle.

'Where are we?' he queried.

The driver looked nervous. 'I think very small trouble, sir. I take wrong road.'

Before Enzo could reply, two armed men had entered the

vehicle and ordered the driver and Enzo to get out, which they duly did. Enzo, wearing his green desert hat, bush shirt and khaki shorts, could easily have been mistaken for a half-crazed insurgent, and it was clear that the military types had their suspicions. Two more men entered the coach, and seeing what appeared to be a coach-load of extras for a *Carry On* film, ordered them all to descend. In fairness to the Indian military, it must be said that the passengers did not look like the normal tourists who visited the backwaters of Kerala.

Enzo looked around. It seemed that they had entered some sort of army compound. A number of military types lounged around an army truck without wheels which was being further dismembered by several men in oily overalls.

'Follow me,' ordered the soldier with stripes on his uniform.

The little group reluctantly picked up their haversacks and did as they were bidden. They skirted what seemed to be a parade ground and were ordered to wait outside a long low building. Enzo and the driver were taken inside where, thanks to a slowly revolving ceiling fan, it was slightly cooler.

The soldier with stripes knocked on a door and on receiving the command, 'Enter,' opened it and ordered his charges to follow.

A man in a well-tailored military outfit and bearing a distinguished moustache, finely waxed at each pointed end, sat behind a desk on which there was a red telephone and an empty filing tray.

'Sir,' said the stripes.

The officer nodded and looked curiously at Enzo. He spoke a few words in what was probably Hindi and then addressed him.

'Let me see in case.'

Enzo opened his holdall to reveal a couple of dozen paper hats emblazoned with his slogan.

'What you mean, Golden Oldie?' the officer queried.

Enzo tried his best but it was very difficult for him to attempt to describe just exactly what was meant by the legend. The officer looked more and more puzzled. Eventually he held up his hand, indicating Enzo should be quiet.

'Bring others,' said the officer.

There was a short interval whilst the other unfortunate members of the tour were marched across and one by one entered the room. As the last few were about to enter, there was a loud bang and a clatter - followed by a cry of anguish. Enzo, thinking that one member of his party had been shot, instinctively rushed to the door, only to observe Sir Archie nursing his dented pith helmet and surrounded by the shattered blades of the ceiling fan. The Chinese-hatted Lady Veronika, showing some concern for once in her life, tried to get nearer to him but was prevented by the wired broad brim of her headgear. A distinctly irate-looking soldier pushed Sir Archie into the room, and as he could not get near to Lady Veronika, pushed her also with the butt of his ancient 303 rifle. This caused her to release a stream of invective in Russian which resulted in another soldier prodding her with his rifle also and forcing her to join the others.

The group lined up before the officer, who examined then with a look of considerable curiosity on his face.

'Why are you here?' he asked in rather good English. 'And why are you wearing disguise?' As he said this he looked intently at the twins. 'You are terrorist,' he said. 'You hide your face.'

'Oh, did you hear that, Philippa?' said Petra to her twin sister. 'He said we are terrorists.' She looked at the officer through the net and brandished her umbrella at him. 'Let me tell you, young man,' she said, 'we live near the Tukituki River and are not terrorists.'

The officer didn't reply but switched on his computer. 'Give me your address,' he ordered. 'I will look on Google.'

Philippa gave the number of their house in the Elsthorpe Road.

'Ah!' he exclaimed excitedly. 'You have a terrorist camp there - Camp David. Is that where you train? You didn't know that would be on my computer, did you?'

'Don't be so silly,' said Philippa robustly. 'That is a holiday camp for young people.'

The officer snorted and once again perused the motley group before him.

'You have entered secret government property,' he said. 'We are now searching your coach and we will search you. This is very big trouble for you. Very big trouble.'

Enzo hitched up his Bombay Bloomers and looked appealingly at Harry, the universal fixer, who had been quiet to this point. Harry was just about to intervene when there was a sharp rap on the door and another officer entered. He babbled something, and the officer behind the desk shot to his feet. As he did so, a very grand-looking military type entered, smothered in gold braid – and who should follow him but none other than the Admiral.

'Good Heavens, Harry – and you also Bigatoni! Have I accidentally dropped in on a rehearsal for the Indian production of HMS Pinafore?'

Enzo, who was now too emotionally exhausted to say anything further, simply sat heavily on a low chair. Harry took the lead and explained the situation.

'Amazing,' said the Admiral, 'that today of all days I should come to this camp. I arranged with some of my old friends from the Indian Defence Staff to take a quick tour of one or two establishments whilst we had time in Cochin – and who should I find but you!'

Needless to say, apologies were issued all round, tea and digestive biscuits were served and the party rushed back to their coach. Much to Enzo's relief, the remainder of the day was uneventful. A military escort took them to Alleppey when they travelled even faster than they had done on the first part of the journey. Despite this they were very late indeed for the boat. Immediately they boarded, a meal of rice and Mezhukkupuratti (fried vegetable curry) was served and much fun was had by all in attempting to pronounce words on the menu. The sisters did agree to raise their veils to eat, and immediately dropped them once it was over. Thereafter, a lovely day was enjoyed by all and Enzo and Harry were thanked profusely by a group of tired but happy Golden Oldies.

Following their frightening experience on the roads of Kerala the previous evening, Albert and Alice decided that they would not travel to the backwaters. As Albert said, 'We have enough canals in England, and Suez was a washout.'

So they gave this unique part of India a miss.

As the ship would be in port throughout the day, they determined that they would take a walk ashore and try to buy one or two souvenirs and a postcard for the Robinson family with whom they had stayed in Southend-on-Sea. The day of the launch seemed a long time ago now, but they had not forgotten the kindness of the Robinsons and wanted to keep in touch.

Fred Batty, after spending hours on the internet, was a mine of information and advised the attendees at his lecture to be careful on shore as the Spice Market was somewhat pricy and tourists would be spotted a mile off. He advised a visit to Jew Town, the part of Cochin where, unsurprisingly, the old synagogue could be found, and which was an interesting place to explore. He also advised that it was a bit far to walk and it would be best to take a taxi or a tuk tuk. Budget-minded as always, despite his vast wealth, Albert decided on the three-wheeled vehicle, the tuk tuk, and somewhat reluctantly Alice went along with his choice. The helpful local guide at the exit from the dock gave them a map and pointed out where they should direct the driver to take them. It all went amazingly smoothly. They were alarmed at one point when out of a small side street there appeared an elephant with a wizened-looking figure riding it. However, they took this in their stride and alighted in a street full of small shops selling coloured scarves, beads, bangles and, believe it or not, postcards.

'By go,' said Albert when they returned to the ship for lunch,' it were crowded out there.'

Alice sat down immediately and started to write on a post-card with a picture of a decorated elephant walking down the same street along which they had walked that very morning.

'*Saw an elephant today*' she wrote slowly. '*Very busy here. Lots of Indian food. Love from Alice and Albert*'.

Albert read it and asked for the pen. He scribbled on the bottom of the card, '*A bit like Grimsby!*'

35

The chaplain was greatly pleased with his clothes. They were delivered to the ship exactly as promised and he tried on the clerical suit immediately. It fitted perfectly, as did the new suit for casual wear. As a little extra, the tailor had kindly included half a dozen silk handkerchiefs and, to the chaplain's surprise, two lady's silk scarves. With them was a handwritten note which read:

Rev Sir,

Your esteemed custom is valued and I have pleasure in enclosing the items that you entrusted me with. If Rev Sir you might recommend me to your Brothers, and especially to His Lord the Archbishop of Canterbury, as we are always ready to serve. I have enclosed a small gift for you Sir and for your charming wife who was with you when you did the honour of visiting my emporium.

May you always be blessed Sir.

Ajatashatru Thomas

The chaplain read the note through twice and blushed. Angela, his wife! He would certainly pass the scarves on to her, but would not show her the note as that would be too embarrassing for both of them. Angela, his wife? It was a totally new thought for him and it played through his mind constantly.

Back on the ship and safely ensconced in his Balcony Suite, Sir Archie examined the damaged pith helmet. He was damned annoyed that it had been hit by the low ceiling fan but, as it had not been holed, only dented, it might be possible to have it restored to its former glory. He had travelled the tropical regions of the world with that helmet and to lose it now would have been too much to bear. As one got older, he reflected, one became attached to artefacts that reminded one of earlier days and this helmet was one such object.

Lady Veronika, who had maintained her customary silence during most of the visit to the backwaters, sat at the small dressing-table writing in a leather-covered notebook in an indecipherable script. Her days spent in the Siberian Secret Service (SSS) had enabled her to form lifelong habits, and keeping a secret detailed record of people and places was one of them. She intrigued Sir Archie, as he could not be sure if she was still attached to the SSS or not. Whenever he had tried to raise the subject she had quickly diverted the conversation (such conversation as she was capable of) onto another subject. He had concluded that, although she was most probably not in the full-time employ of the agency, she still maintained a close relation-ship - but for what purpose he could not fathom. Who supplied her with huge quantities of yak's milk when she was back in England? It wasn't the sort of item one might find easily in Waitrose, but it came to her regularly and, as far as he knew, no bills had ever been received. Who was it who ensured that when the ship docked at various ports around the world, yak's milk was always awaiting to be delivered to the ship? Her husband accepted the fact that there would always be an element of mystery about their relationship - and that was what made it interesting.

Lady Veronika finished her scribbling, closed the book and secured it with a small lock. Why this latter measure was required Sir Archie could never understand as the script was about as readable as Proto-Elamite, a language yet to be deciphered. Perhaps it *was* Proto-Elamite, he mused, and laughed to himself.

Lady Veronika secured the locked book in a briefcase and in turn placed the briefcase in a drawer which she locked. Then she addressed him.

'*Dorogoy*,' she said. (In private she always addressed him as 'Darling' in Russian.) '*Dorogoy*, Captain ask we eat lunch with him. Today. Good?'

'Very good, my dear,' replied Sir Archie.' 'Where shall we eat?'

'Captain say small table on deck. Good?'

'Excellent. Quite excellent,' replied her husband. 'What time?'

'Now,' she answered. 'This minute. We go now.'

Sir Archie, somewhat taken by surprise, found his old rowing cap in a drawer and the couple set off for the deck table.

Captain Sparda was seated when they arrived; he stood up and greeted them warmly, but with some deference due to their titled position.

'Ah, Sir Archibald and Lady Veronika. How good to see you both. Please take a seat.'

Lady Veronika sat down and scowled. The scowl meant nothing in particular. It was purely habitual but it had the effect of putting people off and thinking that they had made some terrible faux pas. It was quite a useful device for Lady Veronika as it made the person with whom she was talking feel uncomfortable and thus gave her an advantage. She had used the scowl to great effect when, posing as a Siberian Orthodox Bishop, she had been able to uncover a major tax-evasion scheme operating in the wastes of her country. Her deep contralto voice and authentic false beard, aided by the scowl, so intimidated the junior clerics that they confessed all. Sir Archie was not aware of this, nor of many other exotic adventures his wife had experienced, but he was familiar with the scowl, especially when it was directed at him and did mean something!

The scowl caught Sparda full on and engendered the usual response.

'Is everything well with you both?' He enquired anxiously. 'I trust you are enjoying the luxury of your Balcony Suite. Later in the cruise I shall be pleased to invite you to dine at my table in the evening,' he said, hoping for a thaw in what he felt was an icy atmosphere.

Lady Veronika remained mute but Sir Archie, always one to promote a warmer climate, chipped in, 'Jolly decent of you, Captain. Lovely old ship this. Quite lovely.'

Sparda, feeling a little warmer, turned to the lunch drinks and the menu.

'What will you both have?' he asked genially. 'I enjoy a cider at lunchtime but please choose what you like.'

Sir Archie selected a small Light Ale. Lady Veronika continued to scowl before speaking.

'A glass of yak's milk with a large vodka on side,' she said to a startled waiter, who had not served her previously.

'Lady Veronika has her own supply,' said the Captain. 'See Mr Tucker - he knows.'

The waiter scurried away and they resumed perusing the menu. By the side of the deck was an iron griddle on which a chef was grilling chops, steaks and sweetcorn. Savoury smoke drifted across the table.

'I shall have griddle,' said Lady Veronika, direct as ever. 'Big steak underdone. Two sausage. One chop. Corn. That is good, eh, Captain?'

Sparda agreed that it was quite excellent and put in the order with a piece of grilled fish for himself and a mutton chop with a baked potato and salad for Sir Archie.

'Now,' said Sparda, as two large plates were put before Lady Veronika. 'This lunch is just the beginning for you.'

For once Lady Veronika managed a half-smile. She was a hearty eater and one of those irritating individuals who eat more than enough and never seem to put on weight.

'We enjoy good lunch,' she said as she tackled the steak. 'In Siberia we eat good.'

'Plenty of frozen foods, I imagine,' said Sparda, in an attempt to introduce some humour into the occasion.

Sir Archie laughed loudly but Lady Veronika resumed her customary expression.

'Well,' said the Captain, getting to the point, 'I am told by Mr Bigatoni, our Cruise Director, that you have won a very special prize. Many congratulations, I must say.'

Sir Archie beamed. 'It was my very clever wife,' he said. 'Nothing to do with me.'

'Well, you will both benefit to the tune of five hundred pounds,' said Sparda.

The observant would have noticed a slight expression of

pain cross the Captain's features as he mentioned the money, but it went unnoticed by his guests. It quickly passed and he continued.

'The ship will provide you with an exclusive excursion at any port at which we call. Everything will be provided to the tune of five hundred pounds.'

'I say,' said Sir Archie enthusiastically, 'that sounds jolly good. My dear?'

Lady Veronika, busy gnawing at a chop bone, said nothing.

'Splendid offer, Captain,' he said. 'I fancy a good rugby match in New Zealand.'

Sparda was just about to applaud this when he became aware that the scowl had deepened. He held back as Lady Veronika replaced the bone on her plate.

'Nyet!' she exclaimed. 'We have TV. We see plenty sport. I want visit in Sri Lanka to see Tigers.'

Sir Archie looked considerably surprised. 'Tigers,' he repeated. 'Tigers? Are there tigers in Sri Lanka? News to me, my dear. What about you, Captain? Have you seen tigers in Sri Lanka?'

Sparda, who for the past thirty years had hardly left the Straits of Messina where he certainly did not encounter tigers, said he had not. Lady Veronika gave a look that would have frozen solid the Light Ale in the Captain's glass had she directed her gaze in that direction.

'Tamil Tigers,' she exclaimed. 'Very interesting.'

Neither Sparda, nor Sir Archie could possibly imagine why on earth Lady Veronika should want to visit such a group - and they were never to find out the real reason. The truth was that some years back, when Lady Veronika was active in the SSS, a group of Tamil Tigers had been sent to Siberia for tactical training. The fact that Sri Lanka was normally sweltering and in Siberia the temperature in the winter was always below freezing did not help matters, nor was it a help that the Tigers were sent over in the winter. Many suffered from frostbite, and learning how to fight guerrilla warfare in snow and ice was not a great asset to them. They only accepted because all expenses were found. Lady Veronika was in charge of a part of this highly secret operation and the visit to Sri Lanka, especially now that there was a peace agreement of sorts in the country, seemed a good time to renew old friendships.

'Well dear, if that is what you want,' said Sir Archie equably. 'I am sure you can arrange something, Captain.'

'I'll get my man Harry onto it,' Sparda replied. 'He knows his way around.'

Lady Veronika ordered a double portion of ice cream with whipped cream, and the others asked for an espresso. Then lunch was over.

'Delightful,' said Sir Archie. 'Quite delightful, Captain.'

Lady Veronika managed a nod of agreement and they parted

- the Captain to visit Harry, and the Willoughby's to retire to their Balcony Suite to enjoy a restful afternoon.

36

The chaplain stood and thanked everyone for coming.

'Good evening, everyone,' he said to the group who had seated themselves in different parts of the room. There must have been about twenty people present, both male and female, and about five male crew members.

'Tonight,' he went on, 'we want to select two choirs: the Golden Glory Choir to sing at the Sunday-morning services, and a smaller group, the Benbow Singers, to sing at the Admiral's birthday. Angela and I will listen to you each in turn and then we shall select which choir you join. Everyone will be in one choir or the other. Now, who will begin?'

Immediately the twins from New Zealand came forward. One could never accuse these remarkable ladies of holding back in life.

'We belong to the Ypuck Singers,' said Philippa.

'And have been members for fifty years,' chimed in Petra. 'Each year we sing at the Napier Art Deco Week, don't we, Philippa?'

'We do indeed,' said her sister.

Felix de Barkley who turned up for every event on board ship, could not remain quiet.

'I suppose that explains why the town was once devastated,' he quipped.

Few people knew that he was referring to a great earthquake that had flattened the town years back and so he did not get much of a laugh.

Ignoring the interruption, Angela asked the ladies what they would like to sing. They could choose anything as Rod played by ear and there was little that he could not manage.

'There is a lovely little song that we have sung many a time at the Arts Festival,' said Philippa, 'but it may be too difficult for dear Mr Saddleworth to play without music.'

'Try me,' said Rod, raring to go. 'What is it?'

'Well,' said Petra demurely, 'it's called There's a Hole in my Bucket. Philippa will sing one part and I shall sing the other.'

De Barkley put his hand to his head. 'Oh God,' he cried. 'What a tuneless load of old cobblers that is.'

'Please, Mr de Barkley,' admonished Angela. 'They may choose what they feel comfortable with. Do begin, ladies.'

Rod struck up and the twins sang the first couple of verses. Alas, the New Zealand vocalists had passed their peak well before the Napier earthquake struck, and their rendering was not in any way aided by the tuneless dirge they had elected to sing. Even the chaplain looked pained and he certainly was not one to talk.

Angela held up her hand. 'That will do now, ladies. Thank you both very much.'

'But Angela dear, there are another fifteen verses yet, plus the ones we added to give the song a local flavour,' said Petra, anxious to continue.

'This is just an audition,' replied Angela patiently. 'We have to keep each item short otherwise we will never hear all twenty-five people.'

She made a mark against their names and asked for the next person. This time a member of the ship's company came forward.

'Ah, Mr Aberdeen!' she exclaimed. 'I am so glad you could get away from the engine room to join us this afternoon.'

There could have been no greater contrast between the somewhat petite sisters from the river valley and Angus Aberdeen, eighteen stone of muscle from Scotland. Few people could understand what he said as his accent was somewhat broad, despite the fact that it had been said that some Scottish people spoke the clearest English going. By listening carefully, Angela made out that he was going to sing a song made famous by the doorbells of the Balcony Suites, 'Ye Tak the High Road'.

His voice shook the room as he indicated in song the road he would take to his beloved home country. The twins, accustomed to what might be described as 'Drawing Room' singing, placed their hands over their ears and de Barkley sought shelter behind a curtain.

'Thank you, Mr Aberdeen,' said Angela, always politeness itself. 'You have a strong voice and ought to be part of a bass section in the choir.'

The audition took a very long time indeed, but by the end of the session a choir of six had been chosen to form the Benbow Singers and the remainder were selected for the Golden Glory Choir. Rehearsals could now begin in earnest.

Sri Lanka was not too far away by now and the ship was holding together remarkably well despite earlier problems. Back in his cabin, Mr van der Loon was congratulating himself on getting another booking on board a ship. Word had got out through emails that his show was amazing, and quick as a flash an invitation had come in to transfer to another vessel immediately the *Golden Handshake* arrived in Sri Lanka. And so Mr van der Loon began packing ready to leave for pastures new.

Back in the engine room after his brief audition for the choir, Angus MacDonald urgently sought a meeting with the Admiral, the Captain and Harry. He was responsible for the Internet on the ship and the move to more amenable opening hours satisfied both himself and the passengers. The quality was, to put things mildly, appalling. Users were being charged from the very second they opened the computer until the last flicker had disappeared from the screen. All too frequently the service broke down completely and, as for speed, or to be more accurate, lack of it, that was something to be marvelled at.

'I could tak the bloody high road and the low road from Land's End to Jimmy Porridge's,' he said, 'and still get there before an email sent from this ship.'

Angus had a unique humour not always understood by Sassenachs or indeed many of his fellow countrymen. By 'Jimmy Porridge's' he was of course referring to John O' Groats, but who was to know that? Despite the internet troubles, that was not the main issue he wanted to discuss with the 'Three Wise Men' as he sometimes called them. On one of the few occasions he had been able to get onto the web, he had come across the Wikiwatts site. Remembering the noxious Toby Troy, he investigated further and came across the following trailer:

"Alarming Revelations - British Admiral in
Spy Scandal.
Innocent Cruise Passengers
Used As Cover for Intelligence Gathering."

'Next week our special undercover reporter, Tobias Troy, will reveal the shocking details of a massive cover-up. He will tell how Intelligence agencies, together with the Church of England, duped innocent

holidaymakers on board a British cruise ship. He will describe the reckless behaviour of the Captain off a foreign coast when his Intelligence-gathering mission was apprehended. He will name names and nail villains. This report is a must for all who love truth and wish for greater transparency by our Government.

Whilst the internet held up, Angus printed the item and it was this he held in his hand as he entered the Captain's tiny office. Angus was a man of few words and, as has been stated before, that was fortunate as no one could understand him. This time he was agitated, and the moment he sat down, he began a long spiel about the discoveries he had made on the web. At least, it was long for him - even though it was only about three sentences in length. The Wise Men stared at him baffled.

'Could you kindly repeat that, Mr Aberdeen,' said the Admiral with a puzzled look on his face. 'I didn't quite catch every word.'

Angus repeated the substance of what he had said but this time added a further sentence. The Wise Men looked at each other and then returned their gaze to the informant.

'Do you have that important information in writing?' asked the Admiral, not having a clue as to whether it was important or not. Fortunately Angus had not forgotten the copy he had made and he handed it over. The trio studied the copy together then the Admiral spoke.

'This could be serious for the whole of Golden Oceans,' he said. 'It could radically affect our sailings in Poole Harbour – and as for the Frinton service, well, I can see this sort of mis-information greatly disturbing the inhabitants of that part of rural Essex. Essex County Council could easily refuse us a per-mit to sail from there – and what then? It's all too bad, Mr Aber-deen. All too bad.'

It was now Sparda's turn to speak and, as his loathing of Troy was so intense, rather than comment on the document before him, he let fly some of the most powerful invective ever to have circulated in his office. Not only was the language colour-ful, the volume was also tremendous, so much so that passengers in the shop several doors away thought a tragedy was about to take place and ran to their cabins to don lifebelts.

It was left to Harry, the fixer extraordinaire, to come forward with a proposal.

'Captain, he said, 'do you not have interesting relatives in Sicily?'

Sparda agreed that there were several cousins in Catania who were in the construction industry; they visited him from time to time, but he was inclined to keep his distance.

'Right,' said Harry. 'You might want to mention to them – in passing, of course – that a certain Tobias Troy is about to besmirch the family name of Sparda along with his accomplice at Wikkiwatts.'

'I don't think I heard that,' said the Admiral. 'We can't have any violence, you know, Harry. Definitely no violence.'

'Of course not,' agreed Harry, 'but they might put the frighteners on Toby boy.'

Sparda's eyes lit up. 'Harry,' he said, 'you're a genius and a gentleman.'

'Leave it to me,' said Harry, tapping his nose.

The meeting broke up and it was a worried Admiral who returned to his cabin to ponder the terrible news. He himself was not at all happy about involving Sparda's relatives. Apart from inciting criminal activity, Golden Oceans would be forever in their debt and he was sure that this debt would never be paid off.

He could speak to his contact at the D Notices Committee, but such a body was virtually useless against the likes of Wiki-watts. Besides, the allegations were total hogwash.

Life takes some strange turns at times. The unpredictable can fall from a clear blue sky without a moment's notice and change circumstances in a trice. As the Admiral worried and the other Wise Men considered their options, Mr Assad Wikiwatts himself found that he was the subject of intense scrutiny. By coincidence, he had actually been in Italy, personally investigating a suspected fraud case, in which ordinary commonplace onions were said to have been liberally mixed with expensive imported

Dutch tulip bulbs, together with a few daffodils. They were sold to the Vatican, at a very high price, to plant in the Pope's private garden. The Pope did not mind an occasional onion, but when hundreds sprouted instead of a colourful array of choice blooms, the Holy Father was more than a little agitated. Mr Assad himself went to investigate this great scam but, unfortunately, encountered an irate Dutchman of almost seven feet tall who chased him around Rome. Poor Assad was obliged to seek refuge in the Vatican itself, or that is what is believed, for he disappeared totally from view. Away from the office, his news outlet collapsed and Troy's story disappeared as quickly as it had emerged.

'I sometimes think,' said Harry when this incredible story had been related to him, 'that our little ship might have some protection from On High.'

He was in the company of the chaplain, who nodded wisely.

'It's certainly possible, Mr Parkhurst,' he replied. 'God moves in mysterious ways.'

'He certainly does,' replied Harry.

And with that they both got up and went along to choir practice.

37

To the great delight of Mr van der Loon and his two companions, a very large group of passengers gathered at the gangway to bid the little party farewell as they disembarked in Sri Lanka. Nelson, the amazing parrot, delighted the ladies by calling from the dockside, 'Goodbye, my lovelies!' which ensured him a place in their hearts for ever!

'You know, Alice,' said Albert, as they considered whether to go ashore before lunch or wait until the afternoon, 'the more we travel, the hotter it gets. It's boiling here.'

Alice agreed that it was very hot indeed and not much better in the Balcony Suite as the air conditioning was not of the best. Mr and Mrs Potts stumped off the ship early, the old man walking with a stick that he had obtained in Cochin and of which he was very proud. Although it gave him a feeling of well-being, he remained morose in appearance and it was doubtful at this stage in his life if that would ever change.

Mr Fennington Barley, the retired dancing farmer, had rather fallen for one of the elderly widows on board who came from a farming family in Iowa. It was strictly against Golden

Oceans policy for a dance host to show favouritism to any one individual – even if, as was often the case, ladies favoured him. To overcome this difficulty he had suggested that he might go ashore with a group of several of his dancing partners, and the lady in question, a Mrs Dora Guttenburg, would certainly sit next to him at every available opportunity. This caused some jostling for places at lunch which resulted in two rather well-built ladies occupying the same seat at a café, until the helpful waiter appeared with reinforcements.

It proved to be a very hot and sticky day, especially for four ladies of ample girth squeezed into the back of a taxi. Mr Barley never actually got to sit next to Mrs Guttenburg and this irritated him as he had gone to considerable expense in paying for the whole group to travel throughout Colombo and to dine also. Normally when in port he would rush back to the ship to enjoy a free lunch and then rush ashore again. On this visit he considered that would appear mean and so he was landed with bills for refreshments for five and also lunch for five. An expensive day, especially when he did not achieve proximity to the widow.

Harry Parkhurst had been totally occupied in making arrangements for Sir Archie and Lady Veronika to visit the Tamil Tigers. Although he had made it up with Enzo, he was still considerably annoyed that the foolish fellow had given away five hundred pounds and made a promise, on behalf of the ship, which was very difficult to fulfil. Admittedly Lady Veronika, because of her previous association with the Tigers, had made life easier for him. She had put him in contact with a private airline who would fly the three of them to some obscure destination. He quailed when he received the quote, as the sum required would leave very little for a grand dinner in the evening. Oh well. He would cross that bridge when he came to it, he thought.

'I say, my dear, these Tiger chappies.' Sir Archie was applying some Blanco to his pith helmet in preparation for another long hot journey. 'They are straight up, are they? We can't afford to be delayed long with them, you know.'

'*Dorogoy*,' she replied with more than a hint of irritation in her voice, 'I know Tigers. OK?'

Sir Archie knew better than to dispute with his Siberian wife or even to question her. Although she was exceptionally quiet in public, she smouldered within, and smoke and flame were released at a time when he was the only unfortunate recipient. He had been singed too often for his liking, so he remained silent and applied himself to the task in hand.

As soon as the ship had obtained Port Clearance and Enzo had come on the primitive address system to announce this, Harry met with his charges. Sir Archie was resplendent in his helmet and buttoned to the neck khaki drill uniform. He looked for all the world like a character drawn from the pages of Kipling.

Lady Veronika wore a long dress that seemed hardly appropriate for hot weather, but Harry assumed that as she had lived in a cold climate, what she was wearing might be considered very light indeed. On her head she wore a 1920's style hat of the type favoured by the late Duchess of Windsor. She carried with her a very heavy case, within which were several bottles of Siberian vodka and a very expensive sable fur coat.

'I think Tiger Chief like coat for wife,' she said, as she showed Harry what she intended to take on the flight.

Harry did not remind her that fur coats were not frequently worn in Sri Lanka. He felt he had enough to cope with, without getting into further discussion.

As they were about to leave, Enzo appeared, all smiles. He was apprehensive about seeing the couple off as Harry was taking them when it ought to have been him doing it. Given the sensitive nature of the visit, there was no way in which Harry would have entrusted Sir Archie and his odd wife to Enzo. The latter's record as tour leader was far from 100 per cent, and Harry could not afford this particular trip to go wrong. Effusive as always, Enzo expressed delight at the destination chosen by the couple, even though he had no idea where it was they were going. It was part of his job to pretend to know everything - and he did that part of his job superbly.

Just as Enzo was about to return to his office, who should appear but the doctor, who was also planning a day ashore.

'By jingo,' he said, as he viewed Sir Archie and his wife. 'If you're filming the discovery of the source of the Nile you're in the wrong part of the world, old boy.'

Harry looked a him sternly, but not sternly enough to silence him.

'Watch out for the crocs, Enzo. They recognise a good dinner at fifty paces.'

Enzo explained that he was simply seeing off the travellers and not going ashore himself.

'Pity,' chuckled the medic. 'The most effective way for you to lose weight would be to have an encounter with a croc!'

Sir Archie laughed and Lady Veronika remained mute as usual. With a cheery 'Pip Pip' the doctor trotted down the gangway. Enzo wished the intrepid couple a very happy day and returned to his inner sanctum.

With the heavy case safely in the boot of an ancient motor vehicle, the trio set forth for the airport. The driver, suitably dressed in peaked cap and gold braided livery, drove at a stately pace to what appeared to be a grass landing-strip some miles away from the ship. Harry, to his alarm, saw two small biplanes parked side by side. Each was open-topped and looked exactly like the planes he had seen in pictures of the Wright Brothers or Amy Johnson. He prayed that one of the antiques was not the aircraft he would fly in, and he was right. One wasn't, but the other was! Sir Archie and his wife were assigned aircraft

Number One and he was assigned aircraft Number Two. They entered a hut, no bigger than a garden shed, where two leather-clad individuals were drinking tea.

'G'day,' said one in an Australian accent that would have terrified the average citizen of Sydney, let alone the UK.

Lady Veronika remained impassive. Bruce, the one who greeted them, nodded in the direction of his companion.

'That's Kevin,' he said. 'Ever since he had to make a forced landing in the Main Street of Sydney, Kevin doesn't say much. I think the police can be tough on that sort of thing there.'

Harry swallowed hard and greeted the two aviators.

'Like your clobber, mate,' said Bruce, eyeing Sir Archie's khaki uniform, 'but you can't wear that bloody beehive in the plane.'

He handed the party leather flying helmets and a pair of goggles each.

'I hope you've got your winter grundies on, it can get damn parky up there.'

Harry wondered at this point if Lady Veronika knew something he did not, as she was pretty well covered for the flight, especially when she slipped the fur coat on.

'Nice bit of rabbit,' grinned Bruce. 'Who got the pie?'

Lady Veronika had yet to speak and the rhetorical question asked by Bruce was treated with the disdain it deserved.

'OK,' said Bruce, slapping Kevin on the back. 'Time to say

our prayers. We're off.'

Sir Archie left his precious headgear in a corner and the case with the vodka was stowed and secured in the spare seat in plane Number Two. The prizewinners were safely placed in the two seats in the Number One plane. It was slightly unnerving for Harry as the pilot in this ancient biplane sat behind him, so Harry was directly at the front.

Kevin came to life when they were on board. 'Strap yerself in, mate,' he ordered, as Harry settled into a somewhat confined space. 'Your job is to keep your mud pies peeled! Look out for jets. Get caught in their slipstream and we are goners. There's no bang seat in this old kite, you know, so you would have to jump.'

In flight Number One Lady Veronika occupied the very front seat with Sir Archie at her side and bringing up the rear, Bruce.

When everyone was as comfortable as they could be, an elderly man, wearing tattered blue overalls, ambled over from nowhere in particular and removed the chocks from under the wheels of both planes. He gave a few swings of the propeller of plane Number One, which soon spluttered into life. He repeated the action for Number Two and then ambled away again as casually as he had arrived. Bruce and Kevin gave each other the thumbs-up sign and both flights bumped their way across the rough grass.

Once aloft, Kevin maintained his lively attitude. Now,

instead of increasing his verbal attributes, he showed what he could do as far as flying an aircraft was concerned. For a while he followed the lead aircraft. After several minutes, he shouted forward to Harry, 'Is the juice safely secured?'

Harry had personally supervised the loading of the vodka in the spare seat and assured Kevin that all was OK.

'Righto,' he responded, then: 'Make sure you don't fall out', and with that he took the biplane into a most terrifying dive.

Harry gripped the edge of the cockpit in terror as Kevin pulled out of the descent and began to climb vertically. By now Harry had lost all sense of direction and had closed both eyes tightly. Suddenly, he experienced more curious sensations as the biplane completed a backward arc and began yet another rapid descent. The little engine groaned and strained as Kevin levelled out and then began to roll the plane over in a circular motion until they were flying upside down. Harry thanked his stars that he had indeed secured his belts properly, otherwise he would certainly have descended at an even more rapid rate than his conveyance. Eventually they resumed their correct flying position.

'Great little bus this,' said Kevin with genuine enthusiasm. 'No time for any more now, mate. Sorry about that.'

It was a greatly relieved Harry Parkhurst who followed the next set of instructions that came from behind, which was to keep a lookout for flight Number One. Try as he might, Harry could see no sign of another plane. Kevin banked to the left and then to the right, but there was nothing to see except blue sky.

'Too bad,' he shouted. 'Bruce is the one who knows where we are going. I don't!'

Harry groaned inwardly. The ship had been plagued with problems since the terrible launch from Southend and, on the whole, they had managed to keep the passengers happy. Now for him of all people to lose two important Balcony Suite passengers was too much.

'I'm going to put down,' bawled Kevin, and began to descend towards a stretch of deserted beach. He flew low to see if it was clear, then he banked, turned and within a few moments the little plane was taxiing to a halt. Both men climbed out and removed their helmets.

'Hold on, mate,' said Kevin. 'I'm bursting. Must go and syphon the python.' He went round to the other side of the plane and returned a few moments later. 'Pity we've no tinnies,' he said, 'but what about cracking open the firewater?'

'Look, Kevin,' said Harry, anxious and somewhat angry, 'the vodka is not ours - it belongs to the guests who I am supposed to be accompanying to an important meeting. Now you have lost them. What do you intend to do?'

Kevin scratched his head and looked hurt.

'Sorry, mate,' he said. 'The radio in the plane packed up last week so that's crook. I think Bruce wrote down some directions which are in my kit somewhere.'

He rummaged in a compartment, whilst Harry marvelled at the casual incompetence of his pilot. Some people on the *Handshake* were bad enough, but this was frankly ridiculous. Eventually Kevin produced a crumpled piece of paper which looked as though it was last used to wrap sandwiches in.

'Got it!' he exclaimed with glee. 'Right, mate, back on board and chocks away.'

Once more Harry strapped himself in, adjusted his helmet and goggles, and they were off along the deserted beach as though they were competing for the land-speed record of Sri Lanka. Once aloft, Kevin kept quiet for about half an hour until he startled Harry by shouting, 'There they are, mate! What a beaut!'

Way down below Harry could see a grass strip with flight Number One positioned to the side of it.

He breathed a sigh of relief as they landed, removed his helmet and goggles and went across to join the small group who had come to meet them. For a moment, Harry thought that there was going to be a stand-up fight. To put it politely, Bruce was very cross with Kevin and told him so. Kevin responded by returning a further string of insults, after which they both went off in search of a beer.

Sir Archie, clearly missing his pith helmet, had knotted a large white handkerchief over the top of his perspiring head. He greeted Harry like a long-lost relative.

'My dear boy,' he uttered, 'when we saw your plane doing those remarkable gyrations we really thought you had been shot down. Thank goodness you're alive and well. We were most worried, let me tell you.'

Harry explained that Kevin had got carried away and then lost the lead plane.

'Well, it's very good to see you,' Sir Archie repeated. 'Come on, let's go and meet the others. My dear wife is having private talks with someone from the Tigers at the moment and so I was just having a refresher.' He poured something from a hip flask and offered it to Harry, who refused.

'By the way, have you got the vodka?' Sir Archie said as he quaffed the drink himself.

Harry confirmed that he had.

'I'm not sure it will be appreciated, Harry, as most of the chappies are Muslims or Hindus. It was my wife's idea to bring it. She thinks the whole world likes the stuff. Well, they say there are one or two Christians up here and they always enjoy a bit of a tipple, what?'

A young man was dispatched to unload the bottles from the cockpit, and whatever religion he followed he seemed overjoyed with the booty.

Harry surveyed the scene around him. A flat airstrip on which the two planes were the only aircraft, and a few wooden huts with several young men milling around doing nothing in particular. Not a sign of any arms. It all seemed most placid.

'I say,' said Sir Archie, when half an hour had passed, 'my dear wife is taking rather a long time, eh? We can't afford to linger, Harry. It's a long way back, you know.'

Harry knew all too well and was as anxious as his charge.

'These Tiger boys are dangerous fellows,' the other man went on. 'I know Veronika knows some of them, but I confess I'm worried. I thought she would be met by the folks she knew from the past, but not so. They took her off, as I thought, to see the chief.'

Both Harry and Sir Archie were beginning to think the worst when there was a sound of crashing through the undergrowth some distance away and several elephants appeared walking in single file and linked trunk to tail.

'Good Lord!' cried Sir Archie. 'Is that Veronika up on high?'

Harry looked at the lead elephant and, sure enough, there was a figure in a long skirt and cloche hat balanced precariously on its back. A little man with a stick guided the procession in their direction, and when the familiar features of Lady Veronika became visible, he could see that the customary scowl was exceptionally severe.

The elephants stopped and the chief mahout gave a command, at which Lady Veronika was gently lowered to the ground. With her usual composure she walked across to Sir Archie and indicated that she wished to speak to him in private. Harry discreetly withdrew but, even some distance away, he could hear her voice booming out in what he assumed was Russian. It did not seem like a happy reunion at all. After ten minutes or so the couple returned. Sir Archie, somewhat red in the face and sweating even more beneath his knotted handkerchief, indicated to Harry that they had better leave now. Harry summoned the pilots, both of whom were fast asleep, and with the briefest of farewells they were airborne again.

It was some time before Harry understood what had occurred on that strange visit to the secret camp of the Tamil Tigers. Somehow, somewhere, instructions had got scrambled. When Harry's contact had heard that two cruise passengers wanted to visit the Tigers, he thought there was a mistake as there are no tigers in the country, only a very rare species of Black Leopard. Thinking that the visitors were animal lovers, he arranged for them to visit an elephant training camp instead, and that is where they finished up and why Lady Veronika was so annoyed. Not only had she handed over a precious sable fur coat, but also a whole crate of the finest vodka, to a character who might well have been portrayed by Kipling in one of his jungle tales.

38

'It is not certain how many islands there are in Indonesia.'

The Admiral was holding forth to a small group of passengers gathered in the lounge of the *Golden Handshake*.

'Some say seventeen thousand, others over eighteen. Whatever, there are a lot,' he said, as he sipped his pink gin.

'Easy to confuse them,' said one of the party.

'Oh, I don't know,' replied Sir Benbow confidently. 'With modern navigation, such as this ship possesses, seamen have little difficulty. I remember when I was in command during my days in the Service of Her Majesty, God bless her, we sailed through these waters without the slightest of problems.'

The group sat back in their seats, glad to be on board a vessel where there was such a wealth of professional ability on hand.

Up on deck, it was sweltering. The primitive air conditioning just about made life tolerable below decks, but even though the ship was at sea where there was a slight breeze, the heat and humidity were considerable. Radley Duvet, the Hotel Manager, decided the time had come to reveal to the passengers a feature that had been kept hidden from them since they departed from Southend. It was now the time to inform them that on deck, bathing facilities would be available immediately.

He imagined, quite correctly, that this news would come as a surprise to all as there was not the slightest sign of a swimming pool on deck. There was, however, an area on the main deck that had remained covered over since the start of the cruise. Very few, if any, of the passengers, knew that the *Handshake* had formerly been a cattle transporter. A remarkable job of conversion had been accomplished and there were virtually no artefacts left on board to give a hint of former days. True, early on in the cruise, there had been the slight aroma of horses - but that passed quickly and virtually everyone on board now believed that the ship was built especially for cruising. The covered area on the deck, however, gave a clue to former days as it was, in fact, a long cattle trough.

It was certainly not possible for anyone, no matter how slightly built, to *swim* in the trough, but it was ideal for passengers to sit and dangle their feet in the water and thus get some cooling relief from the raging temperature surrounding them. Along the back of the trough some rather colourful chairs had been placed so that twelve passengers at a time could occupy a seat and enjoy bathing their feet in the water. It was reasoned by those who thought of this innovation that, as most passengers were of mature years, they would not wish to swim but would prefer to paddle as they did with their grandchildren on a visit to the seaside.

Radley, who was very proud of the pool, requested the Admiral to open it, but, anxious for more of the senior staff to share something of the glory, the Admiral suggested that both Radley and Enzo declare the pool open and that the chaplain be invited to bless it. He further suggested that as the Chief Engineer would be responsible for the pool, he also ought to be with the party and so Angus Aberdeen was once again hauled up from the depths.

It was determined that, after the official opening, the pool would then be available for the first three hours to Balcony Suite passengers, the following three hours to Grade One cabins, and on the following day to the remainder of the passengers. There-after, it was first come first served. Radley had prepared a little notice which said that it would not be possible to reserve seats once the pool was fully operative and no towels were to be left on seats to reserve them. Once a passenger had left a seat, then it would become vacant and available for use by another. During stormy weather the pool would be closed, of course.

On a sweltering morning, when the ship was somewhere en route to Indonesia, a small procession made its way to the upper deck. Radley and Enzo walked side by side, dressed for the occasion in their immaculate tropical whites. They were followed by the Admiral in similar dress except that he dazzled many of the onlookers by an extensive range of medals, which one wit (guess who) said made him look like a mobile Christmas Tree. The chaplain brought up the rear, soberly attired in a white cassock which Angela had had made for him by the ship's tailor.

The famous eagle lectern had been brought into use once again; it stood on a small dais along with several chairs placed there for the processional party. To the side of the stage stood a group of Balcony Suite passengers in bare feet, ready once the pool was officially opened, to take their seats by the trough.

Albert and Alice were first in line. Albert's trousers were rolled up to his knees and he wore a collarless shirt, together with his flat cap, to give him protection from the sun. Alice wore what she called her 'Summer Outfit,' which was yet another flowered dress - this time made up from a pattern in *Floral Life*. Before coming out on deck she had sent Albert off to see what Mrs Potts was wearing, as she would have been mortified had they dressed alike yet again. As Mr and Mrs Potts were no longer Balcony Suite passengers they were not amongst the elite but they were in attendance all the same. Alice was calmed when Albert reported that Mrs P was wearing a trouser suit which made her look a bit on the fat side.

Sir Archie was lined up but, alas, without his lady wife. She had said that there was no paddling in Siberia and she had no intention of paddling now. Sir Archie had paddled all his life in the freezing waters off the Norfolk coast and was delighted to resume his childhood pastime.

There was some confusion regarding the New Zealand twins. They had lined themselves up with the Balcony Suite elite when they were Grade One passengers. No one on the staff liked to challenge them on this matter and so they were allowed to stay in their position. It mattered little anyway as several other Balcony Suite types had elected not to paddle but preferred to watch the opening ceremony from the safety of the deck. Philippa and Petra had dressed for the occasion. They appeared in identical red striped bathing costumes with trouser legs tied just above the ankles with tape and similarly tied just above the wrists. Their outfits were crowned with floral bathing caps that left Alice looking as though her flowers had suffered severe drought.

'This is the outfit we always wear when we bathe in the Tukituki,' they said when meeting the Cruise Director on their way to the deck.

He blinked and remarked that they looked charming and were most suitably dressed for a very important event.

Giovanni and Marco, the musicians, had had their visit to the ship extended by popular request and today were busy playing a selection of popular melodies as the crowd waited expectantly for the Admiral to arrive.

At eleven precisely a crew member gave three rings on the ship's brass bell and the small procession entered the deck to applause from the expectant passengers. Giovanni could not play Handel's 'Water Music' on his accordion, no matter how hard he tried, so it was left to Marko to perform a very passable solo to accompany the processional party. They climbed onto the platform and Enzo went to the lectern to welcome people and introduce Admiral Benbow Harrington RN (Retired), shipping magnate and proud owner of the Golden Oceans Shipping Line.

The Admiral stepped forward and surveyed the crowd before him. He took a red spotted handkerchief from his pocket and mopped his brow. It really was very warm indeed. He was just about to open his mouth when the huge figure of Angus Aberdeen appeared. Although his whites were slightly soiled (a forgivable sin for an engineer), nevertheless he cut an impressive figure. He made his way to the platform and mumbled an apology which he thought was uttered in a whisper but the mike caught every word.

'Bloody rudder again. Sorry to be late.'

The Admiral gave him a stern look and rested his hands on the lectern ready to begin. The eagle wobbled as the ship gave a slight lurch but managed to steady.

'Ladies and gentlemen, fellow officers, members of the ship's company. Today is a proud day for Golden Oceans. We are well into our maiden cruise and are sailing through tropical waters. Many is the time I have sailed the seas in command of a British warship. I have sailed through storm and tempest and felt the full might of the wind. I have sailed through the heat of the day when the sun has burned with relentless fervour and we on board gasped for cooling waters. Now, on a day when the same sun burns with the same mighty power, we long for cool breezes and refreshing water. On a ship of Her Majesty's Navy, conditions were sparse. Here, on this modern cruise-liner, we can enjoy the very height of luxury. Today, for the benefit of all our passengers, I am pleased to be able to open our new innovative refreshing pool. May I invite our selected guests to occupy their seats behind the pool.'

The little party, led by the twins, climbed onto the platform, walked behind the trough and sat in their allotted seats.

'Now, the Cruise Director, the Hotel Manager, the Chief Engineer and myself will invite the platform party to place their feet into the cooling waters.'

At that very moment, as though right on cue, the ship gave one almighty lurch and veered to port. Before one toe could be dipped into the trough, the Admiral, together with his whole party, were tipped headlong into the 'cooling waters'. Angus emerged first and with loud curses rushed from the platform in the direction of the engine room. The Admiral retrieved his gold-braided cap and placed the soaked object firmly on his head. Most of the Balcony Suite guests and Grade One-ers, rather than having been thrown forward into the pool, had been thrown backwards so that they landed in a heap on the deck. The chaplain, the only member of the platform party to remain on his feet, dragged a spluttering Enzo from the trough and slapped him soundly on the back. Duvet emerged, looking very sorry for himself, and it was a few moments before Sir Archie clambered out of the trough, to the applause of the onlookers.

Poor Albert and Alice were very upset as Alice claimed that her best summer outfit was now totally ruined and Albert, who could not swim but had been immersed, vowed never to go near water again. That would prove to be a difficult vow to keep, seeing he was on a world cruise, but at the time he said it he meant it.

Angus must have been able to effect some major therapy in the engine room for the ship quickly resumed course and once again all was placid. The Admiral soon regained his composure and returned to the eagle, which had fallen but was now back in position.

'This part of the world is subject to earthquakes which often cause a minor tsunami,' he said, thinking quickly. 'There is no need to panic, for you have seen how quickly our engineers got things back under control.'

There was applause from the crowd and cries of, 'Good old Angus!'

'It's a mercy not one single person was hurt,' said the chaplain later in the afternoon.

Albert and Alice were not so happy with the events of the day. Back in their Balcony Suite, Albert removed his cap and shirt and sat on the edge of the bath. He turned to his wife.

'You know, luv,' he said, 'it's a rum little ship. It really is. A rum little ship.'

39

The day following the unusual launch of the pool was another sea day - and another sweltering sea day at that. Despite the unfortunate events of the previous morning, passengers had not been deterred from cooling their feet in the waters, and throughout the day all seats were taken. Once the Balcony Suite passengers and the Grade One cabins had had their turn, it was a free-for-all for the remainder of the ship, and there was much pushing and shoving to secure a place in one of the coveted positions. There were a few instances of illegal reservations being made by some cruisers, who flatly disobeyed the written notice and left a towel on a seat. A crew member was ordered to supervise the area and to keep some semblance of order.

It goes without saying that the Admiral's dignity had been somewhat dented at the launch, but he was gratified to see that the pool was such a success and so appreciated by all. Captain Sparda was considerably relieved that, for once, he was well clear of trouble. He had been on the bridge at the time of the official opening, and both he, and the Staff Captain, decided that as the project was the Admiral's baby they would be wise to keep their distance. Indeed they were.

In order to try and compensate those unfortunate individuals who had been on the platform at the time of the accident, the Admiral decided that he would invite them all to dine with him that evening in the Golden Chopsticks Restaurant. The latter was an exclusive dining location on the ship always open to Balcony Suite and Grade One passengers and, space allowing, to other passengers on payment of a supplement.

Although the name indicated an oriental cuisine, it did have a varied menu which was personally supervised by Mike Tucker himself. Although Mike took responsibility for all catering on the ship, 'Choppers', as he called it, was his special interest and he was delighted when the Admiral made it his choice for dinner.

That evening, once again poor Albert was subject to the same old boring conversation that he faced each time Alice had to decide what to wear for an occasion. Even though Mrs Potts would not even *be* at the dinner, Alice could not wear her sunflower dress again as the dinner was too close to the last time she wore it.

'Do you think my Rose Petal outfit will be right?' she fretted, as she produced a two-piece creation from the wardrobe.

'Very suitable,' said Albert.

'You didn't even look,' snapped Alice, annoyed at the casual attitude of her husband. 'You don't seem to realise how important it is for Balcony Suite passengers to set a standard for the ship. If we traipse around in any old clothes, the whole tone is lowered. Do you understand that, Albert Hardcastle?'

Albert said he understood, but inwardly he felt that the whole business was just silly vanity. However, it was more than his life was worth to say so.

'I saw Mrs Guttenburg today,' he remarked, keen to change the subject. 'It's strange,' he continued. 'Although you might be on the same exclusive deck, you never meet some folk. She's taken the end Suite for the whole of the voyage and has it all to herself.'

'You want to watch out for these rich widows, Albert Hardcastle,' replied Alice grimly. 'They are on the look-out, mark my words. I've watched her eyeing nice Mr Barley. He has no choice but to dance with her, of course.'

Albert hadn't noticed a thing and said so.

'Sometimes, I think you go around with your eyes tightly closed,' sniffed his wife.

Further along the corridor, the New Zealand twins were also preparing for the evening in the Golden Chopsticks restaurant.

'I wonder if it's as good as the Patangata Hotel,' said Petra to her sister. She was referring to a roadside tavern by the Tukituki River not too far from where the sisters lived. The most popular item on the menu was fish and chips, but there were also burgers of various descriptions.

'I do like an outing there,' she said. 'It makes such a change.'

'It would be hard for anywhere to excel anything at home, dear,' Philippa replied.

'I don't know why that lovely man Mr Tucker doesn't come and live in Ypuk. He would do very well.'

Petra nodded and agreed.

The sisters turned their thoughts to their evening wear. Eventually they decided that they would dress identically, but this was not exactly an earth-shattering development as they never dressed differently.

'I think I shall wear my black buttoned boots with a flowered skirt and that very nice jacket I bought in Hastings many years ago,' said Philippa.

'Well, dear', replied her sister, 'that is just what I was thinking of wearing tonight.'

Agreement between them both was never difficult to achieve.

'What a terrible tsunami yesterday,' said Philippa. 'The brave Mr Angus saved us all. I do hope he will be at the dinner tonight.'

'I'm sure he will be,' said Petra. 'We shall be able to congratulate him then.'

In yet another Balcony Suite Sir Archie and his wife were in a bad mood. An expert negotiator could have found full-time employment with this one couple alone. They had not been speaking to each other since returning from the visit to the Elephant Training Camp. Lady Veronika was furious and blamed the whole troublesome visit on her husband, which really was not fair. The episode at the pool had further dampened his spirits in more ways than one. The only redeeming feature was that it did cause Lady Veronika to raise a glimmer of a smile when he was plunged into the trough, but that quickly disappeared when they returned to their Suite and her husband continued to drip water over everything.

'First you get me wrong camp,' said Lady Veronika yet again. 'I make one time to Sri Lanka and nothing.'

It had been rather a disaster, Sir Archie concurred, but it was not his fault – but then so frequently he had to bear the blame for the disasters which were an all too common occurrence in his life.

'My vodka!' she exclaimed. 'My good vodka given to zoo-keeper. I spend day looking at elephant. More elephant. Elephant standing. Elephant sitting. I no see my friend Tiger. Just elephant.'

Sir Archie attempted to turn the subject away from animals to the dinner that evening in the Chopsticks, but to no avail. Lady Veronika had to get the whole experience out of her system, and if that could be done without him being the target of flying objects, then so much the better.

'I give my lovely coat. My vodka. All day I give to silly elephant man. I know you,' she continued. 'You arrange to camp because you like elephant.'

Sir Archie, it will be remembered, met his wife when he was hunting the great Mongolian Elephant in Siberia. His protests fell on frozen ground and the tirade continued. Sir Archie resigned himself and hoped that by the time they entered the restaurant that evening, all would be sanguine.

In yet another Balcony Suite, Mrs Dora Guttenburg prepared for an evening out at the exclusive Chopsticks restaurant. A guest-list had not been distributed but all she knew was that several senior staff would be present. Would Mr Fennington Barley be there? He was such an interesting and delightful man, with a farming background like herself. Also, he loved dancing. Dora had learned to dance as a very young woman and continued to dance at the 'hops' arranged by her late husband and held in their barn. It could hardly be described as classical dancing, as in rural Iowa, barnyard hops were the order of the day, and they were what she grew up with. Mr Barley was so understanding and never criticised her when, on the dance floor, she broke into a traditional square dance. That was because of Mr Giovanni, who played the accordion and reminded her of her Cousin Ned back home, who was an expert on the squeezebox. This memory had triggered the familiar routine in her mind. She rather liked Mr Barley - in fact, she could go further than that. She thought he was wonderful. She so hoped he would be at the dinner this evening.

The Admiral was in his quarters looking at the dinner-list. Mr and Mrs Albert Hardcastle. He knew little about them except that they seemed to join in many of the ship's activities, even though they had had an unfortunate incident with the balcony. He imagined that they had saved hard all their lives and were now taking a well-earned retirement cruise.

Sir Archie and Lady Veronika. He was looking forward to getting to know Sir Archie much better. He wasn't clear as to what occupation the chap had followed. He had heard someone say that he was interested in animals, but beyond that he was clueless. As for his wife, well she was a complete mystery. As far as he knew, she had yet to speak to anyone on the ship and he imagined that she would not be an easy table companion.

The Parkinson sisters. A charming couple, he thought. Although they had lived in New Zealand for many years they were deeply infused with English culture and habits. He had heard about them working at GCHQ for a period but that was just a rumour and he had no definite knowledge of that fact. Perhaps they were still living in an England that had long since gone, but they were lovely people and he looked forward to their company that evening.

Mrs Dora Guttenburg. He had seen her on the dance floor on more than one occasion and remembered her because she had a curious dancing style, as though she was stomping around in a pair of farming boots. She was one of the several single ladies on board and would balance out the table, as he himself was alone. Then he suddenly remembered that he really ought to invite the Social Hostess, Angela, as she knew her way around and could deal with the pre-dinner drinks and other such matters. He would have to find someone to partner her, and quick as a flash he thought of the doctor. Stuart Hackett had proved to be excellent in attending to the many minor upsets that passengers suffered and, although he was not very discreet, he was a good type to have at sea. So, Angela and the doctor were included to complete a table for ten. Ideal, he thought, and went to find his best mess kit.

It was as he was looking for his cufflinks that he suddenly remembered the chaplain. The poor fellow had been in attendance at the pool event and once again had not got an opportunity to perform. It was too bad. Every time he was due to exercise his ministry to a large group, something intervened which held him back. He must invite the man, but as he had now already invited the doctor to balance Angela, the padre would be the odd one out. Sir Benbow took hold of the list and perused the Balcony guests. He came across someone travelling alone whom he had no recollection of ever having seen and certainly whom he had not heard of: Mrs Janice Golightly from Worthing in Sussex. He had no other information about her but he got Angela on the phone and asked her to make contact and issue an invite. He was pleased when she accepted. The Admiral was almost ready to leave for the exclusive on-board dining experience when an awful thought crossed his mind. He had forgotten to include the Chief Engineer, Lieutenant Commander Angus MacDonald. As the Chief had arrived late at the opening of the pool and left early, the Admiral had totally forgotten that he was a part of the platform party and an important part at that. Quickly he got through to the engine room and asked to speak to Angus.

'Commander, this is the Admiral speaking.'

There was dreadful interference on the line and one would have thought that the Admiral had been connected to the Arctic wastes rather than a few decks below his quarters.

'Hello, Angus, is that you?'

More interference and then several sentences in a broad Scottish accent which would have been unintelligible to Gordon Brown, let alone Enzo the ship's linguist.

'I would like to invite you to come and have dinner with me and some guests in the Golden Chopsticks restaurant. When, you ask? Why, right now, as soon as possible.'

Again there was growling on the line and between the interference the Admiral was able to make out that Angus had tried the Chinese Chophouse and had no intention of returning. If he wanted to eat with sticks he would have gone to live in the jungle. He was sorry but he was too busy working on steering problems.

Much relieved that he had not committed a major social gaffe,

Terry Waite

the Admiral then made his way to the restaurant. He arrived to find that most of his guests were already there and were being served drinks and canapés by one of the deckhands dressed in a white mess-jacket for the occasion. He ordered a pink gin and then began the laborious task of 'circulating'. He had little love of this type of activity, as he found it totally exhausting. When he was a sidesman, the Archbishop of Canterbury paid a visit to his parish and attended the usual bunfight. The Archbishop had confided to him that there was nothing more exhausting than enforced geniality and he could not have agreed with him more. However, this little gathering was nothing compared with what poor old Sparda had to endure when there was a Captain's reception. Not only did Sparda have to greet everyone personally but he, and Angela, acting as Social Hostess, had to be photographed as well. However, the passengers loved it and it had to be done. In fact, as owner of the line, he insisted that it was done. Thank God Angus was not Captain as, if he were, there would be some very lively receptions indeed.

'Admiral, how well you look in that splendid uniform.'

It was Philippa Parkinson, nursing what was known as a Maori Headsplitter, a lethal concoction which looked for all the world like muddy water.

'My dear sister and I worked for an Admiral in Cheltenham, you know. But he never dressed as well as you.'

Petra, who was by her side, as usual, agreed.

'He was a terror,' she said. 'He could swear in fifteen languages and often did so. It was truly awful.'

The Admiral nodded in sympathy and moved on to chat with Albert and Alice. Albert held onto a glass of Brown Ale and Alice sipped at a sweet sherry.

'So pleased you could come this evening,' said the Admiral genially. 'Have you dined here previously?'

'Not if we could help it,' said Albert bluntly. He had been taking a quick look at the menu and could not make head nor tail of it.

Alice was quick to jump in. 'He means we haven't because we have had too many other engagements to dine,' she said, putting on her most refined accent.

'Well, you will enjoy it I'm sure. Mr Tucker goes out of his way to please.'

The Admiral smiled politely and strolled away to speak with Sir Archie and his wife. The latter was scowling at a vodka bottle and no doubt thinking of her wasted supplies of the stuff.

'Sir Archibald and Lady Veronika, how good to see you. We have met previously.' The Admiral addressed Sir Archie directly. 'I was once invited by Buffy Thompson to dine at the Travellers, and you were at the members' table. I remember he introduced us.'

'By George!' exclaimed Sir Archie. 'I *thought* I knew you.'

'Poor old Buffy. Got eaten by a crocodile, you know. Terrible experience.'

The doctor, who was standing nearby, chipped in. 'Who for?' he said. 'Buffy or the croc?'

Sir Archie looked startled but Lady Veronika actually managed a smile.

'Well, Doctor,' said the Admiral, 'I was truly relieved that there were no real injuries at the opening of the pool. It could have been a very serious incident indeed.'

'How right you are,' nodded the doctor. 'Fortunately, I took the precaution of having the pool swept for crocodiles before we started.'

The Admiral managed to laugh and went to talk to a lady who was chatting with the Cruise Director.

'May I introduce Mrs Golightly,' Enzo said.

The Admiral greeted her. 'We have not met previously, but I hope all is well with you,' he said pleasantly.

The woman did not reply but began to dab at her eyes with a fragrant handkerchief as tears appeared and rolled down her pale cheeks.

'I say,' the Admiral said, alarmed. 'These cocktail onions are rather strong, aren't they? Let me order you some crisps or something.'

She took a sip of her cocktail and apologised.

'I'm so sorry, Admiral, but my dear husband passed away just a few weeks ago and this is the first time I have come out of my Balcony Suite since we sailed. He was a dear, dear man and adored cruising. How he would have loved to be here for this evening.'

'Well, my dear, I'm quite sure he is with us in spirit,' said the Admiral, not knowing what else to say.

Enzo beamed and muttered, '*Vero, vero.*'

The Admiral was about to resume circulating when someone gently touched his elbow. He looked around and saw it was Angela.

'I'm terribly sorry to be late,' she whispered. 'I ought to have been here to accompany you around the room, but I got an urgent call from the chaplain, who could not find his clerical collar. Fortunately, we managed to find an old Fairy Liquid container and cut a collar out of that. No one would ever know.'

The Admiral glanced at the chaplain, who was looking somewhat sheepish, and said to Angela that he understood perfectly. He sighed and moved on.

Mrs Dora Guttenburg was deep in conversation with the Hotel Manager, Radley Duvet. She was showing him some fancy dancing steps that she regularly performed back in Iowa. Unfortunately, the Admiral approached her from behind just as she was demonstrating the Iowan Clog Dance, and her ample foot landed painfully on the tip of his highly polished evening shoes. He could not suppress a loud yelp which, when uttered, made the whole room fall silent. Angela, quick off the mark as always, or almost always, took over and suggested that everyone take their seats.

'Welcome everyone,' said the Admiral when they were seated. 'There will be no formal speeches this evening, but I wanted to say how good it is that you could join me in our Premier Restaurant for dinner.'

Before he could say anything further, Petra, one of the New Zealand twins, was on her feet.

'Admiral,' she said. 'It is we who ought to be giving *you* a dinner tonight. Your officers demonstrated exceptional bravery in the face of such a terrible tsunami. We might have all drowned in our bunks had it not been for the quick action of the dear Chief Engineer, Mr Angus.'

As Petra Parkinson was far from her bed at the time of the imagined tsunami, her analogy was not quite accurate, but the Admiral understood well enough. The doctor did not. He looked up from the menu he was studying.

'Eh?' he exclaimed in a loud voice. 'What tsunami? Was I on the ship at the time?'

The Admiral coughed politely. 'Thank you so very much, Ms Parkinson,' he said, desperate to change tack and conscious of the fact that he had told a white lie at the time of the opening of the pool. 'Alas, the Chief cannot be here tonight as he has urgent matters to attend to, but I shall convey your appreciation to him.'

'Hold on,' continued the doctor. 'I must have missed some excitement.'

It was at this point that the truth was revealed of the saying that God moves in a mysterious way, his wonders to perform. For at that tricky moment, Philippa, the other twin from New Zealand, slipped from her chair and landed with a crash under the table. Immediately there was commotion all round. A couple of chairs were knocked over as Enzo and Radley leaped to their feet. The doctor got on all fours to retrieve the fallen guest and administer first aid. The only person to remain totally calm was Petra who, when order was restored and Philippa was back in her seat, said: 'Oh dear, she is always like this when she has had more than three Headsplitters. This is the only difference between us. I can drink seven and not be affected. Poor Philippa can't manage half as many. We don't buy Headsplitters in New Zealand, you know. It's only when we are away that we allow ourselves a little treat. I do apologise, Admiral.'

'Nothing to apologise for, I assure you,' said the much-relieved Admiral. 'These chairs are particularly slippery, but that is because our excellent team keep this restaurant absolutely spotless. Now, let's turn to the menu, if we may. How do you feel, Ms Parkinson? I do hope you are well enough to stay.'

'Quite well, thank you, Admiral,' said a totally revived Philippa. 'I must congratulate your men on their diligence in keeping this ship so neat and tidy, even though it meant my suffering a small misfortune as a result.'

The doctor, always one to comment on any situation, piped up yet again. 'Did you know, Mrs Guttenburg,' he said, causing all eyes to fall on the clog-dancing widow. 'Did you know that it's illegal to get a fish drunk in Ohio?'

Mrs Guttenburg looked startled. 'I'm not from Ohio,' she said somewhat indignantly. 'I have lived in Iowa all my life and have never even visited Ohio.'

'Oh,' said the doctor in reply. 'Well, all these places sound the same to me.'

'How on earth could you get a fish drunk?' queried Sir Archie. 'They spend all their lives in water so I don't see how it's possible, let alone illegal.'

The Doctor laughed and avoided answering with another amazing fact: 'You can't even fish for whales on a Sunday in that State,' he said. 'They have a real problem with fish in Ohio.'

'I think it's time to order,' said the Admiral, half-grateful to the doctor for steering the conversation in such a bizarre way and a little annoyed that he had startled Mrs Guttenburg, a guest whom he knew little about except that she was extremely wealthy. He was also cross that the doctor had referred to drunkenness. That was the last thing anyone ought to suggest.

Sir Archie had not finished yet. 'I spent many years in Alaska,' he said. 'I was doing some work for a scientific journal and discovered that it's illegal to wake a sleeping bear to take a photograph.'

Quick as a flash, the doctor chipped in: 'I didn't know bears could take photographs!' he quipped.

'I meant,' said Sir Archie, 'that one could not wake such an animal for the purpose of taking a photograph of that animal.'

'Ah, I see,' said the doctor in mock surprise.

Sir Archie continued. 'It is also illegal to get a moose drunk.'

The Admiral, hearing yet another reference to drink and conscious of the New Zealand twin and her Headsplitters, came in now with greater force.

'We really must order, I'm afraid. Time is going by so quickly and Harry and his team will want to get on with preparing our meal.'

Like participants at a bingo session, all heads went down to peruse the menu. It was enormous. Not that there were too many options, but its sheer size was overwhelming. Each menu was the size of a full-blown newspaper before the day of the tabloids.

'You can order the Chinese cuisine,' said the Admiral. 'Or, if you prefer, there are a range of alternatives available, all equally good.'

Before collecting the menu from the waiter Albert had seen chopsticks laid before him and had notified Alice that on no account was he going to eat his meal with sticks. He emulated

Angus by saying that sticks were for tree-dwellers, where sticks were plentiful. Whilst Sheffield was still in England he would like a plain knife and fork.

'You will note,' said the Admiral once again, 'that we have a special innovation in this restaurant. You can order steak, or fish, which will be brought to you in a raw state and you cook it exactly as you like it on your very own, very hot volcanic rock.'

'Good Lord,' chuckled the Doctor. 'Do they want us to do the washing up as well as cook our own food?'

The table laughed at this wit and within a few moments orders were complete. The majority chose the black rock. Lady Veronika put in a special order for food not on the menu, a plate of raw broccoli, some fermented yak's milk and a bowl of unsalted peanuts.

Albert ordered fish and chips with garden peas, as mushy peas were not available. The others took either meat or fish from the heated rock selection.

The evening was a great success. No further reference was made to the tsunami. Mrs Golightly told the Hotel Manager that in future she would come to the main dining room to eat rather than stay in her suite. The twins were genteel and polite, and the only difficult moment occurred when the doctor attempted to converse with Enzo in French. Enzo pretended he had a hearing problem, but if truth be known, he didn't understand a word. The doctor said if he came to the surgery he would fix the problem by putting a water pistol to his head – an offer that Enzo declined. All in all it was a jolly evening and went down in the Admiral's log book as a night to remember.

40

Sea days were the days when the Cruise Director could come into his own. Passengers were trapped on board whether they liked it or not, and many needed entertainment provided for them. Enzo conducted Piddling Pursuits each day and, to be fair to him, it was very popular amongst passengers. He was a master at keeping the quiz moving without too much hostility, for it had been known on some ships for shouting matches to take place and even hand-to-hand fighting between zealous competitors. No other member of the ship's company wanted to conduct the game and Enzo wanted no one else to conduct it, so everyone was happy. His language classes, now moved from the prime time of eleven in the morning, had been shunted around and were as desultory as ever. Because one or two passengers wanted them he kept them going, but they were a disaster and in his heart he knew it.

Norma and Graham Trotter the World Ludo Champions were seldom seen around the ship, as each and every day was spent either instructing novices or arranging and supervising championships. Unfortunately, several days out on the cruise,

Graham developed a severe case of Ludo finger, a condition brought about by too much pressure being put on the digit when excitement is running high in the game. The doctor put him on a course of antibiotics and he was soon well again. Despite warnings from many a health organisation, antibiotics continued to be a favourite standby for the ship's Medical Centre, and passengers paid a considerable sum for a course of the drugs.

Now Graham was back 'on the board' so to speak, Norma was relieved from the terrible responsibility of having to watch out for cheating and intimidating behaviour all on her own. She fulfilled this role splendidly and a passenger secretly nominated her to receive a free allocation of bonus points at her local supermarket back home.

On sea days Mr Fennington Barley danced the day away. He began with warm-up classes, after which there was a mid-morning coffee dance followed by an afternoon spent teaching before he dropped into the theatre as a consultant to the professional dancers. Following that, he was back on the dance floor until the early hours.

Cousin Giovanni and Marko Contoni were exceptionally busy, virtually playing around the clock. Their time on board was now beginning to lose something of its glamour. The two musicians were rushed off their feet. Passengers did not tip, of course, and Captain Sparda was only providing food and lodging, so they were not making any money and thus began to think that it was about time to go home. Enzo was given the task of finding a new group of musicians who would be on board for the remainder of the cruise. It was not an easy task. Finally, in desperation, after searching high and low, he gave up.

'Radley,' he said to the Hotel Manager, with whom he was now on much better terms, 'I am having no luck at all in finding a small group of musicians for the remainder of the tour. I am at my wit's end, really I am.'

'It is a real problem,' agreed Radley, 'but I think we might have a solution. From amongst the passengers there must be musicians. If we could get together a team of four - we have instruments somewhere on board - then they could play in return for a free drink now and again.'

It was only a matter of minutes before an appeal went out, written by Radley himself.

One of the Joys of cruising is being able to be away from home in the company of like-minded people and to experience exotic locations and relaxed days at sea. What is better than, after a day of explor- ing new places or enjoying the delights of the new pool, to return to a sumptuous dinner followed by relaxing with your favourite pastime: a jigsaw puzzle, a crossword or line dancing. Some of you will have learned musical instruments and you may now think it is the time to play them again for your own delight and for the delight of your fellow passengers. If this is the case, please come this afternoon to the

main assembly room where there will be a brief audition and a fur-
ther explanation of what you might do. If you have your instrument
with you please bring it along. If not, then we have several on board
and you can choose what you would wish to play.

Yours in harmony,

Radley Duvet – Hotel Manager
Enzo Bigatoni – Cruise Director

Later that afternoon, Radley, Enzo and Rod Saddleworth the musical cook, were making their way to the reception area to begin the audition. They were surprised when, as they approached, they saw about twenty passengers waiting for the door to open.

'Greetings, Maestro!' shouted someone from the small crowd. Enzo turned and noted the infamous Felix de Barkley, the passenger who was always ready with some witty comment or other. Enzo made a theatrical bow accompanied by an extravagant sweep of the hand, and they entered into the auditorium followed by the budding musicians.

On the small stage was a motley collection of instruments that had been procured by the Admiral before the voyage started. He had had them stowed on board and then promptly forgot all about them, until this moment. 'What an odd assortment,' Radley mused as he eyed the collection.

Apart from the piano, which had always been in use, there was a tuba, two violins, a guitar, a worn-looking set of drums, a saxophone, and a clarinet. Rod took his place at the piano and ran his fingers up and down the keys. It sounded OK . . . just. Radley turned to the budding orchestra and addressed them.

'Ladies and gentlemen,' he said. 'It is so good to see so many music-lovers here today, anxious to share your talents with the whole ship. Thank you for coming. As you can see, we have a selection of instruments here on the platform which should, with care, produce an acceptable orchestra for the ship.'

'At least when it goes down we can have a musical accompaniment like the *Titanic*.'

It was de Barkley again, and Enzo gave him one of his disapproving scowls.

'No need for comments like that, sir,' said Duvet, 'but as you have spoken, may I ask what is your chosen instrument?'

The man was quick to reply. 'I learned the mouth organ at school,' he said somewhat plaintively.

Quick as a flash Enzo replied, 'Yes, we've noted that. I don't think there is such an instrument here.'

'Don't fret,' de Barkley replied. 'I've got mine with me.' And he produced a large German instrument of the kind that Radley used to covet as a schoolboy.

'Right,' said Enzo. 'Rod, if you could accompany Mr de Barkley, we can begin.'

Rod Saddleworth played a few opening bars of 'The Blue-bells of Scotland' and then Felix de Barkley came in - without, it must be said, a great deal of subtlety. He was a mouth organist of the 'suck blow vigorously' variety. Radley made a note in his book.

'Thank you, sir,' he said. 'We will let you know. Next.' He looked up and saw a couple of passengers pushing someone forward.

'Go on,' they were saying. 'You must give it a try.'

To the surprise of the examiners, the person who was pushed to the front turned out to be none other than the chaplain.

'Well, hello, Reverend,' said Radley affably. 'You're very welcome, but I don't think we need an organist at the moment.'

The chaplain smiled. 'No, it's not the organ I play, although I can manage a few tunes in an emergency. No, it's something different.'

'Well, take your pick,' said Bigatoni, indicating the various instruments on stage.

The chaplain stepped forward, jumped nimbly up onto the platform and, to the surprise of everyone, sat himself behind the drum-kit. The next few moments were astonishing. At least, the whole assembled gathering were totally amazed. The chaplain handled the instruments like a true professional, in a way that would have made Phil Collins look like a beginner, and for two or three minutes he kept everyone entranced. When he laid down the sticks the whole assembly broke into spontaneous applause.

'That was very good indeed,' said Radley when the chaplain stepped down from the platform. 'Where did you learn to play like that?'

The chaplain responded by saying that when he was a student, he paid his way by playing in various bars and clubs. What he didn't add was that he had an enormous collection of jazz records and could also play the saxophone.

Both Bigatoni and Duvet were greatly impressed and signed him up immediately. When he was out of earshot Duvet remarked that, now they had had one shock, he wouldn't be at all surprised if one of the twin sisters came forward offering to play the trumpet! This did not happen, but both sisters offered to play the piano and were accepted as it was doubtful that Rod would be able to leave the galley every time music was required. It must be admitted that they tended to play at a somewhat sedate pace, but it was hoped they might liven up once the chaplain got moving on the percussion.

The audition was full of the unexpected, for who should come forward next but Lady Veronika. She was scowling as usual, but her facial appearance was now accepted and no sinister intent was attributed to her simply because she looked combative. Without a word she went directly to the instruments and selected the saxophone. A few quick runs up and down the scale and she was off.

'This is quite remarkable,' said Bigatoni as she played away. 'Who would have thought that she would be able to play like that.'

Without hesitation she was included and now they had the core of a small group: piano, percussions and saxophone.

'An electric guitar would be useful,' said Enzo, and eventually an artiste was discovered in the person of Ron Batty, the former AA patrol man. In his youth Ron had managed to master the guitar and in fact was still quite accomplished. Another half-hour was spent listening to other passengers who claimed to be experts, but both Enzo and Radley were now satisfied with the group they had. When the audition came to an end Enzo requested that the chaplain, the New Zealand twins, Lady Veronika and Ron Batty stay behind for a few moments. He thanked the others and said that he would be in touch with them if further musical help was required. Felix de Barkley was told that the mouth organ might come in very well for a special item on the programme and he would let him know about that.

'I think,' said Duvet to the small group left behind, 'I think that we had better get acquainted and also find a name for the band.'

Without a moment's hesitation, the chaplain, who was gaining confidence by the moment, said: 'It's obvious. The Golden Bells.'

And that was that.

41

Despite the words of Albert Hardcastle, that the *Golden Handshake* was 'a grand little ship', and despite the fact that she had been extensively remodelled, she was getting near the end of her nautical life. Angus, the Chief Engineer, had been able to keep on top of the problems with the rudder, but it was clear to him that major work was required and this could only be achieved by the vessel spending a longish period of time in dry dock. If the Admiral was planning to continue world cruising then, as soon as this venture was completed, dry dock would have to be the next port of call. Meanwhile, on the bridge, the Staff Captain was beginning to worry about the ship's navigation system. As Indonesia was a maze of islands, it was vital that there was precision in this area, and he was not too certain that all was well with the equipment. So worried was he, that he had instructed the Navigation Officer to sharpen his pencil and adopt the well-tried method of plotting a course by the stars and a paper chart rather then the fitted electronic device.

To cut a long story short, old-fashioned skills which were second nature to an older generation of sailors, did not come so easily to the younger officers, with the result that the *Golden Handshake* found herself somewhere amongst the Indonesian Islands, but not quite sure where. Night was falling and the heavens were sparkling with a million navigational points, but despite this, the Staff Captain decided that as land was close by, they would drop anchor and hope that by the morning, full electronic capacity would have been restored.

The night passed calmly enough. Radley Duvet had arranged for there to be a deck party with dancing under the stars, an event which provided the newly formed musical group with an opportunity to demonstrate their skills. With one of the New Zealand twins on the piano (no one quite knew which one, but it made little difference as they both played equally well), Lady Veronika on the saxophone and the chaplain on the percussion, the whole evening was a great success.

'My word,' said Albert as he made his way to the Balcony Suite. 'Yon vicar is a lively lad on the drums. He would have done us proud in the Co-op band.'

Alice agreed and said that all the performers had been very good indeed. The couple paused for a moment to lean on the rail and look over the side of the ship. As it was a moonlit night they could clearly see land not too far away, but no sign of life at all.

'Where's that?' queried Albert, peering across the water.

'Don't ask me,' replied his wife. 'I haven't a clue. It could be anywhere.'

They were just about to depart for their Suite when across the water came the most blood-curdling hissing noise.

'What the 'ell's that?' said Albert. 'It sounds as if someone's geyser's blown up.'

'Don't be daft,' scoffed Alice. 'Come on, we might get a better sight of things tomorrow.'

Dawn broke and revealed another cloudless sky. Once again, Albert and Alice strolled along the deck and by now they could clearly make out a wooded strip of land with no apparent sign of habitation. As they were passing one of the Listening Posts, it suddenly burst into life, revealing the familiar tones of Enzo, the Cruise Director.

'Good morning, ladies and gentlemen,' he intoned. 'It's another lovely day on board the *Golden Handshake*. In a few moments, there will be a special announcement for Balcony Suite and Grade One passengers. Please make sure that you do not miss this special information.'

Albert and Alice waited patiently and were soon joined by Sir Archibald Willoughby and one of the New Zealand twins. Again, they were not sure if it was Petra or Philippa.

The loudspeaker sprang into life once more.

'From time to time, special free tours are arranged for our Balcony Suite and Grade One passengers,' Enzo began. 'This morning at ten o'clock I shall be leading a small group to explore the island you see off the port bow. This is not an island I know, but I am sure we shall have an interesting time. Those Balcony Suite and Grade One passengers who wish to join me, please assemble in Reception soon before ten.'

Enzo indeed spoke the truth, for it was not an island any of the ship's crew knew, as they were still struggling to resume contact with the navigational satellites. As for the paper charts, the less said about them the better.

Shortly before ten a motley group assembled as requested. Sir Archibald and Lady Veronika appeared first. Sir Archie wore his pith helmet, somewhat restored after the encounter with the ceiling fan in India and the hangar shed in Sri Lanka, but not in its former pristine condition. Lady Veronika sported the now familiar cloche hat and long skirt. The twins were back in bee-keeping guise and Albert and Alice wore the same sort of clothes as they would wear on a summer outing to Blackpool. Alice had brought along a new red straw hat that she had purchased on board at a special discount sale when all items were priced under ten pounds. Edna and Felix de Barkley from the Grade One accommodation completed the party.

Enzo led the little group down to the lower deck where they boarded a small boat powered by an outboard motor. Just as they were about to cast off, there was a shout from above.

'Hey, have you got room for a small one?'

Quick as a flash, de Barkley shouted back, 'Make mine a

double if you will.'

Ignoring the repartee, Enzo replied, 'Jump down quickly, Doctor. We can just about fit you in.'

The doctor, wearing a pair of green surgical trousers and a colourful shirt depicting some exotic island, clambered aboard and they were off.

It wasn't far to the island and it was an easy journey as the sea was calm and there was only a gentle breeze. The crewman in charge of the vessel headed towards a strip of sandy beach and Enzo addressed the party.

'I have to admit,' he began, 'that this is a bit of an adventure, for I have no idea what this island is called, nor what we shall find here. Before we land, may I suggest that you remove your shoes and socks as we shall have to wade the final few feet up the beach. Our friend on the tiller will do all he can to get us as near as possible, but there is bound to be a little water to wade through.'

The party began to remove their footwear and, predictably, Felix de Barkley pulled a face in mock disgust and held his nose. No one laughed, as they were now accustomed to his interventions and largely ignored them.

The crewman steered the boat as far up the beach as he could, and his number two at the prow jumped nimbly over the side and secured it with a rope to a nearby tree stump. Enzo and the two crew members then helped the passengers ashore. The only one to present a problem was Lady Veronika and her long skirt. Gallant to the last, her husband took her in his arms and carried her ashore, to loud applause, and the shout from de Barkley: 'Where's the bride's father?'

Once they were assembled on shore, Enzo addressed them again.

'It is important,' he said, 'that we all keep together. I note that there is a small path ahead and suggest we follow that to see where it takes us. We are bound to encounter some interesting wildlife, but I don't expect anything dangerous. I have visited many islands in my time and it's been perfectly safe.'

He wisely did not mention that the 'many islands' he had visited were Hawaii, Sicily, Capri and some of the Scottish outposts.

'I shall lead the way,' Enzo continued, 'and Doctor, if you would bring up the rear, that would ensure that we all keep together.'

Before moving off, Enzo instructed them to follow the same procedure they had adopted on the fateful visit to the Duty-Free Depot in France. That was for each person in file to place a hand on the shoulder of the person in front of them so that they would not get separated. Felix could not resist remarking to Sir Archie as he placed his hand on his epaulette, 'You're under arrest, sonny,' a remark that Sir Archie sensibly ignored.

And so off they went. To say that it was hot would be an

understatement. It was not only tropical, it was boiling. Although Lady Veronika was dressed in kit suitable for a Siberian autumn, she was the only member of the party who did not appear to be perspiring profusely. Albert and Alice staggered along, secretly wishing that they had stayed behind with the other passengers, but valiantly they ploughed on.

They had hardly gone three hundred yards when Albert stopped dead in his tracks, causing those behind to stumble into each other.

'Alice,' he said in a hushed voice. 'It's that hissing noise again. Remember? The one we heard last night.'

Alice listened intently, as did the passengers behind her.

'Come on,' shouted Enzo from the front. 'We can't rest now. We've only been moving for a few minutes.'

'Hold on!' cried the doctor from the rear. 'It sounds as if we are near the station. I'm sure we heard a steam train.'

'No time for silly jokes,' said Enzo in his most commanding voice. 'This is a tropical island and railways don't exist here, as you must know.'

'Oh sorry,' replied the doctor, offended. 'I thought we were on Paddington Green.'

No sooner had he spoken than there was a loud scream from Alice, who immediately ran towards the front of the file, causing the troupe to disintegrate in confusion once more. Immediately by the pathway stood a creature that most of the party had never seen before. It looked for all the world as if it had just emerged from the primeval jungle. It had the shape of a lizard, except that it was about nine feet long with a forked tongue that it frequently flicked from its drooling mouth. The reptile stared at the party, flicking its tongue and hissing like a boiling kettle.

'My God,' croaked Sir Archie. 'I have seen this animal on TV. It's a Komodo Dragon.'

Having said that, he motioned the party to follow him as he backed gently forward along the pathway. Alice, who was near collapse, removed her red straw hat and began to fan her face.

'Stop that immediately!' growled Sir Archie. 'You will attract his attention and he will attack. If its saliva even so much as touches you, that's it.'

Alice would have swooned if Albert had not steadied her.

'Come on, luv,' he said. 'Step back quietly.'

Gingerly, the group moved forward and mercifully the creature remained in place. They had not gone many paces when they heard a crashing noise above them – and lo and behold there was another creature working its way along a stout branch of a tree. This was a smaller version of the first dragon, but equally as fearful. Enzo, who had turned a ghastly shade of pale, motioned the group to gather around him.

'There is a clearing ahead,' he whispered. 'If we could all tiptoe to that place, we shall be safe. I think I heard human voices over there.'

'This is not at all like home,' said one of the twins from behind her veil. 'I have seen longhorn cattle there. In fact, my dear neighbours used to keep two of them as pets – Buster and Dudley they were called. They were very gentle.'

'Shussh,' warned Enzo. 'Be very quiet.'

The explorers, now huddled together rather than in single file, stepped fearfully along the path and entered the clearing. This time they were startled by someone shouting at them. A thin brown-skinned little man carrying a cleft stick had appeared from a pathway on the far side of the clearing.

'Hey!' he shouted. 'Who you? Where you from?'

Behind him, two other small figures appeared – and behind them, six or seven individuals who by their appearance were tourists. Before Enzo could reply, there was a loud scream from Mrs de Barkley as a dragon suddenly appeared immediately behind her. Quick as a flash the little man ran forward and, with his forked stick, poked the animal in the eyes, causing it to rapidly retreat. At the same time, the two other guides motioned Enzo's party to cross the clearing and join the tourists. The tourist group, who happened to be all of Chinese appearance and did not seem to understand one word of English, jabbered excitedly amongst themselves. The little man who had first called out to them returned from his encounter with the dragon looking more than a little displeased.

'Who leader?' he questioned, looking at the Balcony Suite

and Grade One passengers.

Enzo stepped forward. 'We are from the *Golden Handshake*,' he said, 'and are on one of our excursions.'

He might as well have said that he was from the moon as the little man looked even more serious.

'You know this is Komodo,' he growled. 'No one come to Komodo without guide. Very dangerous. Dragon kill and eat you!'

At this information Alice let out a low moan and collapsed into the arms of her ever-dutiful husband, who was quickly joined by the doctor.

'Perhaps we should tell him that the dragon ate our guide,' muttered de Barkley. 'In fact, it might have been a good thing if he *had* snapped up Enzo.'

No one laughed as they were all concerned about Alice, who was gradually coming to.

'Stay still,' the little man warned them. 'More dragon in bush.'

Further hissing noises were heard across the clearing and two more terrible-looking creatures emerged, flashing their tongues, drooling saliva and causing the party to retreat several paces, leaving Alice, the doctor and Albert exposed. Two more little men with big sticks leaped forward and pointed them at the invaders, who once again disappeared into the undergrowth. By now Alice had been hauled to her feet and, with her two helpers, rejoined the main group.

'How you get to Island?' queried the head stick man. 'You no come on pier. You no have ticket.'

Enzo explained that they had come by boat, which was moored nearby.

'You crazy,' said the guide to Enzo. 'You very much crazy. Komodo Island must have guide. Dragon tongue very poisonous. Dragon like meat. Kill and eat you. Yes, true. Kill and eat you!'

'I'm afraid he's right,' said Sir Archie, looking ashen. 'We seem to have made a rather incautious landing on Komodo Island, home of the Komodo Dragon. They are as dangerous as the gentleman describes, and visitors always are accompanied by experienced guides.'

All eyes turned towards Enzo who, for a few moments, was lost for words. Eventually he mumbled an apology and said that he had had no idea that there was an island as dangerous as Komodo.

'Well, old boy,' said the doctor, cheerful as always, 'it'll be good preparation for your visit to the head-hunters of Brazil, won't it. Chalk it up to experience, eh?'

Enzo gave a wan smile and looked towards the stick man.

'Perhaps, sir,' he said in a voice that betrayed despair, 'you and your men might escort us back to our boat.'

The stick man nodded and shouted something to one of his

companions, who stepped forward.

'OK, now, keep behind me.'

He looked at the group,

'Lady,' he shouted so loudly that Alice jumped. 'No red hat. Hat no good. Dragon not like red hat.'

Alice reluctantly removed her straw hat and handed it over to the stick man, who threw it across to one of his other companions.

The journey from the clearing to the beach was only a few hundred yards and it was completed without another sighting of a dragon. To the dismay of the whole party, there was no sighting of the boat either. There were marks in the sand where it had been dragged ashore, and the stump to which it had been attached was clearly visible, but there was no boat. By now Enzo was close to tears. He turned to the guide.

'Our boat,' he said plaintively. 'It's gone.'

In the distance, shimmering in the heat, was the unmistakable profile of the *Golden Handshake*, but the tender was nowhere to be seen. Suddenly all ears pricked up as a loud hissing sound was heard, and before any evasive action could be taken, just a few yards away from the party a dragon emerged from the undergrowth, ran across the beach and entered the water.

'My godfathers,' said de Barkley, 'they can swim as well as climb trees. It looks as though swimming to the ship is out of the question.'

It was never *in* question, as Alice and Albert could not swim and it was doubtful that any of the party, swimmer or not, would be able to make it all the way out to the ship.

'I get canoe,' said the stick man. 'You pay me. I get canoe.'

Once again all eyes turned towards Enzo, who fumbled in his safari jacket pocket.

'Two hundred fifty dollar,' said the little man. He paused as Enzo digested this news and then added, 'Each trip.'

Enzo groaned. 'How big is the canoe?' he asked.

'You take three trip,' said the enterprising guide.

Here Sir Archie intervened and with some careful diplomacy (to which he was well accustomed, having married Lady Veronika), he finally got the price down to $550.

It turned out that the two crew members waiting behind with the boat had also been scared by a Komodo Dragon and had returned post haste to the ship. On hearing the news and having correctly determined his bearings, Captain Peché dispatched another small boat to collect the stranded adventurers. This time the boat went to the correct landing-stage for entry to the Island and was waiting there, while Enzo was parting with his dollars.

'Well,' said Albert when he and Alice had safely returned to the protection of the ship, 'I bet they've seen nowt like that in the Co-op.'

Alice pulled a face. 'And wouldn't want to neither,' she responded. 'Dreadful smelly creatures.'

The twin sisters were less condemnatory.

'It was a real adventure,' said Petra to Philippa. 'Very exciting. But I have to say, I do prefer Buster and Dudley.'

And with that, the good ship set sail for the next destination on her World Cruise.

42

Admiral Benbow Harrington was worried. Although he was well pleased with the *Golden Handshake*, it had some rather severe defects. The steering gear was by no means functioning as it ought, and the breakdown of the navigational equipment was an added concern. Captain Peché seemed sanguine enough about matters, but then the Captain did have Italian blood, and making the impossible work, after a fashion, was part of the Italian genius. They were now on the other side of the world, approaching Australia, and still had a long way to go before they returned to the safety of Southend-on-Sea.

To the Admiral's great relief, the visits to Darwin and Cairns passed off without incident. All passengers who wished to, were able to visit the Great Barrier Reef and there was a general spirit of satisfaction on board. But there was always a nagging fear in the back of the Admiral's mind which surfaced from time to time. However, as both Captain Peché and the Staff Captain seemed reasonably contented, he ignored his anxiety. The Chief Engineer was never happy with anything, and so he discounted his opinion about the *Handshake*, which was far from favourable.

The Voyage of the Golden Handshake

The entry into Sydney Harbour was nothing short of a triumph. The *Golden Handshake* behaved impeccably and they were able to secure a berth by the Harbour Bridge, within sight of the Opera House. This very favourable position more than made up for some of the difficulties previously experienced, as passengers delighted in their new, and most civilised, surroundings.

It was a bright sunny morning and Albert and Alice were sitting on deck after breakfast. They had received a message from Cousin George, who had emigrated to Australia on a Ten Pound Passage thirty years previously. Since he left Grimsby he had not returned to the town. In fact, he had not even returned to the United Kingdom. Alice had kept in touch with him over the years, and had mentioned that they would be passing through Sydney on a World Cruise and hoped that they might meet. He responded by saying that he would keep a lookout for the *Golden Handshake* and contact them when they arrived, which he did. It was decided that they would meet outside the entrance to the dockside at midday, and George would take them to his home for lunch.

'I won't know him after all these years,' said Albert as he gazed across at the bridge. 'By go, Alice!' he exclaimed. 'Look at that!'

Alice looked in the direction he was pointing and saw several individuals making their way over the bridge. Not by the conventional route along the roadway, but over one of the gigantic struts that supported the structure. Alice turned her head away.

'Some folk are plain daft,' she remarked. 'I bet they pay through the nose to make that trip. More fool them.'

Albert reverted to the topic of his long-departed cousin.

'I've no idea what he does, Alice. He's probably retired by now. When he left Grimsby he was working as assistant to a milkman and had to be up at the crack of dawn.'

'Well,' said Alice, 'he's never told us much in his letters. He was never one for writing. We don't have any photographs either. Never mind, we'll find out sooner or later.'

At midday the Balcony Suite couple left the ship and walked the short distance to the port exit. There were several people milling around there, clearly looking for friends or relatives. As the luxury cruise ship the *Regent Voyager* was berthed ahead of the *Handshake*, there were also many passengers from that ship waiting to meet people. Mr Fennington Barley, the dance host, greeted them as he walked out with both Mrs Gutttenburg and Mrs Golightly.

'We're off to lunch,'he said as he saw Albert and Alice. 'It makes a change from dining on board.'

Aye, thought Albert cannily to himself. 'An expensive change, no doubt.'

'I wish we knew what George looked like,' said Alice when several minutes had passed and there was no sign of the long-departed cousin. Just as she said this, a distinguished-looking individual, wearing a tailored suit with a red carnation in his buttonhole, approached them.

'Albert?' he questioned.

'Aye, it is,' said Albert.

Before either could say anything further they were swept out of the hall. In the roadway stood a gleaming Mercedes and they were both ushered into the back.

'By go, you've done well,' said Albert, as the suited individual slipped into the driving seat and they glided away from the docks. 'You've not picked up the Aussie lingo, either.'

George spoke with what Alice described as BBC English and without a trace of the accent of Down Under.

'How's Annie?' asked the driver as they cruised out of town.

Alice and Albert looked at each other.

'Annie?' queried Alice, wondering to whom he was referring.

The only Annie she could think of was Annie Ainsworth who used to work in Woolworth's - and surely George would not remember her, although they might have been at school together.

'I've not seen her for many years,' replied Alice. 'She married Tom Ainsworth and went to live in Wigan.'

'She did?' said the driver, clearly surprised. 'Wigan?' I always thought she lived in Guildford.'

'No,' said Alice, 'it was certainly Wigan. I don't think she ever went South. But what about you, George? How is Jennifer?'

'Jennifer?' echoed George. Never in his life had he heard of anyone named Jennifer. 'I don't remember a Jennifer,' said George as he accelerated out of town.

'But surely you married the girl!' said Albert, now as puzzled as the driver.

Albert looked up and could see George looking intently at them in the driving mirror.

'You are Albert, aren't you?' he asked.

'Right, I am,' said Albert.

'And you are Lizzie, aren't you?' he asked next, addressing Alice.

'Lizzie!' exclaimed Alice. 'Not at all. I'm Alice Hardcastle and have been for many a year.'

'Hardcastle,' repeated the driver. 'Hardcastle, did you say? Good Lord, there's been a terrible mistake. I'm supposed to meet my Cousin Albert Newman and his wife Lizzie from Caterham in Surrey. We've not met for over fifty years but I have to say you look just like him. He's been cruising on the *Voyager*. Perhaps you have met him?'

Albert informed George that they were on a different ship, the *Golden Handshake*, and they too were cruising around the world.

George released his foot from the accelerator and drew into the side of the road.

'I'm terribly sorry,' he apologised. 'We have both made an awful mistake. We must get back to the terminus immediately.' He swung the car round and headed back for the city.

By the time they returned to the terminal building the crowd had lessened somewhat as it was well past one in the afternoon and most people were at lunch on board or ashore. It did not take too long to track down the other George and the other Albert who, because of the long wait, had met each other and were trying to work out where their respective cousins had got to.

'Well,' said Alice, when they had boarded the bus to take them to Cousin George's home. 'What a mix-up.'

Cousin George, who had been thoroughly assimilated into Aussie culture, was unperturbed. 'That's OK, mate' he said. 'No big deal. In fact, I know that bloke who picked you up. He runs a chain of betting shops. Came out years ago like me, but did a bit better! He's lucky not to be in jail.'

Albert laughed. 'Well, George,' he said, 'as one English chap once said, "All's well that ends well".'

'Shakespeare may have said "all's well that ends well", but Aussies say "she'll be right".'

And with that they all went out for lunch.

There was a tinge of sadness in the air as Captain Sparda stood on the bridge and watched the tug prepare to guide the *Golden Handshake* out of the harbour. The visit to Sydney had been a great success. The Admiral, together with several senior staff and a goodly number of passengers, had been fortunate enough to obtain tickets for the opera, and apart from some minor grumbles about the number of steps to climb and the lack of comfortable seating, everyone was well pleased with the performance. Appropriately, it was *The Pirates of Penzance* that was being performed, and afterwards the whole party took Enzo out for a drink as he was still rather depressed about the Komodo incident and had received yet another reprimand from the Hotel Manager.

Norma and Graham Trotter had managed to link up with the local Ludo Club and were fêted as was appropriate to their status in the Ludo world.

The only people not to step ashore were the New Zealand twins, who said that they had had quite enough of Australia and were content to stay on board and have a rest, which they did. The visit to Komodo, albeit interesting, had been a little taxing, they admitted. New Zealand was to be the next stop and the twins could not wait to get there.

'It's a lovely country,' they said to anyone and everyone who would listen.

43

It was early morning when the *Handshake* arrived in the Bay of Islands. The ship anchored in the bay and Enzo informed passengers that they would be able to go ashore in a tender that had been hired for the day. As it was a reasonably-sized boat it could take at least forty passengers each trip and deposit them for the day in Russell, a picturesque seaside village.

'I never thought the day would come when I would set foot on the other side of the world,' said Albert, as he and his wife clambered gingerly out of the tender and onto the landing-stage. 'By gum, luv, it's been a rum voyage but well worth it.'

The warm sun and cheery atmosphere of Russell made everyone feel better and helped them forget some of the more unfortunate happenings of the past weeks.

'Look at that,' said Albert when they stepped off the wooden walkway onto dry land. He was pointing at a hotel immediately opposite, named the Duke of Marlborough. It had an attractive wooden balcony and an outside dining area. 'By go, Alice, I like this place.'

The pathway, lined with small shops, was full of visitors from the *Golden Handshake* buying postcards, trying on hats and topping up with sun lotion. Albert and Alice sat on a wooden bench and watched the comings and goings. Sir Archie and Lady Veronika passed by and Sir Archie politely nodded to them.

'Lovely day, Mr Hardcastle.'

'Aye, it is an' all,' nodded Albert. 'All I need now is a Brown Ale and it would be perfect.'

Next to approach was Mr Fennington Barley, who seemed to have added to his menagerie, for not only was he accompanied by Mrs Dora Guttenburg and Mrs Golightly, but the elderly Mrs Ellis had also joined the party. They stopped in front of Albert and Alice.

'Quite an outing for you,' said Albert after he and Mr Barley had exchanged pleasantries.

'It's a delight to be in such a place,' Fennington replied. 'Reminds me of the summer days we used to get in England. Look,' he said to Albert, 'as you can see, I am a bit outnumbered. What about Alice and yourself joining us for lunch at the hotel there.'

'It's a bit posh for me,' said Albert, thinking of the fact that there would be a free lunch available on board the *Handshake*.

'Nonsense,' said Fennington briskly. 'We can all sit on the veranda and it's not too expensive. We have already taken a look at the menu.'

'A lovely idea, Mr Barley,' said Alice, who had remained

quiet for some time. 'That would be most acceptable.'

'I've no idea why they called this place after the Duke of Marlborough,' said Fennington as they settled themselves around a table for six.

At an adjacent table, Sir Archie and Lady Veronika - frowning as ever - were perusing the menu.

'He was the grandfather of Winston Churchill, you know,' said Sir Archie, overhearing the conversation.

'Come and join us,' said Fennington, who was clearly in an expansive mood. 'Pull the table up.'

Before Lady Veronika could object, Sir Archie had leaped to his feet and, together with Fennington, brought the whole group together.

'Russell used to be known as "the Hell Hole of the Pacific",' continued Sir Archie, who had clearly been doing his research into this part of New Zealand.

'What!' exclaimed Albert. 'This place a hell-hole? Whoever said that wants to visit Widnes.'

Sir Archie laughed. 'I admit you wouldn't think it was once a place with a terrible reputation. It was a whaling station and a centre of drinking and prostitution. A chap named Johnny Johnson bought this hotel and renamed it after the Duke of Marlborough, who was then the richest man in the world. He hoped that such a name might bring a bit of respectability to the town.'

'Well,' said Albert, 'it's a grand little place.'

And with that remark he ordered a Brown Ale and, feeling so contented within himself, bought drinks for the whole table. As for the menu – well, as far as Albert and Alice were concerned, there was no contest. Fish and chips it was to be, with mushy peas. The whole table agreed with the choice and so it was fish and chips for eight on the veranda of the Duke of Marlborough. A perfect day.

Back on board, as it was a mild evening, Radley Duvet had arranged another buffet on deck. The part-time musicians were summoned and there was eating and dancing late into the night. By this time in the voyage, the ship had settled down. Friendships had been forged and disasters overcome. Now the whole ship's company looked forward to a clear run home, firstly across the vast Pacific Ocean when there would be several days at sea without sight of land, and then onwards back eventually to Southend-on-Sea, a place that seemed a million miles away from the Bay of Islands.

There was one more port of call before striking out across the mighty Pacific, and that was Napier in New Zealand. This was the one place that the New Zealand twins had been looking forward to so much. Their home was not too far distant from Napier and they intended to arrange for a local coach company to meet the ship and take some passengers to see the delights of their home region.

'We shall arrive just in time for the Art Deco Festival,' said Petra to Admiral Benbow, as they were taking tea together. 'Napier was flattened by an earthquake in the 1930s and was rebuilt in Art Deco style.'

'It's a lovely place,' said Philippa. 'Our cousin always bought his striped cricket blazers there. They are made locally out of the best New Zealand wool. You must get one yourself, Admiral. You would look very handsome in it.'

'Yes,' insisted Petra, 'you must. You must also go to the Long Late Lunch, Admiral. Mr Pask, a very nice gentleman who started a winery nearby, puts on a dinner for almost a thousand people who all sit at one table. Can you believe that, Admiral? One thousand people all sitting down to a hot meal.'

The Admiral said that it sounded most impressive, and made the tasks of the galley staff on the *Golden Handshake* seem relatively simple.

The docks at Napier were not particularly impressive. Two or three coaches were on hand to ferry passengers the mile or so into town where the Art Deco Festival was in full swing. Mr Robert Jones, the passenger who had been photographed playing cricket, was extremely keen to get into town as, in conversation with the twins, he had heard of the shop where authentic cricket blazers could be bought and he was determined to get one. He was first on the coach and occupied the front seat, giving him a

Terry Waite

fine view of the road ahead. A local resident, Mr Derek Lamb (a most appropriate name for a New Zealander, thought Albert), had heard about the visit of the *Golden Handshake* and, as he was the owner of a travel company, had been able to arrange a most favourable deal for hire of the coaches. It transpired that Mr Lamb was originally from Scotland and, coincidentally, was a distant relative of Angus the Chief Engineer. Angus agreed with Mike Tucker that, before the ship sailed, Derek Lamb and his wife would be invited on board for dinner.

Shortly after lunch, the first coach set off to travel the short distance into town. Members of the crew who were not on duty were permitted to travel on the transport, provided there was space available, and as Udi had a couple of hours free in the afternoon, he was allowed on the first bus out as there was just one spare place. Passengers always got priority, of course. Derek Lamb was there to see them off and had to put up with the rather strained humour of the resident comedian, Felix de Barkley, who, when greeting Derek, asked him if had brought his dog along. Derek eventually got the joke and politely laughed. Albert and Alice, who always tried to get the front seat of the coach, were thwarted this time as the elderly Bob Jones had commandeered it and so they had to be content with a seat further back.

As the coach travelled along the sea-front, Enzo, who had never been to this part of the world previously, gave a commentary of sorts. He had spent the previous evening swotting up on the internet and thus was able to trot out a few random facts and figures.

'This is the Hawkes Bay region,' he began.

'Indeed it is, Mr Bigatoni,' called out one of the twins. 'Its the most beautiful region of New Zealand, isn't it, Philippa?'

'It is indeed,' replied her sister.

Enzo continued. 'It was destroyed by a terrible earthquake in 1930 which –'

Before he could continue, Petra interrupted him again.

'1931, Mr Bigatoni. The third of February 1931. Two hundred and fifty-six people were killed on that terrible day.'

'Yes,' confirmed her sister. 'It was a terrible day, Mr Bigatoni. A dreadful disaster, like Pompeii.'

Enzo agreed it was truly terrible and continued with his recital of how the city had been rebuilt in Art Deco style, a fact which was now becoming evident to the passengers as they entered the town.

'We shall park a little distance from the main centre of Napier,' Enzo told them, 'and will be at the same place ready to depart at six p.m.'.

The *Golden Handshake* was fortunate in its timing, as the annual Art Deco Festival was in full swing as the party entered the town. They all climbed down from the coach and for a while Albert and Alice strolled along the sea-front with the twins. In a nearby park, a seemingly endless table was being prepared.

'Hey up!' exclaimed Albert. 'What's that?'

The twins explained that dear Mr Pask was getting ready for the Long Late Lunch, when hundreds of people would sit down together for a splendid meal. Nearby, in a bandstand, several important-looking men were arranging microphones. Many of the people walking through the streets were dressed just as they would have done in the 1930s. Lady Veronika, who had taken this tour with her husband was, for once in her life, perfectly attired for the occasion. Her cloche hat fitted in admirably.

'You ought to have worn your best suit, Albert,' said Alice. 'That would have been just right for today.'

Her husband said nothing. He was gazing intently ahead as though transfixed.

'What's up?' asked Alice. 'What have you seen now?'

'It can't be,' breathed Albert. 'I don't believe it.'

'Whatever are you talking about, Albert Hardcastle?' Alice huffed. 'I don't understand you at times. I really don't.'

It's old Havergill,' said Albert incredulously. 'Look, that fella there walking with that blonde woman.'

'Havergill?' queried Alice. 'Havergill?'

'He's coming this way,' said Albert.

'Do you know the gentleman, Mr Hardcastle?' asked Philippa.

Before Albert could answer, Mr Havergill himself spotted him.

'Albert Hardcastle!' he cried. 'Good Lord, fancy meeting you on the other side of the world.'

'Aye,' said Albert. 'Fancy. How are things, Mr Havergill?'

'Fantabulous, old man. Never been better. Meet my good friend, Roxene, who lives in the town.'

Roxene looked at the visitors and managed a weak smile.

'Well,' said Havergill, 'spending all your millions, are you, Mr Hardcastle? What a mix-up we had at the bank when you won so much. We were all so pleased for you both. I left shortly afterwards and came out to New Zealand. Change of air, you know. Needed it. Never regretted it for a moment.'

Petra looked at Albert.

'Did you win a raffle, Mr Hardcastle?' she asked innocently.

'You could say that,' Albert replied, 'but I don't talk much about it.'

'Several million, I seem to remember,' said the indiscreet former bank manager. 'Well done, old chap. You can't take it with you, you know.'

'I think we had better be moving on,' said Albert, increasingly embarrassed now that his fortune had been revealed to fellow passengers. 'We have to be back on the coach very soon.'

'Oh, we have plenty of time,' said Philippa. 'It's not due to leave for an hour or so yet.'

'Aye,' said Albert, 'I know that, but I want to see more of this place.'

'Quite right,' said Havergill. 'Roxy and I must also be moving on. We're going to the Long Lunch and we would not miss that for anything. You could afford to pay for the whole event, Mr Hardcastle. I'm sure the organisers would be delighted to see you.'

Albert mumbled something about not feeling hungry and that there was a good meal on the ship.

'Well, if I can't persuade you then we had better say farewell for the time being. Here's my card. If ever you decide to settle here, I can find you a very nice place. It's a very friendly town, you know.'

Here Havergill winked at Roxene, and Alice, who had remained silent throughout the encounter, still said nothing. Havergill fumbled in his pocket and produced a business card which revealed that he was now acting as an estate agent.

'Some lovely seaside places here, Mr Hardcastle. Your lady wife would really enjoy it.'

'Goodbye, Mr Havergill,' said Alice frostily. 'I hope you have a good afternoon.'

'What a very charming gentleman,' said Petra when the couple had departed. 'And how interesting that you won so much money, Mr Hardcastle. I'm sure you would like to become an overseas supporter of the festival. It would be appreciated. They are always looking for funds, you know.'

Albert groaned inwardly. The cat was out of the bag and he

was now known as a man of considerable wealth.

'Mr Havergill tends to lay it on a bit,' he said in reply. 'That's why he's got the job he has. If you're selling houses, you have to lay it on.'

'Not here in Napier, Mr Hardcastle,' said Petra. 'They are all lovely houses, you know. Art Deco.'

'Come on,' said Alice, anxious to change the conversation. 'Let's get a cup of tea.'

Back on board, everyone was chattering excitedly about the visit to Napier. The twins were a little disappointed that they had been unable to have an extra day in port when they would have taken passengers to visit the Tukituki River beside which they had lived for many years. However, the Admiral and all the senior crew members were agreed that they must push on across the Pacific whilst the going was good. No one wanted to be stranded in the middle of that vast ocean with steering problems - or any problem, come to that.

'You must all return one day soon,' said Petra. 'My sister and I will arrange a tour with dear Mr Lamb and we will have lunch at the Patangata Hotel. You would enjoy that.'

Everyone agreed that it sounded delightful and that they ought to make a special note in their diaries for the following year.

Both Albert and Alice were feeling rather cross with their

old bank manager for revealing the fact that they had won a great deal of money on the Lottery.

'The man's a damn fool,' said Albert when they were back on board. 'The fact that we have a bit of brass will now be all over the ship.'

Indeed it was. Petra, in all innocence, let it be known that when they were out with Albert and Alice they had met a very wealthy Englishman who was now living in Napier and this man recognised Albert as a fellow millionaire as they had both belonged to the same club.

'Millionaire?' queried Mrs Potts, who had moved from the Balcony Suite away from the Hardcastles. 'Millionaire? I can hardly believe that. They may be living in a Balcony Suite, but many people save up for the cruise of a lifetime, you know.'

Despite what Mrs Potts thought, word soon got out that one of the passengers was a multi-multi millionaire and was about to take over ownership of the Golden Line. Fennington Barley was named as a likely candidate, but eventually the rumour centred around Albert and Alice.

'I'm going to do what they did in the war,' said Albert. 'Keep Mum.'

'Quite right,' his wife agreed. Secretly she was not too displeased about the rumour, for now she might well be recognised as a lady of substance.

Albert didn't know what to believe when he was approached

by Admiral Harrington in person and asked if he might be interested in a little business venture.

'As you will no doubt know, Mr Hardcastle, my company is growing quickly and we are always on the lookout for private investors. Might you be interested?'

Albert declared that his business days were over when he left the Co-op and he certainly did not have spare money to invest.

'Well, do at least think about it,' said the Admiral. 'The Harrington-Hardcastle Line has a certain distinguished ring about it, don't you agree?'

Albert agreed that it had and promised to think about it, but was not hopeful.

At midnight, precisely several passengers gathered on deck to say farewell to New Zealand. Earlier there had been a party on deck, but some more adventurous souls had stayed on in Napier for the evening and returned to the ship by taxi. It was a warm evening with a gentle breeze. Captain Sparda stood by as the pilot prepared to issue his instructions. The gangway was removed and, very slowly, very gently, the *Golden Handshake* began to edge away from the dockside. A few relatives, and friends of passengers, had gathered, even at this late hour, to wave goodbye. Somewhere on the key-side, Mr Bernard Havergill, Albert's former bank manager, stood gazing wistfully at the departing ship. He waited until the *Handshake* had totally disappeared from sight, then, with a sigh, turned and made his solitary way home.

44

Once the pilot had departed, Captain Sparda left the bridge for a brief siesta in his cabin. The Staff Captain ordered that the *Golden Handshake* be kept on a steady course at a moderate speed and he prayed that the vessel would hold together for the long crossing. By this time he had become rather fond of the old ship and, now that the passengers and crew had really settled in, he hoped that the final half of the World Tour would pass without mishap.

Both Radley and Enzo had been working together for several weeks preparing for one of the highlights of the voyage – The Grand Passenger Talent Show – which was due to take place that very evening. There would be a special meal, when officers of the ship would serve at table. They would not serve all courses, but they would dress in chefs' outfits and serve at least one dish to each table. Afterwards, all the crew who were not on duty were invited to the show, along with the passengers who were not appearing in it.

Mike Tucker had pulled out all the stops for this evening. Although it was not Burns Night, Mike thought it would be a good plan to have Angus, an accomplished piper, to pipe in the Haggis. He made sure that by every place there was a miniature bottle of whisky, and that haggis, neeps and tatties were on the menu for those who wished to order them. Angus duly did his stuff with the bagpipes, to tumultuous applause! The whisky disappeared and larger bottles were ordered by some tables where they were determined to make a night of it.

Once the meal was over, Captain Sparda, in full mess kit, stood and invited those assembled to join him and the crew to take part in what was to be a wonderful and entertaining evening. Of that he had no doubt. They all left the dining room in high spirits.

As the audience trooped into the entertainment area, the familiar musical trio were already on stage warming up. Philippa was at the piano, the chaplain sat behind the percussion and Lady Veronika was giving a very creditable performance on the saxophone. The great surprise for the audience was to see the elderly passenger Mr Coles, who had kept a very low profile to date, holding a microphone and doing a very acceptable imitation of Louis Armstrong.

'I had no idea we had such talent on board,' said the Admiral as he took his seat at the front of the room.

Captain Sparda agreed that the musical group were excellent, but he had no idea what was to come and would pass comment later.

When everyone was settled, the lights were dimmed, the chaplain gave a roll on the drums and, to considerable applause, Enzo took centre stage.

'Good evening, everyone, and welcome to the Admiral's Command Performance.'

Admiral Harrington at first looked surprised, as this was the first he had heard of this command, but he smiled and nodded graciously.

'Tonight you will be amazed, enchanted and entertained by some of the greatest performers this ship has ever seen,' continued Enzo.

'Not difficult, seeing that before it was a cruise ship it was a cattle transporter,' whispered the doctor to his neighbour Mike Tucker, who grinned.

'For the first act tonight,' Enzo continued, 'I would like you to give a rousing *Handshake* welcome to two of the finest Clog Dancers in the world. Ladies and gentlemen . . . Mrs Dora Guttenburg and Mr Fennington Barley!'

The musical trio struck up a lively polka and, hand in hand, the clog-dancing couple entered. Mr Barley sported an old pair of Bombay Bloomers and an Austrian hat, from which sprouted a long pheasant's feather. Mrs Guttenburg wore a long full skirt and a checkered apron. On her head was some form of white cap of the type Puritan ladies used to wear in the sixteenth century. They both wore yellow painted clogs and, for five or six minutes, tapped their way merrily around the stage. They departed to tremendous applause and shouts of 'More! More!' Holding hands, they tapped their way back onto the stage. Fennington bowed and Dora curtsied, and then they tapped their way off the other side.

'Bravo! Bravo!' echoed around the room from an appreciative, whisky-fuelled audience.

'I must admit they are very accomplished,' said the Admiral, agreeably surprised.

Enzo reappeared and appealed for silence.

'What a wonderful start to the show,' he said proudly. 'I'm sure that Fennington and Dora will have a glittering future in the clog-dancing world. Now, some of you will have heard of our adventures on a certain Island in Indonesia. But nothing happened there to compare with what you will hear in a moment. Ladies and gentlemen . . . Mr and Mrs Albert Hardcastle!'

Again there was more enthusiastic applause as Albert and Alice appeared. Albert wore a cap with a red spotted handkerchief around his neck, Alice her best salmon-pink two-piece outfit bought especially for the cruise. They each carried a script and stood, side by side, before the microphone. Albert began.

'We are about to relate to you,' he said slowly and deliberately, 'a very terrible story. It may shock you, just as it shocked Alice and me when we first had it told to us. If you are nervous, you may want to leave now.'

No one stirred.

'Right, Alice, you begin.'

'There's a famous seaside place called Blackpool . . . '. Alice began, broadening her Northern accent and sounding rather like the late Gracie Fields as she read from the script she held in front of her.

'The Lion and Albert' by Marriott Edgar, was a hugely popular monologue about a couple called Mr and Mrs Ramsbottom, who take their young son Albert to the zoo for a special treat, only to see him - and his 'stick with an 'orse's 'ead 'andle' - devoured by a moth-eaten old lion called Wallace.

The couple took it in turns to read the verses, Albert in an even broader accent, and when the story was over, the enraptured audience broke into thunderous applause.

The Hardcastles made their exit and Enzo reappeared.

'What a story,' he said. 'A bit too near the bone for my liking.'

This remark caused much hilarity as they all remembered the hair-raising visit of the small party to Komodo Island.

'Many of you will have been enchanted with New Zealand,' he went on, 'and many of you will have delighted in the musical talent of the Parkinson sisters from Hawkes Bay. Here they are once again to demonstrate their musical gifts, so give a big hand to . . . Petra and Philippa Parkinson!'

The two sisters entered dressed in long skirts and white

blouses and sat side by side in front of the piano. For the next several minutes they both played on the same keyboard at breakneck speed. It was a dazzling performance that had half the audience on its feet and applauding wildly.

Backstage, Enzo was perspiring profusely. The evening was going well. Too well, he thought pessimistically, for the luck could run out at any moment. The twins struck their closing chords and Enzo went forward again.

'Phew! What an act to follow,' he said, smiling broadly. 'But it can be followed, and will be, by none other than . . . Sir Archibald Willoughby, accompanied at the piano by his lovely wife, Lady . . . Veronika.'

Lady Veronika took her place and struck up the first few chords of the famous Boer War melody 'Where Are the Boys of the Old Brigade'. To much laughter, Sir Archie then entered with his trousers tucked into long socks to make it appear that he was wearing puttees. Over his shoulder he carried a wooden rifle and, of course, he wore his famous battle-scarred pith helmet. He paraded around the stage, and then in centre stage, facing the audience, he began to sing the battle song.

'Where are The Old Brigade,
Who fought with us side by side?
Shoulder to shoulder, and blade by blade,
Fought till they fell and died!

Who so ready and undismayed?
Who so merry and true?
Where are the boys of the old Brigade?
Where are the lads we knew?
Then steadily shoulder to shoulder,
Steadily blade by blade!
Ready and strong, marching along
Like the boys of the old Brigade!'

Although Sir Archie presented a comic figure in his pseudo battle-kit, he sang in a fine clear baritone which moved his audience to tears, both of laughter and of sadness. He took a bow and Lady Veronika stood and scowled at the audience, before retreating to collect her saxophone and resume her place with the other musicians.

Enzo came bounding back on to introduce the next act. The Admiral was totally absorbed by the entertainment and even the sceptical Peché had to agree that it was a first-rate evening.

'Laughter is the best medicine,' Enzo cried, 'and who better to administer it than your friend and my friend – the internationally famous . . . Mr Felix de Barkley!'

Felix came on wearing a tailcoat which was far too long for him and a battered top hat, and immediately began: 'Hello-hello-hello. A funny thing happened as I was coming here tonight. I passed two fish in a tank. One said to the other "Do you know how to drive this?"

There was a loud groan from the audience.

Felix continued: 'When we were in Australia the other day, I heard that boomerangs were coming back! Ah – I see that's gone right over your head,' said Felix, as only a handful of the audience got the joke and laughed.

'Let's try another one. What does a clock do when it's hungry? Come on,' he said to the audience, 'keep up!'

No one answered.

'Let me tell you,' he said. 'It goes back *four seconds.*'

There was another good-natured groan.

'Why are there no skeletons here tonight?' he asked next.

'We don't know,' replied one of the crew boldly.

'Because they've no body to go with.' Felix grinned at his own joke. Now warming to his act, he said, 'I say, I say, I say. I saw a Frenchman the other day. I asked him his name. "Phileepe Flop" he replied.'

The audience were left with no time to groan for Felix continued apace with joke after joke after joke, until Enzo walked across the stage bearing a large placard on which was scrawled in large letters INTERVAL. The musicians struck a loud chord and Enzo dropped the notice and applauded, to be echoed by loud clapping from the audience. Felix, realising by now that his time was up, grinned, took a bow and left the stage.

Before anyone could leave, Enzo addressed the audience,

saying, 'Please don't get up, ladies and gentlemen. There *is* no interval. My intervention was simply to persuade Felix to come to a halt, otherwise we would never get to the other items on tonight's glittering programme.'

To cries of, 'Shame!' from one quarter and, 'Well done!' from another, Enzo introduced the next act, which was Norma and Graham Trotter the Ludo instructors. Norma entered wearing a one-piece bathing costume which she had liberally sprinkled with golden glitter and Graham was in top hat and tails. The audience cheered when they appeared and Graham, quite forgetting that his top hat was full of coloured handkerchiefs, which he was going to produce mysteriously at the right moment, removed his hat to give a low bow. Yards of coloured material flowed everywhere, much to the consternation of Graham and, as Norma did her best to collect it up, he tried without success to stuff it back into the hat. Realising that he was getting nowhere, he tossed the hat to one side and took another bow. The audience, thinking this was all part of the act, applauded and Norma, thinking quickly, produced a deadly-looking sword from the side of the stage. Graham then successfully did a sword-swallowing act. Observant members of the audience could clearly see that the blade retracted into the handle, but those at the back of the room were very impressed. Graham and Norma performed several more illusions then left the stage to cries of, 'More!' and, 'Stick to the day job!' from someone at the back of the room.

'Well,' said Enzo when he returned to the stage. 'Our show is nearly over.'

Several people shouted, 'Never,' but Enzo ignored them.

'Sadly,' he continued, 'we now come to the last act. Two of our distinguished lecturers, Mr Fred Batty and Sir Horace Beanstalk, have spent many hours composing a eulogy which they will now recite. Ladies and gentlemen, please put your hands together for . . . Sir Horace and Mr Fred!'

The pair entered together and the room fell silent. They began to recite in unison:

'Enzo, our great Cruise Director,
Decided to go for a tour.
He spotted an island out yonder
And said, 'I've not been there before'.

He assembled a small group of travellers,
And into a boat they did get,
They rowed and they rowed, seemed for ever,
By gum it was hot, they did sweat.

They took off their shoes and their stockings,
And waded the last twenty feet.
Sir Archie was wearing his helmet

The Voyage of the Golden Handshake

But he even felt the great heat

The island it seemed quite deserted,
There wasn't a person in sight
When, suddenly out from the bushes,
They all got a terrible fright.

A monster appeared breathing brimstone
And flicking its tongue in the air,
Enzo said, 'Run for your lives, lads
The dragon has come from its lair!'

Exhausted, they reached a small clearing
And there was a man with a stick.
He said, 'I can see you're not natives,'
As he gave the old dragon a kick.

The dragon ran off in the bushes
And two more great monsters appeared,
The stick man and all his companions
Said, 'These monsters don't make us afeared.

But they kill and eat wandering travellers
And chew them until they're no more,'
With that, dear Alice Hardcastle

Collapsed in a heap on the floor.

The stick man was not very kindly
And demanded a large wad of dough,
Enzo paid up very quickly
As he was most anxious to go.

Then back to the beach went the party,
The stick man was leading the way,
But the boat that they needed to get home
Was floating right out in the bay.

So little canoes were then ordered,
And Enzo paid out some more cash,
And, paddled by several more stick men,
To the *Handshake* they all made a dash.

And so this sad tale is now over,
The party has all left the shore.
The moral of this little story
Is "Take Care When You Want To Explore"!'

As they uttered the final sentence the musicians played a
chord and the poets took a bow. The roof nearly lifted to the
roars of applause. Enzo appeared on stage and was quickly sur-

rounded by all the artistes. He motioned members of the senior staff to join them all on stage.

'What a wonderful evening, ladies and gentlemen!' he shouted. 'Now let's all join hands around the room and sing together "Auld Lang Syne".'

The musicians struck up and the assembled gathering shattered the evening calm of the majestic Pacific with that fine old Scottish Tune.

It truly was an evening to remember.

45

Sunday morning dawned and the chaplain was putting the last-minute touches to his sermon. He had made several attempts to preach, and on each occasion had been thwarted by some unexpected happening. Now, out in the cloudless Pacific, all seemed set for Captain Sparda to conduct the service, as was the custom on a Sunday sea day, and for the chaplain to preach. Angela had given invaluable assistance in many ways, not least in making sure that his notes were correctly typed. This was a new experience for him, as previously he had scribbled points on any old piece of scrap paper and, once in the pulpit, had considerable difficulty in deciphering what he had previously written. The Golden Glory Choir had practised and were in fine form. In fact, all seemed set for a very pleasant morning, followed by a traditional Sunday lunch that Harry was so expert in preparing.

'A very good show last night,' said Captain Sparda as he encountered the chaplain on his way to the service. 'You really are a dab hand on the drums, chaplain.'

Justin blushed and mumbled that it was quite easy and all one needed was a sense of rhythm.

'You're far too modest,' Sparda told him. 'Well, you have a chance to shine in a different direction this morning. I do like a good sermon, you know. Don't hold back, chaplain. You give it all you've got.'

The chaplain said that he would do his best and they entered the room which was now prepared for morning worship. Angela was stationed at the doorway with a pile of hymnbooks and a service sheet to hand to attenders. She greeted Justin and said that he looked very well in his new clerical robes. Justin blushed yet again. He wished he could do something about this affliction but it had been with him since he was a child and he imagined it would continue throughout life.

Gradually the room began to fill with passengers. The chaplain went behind a screen to join the Captain and several senior officers who were to take part in the service. One of the twins was playing gently on the piano and the Choir members were assembled ready to process in. Exactly on the dot of eleven the Choir received the instruction to process and they were followed by the Captain's party.

'Good morning, everyone,' Captain Sparda began, 'and welcome to our Sunday-morning service. As you will know, it is the custom on this ship for the Captain to conduct morning worship and you will find the Order of Service on your printed sheets. The chaplain will deliver the sermon but, before we begin, the Golden Glory Choir will sing a short anthem.'

Philippa Parkinson stepped forward to conduct and the singers delivered a very creditable rendering of 'Sheep May Safely Graze'. Felix de Barkley, never one to miss a joke, turned to his neighbour and whispered, 'You can tell the conductor is from New Zealand, can't you?'

'Shush, Felix,' said his wife. 'Do please be quiet for once in your life.'

The Captain began to read the opening sentences followed by Radley Duvet who read the first lesson. Then there was a hymn and another lesson, read by Angela. The Captain then stepped forward and announced the hymn preceding the sermon.

The chaplain made sure he had his notes, and as the congregation and choir sang the final verse, he stepped over to the lectern. He was just about to announce his text when he was interrupted by a sudden lurch of the ship which sent both the lectern and himself flying. An alarm bell immediately began to ring and Sparda, together with his officers, made a hasty retreat.

'Please keep calm, everyone,' said Radley, who had picked himself up from the floor of the platform. 'If you could proceed in an orderly way to your cabins, collect your lifebelt and then gather at your respective stations, that would be the best thing to do.'

The room emptied rapidly. Angela went across to the chaplain who was retrieving his scattered notes from the floor.

496

'Come on,' she urged. 'This might be serious.'

On deck, small groups of passengers had assembled and the crew were busy checking them off from the passenger-list. No one could quite understand what had happened. There was a cloudless blue sky. The sea was as calm as the proverbial mill-pond and there was no sign of other shipping, or rocks for that matter. Observant passengers noted, however, that the ship, rather than proceeding on a straight course was, in fact, moving round in a large circle.

'Oh lord,' groaned Fred Batty. 'I know what it is. It's the steering gear broken once again.'

Fred, the former AA man, accustomed to making accurate assessments of mechanical failures, was exactly right. The gear *had* failed – and several hours later, Angus Aberdeen had to concede that there was now nothing further that he could do. The ship had to be towed into the nearest dry dock and the essential repairs carried out.

Later that day, when the engines had been stopped and the *Golden Handshake* lay waiting for a rescue vessel to appear, Admiral Harrington and Captain Sparda called all passengers to a special meeting. There was a general air of gloom. After the initial problems experienced by the ship, everyone had believed they were set fair for a smooth passage home. True, some had known that the mechanics were in a frail state, but it was believed that they would last out. Alas, that was not to be.

It was the Admiral who first addressed the gathering.

'I can't begin to tell you what a disappointment today has been,' he said. 'In the past we have been able to manage the problems we encountered, but I am afraid today we have to admit defeat. We are now awaiting a sea-going tug that will take us back to the nearest dry dock where repairs will be made. I can't tell you how long that will take, but it is likely to be two or three weeks at the earliest, possibly much longer than that. I would like to assure you that we have made every effort to repair this problem ourselves, but that proved to be impossible. I am so very sorry. Let me now ask Mr Duvet to address you.'

Radley Duvet had been working furiously during the day to make arrangements for the passengers and, considering that it was a Sunday and they were some miles off the coast, he had done remarkably well. He too expressed his considerable disappointment and then went on to say that the Admiral had been in touch with an old Service colleague who ran a charter airline. An aircraft would be flying out to New Zealand the following day and would transport all passengers who wished to fly back to their home destination - quite free of charge, of course. Everyone would receive a refund to cover the second half of the cruise which they now could not take, and once the *Golden Handshake* was fully repaired they would be offered another cruise with a substantial discount on the cost.

'I do think we have done everything we can at the moment,'

concluded Radley, 'but I must apologise once more. This is a great disappointment to us all.'

It was now the Captain's turn to speak and he said that he would be very brief. He repeated apologies and said that it was a situation quite beyond their control. For a Captain to have to see his ship let down passengers, in the way the *Golden Handshake* had done, was a bitter blow but he could assure them all that once she was repaired, he would certainly be back in command and would look forward to welcoming old friends back to join him for the remainder of this cruise.

'But,' he said, 'it is not all bad news this afternoon. Good friendships have been made during the voyage and they will last for many a year. Tonight we shall be having a very special dinner despite the fact that at that time, more likely than not, we will be being towed into harbour. At that dinner I have been invited to make a very special announcement - one that will bring pleasure to many of you, I am sure. So, until then, I must return to the bridge.'

'Well, Alice,' said Albert, as those present began to disperse to their Suites and cabins, 'this is a rum do and no doubt.'

'Aye, it is, luv. I'd like to come back, wouldn't you?'

'I think I might,' her husband replied. 'Despite some happenings, it's been an adventure. I wonder if the chaplain will return, and if he *will* ever preach a sermon?'

'We shall have to see,' said Alice. 'We shall just have to wait and see.'

There was general agreement amongst the passengers that the Admiral and his Line had behaved very well towards them, and the vast majority said that, if they had the time, they would certainly return to complete the World Cruise at a later date. And so everyone now prepared themselves for the evening and for the surprise announcement.

Despite the acute disappointment felt by the whole ship, passengers were making the best of things. Such were the relationships between crew and passengers that there was no unpleasantness, simply disappointment. There *was* much excitement in the late afternoon when a tug drew alongside and the stricken *Golden Handshake* was taken in tow. When they were under way, everyone went to their Suites or cabins to dress for dinner. It had been announced that the final evening would be a dress occasion and that photographs would be taken. There would be no charge to passengers, should they wish to keep pictures of themselves with their partners, or with the Captain and other staff.

At the entrance to the dining room, a long queue formed whilst the Admiral, the Captain and Enzo posed with passengers for the camera. Mike Tucker was determined to pull out all stops for the Gala Dinner and this he did. Champagne was freely available on each table, as was wine. As the meal was drawing to a close, Captain Sparda stood and requested silence for a moment. The room fell quiet.

'After so long together at sea,' he began, 'I feel that now I may address you as friends, even though you are indeed all Ladies and Gentlemen. Today has been one of the saddest days of my life at sea, and I think I can say that for all the Ship's Company. To have to curtail the voyage when we are only half-way through, and to see my lovely ship being towed into dock, breaks my heart. My sadness has only been made bearable by the fact that tomorrow we shall not be saying "Goodbye". Rather we will be saying "Au Revoir". I am sure that we shall meet soon to complete the voyage.'

At this point there was loud applause and shouts of, 'Certainly!' and 'We shall be back!'

Sparda smiled.

'I said this afternoon that I have a surprise for you, and so I shall not keep you waiting any longer. It is a real pleasure for me to announce to you that the good ship *Golden Handshake* has been a ship that will live forever in the memory of at least four people on board. I am sure that it will remain so for all of you, but for the following four people especially.

'Mr Fennington Barley has delighted many of our single guests with his faultless dancing. He has also demonstrated his skill as a clog-dancer when he partnered Mrs Dora Guttenburg in what was a wonderful display at the evening entertainment. Ladies and gentlemen, I am pleased to announce the engagement of Fennington and Dora.'

Immediately the assembled began to clap loudly and the Captain motioned the couple to come forward and join him.

'That is not all,' he continued, beaming. 'There is one person on this ship who joined by accident and that mistake proved to be most fortunate for him and for many who have got to know him. I am also delighted to announce the engagement of our chaplain, the Reverend Justin Longparish, to our Social Hostess Miss Angela Fairweather.'

There was more thunderous applause and once again the Captain motioned the chaplain and Angela to join him and the other engaged couple.

'As this ship is registered in the UK,' the Captain went on, 'I cannot marry the happy couples. However, they tell me that they intend to be married on the same day at the same church – and that we *all* will be invited to attend.'

There was loud cheering at this announcement.

'Also, they assure me that they will be back for the second leg of this voyage when as many of us as possible will join together to visit the other half of the world. Now dear friends, I ask you to raise your glasses and drink to the health and prosperity of Justin and Angela, Fennington and Dora.'

Glasses were raised and their health was drunk.

'There will be no further speeches from me tonight,' said the Captain. 'May I wish you all a peaceful rest and all the best until we meet again.'

'Ee, what a lovely evening,' sighed Alice when the couple had returned to their Balcony Suite. 'We ought to make an effort to go to the weddings, Albert, and we really should try to come back.'

'Aye,' said Albert, as he removed his black boots, which were hurting him. He tied his pyjama trouser cord into a large bow and climbed into bed.

'I think we must,' he yawned, as he switched out the bedside light. 'As long as we can afford it, mind. I think we must.'

THE END

Acknowledgments

Special thanks are due to: Jenny Coles who braved several storms and did all the donkey work on the script, Joan Deitch who was an excellent copy editor and my publisher Humfrey Hunter who was always encouraging and helped me avoid many a shipwreck.

Terry Waite CBE

Suffolk, 2015